CHARMAINE R. FISHER
114 - 29TH ST. WEST
BILLINGS, MT 59102

# PACIFIC CAVALCADE

## Also by Virginia Coffman

*Marsanne*
*Hyde Place*
*The House at Sandalwood*
*The Dark Palazzo*
*Mistress Devon*
*Veronique*
*Fire Dawn*
*The Gaynor Women*
*Dinah Faire*

# PACIFIC CAVALCADE

*A NOVEL BY*

**Virginia Coffman**

ARBOR HOUSE • *New York*

*Copyright © 1981 by Virginia Coffman*

*All rights reserved, including the right of reproduction in whole or in part in any form.* *Published in the United States of America by Arbor House Publishing Company and in Canada by Fitzhenry & Whiteside, Ltd.*

*Library of Congress Catalog Card Number: 80-66502*

*ISBN: 0-87795-277-9*

*Manufactured in the United States of America*

*10 9 8 7 6 5 4 3 2*

*For Jay Garon, mapmaker of* Pacific Cavalcade;
*for Donnie and Johnny, guardians of the seaway;*
*and for Don Fine and Jared Kieling who got me to*
*port.*

*With many thanks to Peggy Wiig, Paul Wiig and*
*Eleanor Durham, among others, for their*
*eyewitness reports.*

# *PROLOGUE*
# December 5, 1941

IT was a hazy December day, with images indistinct. Even the sharp green Koolau Range, cutting jaggedly into the Hawaiian sky, looked faraway, a dreamlike backdrop for those beloved faces in the crowd under the Aloha Tower.

The hotel band on the dock was briefly silent, but everyone knew what would follow. A slight tap, a signal, then the first poignant notes of the ancient queen's own hymn, "Aloha!"

But despite the traditional farewell, this was like no other sailing in the memory of either the waving crowd or of any of the passengers themselves who lined the rails of the elegant white cruise ship *Lorelei.* With three-quarters of the globe either in flames or under the jackboot, most of the civilians at the Aloha Tower that first Friday afternoon in December of 1941 felt that war in the Pacific was inevitable, and would probably come before spring.

Randi Lombard caught the attention of several men along the rail. She was worth looking at, though she had long since passed her girlhood. Her tall, slim figure, the wisps of tawny hair blowing across her cool face, her intense eyes, attracted the good-looking assistant ship's purser. His eyes kept drifting to her despite the plump yet beautiful redhead who clung to his arm, asking questions he couldn't answer about the possibility of war.

Brooke Lombard Huntington Ware Friedrich was used to being

the center of attraction. The older she got the more she marveled at what men saw in her aloof sister-in-law. Randi had been her friend as well as her sister-in-law for nearly a quarter of a century, but no one—in Brooke's mind, at least—would call Randi Lombard either beautiful or sexy. Still, she was a good companion, and Brooke had had enough of Hawaii for this visit, anyway. All the eligible males were either in uniform or growing too drearily old, she thought.

Both women leaned over the rail to wave at their family on the dock far below. The ship drifted away slowly, serenely, while the band on the dock played its farewell.

The blast of the ship's horn made both women jump. Randi leaned out over the rail to catch her last sight of one man amidst the waving crowd. He was taller, handsomer than the others, she thought, as she watched him running to the end of the dock where he still waved to her and Brooke. She could see her son Tony, too, throwing kisses. The sight brought tears to Randi's otherwise cool eyes, tears which she quickly blinked away.

"I don't know why I'm behaving like this. After all, Tony was born lucky, and Steve—well, he's going back to his 'beauteous Meribel' as Winchell calls her. As for me, I'm going back to—"

"Leo, dear?"

"Well, Hollywood and work."

"Isn't it fortunate Leo lives there as well?"

Randi ignored the remark and tried to focus her thoughts on all her loved ones one by one. . . . Steve would of course be back on the mainland before the powder keg in the Pacific blew up, as it seemed to threaten. As for their son Tony, his wife and their twenty-day-old baby, the Territory of Hawaii was temporarily their home. What would happen to all of them if war broke before spring? . . .

Far below, the faces had already begun to blur as the channels of water widened between the dock and the ship's flank. Randi blinked again. *Sentimental damned Irish! That's me. I know Steve and I are through . . .*

It must be the air, she thought, the dull thick haze that covered the day, the sky and the island of Oahu itself. Depressing . . .

And suddenly she remembered another day. In another time, another age . . . The 1933 earthquake, eight long years ago. That day had been like this, oppressively thick and hazy. The sun had been up overhead somewhere, but unseen. People said afterward that it had been hard to breathe that day. Before the world turned over for her family. And for all the others . . .

Maybe that was true. In any case, it was hard to breathe at this minute, and the lump in her throat made it difficult to swallow.

The crowd shifted toward the end of the dock, still waving. Several thick, moist flower leis, which had been draped around the necks of the passengers, were now being tossed overboard, sacrifices to the superstition that said if they floated ashore the owner would someday return to "paradise."

Randi tried to turn her thoughts away from farewells. "Look at those hills, Brooke. You can hardly see them in the haze. Usually they are the greenest things imaginable."

But Brooke only pulled the sleeve of Randi's raw silk suit jacket.

"Look over there. The Royal. What good times I had there when I was married to Nigel Ware!" She pointed out the pink stucco Royal Hawaiian Hotel on Waikiki Beach.

The young assistant purser moved between the two women. He looked rather like the movie star, Robert Taylor, and knew it.

"Mrs. Lombard? Welcome aboard. We are lucky. You and Mrs. Friedrich, both, on the same voyage. Chief Purser Hatch hopes you two ladies will join his table. His cards are in your suite, but—well—" He looked furtively over his shoulder. "He's in hopes of cutting out Captain Creasey, if you know what I mean."

Randi laughed at such intramural rivalry, though she knew its precise worth. No matter how flattering it sounded, her popularity was greatly enhanced by her marriage to a famous man.

"I imagine you will have no trouble filling up the dining tables. I've never seen so many passengers. And all the children."

"They seem to be everywhere," Brooke put in with a big smile.

"Yes, ma'am. We're sailing with well over six hundred, not counting sickbay and crew. Up to now, the record was five hundred and thirty passengers."

Randi tried to keep a lighter tone than she actually felt. "The ships seems to be racing home for some reason."

The young purser pushed his billed cap back off his forehead with his thumb as the ship's horn gave its traditional last salute to rugged Diamond Head, which jutted out beyond Waikiki. The other passengers moved away from the ear-piercing blast.

"Well, Mrs. Lombard, I'll tell you this. It's common knowledge in the Pacific." He was obviously proud of his boast. "The Japanese navy has a list of twelve passenger ships to be sunk on sight in case of war. That's to prevent their being used by us as troop carriers. The Japs call them the 'twelve monsters.' " He then added with emphasis, "The *Lorelei* would be their prime target between Honolulu and Frisco—that's how important the *Lorelei* is."

Brooke shivered and looked down at the white foam marking the wake of the now fast-moving vessel.

"Then I'd say it's very lucky we're not at war."

The officer noticed Randi's tense face and remembered his first duty. With an overabundance of cheer, he brushed away the disturbing talk.

"Now, ladies, I think the Japs just about have their hands full in China and in the rest of the Orient. They're not going to make themselves any more trouble for the next few months. Even if they did attack, it would be the Dutch Indies or Hong Kong. Maybe the Philippines." He pointed. "Look back there. Way beyond the Aloha Tower. As far as you can see. All our battleships are there protecting us. They won't let anything happen to us, not while they're lined up and ready. So don't you worry."

All the same, Randi and Brooke were relieved to get away from the scene on the deck. They walked down below to their adjoining bedrooms with the wicker furnishings redolent of the South Seas, and the small, open lanai that caught the December sunset.

While Brooke refreshed her makeup, Randi stood at the rail of the little private lanai. She wondered if the family had driven around to Koko Head or Mokapuu Point and were at this minute watching the great white ship. Perhaps Steve and Tony would get out of Dr. Ware's green Chevrolet and stand side by side—Steve, who exuded power and strength and a magnificent authority, and their son, not quite as tall, darker, thin and breezy. Like his father, he was very sure of himself and of the Lombard name.

Though she knew she had let her husband go, Randi had never really stopped loving the strong, determined man who had married her twenty-three years ago this month. Somewhere within the now worldly Steve Lombard was the young, cocky Steve who had asked an ex-waitress named Mary-Randal Gallegher to become a part of his life, and a part of his family—the elegant Lombards of San Francisco.

Brooke called out to her through the adjoining open door. "I really think I can take the leis off now. They're so wet. Randi, do help me."

Brought back to the present, Randi came in and helped her sister-in-law remove the leis one by one, and then removed her own. Both women draped them around the bathtub. Randi took off the last two reluctantly, the *pikake* lei from Tony and the elaborate gardenias from Steve.

"We'll wear just one each for dinner," Brooke decided. "The steward can put the rest in the refrigerator."

There were fewer diners in the elegant Waikiki Dining Room than

Randi had expected as she stared around at the two-deck-high ceiling and the walls with their murals of tropic vegetation. The children were perhaps seasick, she thought, what with the nerve-wracking farewells and the endless trail of macadamia nuts, coconut chips, ginger candy and other such treats. The women who showed up looked as worried as Randi felt.

Brooke noted how few men were present.

The portly chief purser stopped by to welcome the guests at his own table and caught Randi's surprised glance.

"Not a normal voyage, is it, Mrs. Lombard? Let's hope all this war scare dies down before we get to the Golden Gate. In my opinion, we can thank the radio and the newspapers for it. It's their constant harping on the turmoil in the Far East."

Randi tried to soften her reply, but despite her best smile, the sharp edge in her voice remained.

"I'm afraid my husband is responsible for some of that harping. He is always busy with speeches and radio broadcasts about the war. But he and my employer, Leo Prysing, both believe that since the Nazis overran Europe, we will soon be in a—" What did Steve call it? "—a pincers between Hitler and the Japanese."

"Good heavens!" cried Brooke, looking to the purser for comfort.

"Well now, no Jap is going to attack us out here in the front yard of the Pacific Fleet, so don't you worry. We promise to get you safely home. If you will excuse me now, duty calls. But I did want to welcome you aboard."

He shook hands with Randi, and then, taking Brooke's proffered hand, held it a moment longer than strictly necessary. "May I say you are looking as beautiful as ever, Mrs. Friedrich? Let's see. Wasn't it back in '32? Back on the old *Malolo,* nine years ago. And you, Mrs. Lombard," he added, "as lovely as ever."

Brooke said with mischief in her eyes, "You haven't changed a bit either, Clyde. You are as gallant as ever."

How little anyone knows anyone else, Randi thought. *I've* changed, God knows.

Despite the purser's efforts—and he made it a point to circle the bright, tropical dining room with its fresh orchid decor—the mood of the diners was glum.

Captain Creasey came striding into the room. A stocky, impressive man with a smile that relieved his severity, he managed a word of greeting with many old acquaintances, though he never really stopped moving until he reached the purser's table.

He shook hands with the Lombard women, gave them a gallant

salute and expressed the wish that Steve Lombard was along for the voyage.

"I would enjoy your husband's opinion on all this war talk in the Pacific."

"Steve will be flying back on one of the Clippers," Randi explained.

Brooke added proudly, "My brother is interviewing Lieutenant General Short tomorrow. Then he will talk to some businessmen about the situation and what is needed from Washington. And on Sunday he is slated to have breakfast with Admiral Kimmel at the Canoe Club. He's trying to set up an interview with the Japanese consul general in Honolulu but Mr. Kita is busy this weekend."

Randi was astonished at Brooke's knowledge of Steve's doings. If she herself had made an effort, instead of fussing over the new granddaughter, perhaps he would have told *her* all this.

"These are strange times," the captain remarked with a sigh and went on out of the dining room.

A harried-looking woman joined Randi and Brooke at the purser's table, explaining that her son was sick in his bunk, having consumed most of the bon voyage basket given to them by the crew of the battleship *Oklahoma* in Pearl.

"My husband's ship. He's Lieutenant Jack Hibberman. I'm Dora. Thank God there'll be no more of this traveling alone after February. Jocko's swallowing the anchor then. Coming home to Alameda. This'll be my last Christmas alone, I can tell you."

Unfortunately, Mrs. Hibberman began to find the gentle listing of the *Lorelei* troublesome to her stomach, and somewhere between the raw *lomi-lomi* salmon and the delicious grilled *mahi-mahi,* she departed.

It was not a festive sailing dinner.

Even the flirtatious Brooke got sleepy at an early hour and, after a brief tête-à-tête with the chief engineer, went off to bed alone. Randi took a long bath, wondering about what awaited her. Finding no answers, she went to the window which looked out over the Pacific night beyond the lanai. She felt a stuttering motion underfoot. The great liner rolled and creaked as it cut its way through the dark waters.

When she closed her eyes, she saw Steve's face as he looked up at her from the Honolulu dock eight hours ago. It seemed hardly older than the face she so vividly remembered from her wedding day, with his blue eyes laughing as he tried to slip the gold band on her badly shaking finger.

Sleepily, she reminded herself . . . there was so much to decide when this voyage ended.

# *BOOK ONE*
# November 11, 1918

THEIR marriage was built on a dare, a wager and a scheme. That knowledge would always stand between Randi and any accusation she might make against Steve.

She was honest enough to admit to herself that this first and unforgivable fault had been hers alone. The fact that she loved him so deeply was an excuse, not an absolution.

On that chilly November day when it all began for Randi and Steve, the Great War was ending in Europe, but Liberty war bonds were still being hawked in the United States.

TWENTY-YEAR-old Mary-Randal Gallegher finished her deliveries of rally tickets in San Francisco's financial district and made a flying leap to the already crowded steps of a passing California Street cable car. She hung on, her tawny hair worn unfashionably free and lashing across her face, while the little car rattled toward the steep flank of Nob Hill.

She had reserved Liberty bond rally tickets for the Lombard family in order to deliver them late in the day. Brooke Lombard, sister of Steve Lombard, the local war hero and the one idol in Randi's life, was prominent in the city's social work and possessed a great knack for making friends. Brooke's friendship meant a great deal to Randi, who often wished she could have Brooke's frail, gentle-voiced mother for her own.

On the rare occasions when Randi met Mrs. Lombard, the lady had treated her with graciousness and had expressed a genuine interest in Randi's life.

Deeply conscious of her own tumultuous family household, Randi welcomed Brooke's invitations to tea. The tea ceremony, often pale golden sherry served with English cookies the Lombards called "biscuits," or sometimes just China tea served in delicate Spode cups, transported Randi into a world of beauty and culture, allowing her to forget for the moment her own impoverished home.

The fact that Brooke Lombard had an attractive and eligible brother overseas in the AEF was an added charm. There were always bits of news about Steve Lombard, including letters from the hospital near Paris where Steve was recovering after a siege under the debris of a Marne chateau. Having been invalided out of the army, he was waiting for transportation on the first ship that would carry him to an American port.

Hoping she would be invited to stay at the Lombard house for tea, Randi clung to the post of the cable car, with several male hands covering hers as more riders jumped onto the moving car. Usually she paid no attention to the conversations around her, but today the air was buzzing with talk of just one thing.

"The hell it is! We had another fake armistice last week."

"This'n is no fake. It's the real thing, buddy."

Another opinion came from Randi's other side. One of Montgomery Street's stiff-collared young stockbrokers agreed.

"The Huns have given up. The kaiser's hightailing it to Holland. I heard it from Fremont Older himself at the *Bulletin* office."

Cheers went up around Randi. In the good-natured scuffle of celebrants, Randi was nearly pushed off the car as they crossed Chinatown's main thoroughfare. The stockbroker and a horny-fisted bartender from the Embarcadero grabbed her and pulled her in again. There was more laughter, in which Randi joined.

We're all so selfish, she told herself . . . All I can think of is that maybe Steve Lombard will be coming home some day. And if I am very nice to Brooke . . . But it was easy to do that. In her own way, Brooke was nice to everyone. If she seemed to patronize less affluent friends, surely her wealth and upbringing were to blame.

Brooke was probably amused by the notion of Randi's crush on her older brother. Before he enlisted, Steve Lombard had scarcely known Randi was alive. He saw her only behind the lunch counter outside Sather Gate when she was working her way through the University of California at Berkeley. He grinned at her, left a typical ten-cent tip, and often stopped to exchange a few words with her, to ask how she had passed her midterms and to wish her luck.

On one unforgettable day he had jokingly bestowed a kiss on her forehead when she got an A-minus on her bluebook final and he went to the trouble of looking it up outside the lecture hall where it was stacked along with other class bluebooks. Dozens of times he had been kind to her. But would he really remember her as anyone *really* special? He never asked her for a date and he went right on flirting with Alma Cortlandt, who shared his postgraduate business administration course. At times Randi felt that she really was just part of the woodwork to him.

Two years had passed since the days at the lunch counter outside Cal's Sather Gate. Steve Lombard, who had once been all-coast halfback of Cal's football team and the top man in his classes, had gone on to do postgraduate work there. He was the first of his class to go overseas and the only one to receive his bars. Even after he enlisted, the gossip in college circles predicted that "if anybody can fill Red Lombard's shoes, it's his son Steve. Wait 'til *he* comes marching home. The old man will have to move over."

As far as Randi could gather from what she had overheard between Mrs. Lombard and Brooke, these predictions didn't please the tough, leathery Red Lombard one bit. The competitive spirit between the Lombard males was a California legend, as well as a family disaster. Red Lombard's own father, "Mad Tony" Lombard, had camped out on Nob Hill in a miner's tent back in 1851, staked out five lots—five was his lucky number—and had stayed there whenever he came down to the city from the northern mines. The Lombard tent became the foundation for the Lombard mansion, the most prestigious address on the most prestigious hill in The City, as deepwater sailors the world over continued to call San Francisco.

Land was a Lombard obsession. Both Steve's father and his grandfather had made their fortunes and amassed their power not through gold, but through land. While at college, Steve had prepared himself beyond mere buying and selling with geology, paleontology and a summer mining course at the University of Nevada.

In Randi's eyes, all other men faded when compared with Steve. She thought she understood his passion for power and its prerequisites, though he probably didn't even remember her name. But she had secret hopes.

Randi's fierce pride would have forced her to banish Steve from her dreams if it weren't for her later friendship with his sister. On her visits to the Lombard mansion since Steve had gone overseas, she heard nothing but stories of his heroism, his leadership, his strength—with nary a word about girls like Alma Cortlandt . . . Her hopes wouldn't die. . . .

The cable car heaved itself up to the corner of the Mark Hopkins and Fairmont Hotels. Randi swung out, dropped to the cobblestones around the cable slot and started toward the Lombard mansion one block away. With her plaid skirt a blue-green swirl around her long legs, she accidentally offered glimpses of ankle and leg. Several whistles from her recent companions on the cable car amused her, though she did not look back.

When she approached the imposing two-story Lombard house with its twin wings that encompassed an elaborate ballroom on the east and a many-windowed dining room on the west, it was hard to think of anything but its solidity and splendor. Living here would give anyone self-respect, Randi thought. The stone exterior, imported from Italy by way of Cape Horn, had managed to survive the earthquake and fire. An eight-foot-high wrought iron fence surrounded the half block occupied by the Lombard house. Its entwined iron serpents supported lions' heads chewing on iron circlets for the tethering of horses long gone from the steep danger of Nob Hill. Randi passed them, conscious of their empty-socketed eyes staring after her, their stone mouths seeming to form the question, *"What are you doing here, Pete Gallegher's daughter, entering Lombard country? Why aren't you more respectful, Mary-Randal? Shouldn't you enter by way of the servants' door?"*

But of course, she needn't enter by the back way; surely she had become a welcome visitor . . . Insecurities, however, began to bite at her, as they had the first time she called at the Lombard house to deliver stock certificates. It had taken all her courage that day a year ago to walk proudly up the brick walk and bang a lion's-head knocker on the tall front doors of the house. Red Lombard had been just as forbidding and gruff as she had expected him to be, but when his pretty, red-haired daughter came in unexpectedly, he thawed quickly. Brooke made up for any lapses in her father's manners, and had walked to the door with Randi, politely remarking on Randi's straw boater.

Servants came and went in the Lombards' household, a fact that often puzzled Randi. She assumed it was due to Mrs. Lombard's passiveness and Brooke's irresponsibility, both of which traits—so different from her own personality—Randi found endearing.

But she couldn't help being pleased at the compliment Brooke Lombard had paid her one day amidst the chaos brought about by the family's usual servant problems. Randi had asked in all sincerity, "Why don't you just tell them how you want it done? It's your money. They are your employees."

Brooke had stared at her for a moment, then said, "Randi, you'd make a wonderful housewife. In fact, you ought to be running this house. You'd straighten us out." She giggled as an idea struck her. "If only you could marry Steve. Then we'd have some peace in this house. We could leave all these things to you. You're the most competent girl I know."

With that, Randi's dreams were fired again. When Steve Lombard came home, maybe this time he would see her as more than a mere schoolgirl—as his sister's friend, a woman. Counting on his remembering her, Randi wrote a light, impersonal letter to him which Brooke enclosed with one of her own infrequent and haphazard notes. He never replied.

Steve had been caught in the bombardment of a chateau where he and two of his men had taken refuge while on twelve-hour passes. He saved his men and ended up recuperating in Paris. Even in wartime, Paris held its attractions . . .

Today, November 11, 1918, the first day of peace, Randi raised her chin, forced her finely boned, sensitive face into softer contours and tried to look composed.

The girl who held the door open for Randi wore the respectable black dress and starched white organdy apron that other Lombard maids had worn, but her little frilled headband was crooked and her black hair hung in limp ringlets around her pouting face. She was chewing gum and managed to snap it in Randi's face.

"You expected, Randi?"

My God! Randi thought, trying to get a look at her in the dark entrance hall . . . Stella Burkett . . . I went to grammar school with her. *If I hadn't forced my way through college, I, too, would be somebody's Irish maid . . .*

She felt a certain kinship with Stella, although they had never been friends in school. Randi's curiosity about boys and sex might have rivaled Stella's, but she was born with a core of common sense which told her she would get nothing but a bad name if she followed Stella's lead. A few hours of tumbling with a boy in the chilly sand below the old chocolate factory was not worth it, at least not with any of the boys she knew.

Sympathizing with the girl, Randi tried to be friendly.

"Hello, Stella. How are your folks? Ma—mother—hasn't seen them for ages. I have Miss Lombard's tickets."

"Fine. Fine. You know how it is. Dad and the boys are busy down at the docks. 'Course, that'll blow up if this armistice is the real thing. I do hate to see dad and Pat out of a job again so soon. But you know how that is, Randi." She let Randi know she hadn't forgotten. "There was your pa. What a one for lazing around he was!" Hands on ample hips, Stella looked her over. "You picked the right day for your deliveries, I'll say that. But you sure you got on the right outfit for it?"

Stella's remark puzzled Randi. The colors of her plaid skirt were flattering, and though the white batiste blouse was out of date, her short, buttoned bolero jacket caught the exact blues and greens in her skirt. At the trust department of the bank where she worked as temporary help she had been complimented on her appearance by two officers. That counted for something, surely. Still, Randi wondered what Stella meant by "the right day."

"If the bank doesn't expect a special wardrobe, I'm darned if I see why the Lombards should."

Stella gave her a long, penetrating look, shrugged and strolled away. "I'll tell them you're here. You might have to settle for our little princess, after all."

Randi had from the beginning asked to see Brooke Lombard. Stella's remarks were very odd.

Three or four minutes later footsteps hurried down the oak staircase and Brooke Lombard's dainty little figure, crowned by a mass of deep red curls, brought a cheerful light to the entry with its archways opening into the darkened, cluttered Victorian parlor and the formal dining room.

"Honey, what's all this formality? I've got the most divine news for you. Wait 'til you hear." She tugged her tall friend's hand. "Come upstairs to the sunroom. I've oodles to tell you."

"What is it? Tell me!"

They went upstairs together. Randi tried not to seem curious about the shadowy, closed doors upstairs, but she would like to have asked which was Steve's bedroom. She could hear the murmur of voices behind one door. Mrs. Lombard must have guests.

Randi badly wanted to believe that Brooke's exuberant mood was genuine. She had learned very early that the less she revealed of her own affections, the less she would be hurt. Yet deep inside she longed for acceptance and affection, and when it came she warmed inwardly to the offering.

Randi couldn't imagine what her friend's great news was. Knowing how easily roused Brooke was, she suspected it might be something as trivial as new clothing. In spite of the war shortages, Brooke was forever displaying a new muff, or an evening gown of feathers, fringe and beads, or something else that soon after was forgotten and discarded, making Randi acutely aware of how cheaply the Lombard daughter regarded money. And men . . .

New clothes and new men went together for Brooke. Randi was never quite sure how far Brooke's affections were involved in each affair, but judging from the newspaper gossip columns, all Brooke's ex-loves had one thing in common: every man remained loyal to his memories of her.

Randi knew, as did most of San Francisco, that Brooke had been briefly married ten years ago, when she wasn't quite sixteen. Her father, Red Lombard, stormed off to Canada after her, and in the end, after Brooke's son, Alec, was born, there had been a divorce. Brooke returned to San Francisco and the child remained with his father's people, visiting Brooke on rare occasions. Brooke insisted that she was too young to be a mother. And Colin Huntington, an old college friend of Steve's and the father of her son, had died a hero in France during the poison gas attack at Ypres.

One day Randi overheard a conversation between Brooke and her mother as they read a letter from Steve.

"Mother, I always thought Steve enlisted to pay for what happened to Colin at that place in France. All that horrible poison gas and everything." Brooke shook her head. "Poor little Alec. I try to be especially nice to him during the week he visits us. I feel I owe him that, although I almost died when he was born. It made his left leg a tiny bit short," she later explained to Randi. "Hardly noticeable at all. You can't tell, unless he walks fast. Luckily, he doesn't care. He's awfully bookish."

After a moment of appalled silence Randi asked, "Who does he live with now?"

"Colin's mother. She lives somewhere up in the North Pacific, outside Vancouver." Seeing the look in Randi's gray eyes, Brooke raised her voice defensively. "I wouldn't dream of taking him from his grandmother. Why, she adores him!"

Randi had never again heard the name of Colin Huntington mentioned in the Lombard house. She wondered if Brooke ever gave a thought to her son between those one-week-a-year visits. Sometimes Randi wondered about the sensitivity of the Lombard women, but they were kind to her and she could never forget that . . .

"Now, come and sit down, honey," Brooke coaxed Randi, leading her to the cozy back room with long windows separated by a window seat that Randi liked so much. From the seat she could look out over the north slopes of Nob Hill and on down to the Golden Gate, now shrouded in fog. The furniture here was light wicker and the cushions had worn comfortably threadbare. Randi took the window seat at Brooke's invitation.

"What is it? I have your rally tickets, by the way. I guess you know by now that Douglas Fairbanks can't attend, but everyone else will be there, anyway."

There was no calming Brooke.

"Never mind that, Randi. I have an absolutely darling idea. Solves all our troubles. Look at how hard you work. Six days a week, not to mention those Sunday deliveries. What you need is a husband."

Randi sat up straight. She began to laugh before she realized that Brooke was actually serious. But surely Brooke suspected by now that Randi's dream lover was Steve Lombard. She had teased Randi about it often enough.

"Brooke, I don't think you understand. I don't want to get married just to be married. If I don't find—" She broke off, then carefully added, "—a man I could spend my life with, I just won't marry at all."

Brooke giggled. Her sky blue eyes had a curious glow, as if they borrowed light from her bright hair.

"Yes, you will." She looked around as if afraid she would be overheard, and lowered her voice. "Randi, I'll go so far as to wager you will accept the next proposal you receive." While Randi stared, wondering if Brooke's humorous instincts had gotten the best of her, Brooke added with great force, "One month. Give me one month. That's all."

"You *are* crazy."

"One month. One hundred dollars says you will accept the first proposal you receive within one month from today. That will be December 10."

"Eleventh."

"All right. What do you say? You swear you aren't going to marry, so what can you lose?" She clapped her hands like a child and then exclaimed, "Oh, I love it! I haven't had such fun in years. Not since my elopement."

It was an unfortunate comparison.

"Do you know how many months it would take me to pay back one hundred dollars? My salary is fourteen dollars a week."

Brooke's dimpled face glowed with her little private joke.

"But if you *are* married you can simply ask your husband for it. You just say, 'Darling, remember my georgette negligée that you loved so much on our wedding night? It isn't paid for. I need one hundred dollars.' "

"Brooke, you are impossible! Now, what is this secret of yours?"

"Is it a bet? Promise?"

"Certainly not."

"You'll be awfully sorry. Do promise, for your own sake. I'll make it fifty dollars."

Brooke was like an adorable little pup. She just wouldn't let go.

It was such a preposterous wager that Randi wondered briefly whether this might be Brooke's form of charity. She bristled at the idea, then discarded it as unlikely. But really there was no way Randi could lose—there wasn't a man in San Francisco that she had any intention of marrying. She laughed finally and agreed.

"But I'm warning you, Brooke. I'm not the least bit interested in any man you could name in this city."

"In this city. But maybe—somewhere else?" She abandoned her coy teasing. "It's a bet. You must shake on it." She held out her small, dainty hand, which made Randi conscious of her own long fingers. It was such an absurd wager Randi couldn't picture herself losing. The girls shook hands. She decided Brooke must have met some eligible young man who didn't interest her and she had decided to "fix Randi up with a husband" as the girls of Randi's acquaintance said.

"Well, that's settled."

Brooke swung around, rattling the beads of the pink crêpe de chine dress she had intended wearing to one of the lively tea dances at the St. Francis Hotel. Studying that dress with its deep V neck revealing half of Brooke's ample bosom, Randi felt a twinge of disappointment. Whatever Brooke's secret might be, it didn't include tea. Randi untangled her legs and started to get up from the window seat.

"I'll be on my way, then. I just came to leave the rally tickets."

"No, you don't. Don't you dare run away and make me lose my bet!" Brooke pressed her back onto the window seat, enjoying herself enormously. "And don't forget. He must never, ever know. It's our secret."

Randi sighed. This was what it had all been about. One of Brooke's maneuvers. Her "eligible young man" was probably waiting outside the door. With a forced smile and prepared for the worst, she watched her friend rustle across the rattan rug to the door where she slipped out.

Voices in the hall. A man's deep-throated laugh. Not like Red Lombard. Then Mrs. Lombard's languid voice. "Brooke, you tire me, just dancing around us like that."

An arm in a khaki sleeve pushed the door open. Brooke ducked under the soldier's arm and came in to make an announcement.

"Miss Gallegher, may I present the hero of Belloo Wood, Captain—"

"Bell*eau* Wood," the soldier corrected her.

"Who cares? Captain Steve Lombard is home. And all in one piece."

"More or less," he said and came across the room to meet his sister's friend. "Happy to know you. This minx forgot to tell me you were something special, Miss Gallegher."

"Naughty boy!" his mother chided. "He wouldn't tell us when he was due to arrive so we could give him a proper homecoming. His father has been in San Jose all afternoon on some stupid business project. But we left messages and Redmon should be home any minute."

Captain Lombard said nothing to this. He took Randi's hand in his strong fingers. For the first time in a long while she felt almost petite, and very feminine. All the witty and charming words she had dreamed up and rehearsed disappeared and she found herself saying merely, "Welcome home, captain." But while her eyes took him in, he was observing everything about her with that penetrating gaze of his.

He had changed surprisingly little. Unlike his father and sister, Steve did not have fiery red hair, but it looked as ruddy and as unruly as ever, if not quite so thick as she remembered. She remembered, too, the aquiline nose that had been broken during a scrimmage in his first year at Cal. It hadn't changed. Nor had that sensuous mouth that troubled her dreams. As for the rest, he looked taller, leaner, more powerful in khaki. He seemed to have been toughened by what he had been through. But the flicker of warmth about his mouth held her. He could be tender and yet ruthless, one of those tantalizing combinations that would forever intrigue her.

One thing was certain. She realized from his manner that she was entirely new to him. As far as Steve Lombard was concerned, he had never seen her before.

# *Chapter Two*

SOMEWHERE in the back of his mind, crowding out the images of a lifetime, Steve Lombard would always see Randi Gallegher as she looked that first Armistice Day in his mother's sunroom . . . a tall, slightly angular girl, totally unlike the padded and fleshy women of Europe, curled up on his favorite window seat. As she greeted him, she untangled long, lovely legs such as he had dreamed about for eighteen months in trenches, canteens, hospitals and especially in Paris cafés.

Day after day on every café terrace he had laid bets with André de Grasse, the French aviator who had saved his life, that an American female would pass them and somehow reveal the long-legged torso he described in such picturesque detail.

And here she was, in the flesh. He wished André could see her. She had the pride he liked, a regal way of holding her head on the slender stem of her neck, and she didn't assume all the saccharine airs of Brooke's usual friends.

Brooke seemed to misunderstand his silence. She looked puzzled as he held Miss Gallegher's hand and enjoyed the sensation of the thin, fine bones in his fingers.

"I see you have good taste, Miss Gallegher. You are in my favorite window seat," he said.

She looked a bit startled and tried to get up. But he continued to tease her, wanting to hold her there in that fetching position.

"I'll let you keep it today, but you will have to promise me something in return."

She raised her tawny eyebrows. There was none of the coyness he was used to. It was hard to tell whether she teased him in return or really meant it.

"I'd say that depends."

"On what? Whether my window seat is worth it?"

"Whether pleasing you is worth it. I'll have to think about that." But this time she smiled. Her mouth was wide. Generous, an artist would call it.

Behind him, he heard his sister's snicker. Their mother let out a breath of astonishment at Randi's impudence, but he found it challenging. He wished that the fluttery women of his family were elsewhere during this little duel.

"Suppose I give you until this time tomorrow."

"Good. That gives me twenty-four hours." Still smiling, she freed her hand from his clasp and, surprising himself, he let it go.

"Brooke, I know you intended to go out, and I've interrupted you." She explained to Steve, "I only stopped by to drop off the war bond rally tickets." She quickly added, "I am a messenger girl for the San Francisco-Comstock Bank."

So they were using girls now as messengers! Steve found the changes in customs and habits more and more interesting since he had been shipped overseas. His blood raced with an excitement that before had only accompanied a business deal that would bring him respect and recognition in Red Lombard's eyes.

"Look here, mother, whatever happened to that tea business of yours at this hour? Or is that a wartime casualty?"

"No, indeed, dear. As a matter of fact, Mary-Randal often stays to tea." His mother waved her hands vaguely, with a questioning glance at Brooke. "But you were going out, weren't you?"

Brooke seemed delighted, for some reason. It wasn't like her to give up a date just to be with her brother, even a brother triumphantly home from the war.

"Of course I'll stay. Steve, why can't we open that French brandy you brought home? We don't have to wait for daddy. I'll make it right with him."

He was sure she would . . . He had long ago accepted the idea that Red Lombard's son could do no right and his daughter could do no wrong. When Steve was fourteen and nearly as tall as his father, he challenged Red Lombard on the subject.

"Is it because you feel I'm in some way a threat to you, sir?" Steve had once overheard Sam Liversedge, his father's banking friend, say the same thing to a business partner. This was the only time Steve had caught the old man with his guard down.

"Since you know how it is, my boy, can't you make allowances?"

There was no answer to that, no reasoning with him. Gut instinct would prevail. Red Lombard remembered the threat he had once posed to his own father—a threat he had delighted in carrying out . . .

Steve turned to face his sister's lovely friend. "What do you say? Mary-Randal, is it? Will you stay? I'll guarantee to get you home."

With an odd, nervous gesture she brushed aside his offer.

"That won't be necessary. I'll be happy to stay for a little while."

"And I'll be happy to furnish the brandy," Brooke added. "Mama, shall we have our little party right in here? Randi and Steve seem to have fallen in love with this tacky old room."

"That will do, dear. Run along."

While Steve tried to catch Randi's eye, Mrs. Lombard took the little bell off the round center table with its crocheted cover, went to the door and rang the bell to call the downstairs maid.

All the old home touches, he thought. Nothing had changed here. Brooke was as scatterbrained as ever, his mother as vague and out-of-step with all the modern conveniences of life. The maid who had let him in was sloppy and almost rude, but apparently neither Brooke nor his mother noticed. Even the telephone had been installed downstairs over his mother's soft-voiced protests, though she and her friends of the Golden Gate Club, the Beautification League and the Ladies Historical Reading Society babbled away on it often enough. To judge by the Lombard house, one would think there had never been a war.

Steve gazed at Randi and asked if there was room on the window seat for him to rest.

"The old wound's kicking up, you know."

For an instant her face showed concern. Then she must have read something else in his eyes because she laughed, got up and said, "Don't take that straight chair, Mrs. Lombard. I know I've been hogging the best seat."

"Hogging" was an odd word for her to use. Not in the throwaway manner of Brooke's friends, but as if it came naturally to her. Intriguing girl, Steve decided. No—woman.

The maid brought in a tray carelessly laid by the day-cook. Mrs. Lombard sighed.

"Cold again. How often I've asked Mrs. Schultz to heat the pot. Stephen, do you think she does it deliberately? I mean—maybe because you've beaten their dreadful kaiser?"

"I doubt it. Schultz is a born and bred San Franciscan. And mother, I didn't personally lick the kaiser. Didn't even see any Germans until they were prisoners. Or stinking dead."

"Really, Steve!" Brooke murmured as his mother winced.

He noted that Randi Gallegher raised her head as if she were studying him. Steve enjoyed making show-off remarks like that . . . In some way every wince of distaste was a tiny price extracted of civilians, a kind of bloodless offering to those few painful memories he carried. Not for the dead. They were nothing now but part of the rich, dark earth of France. The offering was rather to the men he had known who were maimed, or those so badly burned by the chlorine gas experiments of the enemy that no one could look at these men without shuddering. In honor of the dead Colin Huntington who had been his brother-in-law all too briefly, Steve had visited the hospital ward devoted to the gas victims before they were shipped back to Britain and oblivion. The sight had made him ashamed of the relatively insignificant shrapnel wounds that had invalided him out of the army . . .

Curiously enough, Randi Gallegher seemed to understand his deliberate attempt to shock the women. She did not smile but took the brandy snifter he offered and held it between her palms, warming and swirling it. Steve raised his own glass, got a whiff of the aged liquor that recalled so many moments in France, snatches of memory mostly pleasant. Almost as if fate had decreed it, Randi Gallegher had raised her own glass and was studying him over its gold rim. He tried to translate that look: interest, puzzlement. More. Why should she look at him with such passionate intensity? She had only known him for half an hour. But he enjoyed the curious bond they seemed to be forging. It warmed him in a way that reminded him of his carefree days before the war.

"I really have to go," Randi spoke up, startling him out of his reveries. "I'm afraid I've stayed too—"

"Daddy!" Brooke cried, running to hug Red, who had suddenly appeared in the doorway behind Steve.

Steve noticed with a touch of resentment that both his mother and Miss Gallegher seemed shaken by the arrival of his father. Red behaved well, however. Remembering childhood experiences, Steve had half-expected to be greeted by a rumble of criticism. But his father surprised him by coming into the room and throwing his arms around his son. Embarrassed, Steve patted him on the back.

"Good to see you, father." He couldn't think of anything else to say.

His father had never displayed overt affection, and now Steve didn't know how to deal with it. But Red persisted.

"I knew you'd make it home. We read all about you. Made us all proud, son. Proud."

Well . . . that sounded like him, Steve thought and relaxed. He exchanged a squeeze of the arm and offered him the brandy bottle. For a minute he thought his father was disappointed. Maybe the old man had actually wanted to greet him first, and open the bottle with Steve alone. But it was hard to tell as Red Lombard poured a generous tot of brandy into one of the tea cups and drank it down.

"Good quality stuff. Better be careful with it. They're going to get that antiliquor bill passed, sure as shooting. Imagine this country—this city—going dry. They must be crazy. A bunch of crotchety old battle-axes behind it, you mark my words."

Steve laughed, glad he could agree. "One thing you can count on. The army isn't back of it." His attention was divided between his father and Randi Gallegher. She had sipped most of her brandy and gotten up. She meant to leave. A woman of her word. Steve, who had been lounging against the wall, straightened up.

"Did you meet any of those Bolsheviks in Paris?" Red Lombard wanted to know.

"If I did, I didn't recognize them. Europe is having a worse time with the Spanish influenza than with the Bolsheviks. I saw flu masks down at the Ferry Building two hours ago. Is it very bad here?"

"In the Tenderloin, and among the South-of-Marketers. Not much up here." But his father couldn't get his mind off the Communist threat. "Awful thing, what they did to the tsar's family. Every one of them, children and all. I heard that they actually chopped—"

He's worse than I am, Steve thought, hearing his mother's plaintive interruption. Just like the old days.

"Redmon, dear! Not at teatime."

Randi cleared her throat. "I'm afraid I'll have to go. My mother isn't well and she will be waiting for her supper . . . uh, dinner," she corrected herself, as though the precise word somehow mattered. Steve felt an unexpected twinge of tenderness toward her. Did she imagine that she had to live up to the Lombard family's expectations? He felt a strong urge to break the bubble of that illusion. Her good, strong Irish background might be superior to the weaknesses he saw after only a couple of hours in his own home.

"I'll drive Miss Gallegher home." Randi turned to protest again but he rode right over her objections and asked Brooke, "Has anyone driven my Ford lately? If not, I'll have to borrow your car."

"I've been using yours, Steve. Had a little accident with mine in September."

"Ran into a parked car down Mason Street," Red put in. "Ruined the damned car. They must be made of tin these days. My Locomobile could have stood up to a dozen grazes like that. I've ordered her a new one. Overland roadster. But it isn't in yet."

Steve noticed with amusement that his father still boasted about Brooke's "pranks," fixing her up again as always.

Brooke gave him her most endearing little-girl look. "Something happened to the crank on your Model T this morning. It just wouldn't work. I left it in the garage on Van Ness and hopped on the cable. But it will be ready by the first of next week."

"Want to use my Locomobile?" Red volunteered gruffly.

"Really, the streetcar is handy. I live downtown on Sutter Street," Randi said. "I wish you wouldn't bother."

"No bother."

She was obviously being polite. Maybe she thought she was imposing on him. But to Steve she was a breath of fresh air, the only person in the room who appeared on top of things. He took her arm.

"Thanks, dad, but as Miss Gallegher says, it's easier by cable."

RANDI DREADED having Steve Lombard take her home without first being able to coach her mother. Everything had been so perfect during the hour she spent with the Lombards, and there was Brooke's last whisper as she said good-bye.

"Remember, honey. I dare you! One month. I'm counting the money."

Dear, friendly little Brooke. She actually believed that such dreams could come true.

As they walked, Steve's hand on her arm was warm and strong. He didn't limp; he must have been one of the lucky ones whose wounds had healed and left no visible scars. He had a fast line of talk, but she sensed that there was something more to his manner than mere teasing and flirting. She caught him looking at her now and then.

"Are you a painter?" she asked as they crowded onto the outside seat of the cable car.

"God, no! Where did you get that idea?"

"The way you study people."

"Not people. You. You aren't at all like my sister. How did you two happen to become friends?"

She explained about the stock deliveries to his father and how she had several times been invited to stay for tea. "Or sherry. It was very kind of your mother."

"She's good-hearted, though you have to remind her occasionally. Mother has learned to cope with loud, opinionated fellows like dad and me. There's no malice in her."

"Or in Miss Lombard."

He laughed. "No. But she's a born schemer. Loves to weave other peoples' lives like a knitted shawl, or whatever you call it. But she will never weave mine. I've seen to that."

Uneasily remembering Brooke's wager, Randi realized then that Steve must never hear about it. "I like her very much," she said softly.

"Everybody does. Impossible not to. But Brooke hurts people, so watch out. Like Colin Huntington and his little son. Left them with hardly a shrug. But none of it is intentional. I quarreled with my father over the divorce, even moved out of the house for a few months. Nothing fazed Brooke. She insisted Colin wouldn't want her to be unhappy, so she felt she was obliging him by divorcing him."

Randi laughed rather nervously as her conscience tugged with the thought of the wager.

"Well, it's nice to know one member of that family is free of blemishes."

She had startled him. "Who might that be?"

"Yourself."

Steve reddened. "Did I sound like that? You might as well know. Mother and Brooke are angels compared to my father and me. Talk about selfish! We've never had an idea in our heads that didn't push us onward and upward. That's practically our motto."

"Not a bad motto. I get off here at Grant Avenue and walk over to Sutter."

They started through Chinatown. Steve didn't like the idea of her walking alone at night through these colorful though dangerous streets.

"The Chinese won't bother you. Nor the Japanese. Despite what people say, I've always felt safer here than on Market Street, broad and spacious as it is."

"When I was a boy most of the Chinese here wore queues—this was before the fire. We were actually the savages. We'd pull their pigtails." Randi looked at him, but he went on, his tone unexpectedly apologetic. "I didn't exactly do it, but I didn't stop anyone else. That's worse."

"I don't think so." She looked up at the Japanese lanterns swinging in the wind. "Did you ever hear why all their roofs turn up like that?"

"Tell me."

"To catch the wicked demons chasing after them."

He smiled. "Not the story I heard. But I like it. It's probably the way things really are."

"You *are* a heathen."

"Who isn't in this world? What do you say to a bag of candied ginger? Maybe some fortune cookies?"

She thought of Bridget Gallegher waiting at home. It was always worse when she had too much time to herself. She liked company—male, if possible. Randi understood her mother's needs very well and the two women were often good companions. But nevertheless, her mother's weaknesses troubled her . . .

"They will spoil our supper. But why not?"

They went into the narrow shop and while Steve bought the candy, she fingered her favorite item in all of Chinatown, a tiny paper Japanese parasol which opened and closed. There was a whole box of them in half a dozen colors. Steve reached over her shoulder and without looking, picked out the deep pink one with a blue flower in the center.

"No, don't. I didn't intend—"

"Just say you owe me a nickel. Or better yet, let it be my first offering to you."

"I do love those parasols," Randi finally said.

"I know. I saw it in your eyes."

She explained. "When I was a child pa brought one home. He had been unloading the cargo of a barkentine inbound from the Hawaiian Islands and the parasol fell out. When I played with paper dolls, the parasol just fit."

They walked down the little slope of the street to Sutter. He hadn't turned back yet and they were about to pass the narrow and dark wooden rooming house in which Randi rented two front rooms with a kitchenette for her mother and herself.

"You've walked me home, Mr. Lombard, and I do appreciate it. I'll say good night now." She held out her hand.

He ignored her. "I'll just save that until I leave. Remember. You owe me a handshake. I'll get you safely to your mother."

Randi gave up. As they climbed to the second floor from the gaslit front hall, with its smells of boiled clothes, lye and Argo starch, her heart sank with her shame of the squalor in which she and her mother were forced to live. Curiously enough, though, he paid little attention to it.

"In Paris you got the smell of cabbage. I prefer starch."

"You oughtn't to be here at all. Your folks are probably in the middle of dinner right now."

"Supper."

She gave him a hard look. "On Nob Hill it's dinner. Really, there is hardly room for ma—mother—in our apartment, much less a visitor from Nob Hill. I'll have to say good night here."

They were at the front of the second floor by the door with its broken brass number six. He tried the knob. It opened.

"Are you in, Mrs. Gallegher?" he called out. "I'm bringing your daughter home safe and sound. Hope you like candied ginger."

Randi began to suspect that Steve Lombard could handle anything, including her mother, no matter what Bridget Gallegher was liable to do. For a minute or two it seemed the apartment was empty, though the room was dimly lit from the glow of the ornate glass Tiffany-style lamp.

"She must have gone for a walk," Randi suggested hopefully. "She gets headaches in the late afternoon." But she saw his expression change from mild curiosity to surprise. Worse—amusement. She swung around.

The bedroom door had opened and Bridget Gallegher made her way into the living room, blinking in the lamplight. Her graying but still lustrous dark hair was wild and uncombed. Her pretty, heart-shaped face looked bloated as it did after she had drunk too much beer. She wore a green flannel wrapper which she had pulled around her ample form, though Steve couldn't miss her legs, her bare feet in a man's leather slippers.

"Well now, girl," Bridget greeted them, taking one hand off her wrapper to yawn elegantly. "You'll be making a noise to wake the dead. Who's this? A fine looker, so he is. You're not the landlord's son, by any chance? He's servin' of his country, too. The navy, ain't it, Mary-Randal?"

Before Randi could open her mouth Steve came forward and took Bridget's hand. "Afraid I'm not in the navy, Mrs. Gallegher. Merely the infantry. By the way, my name is Lombard."

"Mother, Mr. Lombard walked me home."

Bridget beamed, pumped his hand with vigor.

"A pleasure it is, Mr. Lombard. If I knew you was expected, I'd of put out some'ut. You wouldn't have a taste for the best beer in town, would you? My friend LeMass rushes the growler for me. He's got connections, bein' in shipping and all." She offered him the rocking chair with its torn antimacassar but Randi, trying desperately to save the Gallegher pride, cut in.

"Mr. Lombard has a dinner engagement, mother. Some other time."

"I do have to be going, Mrs. Gallegher. We'll make it next time, shall we?" He glanced at Randi who retreated to the hall door and, trying to look nonchalant, waved him out.

She had one consolation. The worst was over, or so she thought.

Steve was already in the doorway when the bedroom door squeaked open wider and out came Bridget's gentleman friend, a longshoreman who had altered his original name of Padraic Leamas to the more pronounceable Patrick LeMass and made himself indispensable to Bridget. Though he was a bit of a sponger, even Randi liked the big, brawny fellow with his good heart, his devotion to Bridget and his friendly interest in "his daughter," as he referred to Randi.

But not tonight. She could have killed him, coming out of the bedroom like that, snapping on his blue elastic sleeve garters and pulling up his suspenders.

"Evenin' to you, captain. You bein' one of Red Lombard's kin as I take it, you might give your paw the word that LeMass will be lookin' for work, this war bein' over and all. Just tell him I painted the flagpole at the new Hall of Justice back in nineteen-ought-nine."

Steve grinned. "The very next flagpole that turns up, I'll see that you get the job."

"Great man, Red Lombard. Just bear in mind, captain, I got a head for high places. Like the new Mercantile Building across the bay in Oakland. That's something your paw's got his money into, ain't it now?"

"Probably. He has a hand in half the Pacific Coast."

Randi noticed that Steve's mood seemed to change, though when he said good-bye to her it was difficult to guess his thoughts. The lightness seemed artificial. With a crushing sense of loss she decided that the unexpected look of gentleness in his eyes was pity. And in that moment she hated him . . .

Nothing had been said about meeting again. Nor did she hear from him the next day.

"Damn him!" She thought, and hated him the more because he had made her hope.

# *Chapter Three*

IT was strange to wake up at home now with his eyes closed and wonder where he was. Smells told Steve Lombard a lot . . . the carbolic stench of the hospital, the garlic wafting its way up from the café in that Left Bank hotel on the rue de la Harpe . . . then there was the haunting, faraway odor of spring blossoms . . . then came the closer and more pungent stink of freshly turned earth, rotting wood lining the dugout and the feces of terror . . .

That night of his twelve-hour pass, when he and two doughboys from the adjacent sector dove into the ruins of the Rogier-Grasse chateau to avoid the bombardment, he had smelled the blood even before the last ancient wall of the chateau fell in on them. He had dragged out the two men. The smell overwhelmed the dusty rubble. Must have been dead animals trapped somewhere within. But the rest was hazy . . .

Smells . . . the cabbage in the French girl's room behind the Opera . . .

Like the smell in the Gallegher rooms. How did the girl stand the life and still come out with that proud, clean look? In a few years all that pride might be lost, living as she did. Like her mother's good looks. What a waste . . .

He planned to see the girl again. She fascinated him. There was a tantalizing quality about her that almost annoyed him; for the first time in his life he couldn't get a woman out of his head. But that would have to wait until he got more immediate matters cleared out of the way. He had been home two days and to his sister Brooke's disgust, he spent every hour looking up friends from his college and football days. Alma Cortlandt hadn't changed much. She was going with a doctor—what the hell was his name?—who was very bookish. Alma was still her small, darkly attractive self, and it was hard to tell whether she cared for the doctor fellow or not.

Immediate matters brought him back to the fact that the war was over. Armistice was two days old. It really might not come unstuck this time . . . He opened his eyes. It was over . . . the last great war to end all wars.

He sat up. There were a lot of things to do today. He had to check on the deals he had worked on before his enlistment. Most of them would be gone now, but no one had known about the series of bungalows he planned in tiny hamlets along the Russian River in Northern California. It had been his secret. He needed only the credit at Wells, Fargo-Nevada Bank; for collateral there was the trust fund left to him by his grandmother on his mother's side. Now was the time to build small properties, Steve thought, for the middle class. This was a lot closer to the basic Lombard nature than the Virginia aristocracy he and Brooke had inherited from their mother, a member of the First Families of the Old Dominion. The impressive buildings that Red delighted in financing would remain half-empty during what would surely be a depression after the war boom died out . . .

He thought he had bathed and dressed before anyone else was up to demand the great house's single bathroom. But when he got down to the breakfast room for Mrs. Schultz's memorable crab cakes with fried potatoes, eggs, oatmeal and cream, applesauce and coffee with a jigger of whiskey, he heard his father striding into the little room right behind him.

Steve was glad of the company. They had in common the most important subject in the world: their profession.

Red Lombard served himself liberally from the platter of crab cakes. He stacked freshly baked toast on his bread-and-butter plate and then dug into the rest of the breakfast laid out in the center of the alcove table between Steve and himself.

"Well, son, I suppose you will want to start getting your feet wet today. You always did like to dive right in. Sam told me they'll be mighty happy to oblige you in any way at Wells, Fargo. There's a vice-president and trust officer's job going begging this very minute.

You might just inquire about it today. Ask for Sam Liversedge. You remember him."

It was good of the old man, Steve thought. He had probably given the bank a big talk about his homecoming son. On the other hand, Steve had learned very early on a mild sort of cynicism when dealing with his father. Steve could hardly remember a year when Red Lombard hadn't overextended himself at some time. The family had often failed to pay the servants, and had to get by on tea and Mrs. Schultz's baked bread and vegetables from the wholesale market downtown. But in order to satisfy Red's craving for meat, they always paid the earliest boats of the Italian fleet at Fisherman's Wharf to deliver their best catch. That was family policy. Things were always pleasanter in the house when father's wants had been satisfied . . .

"Sure, I remember Sam," Steve said, carefully casual. He never trusted Red on business information. He had written to Sam Liversedge from Paris asking in confidence if there was a buy with a future along the Russian River, a "sacrifice" of some kind that he could get into with a healthy percentage of his forty-thousand-dollar trust fund.

Red took a toothpick to his teeth and sucked hard as he reminded Steve, "Before you do any big dipping into the investment pool, I'd suggest you get yourself a cushion, just for the immediate future."

"A nine-to-five job, you mean." It wasn't quite what Steve had envisioned and he began to feel concerned, wondering what Red was getting at . . .

Steve had inherited one-third of the Lombard house and its expenses from the original builder, his grandfather "Mad Tony" Lombard, as well as the trust fund from his maternal grandmother. The house gave him asylum, though he suspected that its upkeep had still cost him a considerable sum during his time overseas. Because there was no alternative for a family which despite its rivalries stood together against the world, he had left his power of attorney with his father.

"How have your investments been going, dad?"

"Good. Spreading out. I had some pressure from a contractor in Southern California but I haven't acted yet. Not my line of country, as they say. I'm looking into the north, mostly. Future's there. Climate and all."

"You mean Portland? Seattle?" He avoided that little vision of his along the vacation haven of the Russian River an hour above the Golden Gate.

"That, yes. And around Santa Rosa. I've got a man looking into things in Sonoma County."

Steve concentrated on buttering a slice of toast. It was bizarre, downright scary—the old man could read his mind.

He tried to urge Red away from the north. "When I wrote to Sam Liversedge he said there was a lot of oil interest in *Southern* California. That ought to bring in people—and people need housing."

Red stopped eating, ruffled up his grizzled, carrot red hair.

"Could be something in that. Still and all, if you want my advice, you'll take the job. Frankly—" He hesitated. It wasn't like him to be reticent. "We could use the salary. The house and our womenfolk don't come cheap, you know. Should've seen the bills I got after Christmas '17. And another one coming up."

Steve had heard that before. In bad times they borrowed from Wells, Fargo-Nevada at prime rates, securing the loans with the Nob Hill property.

"Another mortgage coming, I suppose. But dad, I think the time is getting ripe to make smaller investments. Diversify, consider the new buyer and the new renters. One thing about landing in a trench, you get a lot of time to think, and also learn the plans of your buddies who are going to come home and buy from you."

"Not me. Never retreat. That's the Lombard slogan. I like my deals big, shafting the heavens, boy. None of these little rose-covered cottages."

Steve felt a prick of new hope. "Then this business in Sonoma County is just talk. I know you, you old fox. You've been talking about it to throw rivals off the track."

"No such thing. We're putting in a series of summer cottages on the river at Guerneville, right now."

Damn him! Talk about mind readers.

"Good for you, dad. Afraid I'll have to be on my way. A lot of time to make up. Kiss mother and Brooke for me. I'll see them later in the day."

"Sure. Your mother won't be down 'til eleven or so. That's when she makes her phone calls to her old club biddies. She's putting up the first two thousand dollars for the orphans of the Allied countries."

Steve stopped, half out of his chair.

"My God! Do you know how much that is, from one family, when there are a hundred similar drives? Mother has never invested one cent in the house here, or the family."

"It's her money. That was my deal when she married me. You don't think that fine old family of hers would let her marry me without a settlement. Sam Liversedge says it's about quadrupled in the last twenty-five years."

Steve grinned. "And you can't get your hands on it. You could have lost it or doubled it and lost it again in the meantime. Looks like mother trusts her charities more than she does you and me."

"Maybe she knows us too well. Anyway, she had to get the money in fast. It's chicken feed compared to some, but it puts our name first on the Golden Gate Club roster. And that doesn't hurt, in our business. Keeps the Lombards from being fly-by-night real estate operators."

"We'll be lucky if Brooke and I won't have to draw on our trust accounts before we're through.

"Won't be the first time, and it's always paid back in. You know that. Nobody can say I ever defaulted, especially on my own kin."

TWENTY MINUTES later Steve was in the office of Sam Liversedge and looking out over busy Market Street with streetcars passing on each of its four tracks. The war might have ended but the traffic below these windows made the Champs-Elysées look like a country lane. It was hard to believe he had only been away eighteen months.

He saw an entire family crossing the street, dodging streetcars and about four lanes of automobiles. The entire family wore gauzy flu masks. The way they were jaywalking was a lot more dangerous than the flu, Steve thought. But he grinned at old memories. Jaywalking to a San Franciscan established his independence.

"It was ever thus," he murmured as the little banker rolled into the room, his two hands spread over his stomach, the fingers of his left hand playing with his watch and chain. His pudgy right hand shot out.

"Welcome home, Stephen. Mighty glad to see you in one piece. Pretty rough business over there, I guess."

Shaking hands with him and glancing out the Montgomery Street corner window, Steve said, "The changes here shake me up more. Make me itch to get into action. I'd barely started when the war began. Now I get the feeling all those bustling fellows down there are years—and millions—ahead of me."

"Do sit down, Steve—may I call you Steve? Seeing that I knew you when you were being diapered. Well, sir, I don't think it'll take you long to get back in the swim. You Lombards are a tough breed. Remember how quickly your father got that noble old house of yours cleaned up, refurnished and livable after the fire? Seems to me some of the swells of Nob Hill stayed with you a few nights."

Liversedge reached into his right-hand drawer, pulled out a box of cigars, slid it across to Steve and leaned far back in a squeaking leather chair. His soft round face was redeemed by a pair of intelligent eyes.

"I remember. I sometimes think dad can do anything. Even the earthquake and fire didn't defeat him . . . Do you mind? I've gotten used to these." Steve took out a slightly crushed pack of cigarettes and offered it to the banker, who waved it away.

"Getting down to business," Steve began after watching Liversedge fuss with his cigar, clip it and light it, throwing the match in a polished brass cuspidor by his desk leg. There was no question that the man was stalling.

"First of all, did your dad tell you about our hopes for you?"

"He said something about a job. Vice-president and trust officer. In ordinary circumstances I would say it was a tempting offer."

"But then—"

"I'm not an ordinary man."

Sam Liversedge sat up a little, his chair creaking its protest at the gall of a twenty-seven-year-old suppliant with no job, no experience and the conceit of the devil. Steve read his thoughts and smiled.

"I never said I was superior. Just that I do my best work when I have a little responsibility. I like working on my own."

"Just like your father. Stands to reason. Then what did you have in mind?"

"An investment to work on at once. Something to build. No, not one of dad's ten-story skyscrapers, all business and big money. You remember, before the war, that thing I asked you to look up for me?" The banker looked puzzled. Steve added, "Sonoma County. The beach and that beautiful land along the Russian River. Does that come back to you?"

"You mean Guerneville and some other little towns."

"All the way to the coast. The old Russian Fort Ross is north of there. Pretty dilapidated. But it's all beautiful country."

Liversedge puffed. "I know the area. My wife was born in Petaluma. Could make an elegant estate. Often thought so myself."

"Not an estate, Sam. Attractive little places for, well, more modest people. I'd like to try a small area to begin with. Two or three lots to build on."

"But my dear boy, you don't think that lovely area would remain untouched for eighteen months. I'm afraid others saw what you saw. You wouldn't know the place now. Booming. But it's not the only buy in the world." He leaned forward across the desk. "Let me tell you about an investment you're really going to jump at. South of Los Angeles, a beach town called Strand. Ever hear of it?"

Steve ignored the question. "Who saw the potential in the river country?"

The banker was uncomfortable, and explained with a bland assumption of innocence.

"Red Lombard goes fishing up-country. You know that. He often took you. Why would you think he'd miss what you saw? You must remember, Steve, you never told me these dreams of yours, so I couldn't very well have betrayed you."

The probable truth in Sam's explanation didn't make it any more palatable. Steve got up, feeling the pinch of knitting flesh across his ribs. He caught himself massaging his side and pulled his hand away angrily.

"Yes. I've heard of Strand. They discovered oil down there."

"On the outskirts of town. Riggman Hill. Actually, it's a resort city. Lots of newcomers pouring in from the Midwest and the rest of the country. Great climate. That means they will need housing. Middle class, lower middle class, and some very posh oil speculators. And sitting right on a cliff overlooking the ocean and the longest beach you ever saw is a new eight-story apartment building complete with elevator, electricity and several new owners hungry for cash. They are the heirs to the original owner-contractor.

"An eight-story building would take more than my entire trust fund and then some," Steve reminded him, although a vague pride of ownership had begun to blur the bitterness of his disappointment.

Liversedge eagerly pushed onward. "But you can. The Los Angeles Marine Bank has orders to sell shares. The larger the share in cash, the larger the interest in the building. Simple enough for anyone with a minimum offering of twenty thousand and over. I thought of you at once when Red turned it down."

"He knows about it?"

"Says there's no future in that area."

Steve remembered the breakfast conversation. "He told me that, too. I mentioned that the oil would bring big money people, but I don't think he heard me."

"Just so. Consider it, Steve. Look the property over. Then bid in a share or shares. Whatever you feel comfortable with. Or without," he added, chuckling at his own wit.

Steve took a long breath. Whatever bitterness or resentment he might feel over his father's chicanery with the family assets, he had no intention of letting an outsider guess his feelings.

"How much do I have to play with? I don't seem to have saved much from my pay," he managed to ask casually.

"I don't imagine so. My daddy told me he came home from Appomattox with six bits in his poke." He laid down his cigar. The desk top was scarred with cigar burns. He pressed his fingertips onto the desk in the shape of fat, high-bodied spiders.

"You know the Lombard methods. We'll be redeeming all those captive trusts and mortgages within the usual six months. Isn't that dad's habit?" Steve suspected that the banker knew something.

"Oh, absolutely. No fear. He's brought the mortgage on your house down in fine style, if I may say so. Your generosity with the trust funds, yours and that pretty sister of yours, has made it possible to finance A. and R. Lombard and Company. At the same time, the company's investment will pay off handsomely within the next five years. Our analysts predict a boom in about three years, give or take a year."

"Very comforting. Do you happen to know, offhand, how much remains in the two trust funds?"

The banker pursed his lips, confessing, "I couldn't give you the precise figure, but as Red probably wrote you in January, we can predicate your income on the fact that at this minute a minimum of over twenty thousand is drawing interest. That would be your fund alone. Miss Lombard drew twelve thousand more of her own fund when she planned to marry that Russian gentleman this past summer."

"Russian gentleman?"

"A prince, so he says. Your father had him investigated. He's still around, but the marriage talk seems to have subsided."

"I hope so! That means most of Brooke's trust is gone."

"Temporarily, my boy. As I say, the A. and R. investments are a sure thing. I'm positive your father will invite you to examine the assets."

Steve had a gnawing ache in the pit of his stomach. Even knowing his father, he hadn't really expected this. As for A. and R., the company was strictly his father's. No offer of participation had ever been made to Steve. Nor did he wish it, as his father perhaps knew. Red Lombard had simply borrowed to the hilt on his children's funds with the habitual understanding that it would all be paid back with interest, if possible . . . perfectly understandable in a family that never invited outside participation . . .

But it left Steve very little with which to set up his own business. That dream of a fine pyramid of deals which reached or even exceeded his father's acquisitions burst like a child's balloon. What a fool he had been not to anticipate this! . . . Yet he knew that if he had it to do over again he would still have given his father the power of attorney. The Lombards looked inward, to each other. They had never admitted outsiders to their deals. . . .

"All right, Sam. I'll give thought to that Southern California deal you mentioned." He added with cool amusement, "I've got twenty thousand left, more or less. And the shares are twenty thousand. A gambling man would say that's an omen."

Sam Liversedge smiled archly at this.

"Of course, we bankers always tut-tut anything that smacks of gambling. But it does seem providential." He held up his hand in final warning. "So long as a better offer doesn't come through, but don't wait too long—and Steve?"

What other bad news was in the wind?

"I wouldn't have pursued this with you if your father hadn't turned it down. I don't play Lombard against Lombard. Never did."

Steve said he understood, and was already out in the hall when the banker's secretary came rustling out in a neat blue serge suit with a ruffled white blouse.

"Call for you, Mr. Lombard. It came to Mr. Liversedge. You may take it on my phone."

When he got back into the tiny hole-in-a-wall that was the secretary's office, Liversedge stood in his own doorway, very pleased with himself.

"It's your sister, my boy. What a charmer she is! Been flirting with me over the phone, naughty girl. Made me feel like a boy again."

Wondering what had happened, Steve picked up the old black phone and receiver.

"Brooke? Sam says you want me."

"Brother dear, only to make up a foursome. You'd never guess who just arrived."

"Santa Claus."

"Unworthy, Steve. A very dear friend of yours."

"Alma Cortlandt? I had lunch with her yesterday."

Brooke said with controlled impatience, "No, honey, not Alma. Somebody from a long way off. Gay Paree. And Steve, he's the handsomest thing! You never did him justice."

Here was someone who would understand the last two years without being told. Steve could be himself with André, the Comte de Grasse, who had found Steve and his two companions outside the wreckage of his family's chateau. It was André who had commandeered an ancient tumbrel and mare to get his American allies out of the danger zone. Five months before, he had crawled away from a flaming crash, the last survivor of his squadron. Having also lost his mother and his young wife in the original bombing of the chateau, he acted like a man with no future nor any ties to the present.

Steve was not too surprised at his showing up in San Francisco. In his elegant, slightly distant way, he had become Steve's confidant, and vice versa. It was good to know he was in town. He was a friend one could trust—except in one respect. Brooke must not be allowed to involve herself with André.

"Great. Tell you what, Brooke; tell him I'll be on my way. See you all soon as I can make it. Tell André he's staying with us, of course. And by the way, just a reminder. He was very devoted to his wife. Women since then seem to be fly-by-nights."

"I get it. Don't worry, they don't make the man who turns me down. Not that I'll ruin your precious count. Listen, I thought we ought to take him someplace where we can dance; I can tell he's a divine dancer. But since he got off the train in Oakland, all he talks about is the ferryboat ride."

It was going to be awkward. Steven wondered how André himself wanted to handle this matter. Better leave it to him.

"What does he want to do?"

"I thought we'd get him back on a ferryboat and ride across the bay to Sausalito for an early dinner."

"Sounds all right."

"But I need a girl for you. What would you think about my friend Randi Gallegher?"

He didn't know what to say. He did not want any involvements right now. And there was something about that girl . . . He still remembered every detail of their walk through Chinatown the other night, and the wonderful way she held her head when she said good night after what must have been a disaster for her. Later. Some other time. No involvements now. Too much to do in getting started . . .

"No. Better make it Alma. We can spend the day tearing apart old school chums."

"Alma! Hell! I never liked Miss Popularity."

"Now, now, don't get jealous."

She scoffed at this. "Me jealous of that black-eyed witch?" But for some reason she relaxed and was again her sunny self. "Well, why not? See you at home soon. And Steve, thanks for knowing such adorable people."

"Glad you like Alma."

Brooke didn't bite on this. She hung up.

# *Chapter Four*

RANDI Gallegher rushed her mother onto the large white ferryboat just before it wobbled out of its slip and headed around toward the choppy San Francisco Bay. With the foggy wind whipping her face bright red, Bridget demanded proudly, "What's your opinion now? Think I'll pass muster?"

Randi hugged her until she squealed.

"Ma, you never looked prettier in your whole life. And so elegant."

"It's me rabbit coat LeMass give me. Makes me feel like the Queen of Sheba, so it does. I ain't wore it in months. But when he give it to me it was like new. Only here at the cuffs, maybe."

"Nobody will notice. Ma, I'm so proud of you."

Holding onto her blue grosgrain turban with one hand, Bridget looked around.

"I swan! I don't know why you thought Miss Brooke would be askin' to see me, I'm sure. She's your friend. Not mine."

Randi wasn't at all sure herself. The phone call had caught her at the bank as she was leaving to deliver a trust deed across town, and it still seemed highly unlikely that Brooke Lombard would be traveling alone across the Golden Gate and needing Randi's company, no matter what she said. Her brother must be mixed up in it somewhere. Either he had asked Brooke to call, or it was Brooke's attempt to bring Randi together with Steve and thus win her bet.

Whatever the reason, Randi had rushed home after delivering the deed and insisted that Bridget go with her. She was determined that the Lombards see her mother at her very best. They weren't going to be allowed to sneer at Bridget Gallegher.

Randi had changed hurriedly to a blue blouse with bishop sleeves and an overdress of deeper barred silk with a wide sash to match the blouse. The effect was almost spoiled by her old tan coat, but it was too cold to hazard wearing no coat at all. She had pinned on her tiny blue hat, made in imitation of a trench cap, and it was just as well that her hat pins were sturdy. It promised to be a rough crossing. Since Brooke had once remarked that her brother was a "leg" man as opposed to one who looked at bosoms, backs of necks or other such areas, Randi had spent several days' salary on silk stockings.

"You never know," she excused herself. "He just might notice them. Somewhere." She had given up hope of his ever contacting her of his own accord, but San Francisco being a very insular city, he was sure to cross her path some time soon.

"But not today," she muttered, her teeth chattering. "Ma, maybe we'd better move inside. It's so cold."

"Surest thing you know, dearie. Even a flu mask would be warming. There's Alcatraz coming up. Always crosscurrents along here. Begod, it was along here your pa asked me to marry him. We went on up to Vallejo, got us a judge, and you was born legal and all."

Randi teased her. "What? No priest?" But she had heard before how desperate Bridget was to keep Randi from being born out of wedlock . . .

While Randi slid the door open for her mother to enter the main deck interior of the ferryboat, her hooded glance considered all the long, shiny rows of seats facing each other, full of Marin County shoppers returning home from a day's buying in the city. No sign of the Lombards.

A dozen people crowded around the central short-order bar, collecting Orange Crush, milk, coffee, Liberty burgers, frankfurters called "hot dogs," and ice cream cones. Behind these varied pleasing scents could be heard the throb of engines in the bowels of the boat.

Bridget asked pitiably, "S'pose I could be nibbling on one of them frankfurters without I was called the kaiser's friend?"

"Sure. Why not?" Randi tucked a dime in her mother's hand, then considered and closed Bridget's warm, gloved fingers over two quarters. "I'll get paid in two days. Let's enjoy ourselves." On an impulse she caressed the soft, worn fur shoulder of the rabbit coat. "You're looking so nice, ma."

Several young sailors crowded around Bridget, all talking at once, teasing and fighting to offer her a swallow from their beer steins. Bridget often had that effect on young men. While Randi watched her mother's happiness with mischievous pleasure, knowing what was in the steins, Bridget took a sip from each stein, swallowing and then sputtering.

"Root beer!"

"Don't forget, ma. It'll be root beer for all of us when Prohibition comes in," Randi reminded her.

The sailors laughed as Bridget gagged. One of them looked Randi over appreciatively, but her real interest had been distracted by the sight of two young women and their escorts across the wide interior of the ferryboat. She saw Brooke, all in white with ermine trim on her Russian-style coat. She was with a darkly handsome, foreign-looking man, tall and elegant in civilian clothing, though his shoulders were hunched over a little. But he held little interest for her. There in civilian dress was Steve Lombard, looking lean, rugged and powerful. Randi was afraid her heartbeat was loud enough to betray her. She was made acutely uncomfortable by the curvaceous little brunette with whom he seemed to share a joke at the moment. Both were laughing and pointing at Berkeley on the eastern horizon . . . So he still had Alma Cortlandt on his mind . . .

The sailors wandered away to look at the desolate, rocky Alcatraz, the old prison of gold rush days, leaving Randi and Bridget alone. Randi attempted a mental trick she and her friends had used in school. She kept willing Steve to turn and see her. Brooke Lombard, meanwhile, carefully avoided her after one wiggle of her fingers which Randi took to be a signal.

It worked. Steve put one hand up to the back of his neck and rubbed it. It was exactly the spot Randi had concentrated on. Randi, delighted at her success, produced a smile for her mother just as Steve turned around to look at the foggy expanse of the Golden Gate.

She was careful not to look at him, and Bridget unwittingly helped her by talking with great animation. Steve noted Bridget, too, and out of the corner of her eye Randi saw that he was impressed. He seemed to like what he saw. Alma Cortlandt asked him a question, then stared at Bridget and Randi. The little brunette's smile came a fraction too late to be natural.

Randi continued to ignore him. She was having great fun annoying Alma, who though she had never done Randi any harm, nevertheless was making her suffer both envy and jealousy.

Steve hadn't apparently made much of an effort to come over and speak to her, but at least she had caught his interest. Bridget startled her, almost ruining everything.

"Well, I do declare! There's that good-looking Stephen Lombard. Look, dearie. Behind you. Hi, there, Mr. L." She stripped off her glove and waved it with innocent enthusiasm.

Randi felt like sinking. She smiled, nodded and then waved to Brooke. Having done her duty, she turned to her mother.

"Aren't you going to finish your hot dog?"

"Don't want to get my hands stained with the mustard. They're coming over here."

"Who?"

"Whole gang. The redheaded Lombard girl started over first."

"That's what I was afraid of."

Bridget understood.

"Don't you be worrying, baby. He seems definitely interested. Say! That other fellow, the dark one, looks good enough to eat. Wonder who he is . . . well, now, it's a small world, Mr. Lombard. And your friends."

Randi swung around, nodding to Steve and giving her full attention to Brooke who looked ready to burst from the intrigue she had set in motion. Randi said, "Mother, this is Miss Lombard." She added this with a defiant tilt of the chin and a wave toward Steve, whose response surprised her.

"I certainly do know Mrs. Gallegher. Delighted to see you again. We hardly had a chance to get acquainted the other night. May I present Miss Cortlandt, my—our family friend." Alma's full lips pursed, and everyone heard Brooke's familiar giggle.

"And my very good friend the Comte de Grasse," Steve went on. Randi found his manner a bold challenge to her. While he spoke to Bridget, he glanced twice at Randi, looking her over.

Maybe Brooke Lombard knew what she was doing, after all.

Brooke made a fuss over Randi, hugging her and whispering, "Work fast. I want that fifty."

Fifty dollars meant so little to Brooke that it surprised Randi that she worked so hard to achieve her ends. Randi decided the reward for Brooke lay in the victory itself. She remembered that Steve had said that his sister loved to play with people's lives.

While the Frenchman, a pleasant fellow, was shaking hands with the Galleghers, Alma Cortlandt made small talk with Steve, including Randi without specifically addressing her.

"So cold! And that fog! It's usually like this in June and July. Not November. Piedmont is always so much warmer. But you know what a nice climate we have, Stevie." She clung to his arm.

*Stevie?* Randi had the satisfaction of seeing Steve wince. Apparently, Alma had rubbed him the wrong way.

"Why don't you join us, Mary-Randal? We are showing my friend André the Bay Area."

"We'd love to have you come along," Brooke put in. "Do, honey." She added, nudging Bridget, "You, too. You can ask André all about Paris, since you two seem to be getting along so famously."

Randi had not noticed the friendly exchange going on between her mother and the Frenchman. Bridget spoke up with her appalling frankness.

"Don't you be jealous, Miss L. His nibs and me were goin' over how to settle his stomach. The lad is after bein' seasick."

André de Grasse nodded with a remote look. There was polite, restrained laughter from the women, but Steve scoffed at the idea.

"You crossed the Atlantic. You crossed the bay to San Francisco. And you get seasick now?"

André nodded, assuming a demeanor of gravity he obviously did not feel.

"Compared to this they were millponds. If you will forgive me, I will go and purchase a lemon. Madame Gallegher assures me it is the only answer."

Brooke went off with him to implement the purchase, leaving Alma to her own devices.

"I'm afraid the Hotel Belvedere will be expecting only four. We must be sure and call them from the landing to let them know we will be six. If we will," Alma said, hinting.

Steve's eyes questioned Randi and it took all her power to turn away this opportunity. She was sure that he expected her to say yes, and that made it harder. She gave him what she hoped was a look of both promise and regret.

"We are going up-country to visit one of mother's friends, a widow. It might hurt her feelings if we canceled."

Bridget gasped and stared.

"What a shame!" Alma exclaimed with noticeable relief. Then with a puzzled look, she said to Randi, "But don't I know you, Miss Gallegher? I could have sworn I'd seen you before. Your face is so familiar."

Fortunately, Steve broke in. "We won't try to persuade you, Randi. Some other time—soon." He certainly was playing a game with her. She read the humor in his eyes and the challenge. She had done the right thing to hold his interest.

All the same, it was a little disheartening to see the happy foursome go the opposite way when the ferryboat pulled into its slip. Randi had only one thing to hold onto, the memory of Steve's warm, inviting handclasp just before they parted . . .

She had a bad two days before her desperate gamble paid off.

STEVE LOMBARD hated family quarrels, but during the forty-eight hours since he had discovered his father's deep incursions into the two trust funds, he had been unable to treat him with much civility. He should have known better than to expect excuses or apologies. But it infuriated him to think Red Lombard got away with so much and never suffered for it. Even Red's Sonoma County projects looked profitable. He had made enough on a single lot for a Vancouver department store to pay off the latest mortgage on their Nob Hill house.

There was no question about it. The old fox still had his touch.

Meanwhile, there was the household itself. Steve complained to Brooke, "Can't you even handle a few servants? Why must they steal food and liquor? They get drunk and quit without notice."

Brooke gave him one of the innocent looks that always worked well on those who didn't know her.

"That's exactly what my friend Randi says. You remember Randi. You met her on the Sausalito ferryboat."

"Don't be sarcastic. I do know Miss Gallegher."

"Well, she said the identical thing. It's wonderful how she knows things like that. I'd never have thought—"

He looked at her. She backtracked. "All right. I might have thought of it but I'd never have done it. I have too much to do! Steve, have you ever seen André tango?"

He had vague impressions of his friend at a *thé dansant* just off the Champs-Elysées. Brooke wasn't a bad dancer either, but he hoped André wouldn't make a play for her. Having her heart broken would be a new experience for Brooke, but even so, he didn't want her hurt.

Steve felt torn, resentful of Brooke's manipulations of his life, especially concerning his future and Miss Gallegher. Even worse, he resented the fact that this woman he desired physically might be just the person to solve the household mess. The two visions canceled each other out. This woman of such rare qualities seemed to be very much like wife material, and he wanted to stay clear of *that* until he was more independent, more in a position to overpower A. and R. Lombard and Company. And that wouldn't happen overnight . . .

He didn't want Randi Gallegher to be used. Her tenderness toward her own mother was touching. Her pride, her care not to throw herself at him, her smile, her grace and cool dignity all touched him in different ways. He found himself fond of the lively Bridget as well.

He knew that Brooke would certainly try to use Randi. Steve had a pretty good idea of why his self-centered sister wanted a poor girl in the family. Randi could straighten things out, and she would never dare interfere with Brooke's pleasures or Brooke's expensive habits. Brooke would be her benefactress.

Not bad thinking. But then, he seldom underestimated Brooke.

He wondered suddenly if he had made the mistake of underestimating Randi herself. But he dismissed this. As it was, he had been thinking too much about her.

"One of these days I've got to take Alma to that tea dance at the St. Francis Hotel that you're always talking about," he announced to Brooke at lunch.

"She won't like it. She's too uppity. I thought you had better taste. She keeps hinting that André ought to get a job. He started out before breakfast, poor dear. It's plain to me that he wants to stay in San Francisco. Would it be immodest of me to say I know why he's staying on?"

"So he's out looking for a job. I wondered." Steve couldn't imagine anything André would be fitted for in San Francisco. He might resume flying in his own country. It was curious that he wanted to stay here. Could it be possible that Brooke was the reason? If André meant it, it would be a great thing. But Steve had his doubts. Everything André cared about was in Europe. Before the war he had hobnobbed with grand dukes at Baden and Monte Carlo, betting heavily and living with ease. Such a life didn't fit him for much in the postwar American world.

Yet Steve still found André the only one he could really trust to understand his discontent, his jealousy of his father and his hopes for a career that would eclipse Red Lombard's own. But he did wish Brooke was not so eager to win André. The Frenchman had only one woman in his life, his wife, and she was dead.

"Anyway," he warned his sister, "I've known Alma Cortlandt since freshman year, so just talk about something else. You're in no position to criticize my taste. I've heard about that Russian prince you almost married. *You* need a keeper."

"What a disgusting thing to say to your only sister!"

"But true all the same."

"That has nothing to do with it."

An hour later, happening to be in the neighborhood of the bank where Randi Gallegher worked, he wandered in. One of the loan officers who knew his father came over to talk to him.

"Flu's come our way," the banker complained, shaking his head. "The boy who delivers our *Examiner* is down with the flu. The bad kind.

They say the poor kid won't pull through. Back East it's a real epidemic. A lot of returning veterans bringing it out here, they say." He recollected himself. "Present company excepted, of course."

But Steve was too busy staring at the area beside the front cage to take offense. Randi Gallegher stood there looking animated in close conversation with Steve's friend, André de Grasse. He felt a twinge of resentment and was instantly ashamed of himself. André had once saved his life, and had come here to the bank looking for a job. It was only natural that he should meet Randi . . . Still, Steve couldn't help noticing that the Frenchman had more color and looked more alive than usual. Had Randi's company done all this?

"Excuse me," Steve told the banker. "I see a friend of mine up front."

The two seemed happy to see him.

"I was inquiring about Miss Gallegher's enchanting mother. Her remedy spoiled my taste for good wine that day, but it certainly cured my *mal de mer.*" André's dark eyes read a great deal in his friend's face. He added with a shrug, "But this is not attending to business. I am going to be rude and leave you two. I have—as you say—irons in the fire. *À demain,* Miss Gallegher. Steve."

He tipped his hat, American-style, and walked away from them toward Market Street.

Watching him, Randi laughed. "Your friend isn't very subtle."

"But he knows me. That's why we are friends. Are you on your way somewhere?"

She said that she had just returned and would have to hang around and see if she was needed. It took a little doing to talk her out of that, and he motioned to the loan officer who gave him a patronizing beam.

Though Steve had been fairly sure she wanted to go with him, she now seemed a bit cool. Maybe he had taken too much for granted. He still didn't know what he wanted or how far he thought he would, or could, go with her. He was only sure he wanted to be with her.

He walked with her over to the new 1918 Hudson which he had taken directly off the showroom floor and whose cozy roadster look had the advantage of a hardtop. For exhibition purposes it had been handsomely painted a deep maroon with a contrasting golden tan top. He was rather proud of it. Alma had confessed that her father's new Willys-Overland was hardly more elegant. But Randi wanted to know where he was taking her in it. The girl was not easily led.

They agreed on what Steve described offhandedly as "a nice little place at the beach. Nothing fancy, but the food used to be good."

He hadn't consciously set out to do it, but Steve found that with every meeting he was testing her, pitting his desire and his will against hers.

She liked the car, and with an approving pat on the leather, said, "Very nice. Some women like hardtops better because their hair doesn't get mussed up."

"Do you?"

"I don't mind being mussed up. By the wind."

She looked at her hand still caressing the seat between them. He had closed his fingers over her own. They did not withdraw and they were very much alive. On an impulse, he raised her fingers to his lips.

She smiled. "Did you learn that from the Comte de Grasse?"

Annoyed, he informed her, "There *are* some things we know, even in this country."

"Oh, absolutely. It's just that he does it so well."

He tried to grin. "You little shrew!"

"Do you know, this is the first time I've been called that."

"Well, you are behaving like one."

"No," she corrected him. "Not shrew. *Little.*"

That made him laugh. He pulled her over to him, started off for Geary Street and the beach in high spirits. She made no move to release herself and he began to reorganize his plans for the evening. His common sense battled his mounting desire. He wanted her enough to take her now, tonight, and wondered if he would be disappointed if she gave in so easily. It was hard to say.

Either way, she captivated him . . .

They swung down the Great Highway around the glass roofs of Sutro Baths, the largest indoor bathhouse in the world, then passed the Cliff House and the amusement zone, desolate in late November. Steve's "little restaurant" was perched by itself among the sand dunes, far down Ocean Beach and past the Pacific edge of Golden Gate Park. TIDELANDS-AT-THE-BEACH, announced the weathered sign over the two-story frame building painted red with a white trim.

"You're sure about the food?" Randi asked.

As his hopes slid up and down, Steve talked fast—too freely, he thought.

"They're all ready here for Prohibition. This is going to be a real roadhouse where you can get liquor once the black day comes."

"I sometimes wish there had never been anything but Prohibition."

He was touched by the depth of feeling in her voice. Just before he pushed open the red door with its stained glass inserts, he stopped and spoke abruptly.

"I like your mother."

She examined his face. She must have read the truth, because her voice was gentle as she murmured, "Thank you. I'll remember that."

They entered and were ushered with suave assurance by a foreign headwaiter to an alcove table. Steve didn't know the new personnel here but they knew him, or his name. Not knowing whether he was sorry or glad about where they were seated, Steve realized that almost anything could happen in this little window box seat, surrounded on three sides by walls and long Victorian windows, heavily curtained. The other side opened onto the restaurant itself. Only one other set of diners was here at this early hour. It was a threesome of two middle-aged men and a very young blonde. The girl seemed to be enjoying herself.

Checking with Randi, he ordered oysters on the half shell, tenderloin steaks, baked potatoes and a bottle of red wine. If he weren't so ambivalent about his feelings toward her, he thought, he would be able to enjoy himself. As much as he wanted Randi tonight, a part of him suspected she would never again be as much of a temptation if she yielded tonight.

She liked the steak, and he was amazed that so slim a woman could put away so much food. She drank two glasses of wine during dinner, and by the time they had finished the spumoni for dessert Randi seemed to be in a flush of good spirits. Steve offered to show her the rest of the house and how it would be rearranged when it became a roadhouse and rooms had to be cut off from police inspection.

So far, so good . . . But she refused to go upstairs even when he pointed out that the gambling rooms would be situated there.

"I'll wait 'til Prohibition," she told him with a smile that lit up her hazel eyes. "Besides, I might be too drunk to climb those stairs."

"You're no more drunk than I am." He lifted her to the first step.

"I know," she said.

You couldn't find much of an answer to that, he thought. He knew she wanted him. He had only to keep her here, holding her close, her breasts crushed warmly against him as they were now, his flank against hers.

He felt the beat of her pulse, the warmth of her thighs as he pressed her very close. Tight in his arms, she seemed so fragile. He saw the flash of alarm in her eyes.

She whispered, "I do want you so."

"Well, then?"

"Not this way. Not like this." She began to recover her strength. It wasn't much power, as strength went. But the light in her eyes was fierce.

"Nobody takes me cheaply."

The words seared him. He held her for a long minute or two before freeing her, then his foot kicked a trash can in the dark hallway, and Randi jumped. He apologized. "Sorry. I didn't mean to scare you."

She surprised him by laughing. He felt her tears on the back of his hand.

"That's it. The trash can scared me. Can we go back to the car?"

"Sure. Why not?" The huskiness in his own voice annoyed him. Nothing was going quite the way he thought it would, not even his own reactions. He just couldn't seem to get enough of her.

He took her arm and instead of returning through the restaurant, they trudged over the sand around the building to the car, with the ocean roaring in only a highway's width away. He kept holding her arm until she stepped up on the running board and got into the car. When he got behind the wheel, unable to analyze his own mixed feelings, she put one hand out to his on the wheel.

"Damn it, I love you, Steve Lombard."

He turned his head, gave her a quick, teasing smile.

"Well, don't cry about it, for God's sake! I love you too, and *I'm* not crying."

# *Chapter Five*

BROOKE saw to it that the wedding was scheduled for December 10. Triumphantly, she explained to Randi, "One day inside of the wager. You can't ask for more than that. I've won. You must be driving poor Steve crazy. You haven't given in yet, have you? Clever girl."

Every time Randi saw Brooke, she regretted the stupid wager a little more. Though she knew she owed everything to her future sister-in-law, she didn't enjoy the guilt that went with it. She hadn't discussed the bet with her mother but she thought of it constantly, especially in the days after Steve's proposal . . .

She was invited to dinner at the Lombard house one night when war broke out in the kitchen. Stella Burkett, whose ancestors had had their troubles with the British, made the mistake of assuming Mrs. Schultz shared her feelings. Stout, iron-jawed Mrs. Schultz, who prided herself on her patriotism, pursued her out of the kitchen, across the hall and through the long dining room with an iron frying pan. The only one surprised at this behavior was Randi.

"What the hell was that?" Red Lombard muttered, and reached for his wine glass.

Mrs. Lombard, looking delicate and thin in old-rose taffeta that set off her wispy golden hair, merely sighed.

"Not through the dining room, Schultz. Redmon, she knows better. She really does."

Steve demanded impatiently, "Isn't anybody going to stop this racket? Brooke, how often does this go on?"

Brooke denied responsibility. "Randi says we must take a firm hand. But you know I'm not that sort, honey. I never was. Besides, Schultz has an iron skillet. Randi, what—?"

André and Randi exchanged uneasy glances. André was too much the gentleman to interfere. Randi wondered why the devil somebody didn't at least silence the shouting of the two women. She got up, and saw that everybody was looking at her. Steve reached for her hand.

"I'm sorry, sweetheart. You'll have your work cut out for you—when we're married."

So that was his proposal. He stood with her and she pretended not to notice the importance of that throwaway statement.

"If you wouldn't mind, sir, Mrs. Lombard, I might try my hand." She may as well put the cards on the table. "You see, I went to school with Stella Burkett."

"Burkett?" Mrs. Lombard echoed vaguely.

"The new maid," Brooke put in.

Steve would have gone with her but Randi waved him back.

"This is work for a woman," she said, and went out after the two women.

She found them in the gloomy, overdecorated Victorian parlor, Mrs. Schultz swinging her time-blackened pan, Stella waving a foot-long jade Oriental statue that must have cost a fortune. Randi kept her voice low, calm and authoritative.

"Mrs. Schultz, everyone needs you. I'll take care of this woman. You don't want someone else fooling around in your kitchen, do you?"

The cook stood poised for action, but her lips pressed together in thought. Adding fuel to her argument, Randi went on, "I do believe Miss Brooke had some idea of going in and making omelets for the party."

In a panic, Mrs. Schultz swung around, the pan still clutched in her hand.

"Not in my kitchen, she isn't. I know that girl. There'll be not a clean spot left. Nor a pan unscorched."

Randi saw Steve behind the cook. Easily and politely, he took Mrs. Schultz's fingers off the handle. She capitulated, and Steve escorted her back to the kitchen after a quick glance at Randi, his eyes full of fun.

Alone with Stella Burkett, Randi had the harder job. "Better calm down. If you break that statue, you'll never be able to pay it back."

Stella was flippant, waving the jade mandarin, clubbing it at imaginary golf balls.

"Gettin' above yourself, ain't you, Mary-Randal? I see the way he looked at you. Don't think he'll ever marry you. He had a perky brunette here last week and he looked just the same at her."

Seething inside, Randi kept a tight hold on her temper.

"Stella, why don't you put down the statue and think about your job?"

Stella, who was no coward, made another swing with the mandarin. She supported her father and her brother, and could never pay for such breakage. She would undoubtedly lose her job as well, and the last thing Randi wanted to do was get her fired.

Fortunately, the girl recovered her temper and her good sense. She made as if to swing the jade at Randi, but instead set the statue back on its oblong ebony stand. Her grin called attention to her good teeth and her excellent Irish complexion.

"Might as well. Even if I am doin' the work of two. Florrie should be servin'. She went home with a toothache; so she said."

"I'm sorry about it. I'll try and see that you're paid special for it."

"You do that. 'Cause I want cash in hand. None of that business about an extra half-day off. Wouldn't put it past you to go tattling to the sainty madam. You always was a shrewd baby."

Randi defeated her by saying merely, "Thank you. I try to be. Do you want to finish serving?"

"Will I get paid extra?"

Randi hesitated. Her sympathies in the matter of payment were all with Stella.

"I'll see to it." Some way, she thought.

"In that case, you leave it to me. You know, Randi, you and me might get along real good if you was to snap up that good-looking captain and run this old museum."

Randi just nodded and returned to the dining room. There she and Steve, who had just come in with a plate of Mrs. Schultz's sauerbraten, were greeted like heroes. Even Red bestowed his blessing on them.

"What's this I heard about you two getting engaged?"

"Married," Steve corrected him. "I have a lot of time to make up for."

André offered his congratulations to Steve, all the while looking at Randi. It occurred to Randi that she hadn't actually been asked, and that Brooke was eyeing her with a conspiratorial twinkle. But she accepted all the comments with quiet pleasure, hoping no one saw the pulse in her neck jumping. Once she caught a slightly puzzled expression in Steve's eyes. He's not quite sure of me, she thought . . . *My darling, I've loved you for so long. Long before you ever knew I existed . . .*

Somehow she managed to keep her dignity. She wanted him so much it scared her. But there were so many problems! At the moment, the little ones . . . she had no doubt she was welcomed for the sort of thing she had done tonight . . . Brooke would expect to be paid back for her assistance in this marriage . . . Stella Burkett probably thought she could ride roughshod over her old schoolmate . . . Steve's parents would certainly use her . . .

And Steve? Would she be here now, hugged, kissed and welcomed, if she had given in to her own passionate desires this last week? Perhaps the wise, conniving Brooke had called her by the appropriate word. Randi had been clever.

She didn't want to think so. She loved Steve too much for that. But there were times when she knew, in all honesty, that her self-respect was even more important.

BRIDGET, WHO had grown fond of Steve and had been royally treated at dinner by her Lombard in-laws, still made a curious objection to her daughter's hasty marriage.

"They'll be after thinkin' he married you to make an honest woman of you, dearie. It ain't true, is it?"

"I promise you solemnly, ma, we haven't gone to bed together. I held out, and he didn't insist."

Bridget was reluctantly satisfied.

Mrs. Lombard had suggested in her gentle voice that the wedding be held at the Lombard house. Though Bridget wanted a Catholic wedding at Old Saint Mary's in Chinatown, Randi couldn't see her Methodist-Episcopal in-laws pouring along Grant Avenue to Old Saint Mary's and then holding the reception at Sun's North China Tea Shop or the Manchu Pavilion. Eventually it was André de Grasse and Steve who got Bridget's permission for the wedding to be held on Nob Hill. They visited Bridget one day while Randi was working and cajoled her into the idea.

The wedding gown remained a big problem for Bridget, Mrs. Lombard and Brooke. At Steve's request, the three ladies put their heads together and came up with a compromise that would save face for everyone. For years Bridget had saved a bundle of exquisite Irish lace made by a Randal ancestor. This was to be Randi's wedding gown, to be worn over matching cream satin. But Bridget didn't have the satin, nor could she afford to have the gown made in the high-bosomed, slim-skirted Empire style that Randi had tentatively sketched.

Mrs. Lombard flattered herself that the idea was hers. "Do let our present to the bride be the making of the gown. You, Mrs. Gallegher, will furnish the important part, that beautiful lace."

"I must say, I envy the bride," Brooke put in. "If I had it to do all over again, I'd certainly marry in style. I wonder if André—"

Mrs. Lombard beamed. "Such a charming young man. And truly a count. I must say, Brooke, one would have expected a proposal from him before this."

"Or something," Brooke grumbled. "He's a great hand-kisser, but you can't live on that."

After the bridal discussion, she complained to Randi, "I almost got him to bed last Saturday after the dance."

"Has he made love to you, then?" It was a question Randi would have asked no one but Brooke, whose eyes rolled as she described her lack of success.

"Now here I am with hopes of André dashed. And my poor kid Alec just wrote to me. He wants to come and visit."

She showed Randi the neat, ruled page from her son. Randi felt sorry for the boy. His letter sounded much too careful, not the scrawl of a fun-loving, ten-year-old child. And clearly he had tender memories of his vivacious mother.

*Dear mother,*

*Since grandmother passed away of dropsy and I've been staying with my cousins, I thought of what great fun we have when I stay with you and Uncle Steve every summer. Now that Uncle Steve is coming home from the war, it's even better. I have studied hard and am at the top of my form. I would very much like to see the University of California and stroll through Strawberry Canyon, and see Edwards Field where father played American football with Uncle Steve and see the campus and places father liked.*

*It's so long until summer. Do you think I might visit you soon? I wouldn't be much trouble (the* much *was crossed out)*—any *trouble and I don't eat much. I have some money to pay for things. Also, I don't have to have lots of games and buddies. I get on fine by myself. I would like to see Uncle Steve when he comes home from the war. I miss father very much. Father talked about Uncle Steve a lot.*

*Could I please come and visit you now instead of next summer?*

*Your loving son,*
*Alexander Huntington*

The letter seemed a pitiful combination of schoolbook language and the needs of a little boy. Though Randi had little experience with children, she felt that the child's letter was a plea for love and understanding.

"I hope you let him come."

Brooke made a face. "I'd love to, I really would. But don't you see, it would be so cruel. You know how I am," she confessed. "I wouldn't be good for him. I like to be on the go, do what I want, see the men—uh, the people I want. Actually, I'd be a rotten mother, and you know it." She folded the letter, put it back in the carefully addressed envelope and threw it on the ebony highboy. "Remind me to answer that the minute the wedding is over. It's much better, you know, if he comes in the summer. You'll be back from your honeymoon then and can help take care of him."

Behind Brooke's outward charm and generosity, Randi was beginning to see a disturbing self-centeredness. She owed Brooke too much to blame her for her shortcomings, but someone would have to cover for them. . . .

The night before the wedding Steve stopped by the Sutter Street rooming house on his way to a bachelor party with André. He caught Bridget and Randi packing for their overnight stay at the Lombard house. Though Bridget stopped every few minutes for "a wee dram of beer to steady" her, she had promised solemnly not to drink a drop of beer after midnight.

"I'll be sober as a judge," she swore. "No, dearie. Make that 'sober as a minister,' though it goes against my sainted ancestors to admit there'll be no priest in me own daughter's wedding."

When Steve arrived he hugged Bridget, lifted her off the floor and kissed her soundly. "Now, you stay here and charm the socks off your admirer, André de Grasse. I want to confide my bluebeard secrets to your daughter."

In the bedroom which was littered with Randi's half-packed trousseau they embraced hungrily. He was impatient. "The hell with the damned bachelor party! Why don't you and I just sneak off somewhere to be alone?"

She loved his hands moving over her waist to her hips, his mouth touching and lingering on her throat. She clasped her wrists at the back of his neck, edging her arms against his shoulders.

"Tomorrow," she promised. "Only a few more hours, darling."

He took a step, obviously intending to maneuver her back across the bed, but he caught his foot in the hem of her new silk crêpe dinner dress and lost his hold on her. They were both so keyed up they began to laugh. Randi recovered with an effort.

"I'm sorry. I should have been packed by now."

He kissed her forehead and seated her carefully on the bed. "Never mind. It's a relief to find these little imperfections in you. Here's what I wanted to settle." He showed her several legal pages with red margins and a blue backing.

She pushed them away. "Looks like a divorce."

"A contract agreement. As long as Bridget Gallegher lives, she gets fifty dollars a month every month." Randi started to object. He silenced her. "It's backed by these deeds. This one for five lots on the Great Highway beyond Golden Gate Park, which can only increase in value. The others are two small annuities I inherited. No matter what happens, your mother is protected."

"It's too much. And suppose she marries again."

"Don't tell me she can live on less. And further, if I made provisions about marriage, she might have to forego a lot of happiness because of it."

"We have lived on less. But it's so good of you, my darling." She tried to play it lightly but the matter of Bridget's future was too serious.

"Steve, don't tell ma the whole truth. Just send the money each month if you like. I don't want her to know how much is in her future. She might get too—too carefree."

"The drinking. All right. We'll do it your way. I just don't want you or Bridget to have worries about the future."

They went out arm in arm to join the others, and when the men had gone, Randi rushed to the long bay window to watch them walk up the street.

"I'm the luckiest girl in the world," she murmured, and hoped her luck would never change. . . .

THE HOUSE was jammed. Even the silver anniversary of Red and Alicia Lombard, which got a headline and a front-page picture in the *Examiner,* couldn't rival this.

"CINDERELLA MARRIES WAR HERO," André read with a slightly sardonic twist, and showed his friend the front page of the *Evening*

*Bulletin.* The paper had jumped the gun with a sketch of Randi's wedding dress. The willowy sketched creature appeared to be seven feet tall and about half an inch wide.

André asked, "Is it accurate? Or the usual artistic distortion? I refer, naturally, to the gown, not the lady."

Steve, who found himself surprisingly nervous, wasn't sure. "I'm being kept away. I knew mother and Brooke were superstitious and of course, Bridget. But Randi wouldn't even see me this morning, so I haven't seen a thing."

"If she is prettier than her mother," André remarked, looking into the crowded ballroom, "you will have nothing to concern yourself about."

Steve followed André's bow and saw Bridget at the far end of the ballroom. Small and well-curved in her ankle-length blue grosgrain suit with a ruffled blouse and a fetching blue turban, she waved a champagne glass at her admirer, the celebrated French count.

Agreeing with André that Bridget was a charmer, Steve watched her and waved. "My God! I promised Randi there would be no beer."

"Do not concern yourself. I will do what I can." André made his way through the chattering crowd toward Bridget Gallegher. Steve was relieved.

Alica Lombard floated toward him in her wedding party dress of peach velvet and sables. Steve took his mother's hands, but his own were shaking.

"Dear boy! It will turn out well. You'll see. Such a sweet girl, and so capable."

Burly Patrick LeMass, in rented swallowtail coat, made his way among the guests. He joined Steve, paying handsome tribute to Mrs. Lombard who smiled vaguely and moved away. LeMass clasped Steve's hand.

"You'll be getting a fine girl, so you will. Don't know what her mother will do. Mary-Randal was the sole support of poor Bridget."

Steve wondered to himself with amusement how far LeMass could be led on before he came out and asked for money.

"I'm afraid Randi's company will be missed more than her earning power."

"True. Too true. Still and all, it's a blow. Poor little Bridget bein' so unused to going out to work. Chambermaiding, like as not. Or waitin' on table down on the Coast."

Enjoying himself, Steve went on. "Oh, but the Barbary Coast isn't what it was before the fire. And that minister who got all those ordinances passed against it."

"Ay. But to picture sweet little Bridget at the mercy of them fiends, pawing and making their foul demands, it don't bear thinkin' on."

Steve clapped him on the back. "But that can't happen, can it?"

LeMass brightened. "Do you think so, then?"

"Of course. Bridget has you to take care of her."

LeMass's face fell. He managed a gallant recovery. "She has that. If yez'll excuse me, I'm off upstairs to escort the bride."

"Don't let me detain you."

Steve did not laugh until he had gone. Meanwhile, he heard Bridget nearby muttering, "I wish I had a beer. Holy Mary! Could I use one!" But she settled for champagne. Two glasses were emptied rapidly while she and Steve's mother congratulated themselves on having done all they could upstairs for the bridal party.

Steve grew more nervous as the minutes passed, which did not escape André. "Do not worry, my friend. I have the ring. If you know your lines, may I suggest you do not bellow them as you did at rehearsal."

Steve grinned sheepishly. The organist from the Lombards' church had been playing on the grand piano in the parlor, out of sight of the heavily decorated ballroom with its blue, pink and white streamers, its profusion of hothouse flowers and many satin ribbons attached everywhere.

Steve took his place with André at the far end of the room where the Reverend Ericson, a former classmate of Steve's, stood on the dais once occupied by dance orchestras.

The organist struck up the March from *Lohengrin* on the piano as Steve's head turned along with those of the fifty seated guests in the rented chairs. He felt André tense with excitement beside him.

All doubts went out the big east windows. He recognized more than desire when he caught sight of Randi . . . he had desired other women . . . Alma Cortlandt, looking pert and pretty, had given him her best smile when she arrived earlier with her parents. But looking at his bride as she entered the festive ballroom, he lost all memory of any woman but her.

No woman but Randi would have made him feel this intense and passionate pride. It was worth more than all the overnight loves in the world . . .

Her tawny hair was brushed so finely it shone through the veiling which fell gracefully down her back all the way to her hem. Steve heard the usual murmur of admiration go up from the guests and saw only the woman, her shimmering pale skin, her wide mouth that promised passion only to him. Her bridesmaids were a pretty nosegay in their full-skirted pastels and their bouquets of tiny roses and maidenhair, but even red-haired Brooke, the maid of honor in grass green taffeta, could not steal the day from the bride.

Though he was at the far end of the long room, Randi thought Steve stood out from all the others. It was more than his height or his lean, powerful physique. Unlike most bridegrooms who looked harried and solemn, Steve radiated both his love and his pride.

Later there would be gaps in Randi's memory of the ceremony as she moved forward between the silken ropes with LeMass, a bit shaky, at her side. But she would always remember vividly the instant Steve stepped forward to take LeMass's place, and they stood close together. The fingers of his left hand opened and closed nervously and touched her gown. She turned her head. Sharing a common nervousness, they exchanged quick, understanding smiles in unison. It was a wonderful moment between them . . .

Steve gave his vows clearly and with emphasis. Randi had a terrible, unreasoning desire to laugh when the ring proved difficult to slip on her finger, and Steve finally had to force it over the knuckle. She did not dare look down at it, but she used her thumb to feel the smooth gold band with its simple inscription of their two names.

"Mary-Randal Gallegher, do you promise to love, honor and obey Stephen?"

"I do."

On and on. She felt Steve's body beside hers. She imagined warm spots on her flesh where he touched her. It wasn't possible. Not through his heavy suit and her own elaborate gown.

"Steve, you may kiss your bride."

It was an exuberant kiss. The electricity she had felt between them during the vows was lost now in the consciousness of being on parade before the entire party. Several men, beginning with LeMass, claimed her from Steve. She returned their kisses and had to fight her way through them to reach Bridget, who was in a flood of tears and seemed just a bit wobbly.

"Never been happier. Never seen the day I was prou–prouder–prouder of my girl. Give your old ma a big hug."

Randi did more than that. Bridget had stayed away from beer for Randi's sake. It wasn't her fault if the damned champagne hit her hard. She just wasn't used to it.

"Ma, I love you. Take care of yourself."

"Sure-mike. You, too." Then Bridget whispered, "Hug her, too. Your other ma. Only right and p–proper. So 'tis."

Mrs. Lombard stood nearby with actual tears in her pale eyes, and she seemed glad when Randi kissed her. She was followed by Red Lombard who kissed her roughly and, as if he had gone too far, pulled back.

"Nice wedding, girl. Proud to welcome you into the family. Steve's so secret about the honeymoon—where are you really going?"

"I don't know. It's a surprise. Not that it matters. I'll be with Steve." Randi felt giddy with excitement.

"You'd better be." Steve had returned to Randi's side after getting his mother a glass of water. Mrs. Lombard was now fanning herself. "I've such a headache. All this excitement."

Randi knew just how she felt, but Alma Cortlandt had come up to shake hands and wish her happiness. Randi replied with appropriate thanks, aware of how Alma's dark eyes followed every move made by her brand-new husband.

Brooke Lombard embraced her new sister-in-law, whispering, "We did it, partner."

Randi hugged her hard. "Thank you. Thank you forever."

"Just keep that in mind," Brooke teased, reaching for André de Grasse's arm, but he passed her, kissed Randi's cheek, took her hand and likewise wished her well.

Brooke turned back to the bride, whispering fiercely, "If that Frenchman doesn't behave more like a Frenchman after this affair, I'm going to leave town. Find some live ones."

"I'll bet I know someone who would love to see you."

"Who? Tell me."

"Your son Alec."

Brooke jumped back as if she had been stung. She pushed her way out of the crowd that had advanced on the bride. From every angle of the crowded room and the adjoining parlor, Randi kept seeing Bridget. Her mother accepted another of the endless glasses of champagne and seemed to float toward André, waving the glass in her hand. Amid all the shouts, congratulations, laughter and jokes, Bridget's bright, clear voice could be heard.

"Hey, André . . . LeMass . . . s'better'n beer; so 'tis. Where's my girl?"

Randi groaned. Steve braced her. He seemed to find it amusing, and she hoped he would always do so.

"Let her be," he advised her. "She's having fun, bless her. It's only once in a lifetime. André will see to her."

With her blue turban a bit off-center on top of her head, Bridget banged her glass against a mirror-topped tray.

"Toast. S'always done. Ever–body."

The crowd gathered around Steve, Randi and Bridget.

"Fill up. They say, gonna stop s–sellin' the stuff. Gonna pro–prohi–"

"Prohibit," Steven prompted her, and to Randi's relief he kissed the older woman's tear-wet cheek.

"So—fill up. Now! All–'gether . . . Here's to a hundred years of happiness—" she finished triumphantly, "for the gride an' broom."

After a moment of silent stupefaction Steve and Brooke led the laughter. Bridget cried, "Oh, dear Lord!" and burst out laughing too, followed at last by a deeply relieved Randi. The ice had been broken. Gradually the entire party was roaring. Word passed to the hired butler, Stella Burkett, the other maids, the kitchen force, the entire household. After an astonished frown, Red Lombard actually let his own face crack into a grin.

Randi and Steve were maneuvered to the long dining table where blinding pictures were taken of them cutting the four-tiered, silver-trimmed cake together.

Brooke waved her glass at Randi and Stephen.

"Amen to Bridget's toast. May you have ten years of happiness, then ten years of contentment, then—well—after that, you're on your own."

"Very funny," Steve said sarcastically, but he was still amused and pretended to toast his sister.

Remembering Brooke's toast, Randi counted: 1928. Ten years. 1938. Twenty years . . . It was a lifetime away. Surely enough time to assure their happiness forever.

# *Chapter Six*

AFTER the wedding, Steve gave a last kiss to his mother and hers, told his father not to buy up another city and then drove down Nob Hill, pulling Randi to him. She had no idea where they were headed, and only hoped it would not be too far. She did not want to waste the first hours of their honeymoon in a car.

But in this, too, Steve had thought ahead. He drove out wide Van Ness and then back across town to the elegant Palace Hotel on lower Market Street. It was Randi's introduction to this stately hotel. Though born in San Francisco, Randi had never been inside the doors of the Palace Hotel. It was an impressive, solid, gray-white edifice that had always seemed unattainable to her.

They drove the handsome little Hudson up before the New Montgomery Street entrance with Randi's fingers entwined in Steve's right hand. When the car was taken in charge by a Palace Hotel doorman, Randi thought life could provide no greater joy. She had always read about those dreadful old men whom young women married for money, and here she was, married to the handsomest, most important young man in the city, and still treated to all this luxury.

She would have married him if he hadn't a cent. Still, she was the child of poor parents, and had always dreamed of being as good as those "nobs" who went in and out of the Palace. Now she was one of them. Folding the ermine collar of her jacket around her throat, Randi smiled nervously at the doorman. Observing Steve carefully, she saw that he remained at ease. She realized she had a lot to learn.

She walked beside Steve through the long lobby which sparkled with elegance. No one hurried along the thick carpets. Uniformed men and fur-clad women flashing jewels flicked glances at Steve and Randi.

"They're admiring you," Steve told her, turning his head so that his lips brushed her forehead. She reddened, wondering if anyone guessed this was their wedding day. She hoped not. She wanted them all to believe the young Lombards had been married for months. Then, feeling guilty, she clutched Steve's arm and welcomed the warmth of his answering embrace.

He registered for them under the impersonal eye of the desk clerk. Randi confessed in the elevator that her feelings were ambivalent, that she was afraid of any undue attention.

Steve laughed. "Who cares if they know? They've read the papers."

But she was nevertheless relieved that her soft beige doeskin gloves concealed her wedding and engagement rings. The latter was an elaborate sapphire in a Tiffany setting, surrounded by a semicircle of diamonds—overwhelming to a girl who had never had more than a diamond chip on a bar pin.

After the bellman left and the big white paneled doors locked the world out, Steve showed her around the suite with its elaborate, Louis XV gilt furniture in the living room and the big bed in the bedroom. There was champagne in the ice bucket on the sideboard of the living room, and also carefully covered patés and other hors d'oeuvres.

Randi laughed, running her fingers inside his collar, tickling him. "But what if I'm not really hungry?"

"You will be."

"Darling!" She tried to explain but words didn't do it. "You really are a magician. If you'd created this setting with your own hands, it couldn't have been more perfect."

He lifted her off the floor a few inches. "It would be even more perfect if I could ever get you out of this damned outfit. Why the devil did you wear something with a million buttons?"

"Only twenty." Every pearl button was tiny, which caused more difficulty for his large, masculine hands.

"Only twenty? I'll bet it was Brooke's idea. It would be just like her to think this was funny."

As a matter of fact, the design had been her own, based on the new long-torso look she had seen in *Vogue.* The pearl buttons on the rich blue Canton crêpe outlined her backbone to the hips. The rest of the skirt fell in fine pleats to a point three inches above her ankles.

"It was my design," she confessed, touching his knuckles to her lips.

"I forgive you. I think I'm through now. Damn! I lost that one."

"Never mind." She swung around into his arms. "Don't waste time looking for it."

She loved the glitter in his eyes, the sensuous thrill it promised. "Not on your life, sweetheart. I'm not waiting one second longer."

He picked her up and lay her down on the smooth satin damask of the couch. His eyes watched her as she undressed, and he was fascinated by the way she made the dropping of her dress, the unlacing of her corset as enticing as she could. He shucked off his constricting black suit. Like the setting he had created for their wedding night, he was perfect, Randi thought—even the scars were beautiful to her. When she knew him better she decided she would kiss them, soothe them, love them. His naked body was sun-bronzed, muscular and powerful. Unlike most brides, she was excited rather than embarrassed by his nakedness. She held out her arms, enfolding him within her embrace.

With a trace of uneasiness—suppose she disappointed him?—she welcomed his penetration. He surprised her by his early gentleness, but when she enclosed his flanks with her long legs and pulled him to her, she became enflamed by his driving force. She was too self-conscious to let herself go completely, but she held onto his shoulders, kneading his flesh, urging him on. He came again, then they began to recover. She caressed him, softly enclosing his flesh between her hands, whispering, "I love you. You're even more wonderful than I hoped you would be."

"Why? Hey! Don't stop."

"You were so gentle at first."

He grinned. "But not after." He leaned forward, crushing her hands and his flesh warmly between their bodies as he kissed the tip of her nose.

"I think, very soon, I'll know how to satisfy you," she promised.

"You do now. You want to know a secret? I figured your first time would mean a kind of initiation."

"Wasted time, you mean?"

"Right. But it wasn't. Sweetheart, I adore you."

When they had kissed, flesh against flesh, warm body against body, she pushed him aside.

"I'd better clean up."

He laughed and admired her forethought. She had left her new taffeta slip under her body. She picked it up, grabbed her clothes and went into the bedroom to wash and dress. She stuck her head around the big paneled door.

"You were right, darling," she said with a smile.

"Naturally. But how?"

"You said we would be hungry afterward."

Slightly rumpled, but perfectly content with each other, they settled down to champagne and all the delicious hors d'oeuvres. They held hands. He claimed she was teaching him to use his left hand.

She looked around, sighing contentedly.

"I do love it so. That mirror over the fireplace. And imagine having a fireplace in a hotel room! I could stay here forever." She saw his eyebrows go up and corrected herself. "I know. Just our honeymoon. But that's going to last forever. In my mind, at least."

"Matter of fact, we aren't spending our honeymoon here." She looked at him. He added in a charming note of apology, "Only tonight. I should have told you, sweetheart. I meant to, but it's one of those things."

"What things?" she asked, bewildered. For some reason she thought he might have money troubles. If his father was responsible for the Lombard fortune, he might feel that too much money was being spent on their honeymoon. She wanted to tell him it didn't matter, that they could return home if it would help keep the household within its budget. But she felt that he might resent her interference.

"Don't look so disappointed, sweetheart. We *are* going to have our honeymoon. You'll love it. Wait and see."

He reached for her and she surrendered. Who cared where they spent their honeymoon, so long as they were together . . .

STEVE HAD been hesitant about explaining his plan for their prospective honeymoon to her. She was, after all, a woman, and even an exceptional woman like Randi might not understand how important this visit to Southern California would be to their future.

In his more honest moments, however, he knew he was afraid of her disappointment, afraid the mood of their wedding day would vanish. He wanted to preserve it. What a lovely creature she was! And she was his wife. Still, he hesitated to chance the end of this mood . . .

Toward evening, he looked toward the bedroom. She gave him that eager yet wise smile he hoped would always be saved for him, and held out her hand.

"Let's go. It's such a huge bed. It ought to inspire us."

He thought he *was* inspired, but she played to him, loving and exciting, her own passion, if not her knowledge, equaling his. As she had pointed out, the large bed was a fine battleground for their tussles, and they came to a climax together, driven hard by their playful struggle.

Steve came out of it with scratches and bites over his shoulders and forearms. What surprised and piqued him was that rather than being exhausted she merely seemed to breathe a little harder, and she laughed.

*"I do love you,"* she repeated and then they kissed, exploring each other all over again.

When they were both deliciously exhausted he tried to explain about the trip to Strand, the town that had come alive with oil in Southern California. She was thougtful and interested, which was what he had hoped for but had not expected. He saw it in her hazel eyes that so often matched the clothing she wore. She had a genius for picking out modest shades that did not hide but brought out her own unforgettable tawny coloring.

He described the city of Strand—bustling, burgeoning, the main beach town for Los Angeles—but he could see that her thoughts were torn.

"You are going to buy an eight-story building?"

He explained again that he intended to examine the Monte Carlo Arms, and if the investment looked good he would buy in on shares.

Half-dressed, she stopped to consider his project. She couldn't know much about it, but she sat there on the big bed, sexy and provocative to him in her corset and slip. Her lovely skin shimmered in the sunset that reflected off the big Monarch Building across the narrow street below. There were still some business offices open across the street. Randi glanced at those windows.

"I do believe the people in those offices over there can see everything we do in the Palace Hotel."

"I envy them. It must keep them entertained. As a matter of fact, father has an office in the Monarch Building."

Lashed by the memory of his father's use of his trust fund to build his own empire, he pressed on. "Sweetheart, did you understand about the Monte Carlo? It's just a beginning, but if I examine it and it looks like a good deal, I'm going to do it."

"I think I understand." He sensed that she was more interested in his business ventures than women usually were. He didn't know whether to be glad or sorry—there were advantages and drawbacks either way.

She unfolded her legs in the graceful way he always enjoyed watching, and got up to put on her blue dress. "Darling, as you said, it gives one an appetite. Could we have dinner pretty soon?"

"Not only that, but we can eat downstairs in the Garden Court, or—"

"I'd love it. Oh, darling, you are good to me." She hugged him and he drew her close.

"You have a choice, sweetheart. Would you rather order dinner, anything you want, and have it served right here?" He looked into her face and saw her mischievous smile. "All right. Not here. In the living room. Which do you prefer?"

She knitted her broad, pale forehead in thought. "What a choice! Both, actually. But darling, I've never had an elegant dinner brought to me in my room. Let's."

He loved pleasing her. There were times like this when he wondered at his luck in marrying just this young woman . . . He knew the world—and women—well enough to guess that all the trappings behind the Lombard name, the house on Nob Hill and the apparent fortune had something to do with his listing as the Most Eligible Bachelor of his weight and class . . .

Yet here was the girl he had gone after, pursued, persisted and won. She had financial responsibilities, a problem parent, a dozen reasons for trying to trap him. Instead, she had taken care not to throw herself at him. She had even avoided him; yet she loved him. There couldn't be any doubt after today . . .

He told her so. "Sweetheart, you are one in a million."

He called for menus and told her she needn't dress. She could wear that pretty barred silk kimono, or whatever it was called. Let the waiter think what he liked. The worse he thought, the better the joke would be.

But in Randi's curious, ever tantalizing way, she covered up at once, dressed and piled up her hair, putting in all those amber hairpins neatly. "This is the first time I've been here, and I want to do it right."

He complimented her. "Sexy, elegant, proud *and* the most honest girl I ever knew."

To his surprise she blushed and avoided his eyes. He turned her chin toward him, kissed her warm lips. She seemed uncomfortable, but modesty would explain that . . .

# *Chapter Seven*

THEY had their first quarrel over the ridiculous clothing he asked Randi to wear the next morning: a leather jacket, much too long. And anyway, what woman wore leather unless she was riding a horse? There were hiking pants that were meant for a man, and high-laced boots. All mysterious. Even the leather gloves, obviously meant for a boy.

"I got the sizes from your mother. They'll all fit. Try them on, sweetheart. It's going to be a mighty cold drive. It may be sunny, but this is December, after all."

She sensed that he was lying, which unsettled her a little. When she had been bundled into the ridiculous outfit and caught a glimpse of herself in the bedroom mirror, she guessed the truth.

"My God, I'm going up in an airplane!"

His eyes held hers in the mirror and she couldn't miss the excitement she read there. The whole idea of flying gave her the creeps. She was not a gambler, had gambled only once in her life when she made the wager with Brooke . . . That fifty dollars would have to be mailed today. It would clean out the checking account under her maiden name, but it was a debt of honor.

Or dishonor. Steve caught her startled frown. Fortunately, he didn't read the guilt behind it, but it was there. The least she could do was to please him now. She owed him so much. Above all, he had made her love him as she had never thought she could love anyone.

She broke into a smile and saluted him.

"*Oui, mon général.* I will risk my life and limb, but only for you."

She assumed they were flying in one of those crates to the Southern California beach town which interested Steve so much. The more she heard about the shares in the Monte Carlo Arms the more curious she became.

THE AIRFIELD was a real horror. She had always imagined that men sailed off into the skies from flat, carefully paved streets. What she saw in the countryside below southern San Francisco was a field of lupin, yellow poppies and chuckholes. Several tiny toy airplanes were surrounded by groups of young men in khaki. Apparently it was a practice field for would-be pilots who might have been sent overseas if the armistice hadn't come along.

Two planes, one painted yellow and the other blue and silver, were set conspicuously apart from the military at the far end of the field. Steve stopped the Hudson about fifty feet from the blue and silver biplane. André de Grasse came up to them, helping the stunned Randi out of the car.

"What on earth—? Are you the pilot, Mr. de Grasse?"

"Sweetheart, there's nothing to it," Steve insisted. "André's done this sort of thing hundreds of times. He's walked away from two crashes."

"I wouldn't call that a comfort. They do say three's the charm."

The Frenchman, in helmet and goggles and flying togs that looked rather dashing, reassured her quietly. "The weather is perfect. The wind is in our favor and there are no clouds or fog. It is quite safe, Mrs. Lombard."

Her married name sounded good with his slight accent and hearing it put an end to her struggles. She grumbled a bit, but no one paid any attention. André produced a leather cap that buckled under her chin and was a tight fit, thanks to her hair. Steve fastened goggles over her eyes and while she muttered he silenced her mouth with a kiss. Batting her eyelids rapidly in an effort to see out of the goggles, she began to have doubts again.

"Where will you be? Steve, don't you dare leave me up there alone."

"You won't be alone, Randi. André will fly you. I'll be in that yellow plane across the field. I've hired one of André's buddies from the Lafayette Escadrille. American. He's been down on his luck but he's a great guy. Reconditioned a Curtiss that everyone was ready to junk. But it's safe as a house now."

If he was willing to send her up alone in that awful toy, possibly to her death, she could be just as indifferent. The pride of the Galleghers came to her rescue. She found it difficult enough to walk in her cumbersome male clothing, and this kept her from talking to either her husband on her right or André de Grasse on her left.

It was another matter when she was boosted up into the plane. She thought with horror, *What if we never see each other again? What if his plane falls apart?*

She clung to Steve, kissing him with fervor. At the very last second he must have shared her fear. She saw the sudden tension in his eyes. After all, it wasn't as if flying were an everyday occurrence. He kept looking at Randi while he spoke to his friend.

"André, maybe this isn't such a great idea."

"We will never have better conditions. Your pilot is signaling. Trust me, my friend." He spoke in a voice of quiet authority.

Steve studied her. "Sweetheart, would you rather not? You just say so and we'll call this whole thing a stupid idea."

She rose to the occasion. "What do you think I am? A coward? Let's go—wherever we're going."

"To Strand, California, my brave darling. To that apartment house I'm going to bid on." He kissed her again, climbed down over and off the wing and dropped to the ground.

André fastened her to the seat. She tried to watch Steve as he crossed the field where the wildflowers had been mowed down and little dust devils swirled over the bare ground.

André climbed into the cockpit and the next minute Randi was startled by the heavy croaking of the motor as a young man in khaki turned the blades of the propeller, his thin cotton shirt billowing under the stirred-up air currents. The plane itself was light enough to be buffeted as it rested on the ground, but when it began to taxi over the field it shook with a kind of palsy. Randi closed her eyes and found herself beginning to recite the rosary, something she hadn't done in years. Strange things were happening beneath the plane. There was a peculiar lift under her body. She opened her eyes.

The plane continued shivering but the ground was gone and they were actually floating ten, then twenty feet above the earth. The yellow plane hadn't taken off yet.

She surprised herself by yelling to André, "We'll beat them!"

The plane climbed, seemed to glide at various stages and then leveled off high above the field. She could see the little yellow plane as it took off and shakily banked to follow André's trail.

The wind lashed around Randi's face, but she was used to the cold, harsh winds of San Francisco, and had felt much the same sensation many times. With an effort of will she looked down at the ground whose contours, roads and occasional buildings were clearly visible. There was considerable automobile traffic on the highway toward the Southern California area, and some distance south of the nearest army camp she made out horse-drawn wagons and some open trucks driven by men whose trench caps, puttees and greatcoats gave them a distinctive military profile. Watching the land below, she grew so fascinated that she forgot her resentment over the trick that had been played on her.

Randi felt like a famous movie star in a daring war adventure. Actually, she was their superior, she thought, and laughed. None of those actresses went up in planes with the wind in her face and the blue sky so close one could almost touch it, though the plane was never out of sight of the land below.

She watched towns appear and disappear before she could identify them. Beyond Santa Barbara, white and glistening in its blue-green frame of mountains and sea, they soared out over the sunny Pacific, then back across a dark, crumpled mountain range which cut off the sprawling city of Los Angeles from the ocean.

Suddenly, she felt the plane plunging earthwards, as it spiraled, leveled off, fluttered like a bird fighting a huge downdraft and plunged again. It seemed impossible to be scared to death and still want to be sick at the same time, and it was all she could do to keep gulping air and hoping for the best.

André called out to her. "Don't worry. Merely the—what you call crosscurrents."

She heard his reassurance but didn't believe it. She had never felt anything like this awful up-and-down motion, not even at sea.

As quickly as it came, though, the tumult subsided. The plane soared along over what appeared to be giant black skeletons balanced on stick legs.

"Oil derricks," André shouted.

The plane descended gradually, like a seagull gliding in for a landing. But no matter how well the plane behaved now, it couldn't quiet her turned-over stomach.

André called out something. Obviously, this quiet, sleepy town was Strand, where Steve expected to find his eight-story pot of gold. It wasn't difficult for Randi to locate the famous building—it was the only skyscraper in town.

The town itself, spread along the ocean's edge, came as a shock after the frantic pace of San Francisco, where everyone hurried as if expecting another Great Fire momentarily and wanting to make a killing first. Straining to get a better view, she noticed that the people strolled along leisurely even as the plane droned over their heads. Flying at this low altitude, she could even make out their clothing, which would have shocked most San Franciscans. For the most part the women wore flowered gingham housedresses and some of the men were in shirt sleeves. She could spot only a couple of flu masks. But she could not see anyone in this unfashionable crowd likely to be a tenant of Steve's grandiose, eight-story L-shaped skyscraper.

One wing of the tile-roofed white building backed upon the ocean and beach about thirty feet below it and was situated at the head of a wide, mostly deserted street that paralleled the ocean on a higher level. She could see the skeletons of various entertainments in the fun zone on the beach level—a Ferris wheel, not running, and what looked like the beginnings of a roller coaster, stretched out and unfinished.

There were, however, a surprising number of automobiles. She lost count after more than twenty on the main street which bisected the ocean boulevard and which sheltered most of the town's business, wandering northward beyond the oil wells on the hillsides.

She made out a park about two blocks square, one of whose borders was the ocean boulevard west of Steve's skyscraper. The sidewalks around the park were lined with what appeared to be locust trees and in the center of the park a domed building with a pillared Greek Revival front loomed up at the top of the wide steps. A public building of some sort, she thought, probably a library.

With a fluttering motion of the wings, the plane set down in a lot just beyond the last paved street at the west end of town, where small wooden bungalows were scattered.

The plane was met by two young men in shirt sleeves, one of whom wore overalls and who seemed to be familiar with airplanes. Almost before the propeller blades stopped turning, they ran to congratulate André de Grasse.

"You've won, Frenchie. The other one ain't even in sight."

"We had a head start on them. Give us a quarter of an hour. Then we may claim the *Croix de Guerre.*"

André climbed out along the wing. He unhooked and unstrapped his passenger and the two young men helped Randi to the ground. Her knees started to buckle, but the men were apparently used to such reactions from first-time passengers.

Gradually, she recovered her land legs, and stripped off the goggles, unbuttoned her jacket, shook her head to free her hair and peered anxiously up at the pale, hazy sky.

"They are safe," André said, watching her.

"I hope the yellow plane wins. I'm sorry, André. I really do."

He smiled. "They have five minutes yet. Four minutes now."

She squinted, trying to be the first to see the little yellow plane.

"If he is safe," she promised herself aloud, laughing to make it sound like a joke, "I'll love his eight-story stucco barn! I swear I will."

André raised his arm and pointed over her head to the northeast.

"Then begin to love it, Randi. They are coming. Over there."

Excitement and relief washed over her as Steve climbed out and dropped down from the wing, though she wondered to whom he would come first: to her, or to his friends to settle their wager. She was fast learning how important a man's buddies were to him. Before the war there had been his athlete friends, and since his return anyone in uniform won either his friendship or his sympathy. Randi felt she understood, but nevertheless, in a small way she envied them his trust and friendship . . .

Her doubts were dispelled the minute his boots touched the ground and he started running toward her. She met him in the middle of the field, hugging him until he groaned, pretending she had crushed him. While they embraced, André shook hands with Steve's pilot.

"I believe Blue and Silver won by two minutes, seventeen seconds," the pilot announced.

"Now," André turned to Steve when the bills had changed hands, "you must show me your great investment before I leave."

"You can't miss my white beauty. Eight stories of solid brick and stucco."

It had looked like plain stucco to Randi, but as Steve had said, nothing was more solid than brick . . . except those brick buildings in San Francisco that she had seen collapse during the earthquake and fire. Fortunately, this wasn't San Francisco . . .

"You have the building under option?" André asked as the three of them left the field.

"Not yet. I have a folio of pictures, of course. I wanted Randi to see it first. But there are still shares for sale. Twenty thousand each. They're going to be worth five times as much within the next year or two. Liversedge has talked on the telephone to the Wells, Fargo connections in Los Angeles and their trust department has control of the property."

"One brief tour of inspection," André agreed. "Then I must get that little blue and silver beauty back safely to Sunnyvale."

"Don't let Brooke browbeat you, old boy."

André shrugged. "Brooke is sailing for Hawaii. And I think Paris calls me. I must answer."

Randi was disappointed. It had seemed a romantic arrangement—pretty, redheaded Brooke and the handsome Frenchman. What could have happened between them? Whatever the problem was, Steve seemed to understand and he did not protest.

"Maybe it's just as well."

"Oh, enough of that," André said lightly.

# *Chapter Eight*

AS she would later tell her mother, Randi's first impression of the apartment building at the east end of Ocean Boulevard had been amazement at its size and its relative emptiness, except for the few tenants who had lived in it since it opened a year before.

On the afternoon of Randi's first airplane ride, she and Steve and André visited the Monte Carlo Arms. After a rueful look through the glass doors at the inoperative elevator, they all began the laborious eight-story climb to the top floor.

"It's a handsome lift," André volunteered. "A pity the electricity is not on. The brass fittings look very—" He stopped, amused.

Steve agreed proudly. "Very French. Reminds me of the Grand Hotel. I'll show Paris to you one day, sweetheart."

"That sounds wonderful."

"About the Monte Carlo here, we'll have an elevator operator, naturally," Steve promised his bride, who found the last flight of stairs leading to the penthouse almost as difficult as the plane ride. When they reached the top, Randi leaned against the bare white wall and looked out the south window at the ocean rolling along the wide beach that spread all the way to the western horizon.

"It will cost plenty," she said. "But the view is nice from this apartment. You could play that up in your publicity." *Now he's got me talking about it as if it were already his own plaything,* she thought to herself.

The top floor apartment spread over both wings, with the living room, dining room and kitchen in the wing with the sea view. Two bedrooms and a den had a full view of the spreading town to the north and west. She could see plainly now the oil wells on the distant hill and the highway to Los Angeles which extended from the main street.

"Very impressive," André agreed.

Steve grinned, then pointed out the porcelain bathtubs, the fine molding, the white enamel trim on every doorway and even the place where the overhead and bracket lights would go. While the two men talked about plumbing technicalities, Randi gazed longingly at the porcelain tub. Most of her childhood she had bathed in a big, round galvanized tub lugged into the kitchen for the purpose, while jugs, pitchers and kettles of water boiled on the wood stove.

Throughout the building Randi saw few signs that anyone had ever lived here, even briefly, and she noticed faded streaks on the walls where the sun had shone in through bare windows for many months. The builder probably hadn't found anyone who could afford to lease the penthouse, she thought, which didn't make her feel any more confident about Steve's twenty-thousand-dollar investment. At the moment it was simply a great, empty white elephant. Besides, it was interfering with their honeymoon, she thought as she remembered the eight-flight walk down.

When they reached the barren white lobby, Steve spoke eagerly while they tried to catch their breath.

"Look. Mirrors framed by polished brass along the back wall facing the elevator. These square pillars could use mirrors too. Long and slender. Flattering. Not that *you* need them, sweetheart."

Randi held out her arms. As they kissed, she wondered whether the excitement of his prospective purchase was the sole reason for his joy now. André was watching them in the blinding afternoon light that poured through the lobby.

"I will be on my way. I do not fly by night. Not for pleasure. I wish you much luck."

Randi's hand was around Steve's collar. She felt André's lips touch her fingers and linger there. Then he raised his head. She found herself looking into his face over Steve's shoulder, and she read something there she did not wish to see. The look in his eyes came as a jolt, signaling a treachery toward his friend. She wished she had never seen it.

"I really must leave. You understand why." His voice was low.

Steve turned his head, obviously unaware of André's silent message. "I know how you are about your beloved Paris. Don't forget us, André."

"That I will never do. *Au revoir,* my friends." He saluted and shook hands with Steve.

Together, Steve and Randi watched the tall Frenchman stride down Ocean Boulevard, heading for the sandy field fifteen blocks away.

Steve explained. "He knows his affair with Brooke won't get anywhere. He probably feels the decent thing is to leave before it gets serious." He turned away with her hand in his.

"Let's go. The boys left our things at a place called the Cedars Hotel, whatever that is. We'll get our room and see just how much you really want me."

She reached under his collar and rubbed his tense neck with long, sensuous motions. Her eyes were soft and full of promise. She felt especially anxious to prove her love, thinking that somehow it would blur the uneasiness of the last few minutes.

"I love you, Stephen Lombard, even if I do have to share you with this white elephant."

He laughed away her criticism of his beloved project and they went off to find the Cedars Hotel, a two-story wooden structure frequented by oil investors and men of the Pacific Fleet on shore leave.

They made love in a room with blue-striped wallpaper, on a brass bed with a lumpy mattress, and to the sound of loud oilmen next door talking deals over a whiskey bottle.

They ate fish chowder, then frankfurters on rolls at a tiny café in the amusement zone. In order to spare wartime feelings the frankfurters were called "hot dogs," but the new name didn't improve their taste, and the fish chowder was tasteless and watery.

Leaving the café, they walked out on the roller coaster pier. From the heart of the zone the merry-go-round calliope sent out its mournful music. There was only one child and his mother on the merry-go-round.

"I hope they do better in the summer," Randi remarked.

But Steve could see endless possibilities, a future as exciting as San Francisco's great days ahead.

"They will do better," he promised her. "This place will be booming. Look. Up there to the east, beyond the zone. Our building." He caught her amused look and added self-consciously, "By the time I'm through, I may have a controlling interest. I've got a few ideas about raising the money for added shares. See how it shines in the starlight. White stucco over brick."

She nodded as she reminded him, "My memories of brick go back to the San Francisco earthquake. I can't help being afraid of it."

"Darling, leave those worries to builders. They're not really our concern, especially in a place where there are no earthquakes."

"That's true," she said. All the same, he noted that she did not really seem convinced. Randi was definitely a woman of her own mind, he thought.

They leaned over the powerful, five-foot-high seawall that separated the deserted beach from the wide cement boardwalk.

"There are a lot of possibilities over there" he said, pointing behind them. "More than a mile of lots and just a handful of shacks built along here west of the zone."

Randi smoothed away sand from the wide top of the seawall.

"This wall feels as if they probably get high tides here. But I heard something good about that from the chambermaid. It's said they go grunion hunting during a couple of summer nights. These little fish cover the beach, up to that pier where they're building the roller coaster. Wouldn't it be fun, some warm summer night, to wade along the beach and catch the next day's dinner?"

But Steve's mind was fixed on just one subject. "Might be an idea. The Monte Carlo owners could use it in the publicity brochure: *Catch your own dinner.* Let's go on. See what's at the end of this glorious thoroughfare. It might be worth money, someday."

Randi was willing, thinking that it was romantic to stroll through the dark winter night. An occasional short street plunged down from Ocean Boulevard to the cement boardwalk, casting a streak of light across their path. They hadn't spoken for several minutes when Randi looked at him under the last street light.

"Might as well go back. You can put through your bid for a share," she suggested.

Steve agreed with false heartiness, as if he hadn't known all along that he would buy the share. "I've made up my mind. I'm going to go through with the deal. Sam was right. My father didn't know a good deal when he heard one."

But when they entered the lobby of the hotel with its rocking chairs, a worn sofa and a table stacked with copies of the *Saturday Evening Post,* the desk clerk stopped them.

"Telegram for you, Mr. Lombard. I signed for you. That all right?"

Steve grabbed the yellow envelope, but he made no effort to open it . . . It was as if he had a premonition . . . They went upstairs in silence. He jammed the key crookedly into the lock, while Randi merely watched as he got the door open at last. Once inside, he ripped the envelope open with a forefinger and spread the typed message on the bed.

"Not the family?" she asked nervously.

"No." It was from Sam Liversedge. And it was bad.

REGRET INFORM YOU OVER MY OBJECTIONS RED L
DECIDED PURCHASE REMAINING SHARES STOP QUOTE
A AND R NOW LARGEST STOCKHOLDERS IN MONTE
CARLO ARMS UNQUOTE STOP DEEPLY SORRY STOP LIVERSEDGE

So he had lost. And of all the men on earth, he had lost to Red Lombard.

"The bastard! He did this on purpose. He made me think he had lost interest in it."

His sudden outburst of bitterness shocked Randi, but as always she maintained her composure and good sense. She held out her hand.

"May I see it?" She read it in a couple of seconds. "He may not have known how interested you were. You can't be sure about that, can you?"

"Don't defend him, for God's sake!" It would be just like his father to win Randi over to his side, he thought angrily.

She gave the telegram back to him. Realizing at once the extent of her loyalty to him, Steve found her icy tone more effective than any rebuke.

"I read once that Red Lombard fought his father, 'Mad Tony' Lombard. Are you going to fight him the same way?"

He tried to calm himself before responding to this.

"I promise you this, Randi, you married the best of the Lombards. Red beat my grandfather. You'll live to see the day Red comes begging to me, hat in hand."

"Isn't there any other way?"

She had obviously not understood him at all. "I'll break him, Randi, the way it hurts him the worst . . . in those fancy deals of his."

She shrugged. Despite his anger, he was relieved to see her smile.

"Maybe you can beat him quietly. But darling, if you take my advice, you won't exert all that fury on empty air. Just make other deals. Try something he hasn't touched. Like those lots we saw tonight facing the beach. Or in San Francisco, south of Golden Gate Park. Red would never consider them. But—"

He picked it up. "But you're right, the small profits, aggrandized, would be better than Red's colossal projects." There *was* a lot to what she said—yet he still had to pay back Red Lombard . . .

"Sweetheart, would you mind terribly if we cut this honeymoon short and went home?"

"I'm nearly packed."

"Bless you, Randi Lombard!"

"Thanks. I can use a blessing." Though she did not say it aloud, Steve somehow felt that she thought he could use one too.

# *Chapter Nine*

RANDI came home for the first time to the house on Nob Hill with mixed feelings. She had dreamed of walking through the heavy door on Steve Lombard's arm. She would be useful, she told herself, and would fit in, never interfere overtly with the running of the household, but instead try to help behind the scenes. The Lombards might not know it but they would come to need her.

Now, returning with a embittered husband, desperately hoping to head off a confrontation with his father that she was certain Steve would later regret, Randi felt quite unlike herself, nervous and unsure. Standing at the door in the light December rain, she watched Steve try the knob and then rattle it impatiently.

"What next? They've locked the doors."

"Maybe they're all out."

"We do have servants."

She had forgotten that; the habits of a lifetime were hard to break. Placing her hand on his sleeve, she sensed that anything more than this quiet gesture would set him off and perhaps bring on the disastrous conflict between father and son she hoped to avoid. Neither man must be allowed to say things that could never be forgotten—or forgiven. The man she loved would be destroyed, just as Mad Tony had been, and Red would follow. These stupid father-son feuds must end, she thought.

Nevertheless, she shared with her husband his ambition to become a great success in the world. Her own problem was to find a place for herself in that world. There must be one, she thought—or she would create it . . .

Meanwhile, the door was unquestionably locked. Steve raised the brass knocker and banged it loudly. It was Red, of all people, who opened the door for them. In the dark, gloomy hallway he looked old and somber.

"Steve! Knew you'd get here. Couldn't get you on the phone. They said you'd left. Guess you were a mind reader. Come in, come in."

"I'm with my bride, Red. Or have you forgotten?"

Obviously Red was used to having his son call him by his first name. He went to Randi and hugged her.

"Good to have you home, daughter. In other circumstances, I guess I'd say welcome home. We sure do need you. Didn't you get my telegram? I telegraphed too."

"We got one, all right. From Sam Liversedge. Is that what you mean?" Steve snapped.

"*Sam* knew about Alicia?" Red asked, confused. All of a sudden, Randi began to understand.

"Wait, Steve. Something is wrong. Your mother—something's wrong. Red, isn't that it?"

Steve elbowed his father aside and swung around.

"Is it true?"

Red nodded, pointed upstairs. "She's got it bad." His gravelly voice broke. "I've been nearly out of my head. Isn't that why you two cut your honeymoon short? Your mother's come down with the flu."

"My God!" Steve said, and took the stairs two at a time.

Badly shaken, Randi asked Red, "Is it the dangerous flu?"

He nodded. "It's the killer kind." His face ashen and his hair all awry, he looked as if he were about to break down. She tried to brace him, holding him by the shoulders, and looked into his eyes.

"How long?"

"Started the night of the wedding."

"And she's still alive. That's a very good sign."

He sniffed, rubbed his nose briskly. "You know what I thought at first? Damned if I didn't think she—well—it was one of those female things."

Despite all the trouble with her husband, she pitied him. "I'm sure it's understandable."

"Sure. But next day she had this awful headache and fever, and she didn't seem to recognize me. I'll tell you, I was scared! I came right home from Sam's office—you know, Liversedge; he's a banker friend.

Anyway, servants called the doctor. Schultz, the cook, she hotfooted it right out of the house. Now everybody's gone."

"You're all alone?" She had watched him bring in their suitcases himself. "But your wife needs someone to prepare things. Food. Clean bedding. Medicines."

"Doc Humphreys sent over a nurse. She's a fright, but she knows her business. We're not allowed near poor Alicia without masks and things. And then there's that young Irish wench. She's been helping out."

"Stella Burkett?" Randi was surprised.

"Great girl. Kind of sloppy and not the cleanest in the world, but that's all right. I grew up with her kind, over in the Comstalk. Anyway, she wasn't scared. That other maid is still running, for all I know. The handyman—God knows where he is. So that's how things stand right now. You wonder that I'm glad to see you?"

Randi hurried up the stairs, leaving Red still talking. Before today, she had paid scant attention to the flu scare; her fears were mostly for Bridget. She understood now what Steve was going through, and despite her concern for Alicia Lombard, she was anxious about Steve. She sensed that the more he turned from his father, the more likely he was to feel a deep attachment to his mother.

The forbidding nurse, a powerful woman with muscular arms, heard her running up the stairs and met her in the dark hall. The starchy look of a white uniform on such a frame was enough to emphasize the seriousness of Alicia Lombard's condition.

"You'll be young Mrs. Lombard," she greeted Randi. "I'm Willabrandt, your ma-in-law's nurse. Don't make too much noise. It's been touch and go. We've been on the look for you. She was calling for Mr. Stephen last night."

Though it was hard to see how they could have done anything differently without using André's airplane, Randi nevertheless felt guilty about not having been there sooner.

"We didn't know . . . we had no idea. Is Steve with her now?"

Nurse Willabrandt nodded. "You can't see her yet. If she's able to sleep tonight, though, you might spell me. I've already decked out Mr. Stephen in a mask and one of my uniforms. But he can only stay with her a few minutes. If it had been anyone else, they'd have been sealed up in a hospital a long time ago. But now all the hospitals are jammed full, so maybe this is just as well."

"I'll be happy to spell you. Do you have any other help at all?"

"Got a problem there." Nurse Willabrandt pulled Randi into the empty sunroom at the back of the upper hall. The view through the windows of gray stone buildings and gray sky made the whole place seem even more depressing.

"I like to sit here and rock away and drink my tea while I'm off duty," Nurse Willabrandt explained. "Real comfortable. And a great view." She added, "On a nice day."

"You mentioned a problem."

The nurse lowered her voice. "The other nurse came down sick last night and had to be sent home. Doesn't look good."

"She caught the flu." Randi was unable to conceal her rising fears. How far would this terrible thing go? she thought, and immediately her fear for Steve caught hold.

"No question. But the girl must have been exposed before she came here. They stuck her in the hospital this morning. Dr. Humphreys is hoping to get somebody else soon. You can see why you're a welcome sight, Mrs. Steve."

Randi was already unbuttoning her coat.

"I'll get to work at once. Who is handling the washing up and cleaning? I understand Stella Burkett has been a great help. Where would I fit in best?"

"The colleen, that one! Spends half her time making eyes at Mr. Red, not but what she's right handy to me when she wants to be. Terrible cook, though. You could help there. And nights, watching the patient." She squinted, looked Randi up and down. "You still on your honeymoon?"

Randi shrugged herself out of her coat. No point in thinking about lost honeymoons, she thought. She had a feeling their honeymoon had ended the minute Steve lost his real estate dream, the Monte Carlo Arms—though his loss had seemed to draw him even closer to her . . .

"Are we allowed to leave the house? Or are we under quarantine?" Randi asked, her mind racing with thoughts of food, medicines, sickroom supplies, endless things needed from outside.

"Sorry. Anyone visiting the patient's got to stay inside. This thing is spreading. I don't know how we're going to get through it, the shortage of help—sickroom help—being what it is."

Randi thought of her own mother, who didn't even know she was back. Bridget might have caught the flu as well. Right now, though, it seemed clear that Randi was needed here.

"I know. But my husband and I are two more willing hands. We'll get through."

Red Lombard heard Randi from the hallway. "Thank God you folks did get back. I feel a hell of a lot better, Mary-Randal—you being such a capable girl."

*Capable.* Not what a newlywed woman likes to hear. Randi's grimace was caught by Nurse Willabrandt who winked and patted her shoulder.

"Don't give it a thought. They always said that about me, too."

Randi changed the subject quickly. She took her father-in-law's arm and asked him to show her the kitchen and pantry.

"And nurse, if you could make out a list of everything you need, we'll get organized. Meals for the household, hours for eating, and especially all that Mrs. Lombard will need. And at what times."

Nurse Willabrandt rubbed her hands. "That's the right spirit. I was hoping we'd get that kind of help from young Miss Lombard, but I reckon we'll have to wait a while for that."

"I cabled Brooke," Red explained as he and Randi went down the back stairs. "But there is no way she can get home inside of eight days. She's still three days this side of Honolulu."

Randi suspected that Brooke might not shine her brightest in a sickroom. "Let's hope Mrs. Lombard is on the way to recovery by then."

Red seemed to be comforted by her words, however banal she herself felt them to be. Unlike his son, Red seemed helpless without the quiet, gentle support of his wife, and at this moment Randi felt more sorry for this otherwise rugged and powerful man than she would have thought possible just two days earlier.

Grabbing Mrs. Schultz's apron off its hook in the pantry, she bustled around the messy kitchen, throwing endless dirty dishes, kettles, crockery and silver into the big, old-fashioned sink. She piled sheets, pillowcases, uniforms, aprons and other articles of the sickroom into a tin tub, which she tried to move to the stove.

Red Lombard watched her, fascinated. He looked big and lost, but at least relieved now by her presence.

"I'll call you Randi. May I?"

"Of course. I want to boil this tubful. Would you mind?"

He lifted the tub from the sinkboard to the stove, happy to help, and she turned on the gas under it. Trying to make him relax, to ease his tension, she thanked him with her warmest smile, deciding he would be better off kept busy.

"If you could get our suitcases to our—to Steve's room?"

"Right away. Wouldn't be the first time in my life I played bellhop. How do you think I earned my first hard gold piece?" Red started to add something else, but then cleared his throat and suddenly hugged her.

Before Randi could break away, Steve came in and saw them together. He hesitated, scowling, then held out his hand to her, ignoring Red.

"How is she?" Randi asked, wasting no time on explanations.

His strong features looked haggard. "That nurse says there's no change. She looks so thin, so frail." He brightened a little. "She knew me, tried to take my hand. The damned nurse wouldn't let me touch her. But she thinks my being with mother might have been a help."

"Of course it was. The sight of you could make all the difference."

"She's right, Steve," Red said. "Alicia began calling for you and Brooke last night. You may have saved her life, getting back so quick. Thank you, son."

Steve looked at his father's proffered hand, read the hope in Randi's face and accepted the handclasp. Randi wondered uneasily if he meant it. It was hard to tell . . .

"Mighty good to have you home," Red went on.

"Thanks. Good to be here."

"I'll just get your bags put away. And Steve, some time when you have a few minutes, we can compare notes. Find out what the other guy is up to. I guess you heard I covered the remaining shares in that Strand project. You could never have swung it, you know. But I owe you something for that tip you gave me."

"Tip?"

"You reminded me about the oil down there. Those big operators looking for a fancy place to live."

Steve rolled his eyes, but Randi suspected there was actually some truth in Red's remark.

Red went on in all innocence. "But I'll be glad to let you in on anything comes up more your size, so to speak."

Again Steve looked at Randi. He grinned, but there was a militant sparkle in his eyes.

"Sure, Red. Something cut down to size, as it were."

"I'll go get your bags. Just remember, one of these days soon," Red promised him, "You'll be filling your old man's breeches. Hell, you can pretty near do that now. But you just keep your patience. I pride myself you can always learn a little something from Red Lombard."

"I can indeed, father. And don't bother about the bags. I took them up to my room temporarily."

Red stopped and frowned. He had been prevented from carrying out his little errand of peace.

"Temporarily? You've got other plans? Your mother wouldn't like it when she gets better to find you've moved out."

"Nothing like that." Steve put his arm around Randi's shoulders as she pressed down the boiling sickroom clothes with a broomstick. "But Randi and I will be wanting better quarters in the house than my old room. That light, airy den of yours might do very well. You'll want to stay with mother as much as possible. And when you have your cronies over, you can use my old bedroom. It wouldn't require much fixing up. I notice you used it a bit while I was overseas."

Red opened his mouth to protest, but recovered himself. "Wouldn't want overnight friends too close to Alicia's room. They get raucous now and then when they're liquored up. However, we'll discuss all that later on, when your mother is feeling more herself."

"We'll do that, Red."

Randi was relieved when the older man left them—she didn't like the crosscurrents. Though she knew Steve's loyalty to the family, knew that whatever *he* did to defeat his father, he would never let an outsider hurt Red, she still had a deep foreboding about the intense jealousy between father and son.

# *Chapter Ten*

"SURE now, your first night home ain't gonna be what you'd call romantic, Randi-ma'am," Stella Burkett jeered when she came to the sickroom with washcloths and a basin later that evening. "Here's for to clean up the old lady. You ought to see how dead it is out there in the streets. Even the Mark ain't doing no business tonight. Every day folks get more scared."

Randi looked at her. "And aren't you afraid?"

"As bad off everywhere else as here. Besides, the old red-haired guy is real sociable these long hours."

Randi didn't know quite how to respond to this except to warn Stella that she couldn't rely on Red Lombard after the present crisis was over. But she felt that the warning would seem pompous and go unappreciated from one who had been a member of the Lombard family for less than a week.

Stella looked as slatternly and lascivious as ever, but in the circumstances, even her apparent attempts to seduce Red Lombard failed to strike Randi as dangerous. The condition of the fragile Alicia Lombard required everyone's help, and Stella worked as hard as anyone else.

Randi crossed the sickroom to pick up her mother-in-law's tray, of which nothing had been touched.

"Couldn't get the liquids into her?" Stella asked.

"Not yet. Leave the tray."

Randi sat up straight in a cane-bottomed chair beside the dainty white-and-gold painted bed with its carved Empire head-and-footboard. She had deliberately chosen a stiff, uncomfortable chair so she wouldn't fall asleep.

"Whatever you say. I guess you know Steve—I mean Mr. Steve—sneaked out this evening."

"Sneaked out?" Randi raised her voice, then remembered her patient and whispered, "Where did he go? If Dr. Humphreys catches him, he could be in bad trouble."

"Yeah, that's what I thought."

"What on earth is he doing?"

"He's pretty slick, Mr. Steve is. Must be some good reason." Stella scratched her neck and added thoughtfully, "Real good-looking. Another Wally Reid, but even more rugged. You ever see Wally Reid? I tell you I could swoon over—all right. I'll go. But she don't hear me anyhow. Got to have *some* fun in this morgue."

How true! Randi thought to herself. The house was a dark, gloomy morgue. She would fix that up the minute she was given the chance, she thought, and couldn't condemn Stella for pointing out the truth.

The flu mask with its ticklish gauze made her want to sneeze, and she had hoped Steve would not notice how she looked in one of Nurse Willabrandt's uniforms. She had wrapped the extra inches around her waist with a belt. But the first time Steve saw her he had to go out in the hall and laugh. Randi herself had enough sense not to laugh at *his* appearance in the starched white aprons she and Stella found for him.

When Stella had left the room, Randi went to the head of the bed and gently washed Alicia Lombard's face and hands. The patient's skin looked translucent, but at least her temperature appeared normal. While Randi was setting her delicate hands back on the clean, well-worn sheet and the quilted comforter, Mrs. Lombard roused herself, blinked and stared. She snatched her hands away.

"Where am I? Who are you?"

Randi at once thought of the frightening picture she must present to the sick woman who had just come out of delirium. She did not dare to lower the gauze mask, but she tried to soften her voice.

"You are much better, Mrs. Lombard. Doctor says you will be fine. I'm Steve's wife, Mary-Randal. Do you remember the wedding?"

Alicia Lombard murmured plaintively, "Such a headache."

"Does it hurt now?" She hated to wake Nurse Willabrandt unless it was necessary.

"I mean the headache at the wedding. My son was married, you know. Odd sort of girl, but Brooke likes her . . . Where *is* Brooke?" She tried to rise on her elbows.

Randi applied pressure as gently as she could, anxious not to upset her any more than necessary.

"Yes, yes. Brooke is way out on the high seas. It will take her time to get back. Would you like just a little broth? A sip or two?"

She lifted the cup, but the sick woman was too weak.

"No. Not hungry. Where is Redmon?" Her eyes filled with terror again. "He's dead. You won't tell me."

"Your husband is perfectly well. He was with you half the day. He's sleeping now. But I'll get him. Shall I?"

Mrs. Lombard's voice went on querulously. "I want my children. I want Redmon. You are keeping them from me."

Desperate at last, Randi set down the cracked Spode cup. She didn't want to further upset the sick woman by ringing the little bell, so she went to the door and called Stella, although she realized the girl would probably be downstairs having a bite to eat before bed. Fortunately Red Lombard stuck his head out of his big, comfortable den down the hall.

"How are things?"

Randi beckoned to him. "She wants you."

He ran down the hall. He hadn't undressed yet, but was wearing a red foulard dressing gown over his trousers and undershirt.

"See if she will sip any of the broth. She is so weak, now that the fever has broken."

Randi held him back from entering the room until she could mask him, get him into one of the nurse's newly laundered white uniforms and a pair of gloves. She wasn't sure if all these precautions were necessary, but decided to be cautious . . .

Red's visit seemed to help. His wife recognized him, was relieved and before she knew it she was absently sipping the now lukewarm broth. When she fell asleep Randi sent Red off to bed.

She sat stiffly, thinking of Steve and wondering where he had gone, trying not to give way to the lassitude which would be only one step away from sleep. All of a sudden she was startled out of her doze by Steve, who was kneeling before her, peering into her face.

"Sweetheart, you look so tired!" he said. But she was delighted to see him.

STEVE LOMBARD had done what he could in the house that day and early evening but no one knew better than he how useless he was in his mother's sickroom. He had obeyed the women's orders, including the dragon Nurse Willabrandt, and was impressed by his wife's handling of household matters. It was a far cry, he thought, from the usual haphazard chaos that attended any crisis in the family when either his mother or his sister had been asked to straighten things out. How right Brooke had been in urging him to marry her friend . . . But he also realized that this wasn't much of a homecoming for Randi, whose honeymoon he had cut short as well. Fine promises he had made! She wasn't even able to let her mother know she was back in San Francisco.

There *was* one way he could please her now, he thought. Stripping off the nightshirt thing they had him wearing, he got into his khaki overcoat and walked out the back door and through the heavy, ornate iron fence.

It was easy. No one paid the least attention to him. In fact, the rain-swept streets looked far emptier than usual. Only a month ago at this time of evening he had seen couples hurrying along to the Fairmont or the Mark Hopkins, laughing in the foggy mist. Tonight those few who were out huddled into their coats or under umbrellas and avoided each other as if they feared the plague.

It was not surprising. The Spanish influenza had done the damage of a plague, with millions dead already, and the disease had not yet run its course.

Steve thought of his frail mother with concern, but felt optimistic that she would come through the disease safely, having already passed through the gravc early crisis. The idea of Randi catching the flu from his mother, however, was too appalling to consider.

"I hope Red doesn't catch it," he told himself. "I want him alive and kicking when he comes to me, hat in hand." But the bitter satisfaction in that picture did nothing to cheer him up.

He got into his Hudson and headed down off the hill to Sutter Street. The weather depressed him as did the deserted streets. Steve was used to the hurrying crowds, the constantly busy look of the streets, especially at this hour. Although some people were wearing flu masks, in general they kept to the confines of their own homes, avoiding unnecessary contact.

He had no trouble parking. Careful to wear gloves, he went rapidly up the stairs of Bridget's rooming house, relieved to find the smell there of boiling potatoes rather than the ubiquitous cabbage.

Fortunately, Bridget was in. He heard her Victrola playing a Caruso aria, and knocked on the door.

"It's Steve Lombard, Bridget."

Inside, he could hear scuffling sounds, then the screech of the record being pulled out from under the needle. The door swung open. Bridget would have thrown her arms around him but he backed off, holding up his gloved hand.

"No! Mother has the flu," he said quickly. "That's why we came home. Bridget, me darlin', I came to find out how you are doing. I knew Randi would be frantic to know, and she couldn't reach you by telephone or in any other way. Tell me, are you all right?"

Bridget backed away. She didn't like the flu any better than anyone else did, but she managed to laugh. "I'm not scared. I'm feeling me best, dearie. Pardon the brogue but I've been dosing LeMass. It does rub off. Tell me about my girl. None of this Spanish flu with her, please God."

"She is an angel."

"What? You and me talking about the same girl?"

He told her about their sensational honeymoon and the wonderful way Randi had taken over the running of the household during his mother's illness.

"Ay, now that sounds like her."

He scarcely heard her comment. "As soon as mother feels better and Brooke gets home, then Randi can relax and just be my wife."

"Don't sound like Randi to me. Listen, Steve, anything else I can do for you?"

"No. Nothing. I want you to have a telephone. Then Randi can call you and vice versa."

"Sure now, phones cost money, me lad. But later. Later." She looked back into the room behind her.

He hesitated for a moment, then spoke. "I thought, since you've become a lady with an income, it might be easier."

She understood.

"Oh, you were the dear man! I wish I could kiss you for it. I never dreamed it would be so much. I had a sneakin' notion it might be a little something. But fifty dollars! Every month, too. I asked the bank."

"Don't spend it all in one place." He lowered his voice. "And Bridget, don't take offense, but I wish you wouldn't let LeMass get his hands on it."

The door to Number 6, which had been ajar, opened, and a huge man appeared in the doorway. Steve was slightly embarrassed to see LeMass, but the man's grin told him he was prepared to accept the insult graciously.

"She's that fussy, you'd never believe it. Not a nickel do I get, even to rush the growler."

Steve laughed. "Sorry. No offense meant."

"And sure, none'll be taken. Though I'd recommend some sound investments, was it me doin' the receivin'."

"Well then, I'll trust you to take good care of her and if you have any influence at all, see that she gets a telephone installed. I want Randi to be able to talk to her any time."

"I'll do that."

Before Steve could back away LeMass took his hand and shook it. "And I'll bet me bottom dollar you spent your honeymoon buying some fine property."

Steve shrugged. "I've let one go by. Not my sort. I want to be an independent owner. Some day when this flu thing is over, I intend to drive you out to the beach. Show you some lots. I think they're the start of really big things. In a few years, that is."

"Sounds mighty smart. Myself, I'd rather have the little places than a big white elephant like Mr. Red buys up, savin' your presence."

"Would you?" Suddenly, Steve wanted to get away. The Monte Carlo Arms was still a sore spot with him, and LeMass's easy dismissal of it made him frustrated and angry. He had felt this way earlier in the afternoon when he saw Red embracing Randi as if he owned her. Steve knew that Randi had been doing nothing more than comforting the old fox; still, the sight had galled him.

"I've got to be on my way. I shouldn't be out at all. We're prisoners, you know. You two take care of each other. We'll get together as soon as this damned flu scare is over."

Bridget was nervously walking up and down the hall.

"Don't you be letting my girl catch the flu. You look out for her, you hear? I'll go over to the drug store and call her every day without failing. And I'll come to your back door and bring a bit of a meal. Might just come in handy while you're all stuck away in that old barn."

Going down the stairs, Steve waved good-bye to Bridget without turning around. He missed André. He wished he could talk over the failure of the Monte Carlo Arms with his friend, who would have put it all in perspective in his own quiet way. Instead, he vented his smouldering anger toward his father by whirling his little car around the slippery street and heading back up the hill with a screech.

It was past ten by the time he parked the car behind Brooke's in the garage and started walking toward the Lombard mansion. The mist has risen and the moonlight illuminated the brass knocker and the lion's head on the big front door. When he reached the gate, he saw a small figure, less than five feet tall, in a black coat, with bare knees visible above his socks and shoes. A child knocking on the Lombard door at this hour? Steve wondered if the child was a runaway.

Turning nervously at the sound of Steve's approaching footsteps, the boy shifted his weight awkwardly, and Steve could see that the boy was crippled. The left leg dragged a bit and appeared to be slightly shorter than the right. And yet, he looked familiar; towheaded, with freckles, a sharp nose and spectacles which befitted an adult.

My God! Steve thought suddenly. This forlorn little intruder was his nephew.

"You're Alec! Why the devil didn't you call me? I'd have come down to the depot to pick you up." He started to hug the boy, but stopped as he remembered that he himself could be contagious. He felt helpless to show his affection. The boy spoke in a cool, businesslike tone.

"It was late and nobody answered. Then I couldn't get a jitney and I forgot which car to take, so I asked the conductor on the cable car line."

Steve turned the boy so he stood in the tiny pool of light above the front stoop.

"You've grown. I'd never have known you."

"Granny's dead. My cousins have to adopt me. They don't want to. I heard them talking. They've got too many to care for and granny didn't leave any money like they thought. So I thought I'd come down and see mother for a little while before somebody adopts me at home."

"And quite right, too. No nephew of mine is going to be adopted by people who don't want him. You don't belong there any more. You belong here. You always did."

"With mother?" The boy's face lit up. He depends on Brooke, Steve thought. Poor little devil . . . Steve was touched by the boy's uncompromising acceptance of the hard facts of his life.

Steve tried the front door, but it was locked again. All of a sudden he realized that young Alec could very well contract the flu in this house.

"Never mind. We'll go in through the kitchen and pantry."

The boy reached into the darkness and lifted a heavy leather suitcase that had obviously belonged to his father. Steve tried to take it from him.

"I can do it. I got it this far," Alec insisted.

True enough, Steve thought, and let him carry the case.

"Don't touch anything. We have the flu in the house. I'm going to call someone to help you until you can move in with us properly."

Alec made no protest but merely said, "I want to see mother first. Then I'll go wherever you say."

"I'm afraid your mother is a long way off. But by the time your

Grandmother Lombard recovers, Brooke will be back in town. You can see her then."

"I wrote to her. I told her I might be coming," Alec said, his plaintive voice belying his otherwise calm demeanor.

Steve wished Randi were here. She would be able to handle this more delicately.

"I'm sure you did, but maybe your letter missed Brooke. Anyway, I want you to meet your Aunt Randi as soon as it's safe. You'll like her. She is a wonderful girl."

Alec nodded blankly.

"You wait right here. Remember, don't touch anything." Steve felt helpless against the boy's pretense of indifference.

Leaving the boy in the warmth of the kitchen, Steve picked up the phone in the hall and called the Fairmont Hotel's new assistant manager, who happened to be a fellow alumnus of U. of C.

"Bud? Steve Lombard. Thanks . . . Of course, I beat out most of them. I was home the day of the armistice . . . You remember my Canadian brother-in-law, Colin Huntington? . . . Yes. Rotten business. The damned Huns and their chlorine gas or whatever it was. Anyway, his boy—my nephew—is here for a visit. But we've got flu in the house. My mother . . . she's much better this evening, thank God. Can you send someone across to pick up young Alec? I'll see that he's entertained after tonight, but right now he needs a room and a friendly face."

Bud Classen laughed. "And mine is the friendliest you can find? The poor kid. We'll make him comfortable. Anything I can do for old Colin's son!"

"I owe you for this, Bud. And of course, put my nephew's room and meals on our charge."

"We'll see about that. Personally, I feel we owe old Colin something."

After an exchange of mutual good wishes, Steve hung up and saw Alec standing calmly in the hall. Too bad the kid couldn't stay here tonight, Steve thought. Nevertheless, Randi was upstairs sweating out a dangerous watch over his mother. He was relieved when the good-natured housekeeper from the Fairmont arrived and Alec was turned over to her, still dragging his suitcase.

"Do you really think mother didn't get my letter?" He looked back from the sidewalk.

"She certainly wouldn't have gone away if she knew you were coming to visit her, would she?" Steve reminded him.

For the first time the boy's face brightened in a smile. He nodded, took the housekeeper's hand and limped across the humming cable car tracks with her.

Steve called after him. "Use the telephone. Call me or Randi every day. Every evening, too, if you get lonesome. You're going to love Randi."

He hurried inside, started up the stairs to his wife. Then he had an idea about the boy's entertainment the next few days. Alma Cortlandt. She had gone out on a few dates with Colin Huntington, and might now want to help his son. He swung around the newel-post and picked up the telephone again.

Alma was her usual obliging self, explaining that she had just come home after a date, and teasingly asked if he was calling in the middle of his honeymoon. Steve explained about his nephew, but Alma seemed to find his request amusing and could not contain her giggles. Steve cleared his throat, somewhat put out by her mockery.

"Well, just thought I'd ask. I'll get André de Grasse and Bridget Gallegher to help. I've told the boy to call me whenever he gets lonesome, so he'll probably be all right. Sorry to call you this late."

Alma suddenly recovered herself. "Oh, I don't know. Wait. I think I'd like to show the boy around. And I'll see to it he calls you. By the way, father would like to talk to you about some acreage you bought out near the beach and Golden Gate Park. He has all sorts of plans. He tried Red but Red isn't interested in individual properties. Too small, he says. You know your father." She went on, " 'Night, darling. Sorry! It slipped out. You'll hear from Colin's boy—and me—regularly."

"Thanks. That's a big load off my mind." He pushed the phone back, went upstairs and found Randi sitting in an uncomfortable chair, half-dozing but ready to leap up in an instant. After a quick glance at his mother sleeping peacefully, he knelt before Randi with a feeling of such tender possessiveness as he never remembered feeling before.

"How would you like to have a child?" he said, grinning.

"What? Right now?"

"As soon as mother is feeling better."

"Mother? What's this all about? You mean you and I—?"

"Only for a visit. He's ten years old." He then explained about Brooke's son. Randi was enthusiastic, and liked everything except the idea of Alma Cortlandt's involvement.

She's jealous, Steve thought, and was amused and flattered. He didn't mind a bit.

# *Chapter Eleven*

WHEN Alicia Lombard forgot her indifference to her new daughter-in-law, whom she had so clearly neglected in her delirium, Randi knew she was well on her way to recovery.

"My boy's brave, capable bride," she murmured. "How kind you are to your poor old mother-in-law!"

Randi fluffed up her pillows. "You're fishing for compliments. You are far from poor and old. Shall I give you a mirror to prove it?"

Mrs. Lombard smiled and asked if she could see her husband and her son. Dr. Humphreys, who had assured the family of their good luck in the patient's recovery, spent the next half-hour examining Randi and Stella Burkett. He was finishing up when Steve came out of the sick-room.

He went over to Randi and kissed the back of her neck. She laughed, reached around and rubbed his cheek with the palm of her hand. Then Steve pulled Randi's apron strings, let the apron fall and announced that with the doctor's permission he was taking his bride out to lunch.

Stella Burkett did not take her eyes off the two of them.

"Don't forget, Randi—I mean ma'am," she corrected herself. "We got to have a cook in the house by tonight. They're all refusing my food, and they're not too keen about yours, if it comes to that."

As usual, Stella was throwing up obstacles. But Randi's thoughts were elsewhere . . . Buoyed by her mother-in-law's recovery, Randi hoped that Alec could come home and so end the twice-daily conversations between Steve and Alma Cortlandt. Randi had spoken on the phone with Alec several times and tried hard to make conversation. She felt that someone had to make up for Brooke's absence, but it soon became clear that it would take more than good will to make the boy forget the one person he really wanted. No matter what conversational gambits she attempted, they were clearly of no interest to her unexpected nephew . . .

Now that the family was free to move about, a dozen important matters had to be settled before Randi and Steve were free to enjoy themselves.

"Steve, I've got a million people I must call or none of us will eat tonight, or have decent bed linen, or a place for Alec or a house that doesn't smell of disinfectants. I wish mother had a phone. Perhaps I should visit her right away. She could help, too."

Steve aroused her suspicion with his immediate objection. "Bridget will call you this evening as usual from the drug store. I wouldn't drop in on her unexpectedly."

"Good Lord! If you mean I might catch her and LeMass together, it certainly wouldn't be the first time."

Steve grinned. "Just so you know what to expect."

Randi smiled tenderly at his naiveté about Bridget. "Darling, mother needs a man. She's had LeMass so long I almost feel he's a parent. She's not foolish enough to marry him and support him the rest of her life, but he means something to her now. He'll go some day. They all do, unfortunately."

Steve quickly changed the subject. "Get ready, sweetheart. I'm going to show you off to young Alec and to the rest of the world. We'll take in that afternoon tea dance Brooke is always talking about at the St. Francis Hotel. Wear that blue thing with all the buttons, your going-away outfit. Remember?"

"I remember." How could she forget that perfect wedding afternoon and night? The memory had carried her through the long nights of sickroom vigil she had divided with Nurse Willabrandt and Steve ever since. "I'll get ready as soon as I get things settled on the telephone and get Nurse Willabrandt's things together."

"Can't father—can't Red do that? I want you out of this place as soon as possible. At least for the afternoon."

She appreciated his concern for her, but it wasn't practical. Brooke Lombard had taken the first coastal-bound ship from Honolulu and was due in that afternoon or the following morning. Her arrival would make it even more necessary to have the household organized, a cook and servants on the job, plus arrangements made for Alec.

"Look, honey, I know you want to get out of here fast. Why don't you leave now and I'll meet you in an hour or less. As soon as I can settle things."

He didn't like it, but the bright December sunshine made him anxious to get outside. He kissed her, then touched her lips with his forefinger.

"If you promise to make these weighty decisions in one half-hour exactly. But I want to have you meet Alec as soon as possible."

"I promise." She would try her best, she thought. And thanks to the advice of Mrs. Schultz, the cook, she managed to settle the Lombard staff problem in the alloted half-hour. The only remaining problem was Stella Burkett, who needed some reassurance.

"We won't forget how you stood by us during the bad time, Stella," Randi said. "Don't worry about that. I intend to see that your salary is raised a dollar a week."

"*We.* And *us.* My stars, ain't we highfallutin now we're married into the Lombards?" But she heard Red Lombard leaving his wife's sickroom, and her dissatisfaction faded. "Well, I'll see how it goes. But I ain't promising nothing."

Stella's interest in Red made Randi uneasy, but she really could do nothing about it. Red was obviously devoted to his wife, and sooner or later Stella was sure to find a man more appropriate for her.

Randi rushed into the small, dark room she had been sharing with Steve. With considerable stretching she got the pearls buttoned down the back of her dress, changed to silk stockings and high-heeled pumps. She adjusted her honeymoon hat of blue felt so that it perched over her right eye, and added an egret feather to accentuate the tilt.

Still not accustomed to the idea of a taxicab, she walked down steep California Street to the Powell Street cable car and rode down to the St. Francis Hotel.

There seemed to be no flu scare here. The pillared lobby was jammed with pre-Christmas crowds, mainly women in elegant, beaded tea gowns and accompanied by their men. A sprinkling of soldiers circulated among the females but they were outnumbered by the younger and more eager sailors. Two sailors surrounded Randi as she crossed the lobby.

"I'm the real dancer. Wait'll you see my tango," one teased.

"Everybody but this nut will tell you my castle walk is the best in Frisco," the other countered.

"Try us both."

She saw Steve's tall figure near the open doors of the celebrated Rose Room, flanked by Alma Cortlandt and a thin boy with sand-colored hair, apparently involved in conversation with a pudgy man Randi recognized as Buckleigh Cortlandt. Watching the animated discussion between Steve and Alma's father, an investment counsel, Randi suddenly realized that her great rivals for Steve's attention would always be the Buckleigh Cortlandts of the world—not the Almas.

But it was hard to believe at this moment. Dark-eyed Alma looked sultry and beautiful in a maroon coat and hat with sable trim. She wore lipstick which made her lips pout seductively. Randi touched her own lips self-consciously, and half-decided to look into the matter of makeup. Though she had always been proud of her complexion and good color, there was no denying the effectiveness of those bright lips.

Meanwhile, Randi shook off her navy blue Lotharios and strolled over to meet her husband, careful not to run like a nervous bride, not with Alma Cortlandt's eyes on her. Though Alma said nothing, she watched Randi as if she were studying her.

"Go to it," Randi thought, keeping in mind that Steve had chosen *her*. It was simplistic reasoning, but it gave her satisfaction. She squared her shoulders and walked over to the little group.

"Hello, darling. I made it as fast as I could."

Steve kissed her lightly on the cheek and presented his nephew, Alec Huntington. She started to give him a hug, but instead shook hands with him, realizing that he was every bit as proud and as reserved as she was. Buckleigh Cortlandt, however, was far less reserved.

"Must say, Steve, with a bride like your Mary-Randal here, I'd have little time for talking business. Which we've been doing, Mary."

Alec studied her, and she was aware of his thoughtful gaze. "Do call me Randi," she urged Alma's father.

"Nothing would give me greater pleasure. I understand Alma wanted to show you off to her friends in this noisy *thé dansant*, as they call it, so I'm afraid you and I will have to shout over the music."

"I adore your dress, Randi," Alma said.

"Let me return the compliment. That style is wonderful. Is it Russian?"

"It's a Christmas present from daddy. I like maroon. It's exactly the color of that new Hudson of yours, Steve. I adore it. It purrs like a kitten."

No cable cars for Alma, Randi thought. He must have driven her and the boy down to the St. Francis . . . Well, it's my fault, Randi confessed to herself. I should have gone with Steve in the first place . . .

Steve led the way into the Rose Room where the suave headwaiter found them a table elbow-to-elbow with all the others, just as a tango ended on the crowded floor. Everyone ordered wine except Alma, who gave Steve a special smile and asked for a brandy alexander.

"I heard they're all the rage in Paris. Is that true, Steve? Or am I being bold?" Alma giggled.

Steve pinched her nose. "You always were, so why change now? Alec will have tea."

Alec made a face, and Randi asked him how he liked San Francisco. The boy shrugged.

"It's all right. I like the museums. And the ferryboats."

It was the first time she had ever heard a boy say he liked museums. She was beginning to wonder about him, but his serious face suddenly broke into warmth.

"Is it true? Is mother coming home tomorrow?"

"We certainly hope so. We are counting on it." She wanted to preserve that happy light in his eyes. "She will be mighty glad to see you," she added.

The orchestra started up again and dancers moved onto the floor. Steve turned to Randi.

"Remember what they were playing that night at Tidelands, sweetheart?" He got up, held out his hand.

Randi went into his arms, laughing at the memory. "Isn't it 'I'm Forever Blowing Bubbles'?"

"I was blowing them for nothing that night. You know what I think?"

"Tell me." How good it was to be in his arms, she thought. With Steve guiding her around the crowd, she felt as if she were floating.

She couldn't help being proud that he had chosen . . . No! She was chilled by a memory. *She and Brooke had chosen Steve.*

"Are you cold, sweetheart? In all this mob?" Steve asked curiously.

"Shivering at a memory."

"That's better." He pulled her tightly to his body. They circled the room and Randi caught a glimpse of Alec's face. He looked puzzled. Either their particular happiness surprised him or he wasn't used to all this liveliness.

Randi tried to be generous when Steve danced next with Alma Cortlandt. Mr. Cortlandt pleaded his weight as an excuse for not taking Randi onto the floor. Randi noticed with a tug of envy how petite and delicate Alma looked in Steve's arms, and as if to cancel her jealousy she remarked on this to Alma's father. He accepted the compliment with the manner of one who heard such praise every day.

"Yes. Alma was always a beauty. I remember she always had at least two beaux. Many's the time Steve and a Canadian friend of theirs—well, by thunder! It was the father of young Alec here—fought over who'd take her home."

Randi smiled and sipped her drink. Alec, however, pricked up his ears.

"She's fun. She went all over the city with me. And every single time she telephoned Steve for me and told him all about it. She said to call her Alma. That's a pretty name."

Buckleigh Cortlandt's eyebrows raised. "I suspect someone we know has added his heart to my little girl's collection," he said as if the boy were deaf.

Alec's expression cooled. He did not seem to like being the butt of grown-up jokes.

Randi had never been around children very much and found it difficult to think of a subject that might interest Alec without insulting his intelligence. His maturity, however, made it easier than she would have imagined.

"You are in the investment business?" she remarked to Mr. Cortlandt. "Large business buildings, like my father-in-law?" She wanted to find out whether he was likely to be on Steve's side or that of Red Lombard. Judging by Red's conduct in the Monte Carlo Arms affair, she agreed with Steve that he was not to be trusted—neither were his business friends.

Buckleigh Cortlandt, however, did not appear to be one of them.

"Lord, no! Not like the old fox. Matter of fact, Randi, I'd appreciate your not mentioning to Red our talk about the Pacific Dunes Estates. Very hush-hush."

She was delighted. Even Alec showed interest in the conversation.

"Are you talking about Steve's lots out near the beach? I had no idea the project had advanced so far." All this must have transpired during Steve's many telephone calls throughout his mother's illness. She wished he had discussed it with her or at least mentioned it.

"Well, it's the coming area. The city's got to expand somewhere. All they've got is this peninsula, so every foot counts. I wasn't too keen on all those sand dunes. But that husband of yours is a real man of vision. Claims he's been thinking it all through while he was trapped in that old museum of a house. We're going out to look it over late this afternoon."

So much for Steve's promise that he and Randi would share the afternoon, she thought glumly. Yet she refused to admit even to herself that she was hurt.

"I hope Steve won't exclude me. I'd love to hear all your plans. It's rather like being present at the birth of a city."

Alec looked from Randi to Cortlandt. "Alma took me out to the beach. A man at the Cliff House was talking about wireless. It was exciting. He was building himself one. Well, not exactly—a radio has wires. Did you ever see a radio?"

"I never did," Randi said while Cortlandt brushed away the shift in conversation.

"Yes, yes, my boy. And very useful they are, for short distances."

"Oh, but—"

"Never interrupt your elders, my boy. Now then, Randi, I don't think a nice young lady like you wants to waste hours of her time wandering over sand dunes and discussing acreage."

"I would like it very much. Those houses are going to be for people, not giant corporations like—well, like others."

"And we know who that is, don't we? That's all right, Randi. You're a loyal wife. Red's made his pile, and now it's Steve's turn. Both Alma and I agree with you."

"I agree to what?" Alma asked as she arrived at the table on Steve's arm.

Her father's explanation was embarrassing. "Randi wants us to show her what you have just christened Pacific Dunes, my dear. And we all give *you* full credit for that name. Steve, your wife thinks you can show up the old fox, and I agree. So does Alma."

Steve shrugged, and took out a cigarette, frowning. He clearly didn't like his wife brought into his business deals like this. But he *had* discussed it with Alma Cortlandt, and she *did* come up with that name . . . He turned to Alec. "Why are we all talking business? How do you like the *thé dansant?*"

"I don't see anybody drinking tea, except me."

They all laughed and the tension was broken for a moment. Then Cortlandt remarked, "I hope you understand, Steve. Besides your lots there should be a good faith investment on both sides. The development will run into a small fortune."

"Certainly. I've been giving it a lot of thought. My sister Brooke is returning tomorrow. Since Red has used my money to back his investments—all quite legitimately, I might add—Brooke will be delighted to make this loan to me. At interest, of course. It's just a matter of approaching her the right way."

"That will be eminently satisfactory. Keeps it in the family, so to speak."

Everyone understood, but Cortlandt persisted with a chuckle. "I mean *your* family, of course. You and Brooke."

Alma picked up on this instantly. "Father, no one thought you meant Steve and *me.*"

Randi was sure both comments had been deliberate.

Things kept going downhill from that point and Randi was relieved when everyone followed her lead in preparing to return home.

"Just in case Brooke's liner has docked," she reminded them.

Steve agreed. "Fine. Then later today, Buck, I'll pick you up and we'll drive out to the beach to make our plans."

Randi was not included. Subdued and thoughtful, she drove up Nob Hill with Steve and Alec, trying to figure out how she could talk Steve into letting her in on his business dealings as he had in Strand. She wouldn't dare appear pushy, she thought, but she did want to be useful in his work, to have him trust her and, once in a while, listen to her advice. It would take some time, but sooner or later Steve would have to see that his wife was just as capable as Buckleigh Cortlandt's daughter seemed to be.

Randi decided that she would not be foolish enough to remind him that she had urged his interest in smaller properties. He had obviously forgotten that.

# *Chapter Twelve*

WITH Alec between them, Randi and Steve walked into the Lombard house. Despite Alicia Lombard's recovery, the dark woodwork and heavy Victorian furniture made the place look as gloomy as ever. Randi marveled at how glorious she had thought this place was when she was still just a visitor. But there was still the sunroom, and as soon as the tea ceremony was reinstated, she would preside over the elegant ritual.

She started to speak, but Steve wasn't listening. He had heard his father coming down the front stairs, rattling the heavy bannisters in his haste.

"Brooke's here, Steve. Didn't even call us. Just up and took a taxi-cab. She's in a real good mood."

Steve set down Alec's heavy suitcase. Alec was jumping up and down.

"She's home! Mother must've heard I'd come."

Steve was in great spirits. "Randi, shall we take this young fellow upstairs and hear all about the beauty of the tropics and romance on the high seas? I'll bet it ought to mature him fast."

Randi was herself pleased to have Brooke back home where she could help solve the new problems of the household. But one thought disturbed her . . . Did Red Lombard's excitement over his daughter's return involve the hope of a loan from her? . . . He called up the stairs after them.

"The trip was good for Brooke. We had a real nice chat. She wanted to know if that Frenchman was gone. Good riddance, I say. I wouldn't be surprised if my little girl hightailed it off to the islands just to get rid of him."

"Probably," Steve agreed, not looking at Randi.

His father went on. "She's got more sense than I give her credit for. I even talked business with her—investments, household expenses. That girl winds you right around her little finger. Told me we didn't have a thing to worry about. Randi here would take care of everything. You're a very capable girl, Randi."

Randi was certainly willing to bet Red had done some winding around his own finger, and she reminded Steve in a low voice, "If you want Brooke to invest, you had better discuss it with her immediately."

Steve glanced down the stairs, understanding her. His father had gone. Then he shrugged. "I can hardly rush in, say 'Welcome home, Brooke. Can I borrow your money?' "

Alec looked up at Randi, scowling. He probably thought they were robbing his mother. She couldn't help admiring the boy for his loyalty to his mother, even if it threatened Steve's future.

Brooke was in the lovely front room opposite her mother's sitting room. She had never been busier. The four-poster bed with its frilled white dimity tester and curtains had taken on the appearance of a dress shop. Bright colors dazzled the eye. Scarlet kimonos with blue dragons, blue kimonos with red dragons, were all spread over the bed. Before she even said hello, Brooke pointed out an odd, floor-length silk gown.

"That's a *holoku,* like the last Hawaiian queen wore. It will be perfect for a New Year's masquerade. And look at the slippers. *Gatas.* No, *getas.* Well, something like that."

She dropped the black Japanese clogs and threw her arms around Alec.

"Darling, darling boy! To think you made that whole trip all alone. Your mama's so proud of you."

Alec reddened with embarrassment, but he returned her hug so enthusiastically she accused him of trying to strangle her. It was a warm and tender moment, and Randi found it difficult to believe this same loving mother had wanted her boy to remain in Canada.

With one arm still holding Alec close to her, Brooke beamed at her brother and Randi.

"You may kiss me, both of you, but I refuse to let this young man go. He might disappear again for a whole year." She sealed this by kissing the top of Alec's head. He squirmed but both his hands clutched her free hand. He was obviously mesmerized by her warmth and charm.

"We would have had you here long ago, darling," Brooke said, "but you can't expect newlyweds to welcome a little boy who will take all the attention away from them. Even a boy as bright and intelligent as my very own young man."

Randi opened her mouth to object, but closed it abruptly when she saw Steve's expression. He would have corrected his sister with brutal frankness but Randi nudged him. This was no time to disillusion Brooke's adoring son who had by himself traveled down the Pacific Coast just for the assurance that his beautiful mother loved him.

Nor was there time for business talk. Steve soon tired of Brooke's ceaseless remarks about her new wardrobe, and reminded Randi that he had to meet Buckleigh Cortlandt at his office and drive him out to the beach properties. Randi wanted very much to go with him, but there was no getting away once Brooke piped in.

"We are going to have a decent dinner tonight. Do say we are. I'm really tired of raw fish and poi and long pig."

"Long pig!" Steve shouted. "That's human flesh, old girl."

Alec Huntington laughed and hugged his mother, who only waved her free hand impatiently.

"You know what I mean. The pork roasted in the ground with all that grass and stones and stuff."

But Steve was already bored with his sister's chatter.

"Sorry I can't stick around to hear this cannibal talk but I've got business to go over before dinner." He turned, kissed his wife and squeezed her arm. "See you then, sweetheart. But please, no long pig."

She went out in the hall with him, realizing, not for the first time, how awkward it was to share a house with two other families.

"Steve, we should at least pay something on account when they deliver the groceries Mrs. Schultz ordered."

He looked surprised. "Sure. Why not? By the way, when Bridget calls, invite her. André too. There'll be plenty to talk about."

It was generous of him to know how anxious she was to see her mother. But he hadn't understood quite what she meant.

"There's no money left in the household account. Today I used what change I had, but I'm afraid I'm broke now, too."

Steve's eyes were angry. "Don't do that again. I'll have to give you an allowance."

"But meanwhile?"

"Meanwhile, get it from father." He hurried down the stairs.

"Good luck," she called. He waved and was gone.

Less than an hour later the matter came to a head. Mrs. Schultz, looking stouter than when she had fled the house ten days ago, came bustling up to Randi.

"Got to have eight dollars and six bits. The boy's here with roast beef, a loin of pork, the lobsters and the vegetables." She examined her list. "The yellow wheat cereal for the missus, the eggs and bacon for the two gents—and the rest. Here. No more credit, the grocery says."

"Never mind. I'll get the money from Mr. Lombard."

"Ha! I wish you luck then." Mrs. Schultz knew Red Lombard all too well.

Randi stopped outside the door of his den, took a deep breath and knocked. Inside, there were scrambling noises. She knocked again. The door opened and Stella Burkett slithered out with a feather duster.

"Cleaning up here and there."

"So I see." She looked around Stella to Red Lombard, who seemed totally absorbed in the *Evening Bulletin.* "Mr. Lombard?"

"Oh. It's you, m'dear. You're to call me Red, you know."

"I wonder if I could have eight dollars and seventy-five cents. For the groceries." He put the paper down, felt in his hip pocket, came up with the lining inside out. His sheepish grin reminded her of Brooke's.

"How do you like that? Penniless." He tried his vest pocket, came up with a fifty-cent piece and tossed it to her. "How about four bits?"

She caught it by clapping it between her hands. "I really must have the eight dollars and twenty-five cents as well, sir. The boy is waiting."

"Tell you what. Why don't you get it from old Steve? He's always got a pocketful of change."

She stood her ground. "He isn't here."

"But you must know where he keeps his small change."

"Small or large, I really don't know. May I have a check, sir, if nothing else?"

He sighed, beat the folded paper thoughtfully against his thumb. "Damn! To tell the truth, I'm a little overdrawn this month. But there is Brooke. Did you see all the junk that little girl of mine brought home? There's the baby with the money on hand."

She gave up on him for the moment and went to see Brooke. Holding up dresses in front of herself and parading before her bright-eyed son, Brooke was delighted to see Randi and began to chatter before Randi could get in a word.

"Alec has such good taste. He likes the blue one and the black and white. He thinks I shouldn't cut my hair. I told him it's all the rage. But he says—isn't he sweet—he says my hair is too pretty."

"He's certainly right about that. Brooke, may I borrow eight dollars and twenty-five cents? It's for the groceries."

Brooke threw clothes onto the bed in a colorful heap. "Sorry. Rule number one. Never lend a cent of cash to this family. You'll never see it again."

Torn between anger and panic, Randi reminded her, "In that case, it looks like no dinner tonight. I'll have to send the delivery boy away."

"Don't be ridiculous. We've never starved. This is always happening." Brooke laughed, pointed a finger like a pistol at her. "Now you know how you can be useful in this family. We expect you to manage things, honey."

"I know. I was married for my money."

Brooke overlooked the irony of her statement.

"No. But partly to prevent this happening again. It just spoils my mood to come home and run into the same old problems. First, father wanting my money. And then this grocery thing."

"You didn't lend your father the money he wanted?"

"You think I'm crazy? If anyone wants my money he pays for it. I'm like a bank. I don't give. I invest."

"Then you do invest."

"Like I invested in that wager with you, honey. And don't you forget it."

Brooke's words startled Randi, but fortunately, her remarks about investments distracted her . . . She couldn't wait to tell Steve. He could offer Brooke a deal involving a short-term loan at a substantial rate of interest . . .

But meanwhile, there was the grocery boy waiting in Mrs. Schultz's kitchen.

"I wonder if Mrs. Lombard might have a piggy bank or something. Otherwise, it looks as though we won't eat tonight."

Alec Huntington reached into the big patch pocket of his jacket and pulled out a snap purse.

"That's all right. I have plenty. My whole bank account."

Brooke hugged him. "You darling boy! You've saved your poor old mother from starvation."

It took Alec two offers before he could press the eight dollars into Randi's hand. As she left Brooke's room, Randi began to see the pattern of her life before her . . . She had always wanted some responsibility in her marriage. But encouraging a vulnerable boy of ten to support the wealthy Lombards was not part of her dream.

# *BOOK TWO*

# 1919-1926

# *Chapter One*

AFTER his father's death, Alec Huntington had made up his mind never again to let himself care about anyone. Then it couldn't hurt when that person was taken away. So it was easy enough not to love Aunt Randi at first—she was too much like himself, reserved with her affections. Though he understood and respected her, he still needed the warm, soft sweetness of his mother and grandmother, who made a fuss over him no matter how much he pretended not to care. Uncle Steve and Grandpa Red became part of his life, too. With them, it was almost like having his father back. Even strangers like Grandma Bridget and LeMass welcomed him. He never wanted to go home.

Toward the end of the first week after Christmas, he lay awake night after night wondering what he would do when they sent him home . . . By New Year's 1919, it became worse, and Alec found himself more attached to the Lombard family than ever. He bit his nails and tried not to become too used to their affectionate way with him.

All but Aunt Randi—she always behaved the same way. Friendly, brisk and businesslike. It took him a long while to figure it out. Only after many months did the answer come to him—Aunt Randi treated him just the way she treated the rest of the family, like a grown-up. It was very odd, and he couldn't decide whether he liked it or not.

He definitely resented the way she ran the household. Everyone had to come to her. Grandpa Red, Grandma Alicia, and worst of all,

Brooke, had to depend on Aunt Randi's "household money," which Aunt Randi insisted on collecting every month from Grandpa Red, Uncle Steve and even mother.

By springtime every month's end seemed a new torture to Alec. Being sent home now would be that much harder. But early in April his world changed and became anchored on the firm foundation of Nob Hill. Oddly enough, it was the fact that Aunt Randi and Uncle Steve were going to have a baby that cinched Alec's position.

"Our son is going to start out with his very own, ready-made brother. What do you say to that, Alexander Colin Huntington?" Steve asked.

Randi laughed at the idea that Steve had divined the sex of the child without any foreknowledge save his own stubborn will.

"Will he have my room?" Alec asked.

Steve looked to Randi for advice. "What about that? Have we enough rooms to go around? Or must we throw out the newcomer?"

Brooke was home that evening, a rare treat for Alec. "Darling, they're only teasing you. We'll manage somehow. Won't we, Randi?" Brooke winked at Steve.

"I'm sure we'll work something out," Randi said. "In fact, I hope Alec will never want to leave. He's very helpful to me. I count on him a lot."

That evening, when Alec went around saying good night and shaking hands in his prematurely grown-up way he gave Randi's hand an extra squeeze. The arrival of his "younger brother" would be the best thing that ever happened to him, he thought. He could see why all the grown-ups were so happy, especially Steve, who insisted that his son be given a good Lombard name, which naturally perked up Red Lombard. But then Steve came up with the name of Anthony, after Red Lombard's father, Mad Tony, the founder of the Lombards' San Francisco fortune. Alec knew it hurt Grandpa Red, but the old gentleman only laughed and said he hoped the baby would be as successful in life as was his namesake . . .

Alec's happiness was compounded when one morning Randi came in after discussing the next day's menu with Mrs. Schultz.

"Would you mind balancing this morning's bill from the wharfman, Alec? I can't get the thing to come out right. I'm positive there were only two lobsters and five crabs delivered this week."

Alec was ecstatic. He was finally being asked to do something he knew he could do extremely well.

Uncle Steve was out that evening at the opening of the first stucco home built on one of the Pacific Dunes lots. The Cortlandts were there—father and daughter. Alec had overheard his grandmother's remark to Brooke. "It's too bad Randi isn't feeling well tonight of all nights. Alma is so pretty. And Steve used to be rather fond of her, you remember."

"Don't ruin my investment, mother. I have ten thousand at twelve percent tied up in Pacific Dunes. Besides, Alma is old stuff to Steve. And Randi keeps him hopping. There's nothing like providing the family heir to the Lombard name. Alma can't match that."

Alec liked Alma Cortlandt, but he resented her intrusion in Uncle Steve's life. It was only when he was in bed and rubbing his bad leg, which still ached sometimes, that he had a small, nagging thought. *If Anthony Lombard is to be heir to the Lombard name, then who am I? . . .*

Right after his eleventh birthday in January he decided to make himself indispensable—just in case. He learned how much money would be saved if he were allowed to visit the various grocery stores, the North Beach meat market and Fisherman's Wharf for seafood. First he went with Aunt Randi, but later he proved he could handle the orders himself. When she heard about his journeys, his grandmother was indignant.

"The poor little tyke may get lost. Or hurt. Anything might happen. He's crippled, you know."

Alec treasured Brooke's exasperated, "Oh, mother! He just has a teeny limp. It hardly ever shows. If he can help Randi, why shouldn't he?"

By summertime, the usually foggy and cold months in San Francisco, Alec was convinced that they couldn't get along without him. He had achieved his goal, made himself indispensable to the family. For the first time he felt safe. Surely, they wouldn't send him away now! . . .

In early October it was with a sense of personal triumph and responsibility that he joined his Uncle Steve, his Grandma Alicia and Bridget Gallegher in the long vigil the night Aunt Randi gave birth. Anthony Lombard, his new cousin, arrived in the morning.

Alec was astonished to catch Uncle Steve with tears in his eyes. He had never seen a grown man cry before and while he didn't approve of it—after all, it wasn't manly—he felt proud of his own conduct. He had comforted Steve with the repeated assurance, "The baby will be great. You'll see."

Steve clenched and unclenched his fists and kept looking up the stairs. "I know, Alec. But Randi! If anything happens to that girl—someday, you'll know what—My God! It's taking an eternity."

Then it was all over and Alec found it embarrassing to see the way his aunt and uncle kissed each other and carried on. Alec, who had seen numerous cousins and their mothers at birth, was surprised that Aunt Randi came through so well. The strain of the long labor vanished after a few hours, and Randi was pleased with her perfect son. Bridget and Grandma Alicia hovered around Randi's bed and the baby's crib, and Uncle Steve kept saying young Tony Lombard was the handsomest baby ever.

Almost at once, Alec was aware of his changed position in the family. His charm as the only youngster in the family was eclipsed by his cousin Tony, who was born a handsome, healthy infant with a shock of dark hair and hazel eyes which were much admired.

Fishing for a compliment that would restore his confidence in himself, Alec said to Randi one day, "I'll bet you wish Cousin Tony was helping you market."

"Not likely. If he takes after his father or me, he will need somebody with your brains to tell him what these fishmongers are up to. You've amazed us all in school, incidentally. I never saw such grades."

"Don't you think Tony will get good grades some day?"

"I don't think they'll matter to him. Heaven knows what will become of him, but whatever he does, I suspect he will rely more on charm than brains."

"Uncle Steve doesn't think so. When he was carrying Tony around last night he said his son would be president of the United States if he wanted."

Aunt Randi's high-boned face softened the way it often did when she looked at Steve. "President Wilson might have something to say about that."

"I wished I was him when he went over to France to settle the war and all. But now that he's so sick, I wouldn't want to be him. Grandpa Red says he may die with his stroke."

"It's a very hard job. I don't think I'd want my son to be president." She rapped his nose playfully. "You'd make a good president. You're smart enough."

It was the kind of remark that kept him going, riding on the hope that everyone's interest in him would return after the novelty of the new baby wore off.

ALEC WAS not the only one who wondered whether the baby's charms would soon wear thin. Randi had been delighted that Steve seemed so attached to his son and heir, but she feared that when Tony's crying disturbed his sleep a few times, he would find the baby less enchanting.

After that, like many fathers, he would merely tolerate the baby until he was old enough to exhibit distinctive traits.

Nothing turned out that way. Randi suspected that out of the whole family only she and young Alec saw what was happening . . . The baby was too attractive for his own good, and it didn't help matters that everyone spoiled him. He couldn't raise his soft little fist without having the household jump to oblige him.

He *was* enchanting. But as much as she loved her child, she was determined not to let Tony grow up spoiled rotten. . . .

Tony was little more than six months old when Red Lombard began to come home early and spend time with him. Randi came upon them quietly one day, wondering what Steve's father could possibly have to say to his infant grandson. There was Red, bouncing the laughing baby on his knees.

"You're going to be bigger than your old man. You're going to show him you can beat him three ways from Sunday. Just you remember what Grandpa Red tells you. You're going to lick Steve at his own game. And Red will help you. Just count on the old fox."

He peered into the boy's big eyes that reminded everyone of Bridget Gallegher. He was a throwback to his dark Irish grandmother, and already learning to use his winning Irish ways.

Randi spoke calmly.

"Red, please be careful of how you joke with the baby. One of these days he may begin to understand you."

"Hope he does." He jiggled Tony up and down, to the child's delight. When the big gold watch chain across Red's chest caught the late afternoon sunlight, Tony made a grab for it, crying imperiously.

"Da! Dat!"

"You hear that?" Red demanded. "He said 'give me that' just as plain as anything."

"Well, for heaven's sake, don't."

The baby pursued his object, grabbing with both hands. Red lifted out his watch, detached the chain from his vest and hung them over the baby's wrists. When it slipped off, he hung it around Tony's neck over Randi's protests.

"Don't you worry, little Tony. You're starting out right. Always go for the best."

It was the answer Randi had somehow expected. Later, having wrapped and put the watch and chain in the little rosewood jewel chest with other presents given the new baby, she complained to Steve.

But Steve only laughed. "Let Red try his bribes. He's wasting time. My boy is going to grow up my way." Her eyebrows raised. He corrected himself. "*Our* way, sweetheart. I expect him to be the greatest Lombard of us all."

She murmured, "I love that grin of yours. Grin for me."

"Abandoned female."

"Abandoned to the right man."

"That had better be me."

He fondled her, pushed her back onto the bed. She drew him to her, caressing his head and shoulders, working her way beneath his shirt and undershirt, under his belt. He began to respond.

"Sweetheart, you look so cool, but in bed you're so hot. With most women it's the other way around—did you know that?"

She playfully dug her hands into his groin and he stifled a yell.

"Point is—how do you know?"

They laughed, rolled together on the bed and loved each other until young Tony began to cry in the bassinet that had reared five generations of Lombards.

Quieting the baby, Randi asked nonchalantly how Cortlandt-Lombard Dunes District was coming along.

Steve dismissed the subject. "Five more houses. Some of the Johnny-come-latelys are already buying the area beyond our district. But Alma is working on her father. He may save the whole project by buying up to the avenue. When that's done I've an idea or two about Strand and those lots facing the ocean. You remember that aborted honeymoon of ours, sweetheart. But let's not talk business. Come here, woman."

And that was that. . . .

In January 1920, the family threw a lamentable "celebration" the night before the enforcement of Prohibition.

Alec had curled up on the parlor davenport and dozed off after a watered glass of wine, but it was clear that he delighted in the honor of being included with the grown-ups. Randi, Alicia Lombard and Mrs. Cortlandt favored Prohibition, but they were alone in the two families. Bridget Gallegher, together with the Lombard men, Buckleigh, Alma and Brooke, all thought the law a barbarous fraud.

"It is impossible to legislate human nature after four thousand years of alcohol," Brooke claimed. "In my opinion, wine has always been necessary for civilized people like us."

"Amen, darlin'!" Bridget cried. "They're the very words of that French count, bless him. He said it to me at my girl's wedding, so he did."

Brooke gave her a less than friendly look, resenting the easy mention of a man who still intrigued and baffled her.

The party, held throughout the first floor of the Lombard house, was enlivened by the antics of Bridget Gallegher as well as the chatter of Alma Cortlandt. Bridget's old friend LeMass was there, adding to the festivities. He broached the subject of money, first to Steve, then to Buckleigh Cortlandt and finally to Red. He had a scheme involving alcohol shipped up from Mexico to Half Moon Bay along the coast, but only Red Lombard bit at the idea.

"May be something to it if this Prohibition lasts more than a year."

"Six months," Steve pronounced. "Then they'll be marching up Market Street demanding repeal."

While Red and LeMass retired to the dining room to discuss the business aspects of whiskey-and-rum running, Steve put "Wearing of the Green" on the Victrola and urged Bridget to dance.

"Show us your Irish jig, or whatever you call it, Madame Colleen."

"Oh, please do," Alma put in enthusiastically. She was drinking with care and seemed, Randi noted, at once pleased and faintly upset that Steve treated her like one of the family.

"Join Bridget, sweetheart," Steve urged. "There you are in your new green dress and never looked lovelier. Show them that wild Irish footwork of yours. Bridget says you used to dance the reel when you were a child."

Randi shyly shook her head.

"Go on, Randi. Bridget can't do it all alone. Give us a breath of the 'Auld Sod,' " Brooke teased.

The scratchy record began. Randi finished her brandy, and found herself tapping out the rhythm. Steve nudged her and, raising the carefully twisted hair at the nape of her neck, he kissed the soft warmth of her flesh.

Inspired to show off, Randi leaped to her feet, strutted to the middle of the ballroom floor with her hands on her hips and stamped her feet, dancing along with her mother.

Drawn by the music as well as the rhythmic clapping of the audience, LeMass came sprinting in with a partner. He had found Stella Burkett in her bedroom upstairs and induced her to come down and join the celebration. Bridget was having too good a time to really care, but she nevertheless gave Stella several dirty looks as the two Irishwomen decorated the scene with spontaneous gaiety. Alec, heady with the watered wine, wandered in and also joined the dance.

A minute later, the needle slid to the end of the record and Steve wound it up and started it once more. Alec opened up the dance to all comers. After hugging her son, Brooke moved onto the floor, shaking all four rows of fringe on her new red crêpe de chine dress. Steve joined, teasing Alma to come along. By this time Bridget seemed to be more interested in sneaking a last glass of brandy between steps than in finishing what she had started, and Stella Burkett was voted the best dancer in San Francisco.

Randi's attention was distracted by Alma Cortlandt, elegant in black and white, and just tipsy enough to keep prancing toward Steve, who always seemed to be out of Randi's reach.

By midnight the noise of the city's last legitimate fling reached Nob Hill. Celebrants started pouring out of the great hotels, throwing an empty bottle here and there, and the sounds of cars honking their horns resounded throughout San Francisco.

Steve made a point of sharing this final moment with Randi as they all stood outside in the starlit January night.

"It's going to be a great year, sweetheart," he whispered, and began to pull her hair down.

Under his caressing fingers she shared the thought. Nineteen twenty was going to be a very good year, even with Prohibition, a presidential campaign and the depressed condition of most businesses since the war. Randi didn't even mind when Alma joined them.

"Daddy says he will put up the money for the full district. All you have to do is put your year-end profits back in. Isn't that sweet of daddikins?"

"Hmmm," Steve murmured, running his fingers through Randi's hair. Randi felt she could at this moment afford to be generous in her thoughts of Alma. Vaguely, she heard Alec's boyish voice behind her.

"Grandpa Red, are you asleep?"

"No, my boy. Just thinking deep thoughts about business. Buck, you and I ought to have a little talk one of these days. There's a place I've been meaning to talk to you about. Right in your own bailiwick. Downtown Oakland."

"Not right now, Red. I'm up to my ears in this Pacific Dunes thing."

Steve hadn't missed a word. He whispered, "Sweetheart, did you hear? We're going to beat the old fox."

# *Chapter Two*

IN the months that followed, the problem of her son occupied Randi completely. The fact that the baby was being spoiled became far more serious when Brooke also showed her preference for her nephew at the cost of her own son's feelings.

Brooke's return from a trip down the peninsula with her onetime lover, the Russian emigré, brought matters to a head. Loaded with gifts for Tony, she emptied out her suitcase in the middle of the floor beside his crib. Before Randi could stop her she held up various stuffed animals before her nephew's eager eyes. He grabbed at everything but clung to a green puppy dog with floppy ears.

Alec called from the hall. "Is that you, mother? We're having lobster for supper, the way you like."

Brooke was busy but managed to glance over her shoulder with a pink bunny in her hand.

"Come in, darling. See what I've brought for the baby. Look here, aunty's own sweet boy . . . See what aunty has for you? Isn't he lovely?"

Alec quietly left the room.

They could hear muffled voices at the end of the hall.

"It's nothing. I'm all right, I tell you. Let me go." It was Alec's high-pitched, broken voice.

"That boy!" Brooke sighed, then held out her arms as young Tony crawled to the side of the crib.

"Come to aunty, darling."

Out in the hall the voices continued. Randi looked up, but her focus was on her son at the moment. Tony was rapidly learning all the tricks. He beamed at Brooke, then turned and held out his arms to Randi.

"Mommy." He giggled madly as Randi picked him up and hugged him. Over his dark head she reminded Brooke apologetically, "He's like a puppy. He likes to play tricks."

Brooke was hurt but she quickly recovered herself. "So I see. I hope you haven't been putting him against me. That wasn't part of our wager, old girl. When you bet me that hundred dollars you could land poor old Steve, this wasn't part of the bargain."

"It wasn't one hundred, it was fifty, if you recall. And furthermore, it wasn't—"

"—Worth it?" Steve asked in the doorway. He had the struggling Alec in hand, and he was smiling.

It was not a reassuring smile, Randi thought.

EVEN ALEC knew that something disastrous had been said. The words almost seemed to echo from the walls, returning to Randi's ears like bells tolling the end of their marriage. Only young Tony remained oblivious.

"Dada! Dada!" he called, overjoyed, and started to jump up and down in his crib.

"Dear God!" Brooke muttered, looking at Randi with a scared expression. Steve let go of Alec's collar and strode across the room to pick up his own son.

At first, he himself wasn't sure how he would react—or what the two women's remarks really meant. Hearing Randi's tacit confirmation had been worse than what he at first imagined was merely Brooke's twisted sense of humor.

He had always felt he was lucky that Randi had married him . . . She was unlike any other woman, though he had never really known all of her. The mystery remained, and that was the perfection of their marriage. He could never tire of her . . . But this was something he hadn't dreamed of. It was as if she had deliberately set out to marry into a rich and powerful family; she had been conniving and careful, even making a wager with Brooke. How his smug little sister must have enjoyed the knowledge all this time, Steve thought bitterly.

He tried to remain calm while he held his son, but he felt as if he would explode. He wanted to shake her, demand what she had really felt for him before they married, if she had loved him at all. Had it always been the Lombard name and money? . . . He didn't want her to lie, to tell him neither the Lombard name nor the money mattered. They should matter. He had thought they did matter to her. But not to the exclusion of every other feeling . . . What did she feel? . . .

What was even more maddening, Steve thought, was that Randi neither apologized nor attempted some fumbled explanation. As he played with the laughing baby, Randi made the most ordinary conversation, asking how his day had gone.

With equal nonchalance he replied that it had been profitable. *Profitable* . . . And to think he had broken all speed records getting home to tell Randi the Dunes had sold out to the last house and the last lot . . .

"I've got to go and wash. It's been a hot day," he said. Evidently Randi could take this more easily than he could.

He left his son with Randi and the nurse. Out in the hall Brooke stopped him.

"Don't waste your breath, Brooke. You always did like to stir up trouble. Fortunately, my sense of humor is still intact. Now, what the devil ails you, Alec?"

The boy's earlier upset had subsided; in his adult way he somehow understood what he had heard.

Alec began to shuffle away but he stopped.

"Aunt Randi likes you a lot, you know."

Steve agreed in an even voice. "I know." His sense of humor was gone, and he could find nothing conciliatory in the boy's attempt to act as intermediary.

"I just wish my mother really liked me."

That startled Steve out of his own self-absorption. "But she does, Alec. She loves you very much."

"Maybe. But she doesn't *like* me much."

"See here, you mustn't be so sensitive. You spend too much time over your books and not enough in the open air. What do you say we go out to Sutro Baths and have ourselves a swimming race? No women allowed. Just us."

Alec brightened. "Sure. I'm a good swimmer. I beat Grandma Bridget's friend LeMass at Eastertime."

Steve was pleased with his suggestion, somewhat selfishly thinking that it would give him time to figure things out. And the boy was a good swimmer. It was the only real sport in which he excelled, despite the handicap of his shorter left leg. It intrigued Steve to see how Alec was learning to pace himself and thus hide the limp when he walked. He would go far in life, Steve thought, if only he could unbend and loosen up. He was far too sensitive, keeping everything bottled up inside.

"Rather like Randi," Steve remarked aloud, to his own and Alec's surprise.

They drove down Geary Street toward Van Ness, the wide avenue that had been the western boundary of the Great Fire fourteen years before. Alec was talkative and wanted to know all the particulars—where Steve and Brooke and Aunt Randi had been when the earthquake struck and the fire afterwards started.

"Far as I know, we Lombards were all sound asleep when the quake hit. Brooke and I were in grammar school at the time, so we'd have been up in two hours. But only the cook and handyman were awake at 5:13 A.M. We were lucky. We all got out. The fire started later. Up on Nob Hill we weren't burned out until the second day, after they started blasting to halt the spread. That's how Nob Hill got it."

"It must have been very exciting."

Steve's thoughts shifted to more recent horrors, the collapse of the 800-year-old Rogier-Grasse chateau in France, his dead comrades in the trenches, the sight of the ward containing the gassed soldiers. . . .

"Funny thing," he said after a while. "Those things fade with time. Maybe someday I won't even remember what happened in France last year."

Alec grasped the steering wheel, his fingers near but not touching his uncle's hand.

"Maybe then you'll forget about today too."

Steve was shaken by the reminder. Today's whole episode was shallow and stupid by comparison, he thought, and yet he still felt the bitter ache of it. Did Randi regret that the truth had gotten out, afraid she would lose all she had won? But if she was that kind of a woman, Steve thought, she would have made excuses, begged forgiveness and, above all, explained. . . .

In the immense, echoing interior of the great bathhouse, Alec was the first to spot Alma Cortlandt at the pool's edge. Though she was wearing the black one-piece bathing suit worn by all patrons of the baths, she still looked especially well, with the black suit a stunning contrast to her ivory skin.

Steve, in the mood for some talk, greeted Alma casually and asked her to wait while he went off to the dressing rooms with Alec.

They dove into one of the smaller pools, showing off while Alma shouted encouragement. During several brisk races down the length of the pool, Steve let Alec win only once and then by a matter of inches—Alec was too wise to be fooled by any greater break.

Dripping wet and shaking himself like a friendly pup, Alec joined Alma and Steve at the pool's edge.

"It's so nice to see Alec laughing like this," Alma said. "You know, Alec, your father was a jolly sort, awfully popular. And heaven knows Brooke would laugh at a hanging—" She stopped herself. "There. I'm sorry, Alec. You really are a remarkable swimmer for your age. Show me that backstroke again."

Rather pleased with himself, Alec dove into the water and showed off appropriately with a good deal of splash. Meanwhile, Alma, who had succeeded in getting rid of the boy, cuddled up close to Steve.

"Heavens! My teeth are chattering. It's quite cold in here today. I should have brought another dry towel."

Amused by her public demeanor, so unlike that of his reserved wife, Steve put his arm around her, marveling aloud that his cold, wet body didn't give her another chill. She pouted reproachfully.

"You always could warm me up, Steve. What fun we had in the old days! Remember the night after the big game, how a gang of us banged on old Pop Nate's door outside Sather Gate, and how we demanded he stop serving frankfurters and sauerkraut? Unpatriotic to the Allies, we said."

Steve, however, remembered something else. There was a girl at Pop Nate's. Reserved and intelligent. Just a kid, of course—but with beautiful hair and a rare and lovely smile. And those high cheekbones. Then he remembered.

Randi Gallegher! He had never associated her with his college days, or with having been a waitress. Then his thoughts took a different turn . . . Had her plan begun as long ago as that? And the bet with Brooke? She could have known Brooke, who was in Cal at the same time.

Steve felt manipulated. It was exactly the kind of thing Brooke had done all her life; the idea was probably Brooke's in the first place. Had it happened to anyone else, Steve would have laughed about his sister's foolishness . . . But that it should happen to Steve Lombard . . .

He looked down at Alma and kissed her bare shoulder, wanting to stir things up. Alma had let him make love to her before his marriage, and she wasn't shy about her desire for him even after all this time.

"Naughty, naughty," she warned, with an eye on Alec in the pool.

"Watch me, Uncle Steve. Watch me," Alec called out.

Slightly uncomfortable, Steve leaned forward, reached out at the end of the pool and caught Alec's hand.

"Winner by a lap," Steve said and rejoined Alma, who was tugging his arm with surprising determination.

"Stevie darling, no harm done. He wants to show off. Let him. Steve, tell me, when can I see you?"

"You are seeing me," he teased, wishing she would keep it light.

"Don't be funny. I know you aren't happy. Anybody can see that."

Damn Randi! But he discovered, to his own surprise, that he wasn't in the mood for a friendly dalliance. As revenge against Randi, it appealed to him only as a thought.

Infuriated by what he felt was his own weakness, Steve found himself making excuses for his wife. He grabbed at the chance to escape when Alec climbed out of the pool shivering and huddled in his towel.

"Young man, you need home and a hot bath. Alma, can we take you to the ferry?"

After a moment's pause, Alma assured him she had her own car. "But I'll see you again soon, Stevie. Won't I? To talk about those great old days."

"Can't miss."

Fifteen minutes later, Steve was driving Alec through Pacific Dunes, the new district. Its stucco and frame houses peered out of the fog like elegant white ghosts where two years ago there had been nothing but sand dunes.

Alec admired the symmetry of the houses standing one after the other along the streets, with each roof, front windows and red steps exactly alike.

"My kingdom," Steve joked. "As soon as I buy out Buck Cortlandt. You know how far my father had gotten when he was my age? A tired warehouse and several rooming houses out on Fillmore. He hated it because his father, Mad Tony, had made and lost a million by that same age."

Alec looked at him in a puzzled way. "Why do you hate Grandpa Red?"

Steve was stunned by the boy's simple question. "Hate him! He's my father. A man doesn't hate his father. It's just a kind of game in our family. It's only natural to want to excel."

"Like when I'm swimming . . . ."

They drove back across Golden Gate Park toward Market Street, where Steve said he had an errand. A little of the curse was taken off the day when he bought Alec a radio and watched the boy's face. The box was clumsy and the parts probably couldn't be repaired if they failed, but Alec insisted on carrying it in his lap.

When they returned to the house, Steve's apprehensions returned and his sudden tension was not missed by Alec.

"Please don't divorce Aunt Randi."

In that moment, Steve knew suddenly that he loved Randi more than when he married her, and the thought of losing her was like a black curtain descending over his world. She *was* his world, he thought, and the knowledge only heightened his uncertainty and his fear. . . .

Randi was dressed for dinner when he saw her come in to witness Alec's proud demonstration of his new radio. Bridget had arrived for dinner and been marched straight over to see Alec's new marvel. Brooke, cornering her brother alone, tried once more to force an explanation, but he cut her off.

"Forget it. A joke's a joke, and I think that one's had its day."

Still nothing from Randi, he thought. He hadn't seen her alone since he and Alec returned. She smiled. Steve smiled. She asked if they had had a good time and remarked that Alec's hair was still wet. All very normal, very polite. Neither so much as touched the other . . .

Dinner went off fairly well, thanks to the chatter of the senior Lombards and Bridget. Brooke was nervous and she kept sneaking anxious looks, first at Steve, then at Randi.

Later in the evening, while everyone was listening to the local jazz band heard between bursts of static on Alec's radio, Brooke pinched Steve's hand.

"I taunted her. It was all my idea."

"I never doubted that," he said lightly and walked over to congratulate Bridget on finally acquiring a telephone.

Bridget surprised him with a proposition. "Never you mind, my lad. I've been meaning to ask you. A certain gent, my son-in-law, I'll have you know, has been mighty generous. LeMass wants me to invest. He's working on the docks again, and he made me save a little here and there until I've got near a hundred. I want to put it up in one of your deals. You know, add maybe five or six dollars a month. Depending on what that bootlegger charges me."

Steve found it amusing that she was able to save from the annuity. "Wonderful! You'll be a genuine investor." He kissed her on both cheeks, hugged her and saw Randi watching him across the room. Her smile showed her pleasure in his relationship with her mother.

No wonder she was pleased, he thought. This was the girl who had known what she wanted long ago at Nate's café . . . Well, if she could be bought, he meant to go on owning her. He convinced himself that he felt better, that at last he understood their relationship. . . .

When the visitors had gone and Brooke had herded the family upstairs, Steve found himself alone with Randi in the darkened entrance hall.

Randi moved up the stairs, slowly, not like herself. He joined her . . . It had to happen sooner or later . . . Her head turned, so close it was impossible not to kiss her. She responded at once, putting her arms out, holding him close.

They clung together, lips, mouth and body, until they were startled by the sound of Stella Burkett slamming the parlor doors downstairs. Though they moved slightly apart, he couldn't let her go now.

She whispered. "I love you so much . . . so very much."

He looked into her eyes, studying her. "Do you, sweetheart?"

The honesty in her eyes caught him by surprise.

"I've loved you for so long. You don't even know when I first started loving you. Do you want me to tell you about the wager?"

"No!" He said it too quickly, then added with his best grin, "I know Brooke and her damned games. Forget it."

He pulled her to him again, thinking that maybe, after all, there had been love somewhere in that wager. There *was* love in their marriage—he had never doubted that. Nothing in this world was perfect, he thought, and decided he would make do with what he had.

# *Chapter Three*

RANDI found it difficult to go on blaming Brooke for the betrayal of the wager. She had known all along that the story had to come out somehow, and she was almost relieved that it was over with. Steve, she thought, seemed to be taking it rather well. Brooke came to her the next day, complaining that her brother wouldn't let her explain.

"I'm sure it is going to be all right," Randi said. "Let's just put it behind us. Steve himself keeps saying 'forget it.' "

Brooke was doubtful. "I don't know. It isn't like Steve. But nothing's like it ought to be any more—including me."

Randi stopped what she was doing in the linen closet. She noticed that Brooke was not looking her best and she seemed jumpy. She had resorted to a new and unflattering hair style; her thick, curly red hair was cut short above the nape of her neck and over her ears in the latest style. Her dresses were in the extreme of fashion, with bandeaus binding her breasts flat and dropped waistlines fitting below her ample hips. It seemed to Randi as if she were trying to be something quite different from her usually pert and curvaceous self.

"Are you unhappy, Brooke? If Steve hasn't taken offense, why should you feel badly about it? It's something wrong in your own life, isn't it?"

Brooke threw up her hands. "Everything. Why do you think I went to the islands?" She breathed deeply and swung around, doing a model's slouch. "How do I look? Did you ever know a man I couldn't get? I'm not being conceited. I'm just asking you an honest question."

Randi tried not to smile. "Honestly, you could get any man."

"Then why couldn't I hold on to André, the one man I really wanted? I cared about that Frenchman. I really *cared.* And he hasn't written in months."

Randi slammed the closet doors. André should never have given the wrong impression to a young woman like Brooke. For a short while he had even made Randi think he liked her too much. Knowing how much Steve thought of him, she was very glad the Frenchman had left the country . . .

"I think he is still in love with his dead wife."

Brooke thought this over. "I suppose I always knew. Steve said something like that. But you see, I have to prove I've got what it takes. I have to keep proving and proving . . . You don't know my family."

"Why, Brooke?" Brooke reminded her of Steve and his father when they talked of the family.

"I don't know, damn it. It's just the way we are. And André was so attractive. You know," she said, her bright eyes lighting up, "I could have been happy with him. I mean, maybe forever. But if it's the memory of his wife, then it's not my fault. *I'm* not inadequate."

"Anything but that. It is André we must pity, not you."

"Well!" Brooke sniffed. "That's better. Poor André." She walked down the hall, looked back suddenly and giggled. "Of course, as long as there's life, there's hope."

But from that time on, Randi wondered whether Brooke's eccentric behavior with men stemmed from the terrible Lombard drive for conquest, or from unrequited love. It was hard to believe that Brooke could feel so deeply about any man; yet those few moments with Randi did seem genuine.

WHEN RED Lombard put together the biggest Market Street deal of 1922, Randi worried about Steve's reaction. He had just come back from Strand, having failed in his attempt to completely finance his dream project—eight-unit courts on six lots facing the big boardwalk, the beach and the ocean. He had ended by financing only the building of three courts around narrow cement walkways on three lots.

Meanwhile, though, he had managed to buy off sixty-five percent of Buck Cortlandt's interest in Pacific Dunes. Randi encouraged these moves, eager to remove the Cortlandt influence from Steve's newly formed companies . . . .

Randi, however, was not enthusiastic about spending all her hours running the household, catering to the whims of her in-laws or even looking after young Tony, though this task was by far the most enjoyable. She made it a point to walk down the hill with Tony's buggy on sunny afternoons, and when Alec wasn't in school he pushed the buggy for her, discussing with her such matters as international relations and the future of radio. Young Tony's adorable charm and eager arms took up much of her attention, but she also appreciated and enjoyed Alec's intelligence and helpfulness.

Once Randi had organized domestic matters so they ran smoothly, she suggested that she might be of help to Steve in some of his paperwork. He dismissed the idea casually: she would be bored; it would be like playing secretary. When she persisted, she realized he was not listening. He seemed to her to be obsessed with their financial worth, as if that were somehow terribly important.

"But I don't care about the money," she insisted. "I simply want to do something creative, something that utilizes my own abilities."

"You've got young Tony. What could be more creative than that?"

It was maddening. Clearly, he assumed money was the only thing that would satisfy her. She couldn't imagine where he got this unpleasant idea. Only when she made love to him could she manage to convince him for a brief time that profits were not what she was thinking about. . . .

Much to Red Lombard's satisfaction, his purchase of the famed Monarch Building on lower Market Street aroused nationwide attention. The Lombards were celebrities when through an *Examiner* headline it became known that President Harding himself had sent his congratulations and declared that if and when he visited San Francisco he would certainly stay in the Palace Hotel so he could look out the windows at Red's building across the street.

When the president was still a senator, he and Red had played poker together in certain smoky rooms in Washington and the relationship remained a friendly one. Through another of the president's friends, Mr. Fall, secretary of the interior, Red had become interested in oil exploration and had invested in the Sinclair discoveries in Wyoming.

When he learned about his father's new venture, Steve was upset, and complained to Randi that if he himself had loose cash, he could have beaten his father to those Teapot Dome discoveries. But she objected.

"Your father knows nothing whatever about oil. The whole thing sounds risky to me. It's not like real property, buildings you can see and touch. They keep talking about explorations for oil. With a house you don't have to explore. You build it or you buy it."

Steve was patient with her. "Randi, this is not something you are equipped to discuss. He's not relying on his own knowledge but that of the president's friends. And if Albert T. Fall doesn't know, who does?

She couldn't answer . . .

Once his profits were known outside his own office, Red paid back what he had borrowed from his children's trust funds. With money coming in now after the postwar depression, Brooke could afford to travel. She kept busy with love affairs from Europe to Hawaii. Her Russian prince had followed her to Paris where she discovered that he was not a genuine prince.

She put the affair in perspective in a letter to Alec. "My darling boy," she wrote, "Aside from his fabulous tango I am almost glad to be rid of my so-called prince. Imagine drinking vodka at each meal. Ugh! But now you are my only little man and I am more proud of you every day."

The letter was not something Alec could take lightly, and he kept it pressed tight under his pillow.

Brooke had also written briefly to Randi. "Tell Steve I saw the gallant count the other night. He was with a young *chanteuse*, as they call them, in a Russian cabaret. We'd call it a speakeasy. He was disgustingly polite, asked about Steve, and wanted to know how you were. He asked if you and Steve were happy. I do believe he was trying to make me jealous, but he didn't succeed."

Soon after that, Brooke went to the Hawaiian Islands.

Alec was pretty much left to the benign indifference of his Grandmother Alicia, and the more stringent concern of his Aunt Randi. His Grandma Bridget was always a favorite companion. Thanks to LeMass's advice, Bridget was investing her money. Every penny she made out of her one-half-of-one-percent interest in Steve's Pacific Dunes and Strand properties was now a triumph for her, and she found it impossible to sacrifice these winnings to the bootleggers . . .

Red Lombard's big ribbon cutting celebration accompanied the announcement that his Monarch Building, a deserted hulk during the 1920–21 depression, could now boast an eighty-five percent occupancy. He admitted only to the family that he had fudged slightly on the tenancy figures.

"But who's to know? By the way, I'm moving my own A. and R. Lombard Company into the Monarch. I can give your organization a good deal too, Steve, if you would like office space. Not that you will need much. But your Wells, Fargo lease runs out in October, Liversedge says."

Steve was busy feeding Tony, and responded with indifference. "Overhead down, profits up. That's my motto. Why the devil don't canned vegetables taste like fresh ones? No wonder the poor kid doesn't like them."

Randi, however, was not deceived by his preoccupation with Tony. She calmly took over the feeding, and considered the discussion. She was glad Steve had held out against his father's grandiose ideas.

Randi had gradually discovered that Steve's simple office arrangement consisted of an accountant, Mr. Tillingsworth; an elderly secretary, Mrs. Midge; and a statuesque blonde telephone operator, Miss Connie Blowers. Most of his rentals were handled by professional concerns and audited by Mr. Tillingsworth who, like Mrs. Midge, was devoted to his work. Randi approved of this arrangement, but she suspected that once Steve reached a certain level in his career he would exchange all this sensibility for elegance, plush, lots of new glass walls and Art Deco everywhere.

But when Red announced at the family dinner table the cutting of the Monarch Building ribbon, Steve put a damper on things. He told everyone he'd had a letter from Brooke and would read it to them after dinner.

"You should have made the date a month earlier, Red. I told you that this spring," Steve said.

"What? What'd you tell me this spring? Alec—pass the ketchup." He shook it like a banner overhead. "I tell you one thing. This bottle is the greatest food invention of the twentieth century."

Randi was puzzled and uncertain as to what Steve was planning to tell them. All the Lombards would be expected to arrive home for Red's great moment. Brooke was in the Hawaiian Islands and was being asked to leave her current interest, a Dr. Nigel Ware, and make the quickest coastal sailing in order to meet her father's deadline.

"Sorry, Red. As I told you, you picked the wrong month. Do you realize I've been promising Randi a Pacific voyage for at least a year, and I'm not going to go back on it now. All we've done year after year is spend two weeks in Santa Cruz. A nice beach but not quite Waikiki."

While Randi stared, even more surprised than Alec and the senior Lombards, Steve produced two very impressive mint green booklets.

"Tickets. We're sailing Friday for Honolulu. We spend ten days there and then sail home with Brooke."

"You mean Brooke can't get back either?"

Steve showed them Brooke's letter. "Unfortunately, they've taken the *Sonora* off that run, so there's no way any of us can get back in ten days."

Red's face fell. Alicia reached over, covered his burly hand with her delicate fingers.

"My dear, it isn't a life and death matter. I will make it a point to be there. And I'll see to it that every member of the Bayside Beautification League shows up with her husband."

"I don't think we should miss it. We owe it to Red to stand together," Randi said firmly.

Steve looked at her for an uncomfortably long time. She had the feeling he was attaching motives to her remark that were entirely false. Finally, he shrugged.

"I guess I can change them. Randi is right, of course. I hadn't thought of it but there should be a show of Lombard unity."

Alicia beamed at her daughter-in-law. "Dear child," she murmured. Red relaxed.

"SPEAKING OF the children," Randi reminded Steve that night as she was undressing, "Alec is old enough, of course, but who is going to look after Tony?"

She saw his reflection in the three-way mirror of the vanity table. Steve had just come in from the bathroom with a towel around his waist and another over his shoulders. He seemed to her the handsomest man she had ever seen. . . . He was past thirty, but his ruddy hair and penetrating blue eyes still excited her. She wished, however, that there were more confidence in his gaze . . .

Steve looked her over in the white satin nightgown he had bought her for her birthday. He came up behind her, ran his hands along the smooth material from her breasts to her upper thighs. She shivered with pleasure. He followed the curve of her right hip with one hand, then abruptly gave her a swat with his palm.

"Get into bed and let's go to work."

She had meant to discuss something serious. Oh, yes, she thought —the children. Well, that subject could wait until tomorrow . . .

Randi resigned herself to the fact that the adults—eight, including Bridget, LeMass and the servants—could look after one child who was almost four years old and one very adult fifteen-year-old, who was now the youngest member of his freshman class at Berkeley, his father's alma mater.

Someone, though, had to be in charge; Randi was firm about that.

In the end the last person she would have counted on volunteered—Stella Burkett.

"Look, Randi, I can handle it. The kid obeys me. Young Tony and me, we get on fine. How about it? I'd like to make a little money. I kind of need it. What say?"

Randi wondered why she suddenly needed the money, but could not bring herself to turn Stella down. Randi had always felt guilty about her schoolmate, believing that her own luck, together with the cooperation of Brooke Lombard, had given her a man she loved, little Tony and a reasonably happy life. But at the same time she knew Stella was in and out of Red Lombard's den at all hours. There had been no outward impropriety, but for Randi the suspicion remained.

"Stella, you are perfectly capable of taking care of Tony. It isn't as if he were a baby. But he is a mischievous child and I wouldn't put anything past him when he wants his way."

"A wheedler. I know. I can handle him."

"But your private life. Your gentlemen friends."

Stella shrugged. "They don't interfere. To tell the truth, I'm sort of—I guess you'd say I'm finished with all that."

There was something furtive about her movements, the way she went on working, waving the feather duster, spreading dust. But then just as Randi moved away, Stella turned back and Randi couldn't ignore the sincerity in her voice.

"I really mean it, Randi. I swear I do. I kind of need the extra money. Pa and the boys, you know."

That made a lot of sense. Stella was a good provider for her family. So it was agreed between them, though Randi made other arrangements to back her up. Alec would be home in the evenings, and she trusted him more than anyone in the house. During the hours when he had classes she would arrange to have Bridget there. Alicia and Bridget had become close friends when they discovered a common interest in, of all things, tatting.

Tony would burst into tears of rage if he had to wear one more jacket collar trimmed with little tatting circles, but the ladies had a great campaign lined up. They were now tatting for the Ladies Auxiliary of the Mission District Betterment Order. The worn clothing given to the deserving poor was to be renovated and tatting added.

During their hours together Alicia sipped the "medicinal compound" furnished by Bridget and her spirits were raised enormously. Randi was afraid to guess the real reason for Alicia's high spirits and occasional girlish giggle.

"I think I'd better test that 'medicinal compound' of Bridget's. So far, it's done wonders. But we don't want my poor mother rolling down California Street drunk as a lord, do we?" Steve asked, amused.

"Oh, God! Is it that bad?"

"A word to the wise, that's all. I'll just hint to Bridget."

"You won't hurt her feelings?"

"Now when have I ever hurt my mother-in-law's feelings?"

In the end the Lombard family joined forces, with Alec representing his mother, at the ribbon cutting before the street foyer of the Monarch Building. The mayor and the governor arrived on time but were upstaged by President Harding's personal representative who spent most of the time during the speeches discussing the oil investment with Red.

Steve stood by his father the whole time, beaming at the praise heaped on Red Lombard and even joining the congratulations when a telegram was delivered to Red announcing that for the first time every luxury apartment in the Monte Carlo Arms was under lease.

Randi squeezed Steve's hand. She had felt his reaction, seen him wince at the news from Strand. But Steve only grinned at his father, said "Great!" and assured Randi in a low voice, "It doesn't matter any more. Forget it."

She knew that it did matter, that it would always matter. But she was grateful for his outward composure; besides, she thought, there was Tony to be proud of. Not yet four years old, he stood like a little soldier, proud of his grandfather and announcing to anyone who would listen: "I'm a Lombard, too. My name is Tony Lombard."

"Look at that," Steve nudged Randi, delighted with his son. "Little devil is a Lombard through and through."

"Not a doubt of it," Randi said.

Alec stood beside Bridget among the guests of honor on the small, unpainted stand. He watched and listened to all the Lombards and Lombard sycophants, and wondered what would happen if their glistening world collapsed, if one day a man named Huntington took over and really showed them. Colin Huntington's son was as good as "Mad Tony" Lombard's progeny any day of the week!

Glancing at Alec, Randi wished she could read his mind. He looked impassive, the freckles now faded, his light brown hair combed back, neat and straight. One could not notice his limp from the way he stood, but she supposed his leg must ache. A faint wrinkle appeared across his forehead, and he shifted his weight. Randi's heart went out to him, though not for the world would she have let him know . . .

Between them, Alec and Stella could be depended on to keep Tony out of trouble. In fact, Stella was taking more care of herself lately. Her uniform collars were turned in to be laundered frequently, and she wore her dark hair neatly and nicely combed. Even her disposition had improved, Randi thought, and often heard her singing an Irish tune while she worked. The only men Randi saw her with these days were the Lombards and such frequent visitors as Paddy LeMass with Bridget, and Buck Cortlandt, both of whom flirted decorously with her. Stella deserved a great deal of credit, Alicia Lombard had remarked to Randi.

Randi noticed however that Stella had gained weight lately, but wasn't surprised. She had a good appetite and she worked hard. Randi cautioned her not to overdo the work while she and Steve were in the islands.

"Sure," Stella said brusquely. "I get you. I'll be careful. I always was. Well, mostly."

Tony seemed satisfied. He was fond of Stella, and it was painful for Randi to think that with enough spoiling, he might not even miss his father and mother.

STEVE HAD more than one reason for planning the Hawaiian trip. In a sense, it was an act of contrition toward Randi.

When he married her he expected to be reasonably faithful, but like many of his university and army friends, he had considered for himself the possibility of occasional infidelities . . . What he hadn't known was that Randi would satisfy him so completely as to eliminate other temptations. . . . Except once. It was this one occasion—no, two occasions—about which he couldn't free his conscience. . . .

Some months ago, Randi had for a while seemed to slip a little. Too many housedresses, too much work running the house and supervising the relatives and the children. He should have thought of the Hawaii trip earlier, given Randi something to brighten her life. Instead, he had done a stupid, pointless thing which only reinforced his need for Randi.

It began when he took the night train to Los Angeles, where he intended to supervise the buying of desert property in the San Fernando Valley and while nearby, drop in on Strand and collect the last three months of rent from the cheap but profitable stucco courts that lined the long cement boardwalk.

During the train ride someone knocked on his compartment door and walked in. A whiff of sweet perfume took him by surprise . . . Alma Cortlandt closed the door carefully behind her . . . He had never seen her more tempting. She was looking her best in a black faille suit with white lace at throat and wrists, a white scarf binding her black hair fashionably and floating down one cheek in a way that Steve found very seductive. Though her smile was demure, the nervous flutter of her gloved fingers betrayed her.

"You hate me for this, don't you, Stevie?"

"Why would I hate you? It's public transportation. Come in. Let me get a good look at you. How the devil did you know I was on board?" He took her arms, held them out, looked her over. "Terrific! You must have seen me hotfooting it for the train. Just made it by the skin of my teeth."

Though his bed was already made up for the night, Alma sat down on it self-consciously, her black eyes shy and adoring. Her gaze made him uneasy, but he couldn't bring himself to tell her so.

Alma's voice was velvet smooth. "Stevie, darling—oh, promise you won't be cross, I didn't mean to call you that. It slipped out."

He very much wanted to keep things light. If there was one thing he didn't want, it was the messy affair seemingly in the offing.

"Call me anything you like. I'm democratic." He sat down on the cushioned top of the toilet seat, facing her. "So you're going to L.A. too. I call that a coincidence. What's waiting, or should I say, who's waiting for you? You certainly are looking great. Got a boy friend in Hollywood, I'll bet."

She heaved a big sigh, and the ruffled bosom of her blouse rose and fell. She reached out, found Steve's hands.

"Oh, Steve, don't be cross. I was in Mr. Liversedge's office with father today. He told us you were leaving tonight on business. I told father I was going to stay in San Francisco overnight. Go to the theater with Dorothy Cortapassi and Edwin Gault. You remember Doro? In our Geology 1–A with us."

"Sure. I remember Ed Gault too. He always wanted to marry you."

Though he was obviously teasing her, she chose to take him seriously and even blushed. "As if you cared! Anyway, here I am. I thought maybe we could see each other in Los Angeles. That is, if you haven't forgotten all about our good times together in those great days before the war."

Thinking that things were getting out of hand, Steve sensed that Alma was not behaving like someone looking for a casual affair; she was far too serious and tense. Women like Alma Cortlandt should never play at this game, he thought—they didn't have the light touch.

He clapped her hands together between his heartily.

"Great idea. Tell me where you're staying. Unfortunately, I'll be in Strand most of the time but I'll sure try to leave an evening free for us."

"I knew you would. I guess I'd better be on my way or the porter will be suspecting the worst. I have the drawing room at the end of this aisle." She shifted her position on the bed, crossed her legs in their peach-colored silk stockings and removed her gloves finger by finger. Then she blew daintily into each glove finger while her black-lashed eyes stared up at him mistily. "Must I really go?" she whispered.

The sweet cloying scent of her perfume served its aphrodisiac purpose and he could feel his body's rising response.

He would kiss her, he thought, and then send her back to her pullman drawing room. Propping one knee on the bunk and leaning forward, he drew her to him. But she had already shaken out of her jacket.

Her hands defied his original intent, and she began to unbutton his shirt, moving down to his trousers. He touched her full breasts, trying to seem more enthusiastic than he actually felt, trying not to make the inevitable comparison . . . This was not Randi . . .

Alma's body was lush and unusually receptive. But even as he held her, his heart was not really in this lovemaking.

He was thinking up excuses as soon they both relaxed on the narrow bunk. She clung to him, her skin hot and suffocating, and he was relieved when she became fretful and sat up, rearranging her disheveled clothes.

"Darling Steve, it was heaven. I'll go now. But you will be a dear and remember this. Promise me you will remember tonight. Our little heaven."

He bounded off the bunk and helped her to the door. As she was leaving, she kissed his knuckles, white from holding the compartment door so tightly. Embarrassed by her humility, he pulled his hand away, then saw her face turn up to his. Despite her beauty, the expression on her face was pitiful.

"Take care of yourself." It was all he could find to say. . . .

The memory of the scene faded almost immediately to a dim sense of his own inadequacy in dealing more wisely with her. Because he felt guilty he made it a point to see her off as they left the train and to carry her bag to her taxi. He refused to admit he was going in the same direction, and got into another cab.

BY THE time he had been driven out past the burgeoning suburb of Hollywood, through narrow Cahuenga Pass, and beyond the Universal movie studios at the mouth of the pass, he had one thought in his mind: to get hold of the bug-infested desert that rolled over hill and gully to the distant Santa Susana Mountains on the horizon.

He was met at his destination by Harry Munoz, vice-president of the Marine City Title Company.

"Sorry, Mr. Lombard. We've got all this laid out. Town planning for miles. Over there is Burbank. This here is Hollywood too, the north part, they call it."

"And priced accordingly." But Steve wasn't interested in the superficial home lots he was being shown.

"Among other investments, I own one subdivision moving back from the ocean in San Francisco and several ocean-courts in Strand. Land in Culver City, and some in San Jose. I'm thinking now in terms of large parcels with a future. Maybe ranch land, if it isn't too steep," Steve said.

Munoz stared. "You're interested in ranching, Mr. Lombard?"

Although he had hardly ever been on a horse in his life, Steve didn't bother to laugh.

"I have other plans. I want to hold some large pieces here and there. All these little communities have got to expand. It's inevitable."

"Going to be pretty dear, right next to these towns."

"I can imagine. That's why I'd like to have you get hold of some of those outer parcels for me. Cheap ones. Nearer the Santa Monicas, or the Santa Susanas. Not too near. Say a nice medium where the ground goes cheap. Couple of dollars an acre." Munoz grinned. Steve backtracked. "Okay. But nothing ovepriced."

Munoz nodded. "I know just the outfit to make the purchases, leaving your name out all around. You give me the limits you want set."

Steve decided the trip was a profitable one. Though there was a big outlay for what was essentially desert, full of jackrabbits and black widow spiders, he told himself that if he could hold out long enough, the profits were there.

The immediate small money was in Strand, with the rents from each little apartment in the courts, including the new ones above Ocean Avenue. Three months' rent was waiting for him at the agency office on Cedar Avenue. Rentals this year would clear up his original investment and except for the modest taxes, from now on it was pure profit.

HE COULD hardly wait to call Randi that night. She usually worried over the expense of the long distance telephone calls, but tonight it would be worth it. Hearing her voice later that evening reminded him of their honeymoon, and her warm, low chuckle almost made him feel that they were making love long distance.

It was impossible to sleep afterward. He had never needed her so much. He would even have taken Alma up on her offer had she been there, so great was his need . . .

When he came into the hotel lobby in Los Angeles the next afternoon, Alma Cortlandt was waiting for him as if she had read his mind. She walked up with him to his single, unimpressive room, acting coquettish, with a kind of false gaiety that aroused his pity. She was a pretty young woman, he thought, but she was trying too hard.

Alma sat down on the old brass bed and leaned back on her hands so her breasts showed prominently in her lavender sweater.

"Come and sit down, darling—sorry, I mean Steve. And tell me all about your big deals in Strand."

He kissed her lightly. "Can't do it, honey. Got some appointments lined up."

"Don't I look nice in my new outfit? I bought it just because you used to love me in lavender. Don't say you've forgotten."

He had. But her words vaguely reminded him that he had complimented her once in college.

"Far from it. You're looking particularly beautiful today. Unfortunately, I'm pressed for time."

She pouted, got up and moved toward him, clinging, playfully trying to lock her arms around him.

"I love you so much. You must love me just a little, don't you, Steve?"

"Honey, everybody loves you. They can't help it. But I'm a married man, remember?"

"I don't ask much, Stevie. Only once more. To last me all the rest of my life."

She was here. And she was determined. Randi was over four hundred miles away.

Against his better judgment and even his own inclinations, he moved over to her on the bed. They did not undress, and there was little foreplay. He climaxed quickly, almost as if he were trying to avoid thinking about it. Alma's eyes were glazed with disappointment as she straightened her lace teddy and her wool skirt.

"All the rest of my life?" she murmured.

Pity, a poor epilogue to sex, welled up inside him.

"I *am* a married man," he said, and patted her cheek.

"Otherwise—?" She clung to a last hope, but he knew to avoid that pitfall. "But there isn't an otherwise, Alma. Can you forgive me? I do have to see some land developers in the valley. By the way, when are you leaving?"

"You?"

"I've no idea. It depends."

She gave up and began to gather up her vanity case, her hat and gloves.

"I have tickets for tonight's train. If you can make it, promise you will."

"If I can make it."

"Good-bye, Stevie. Maybe tonight?"

When he returned to San Francisco, Steve saw to it that business and family kept him out of reach of the Cortlandts.

# *Chapter Four*

THE departure for the Hawaiian Islands suddenly took on new importance when Brooke wrote that she was marrying a Dr. Nigel Ware at his home outside Honolulu and wanted the family present. She said she would not ask her mother, knowing how seasick she got, but since Steve and Randi were coming anyway, they must stay with her at the doctor's large, comfortable house until the wedding.

No one at home had much faith in the success of this marriage; they didn't even know the man, and he probably didn't know Brooke. Besides, the bridegroom was fifty years old and had an eight-year-old daughter. But they all wanted to make Brooke happy. . . .

That November, before their departure on the little ocean liner, Randi noticed that Steve was trying almost too hard to show his wife off at her best. Since this westbound trip on the *Mahala* originated in San Francisco, the passenger lists included various celebrities who had come up from Southern California, especially Hollywood. Knowing this, Steve checked on Randi's entire wardrobe. Instead of her old cloth-sided valise, she now had a wardrobe trunk, the first in her life, to go with the suitcases he had given her for their honeymoon.

When the family came down for the sailing, a polite Oriental room steward brought in baskets of fruit, bouquets of flowers, a box of chocolates and many leis. Randi had never seen them before: chains of tiny orchids, garlands of white and cinnamon carnations, baby roses and exotic gardenias. The gardenias especially fascinated her. She had been given a corsage of gardenias once, but never an entire chain. The scent was intoxicating, and Steve laughed at her enthusiasm.

"It's like being drowned in perfume," he teased.

But as long as Randi lived, it would remain for her the definitive scent of the Pacific islands. She adored it as much as the wardrobe trunk, which she displayed to the great satisfaction of young Tony and of Bridget.

"Look. All the drawers. And on this side, hangers. Down here in the bottom drawer, the shoes. You could live a lifetime out of this trunk."

Alicia had not felt up to making the bon voyage trip with all its attendant crowd and noise. Nor did she care for the bootleg liquor served in water glasses or drunk out of hip flasks. But Red Lombard and Bridget Gallegher were in their element. Bridget had such a good time investigating every hole and corner of the ship that photographers from the four leading newspapers asked her to pose on the ship's rail, with her hat tilted over one eye, her legs crossed and her right hand waving.

Randi was so excited by the prospect of the voyage and her new wardrobe that she was almost as obliging with the photographers as Bridget. While Steve was showing little Tony and his cousin Alec the ship, Red Lombard managed to get in the *Chronicle* and *Call* photographs with Randi.

Alma Cortlandt's late arrival at the Lombards' cabin took a small part of the gloss off the sailing. She flashed an impressive ring in a Tiffany setting.

"Engaged at last, would you believe it? Edwin has been after me since the war. Stevie used to tease me about him. I finally broke down. Edwin Gault, you know. In daddy's company. He's got important Sacramento clients in his office, or I'd have brought him down and showed him off."

Randi was delighted and told her so. Both women understood each other. Alma then rushed off to find Steve and regale him with her news. He was quite indifferent when Randi mentioned it later, while they were throwing serpentine to the family on the dock far below.

"Yes, I knew Ed. Gault's been hanging around after her most of her life. Well, I wish them luck. Alma means well."

The ship set sail at 4:00 sharp amid lashings of multicolored serpentine. The fog was already rolling in, and although she could hear the eerie moan of foghorns terrifyingly close, Randi wasn't able to see a single landmark as they sailed out the Golden Gate.

Steve tried to show her the forbidding Farallone Islands a half-hour later, but by that time the ship was being tossed by usual rough swells outside the Golden Gate and Randi began to feel an extraordinary queasiness in her stomach.

"Don't think about it, honey," Steve said. "Look. Right off there. That dark ridge above those choppy waves. That was the first landfall the old deepwater sailors saw. And the last. The Farallones."

"Fascinating." It was an uncomfortable sensation, with her stomach jumping and her head aching. "I think I'd better go downstairs."

"Below."

"I don't know where it is. My stomach. My—I feel rotten."

"No. I meant, you go below. Not downstairs," he said, laughing.

"Either way, I'm going down those stairs. I've got to lie down."

"Worst thing you can do. You should be up here in this fog. It kind of caresses you. Just breathe deep."

"Not while the damned ship keeps rolling from side to side."

He put his arms around her, smoothed her hair and her new rust straw cloche.

"Sweetheart, it isn't rolling. Your stomach could stand that. It's pitching and tossing, which is nastier. If you're really suffering, mother gave me something she swears by: Mothersill's Seasick Remedy. Come on."

"Bless you. You can be human, after all, Let's go."

STEVE COULDN'T help smiling at his wife's discomfort, which aroused his latent tenderness. He knew she would be her strong, unruffled self again as soon as this bout of seasickness cleared up, and he was anxious to show her off to their tablemates at dinner that evening. He knew that she had needed to get out and show herself, and thought this trip was a great idea for her. It had also signaled to Alma Cortlandt that the Los Angeles episode last spring was over. . . .

Steve still blamed himself for the affair, and it was no use telling himself that Alma had been pressuring him for years, or that she followed him down to Los Angeles with one object in mind. He knew very well that he could have turned her off.

His deep-seated insecurity about Randi remained, however, and this brief adultery became a poor revenge. He only wished Randi could have loved a Steve Lombard who was poor and who didn't live on Nob Hill. But ever since the story of the wager he felt grateful that he really was Steve Lombard. . . .

Earlier, Alma had come to the ship's galley, flushed, with tears brimming in her big dark eyes as she blurted out the story of her engagement. He had been relieved, and worse, he had shown it. Then came her plea, in the presence of little Tony and Alec. "I won't go through with it if you tell me not to."

"All the best luck. He's a mighty lucky man," he said, and kissed her lightly on the forehead.

As if by divine intervention the "All ashore!" whistle blasted at that minute and Steve hustled the children up to the deck. The first person they saw on the passenger deck was Randi, dressed in a rust-colored raw silk suit and French-heeled shoes. A short, dark-haired man standing back from the rail was also watching her. He lit a cigarette, while his attention remained fixed on Randi.

The man looked vaguely familiar to Steve, and he wondered if they had met in some business deal. The fellow looked European, and his face was interesting, his eyes keen. He seemed to radiate a powerful presence, slightly Napoleonic. As he stood on the fog-shrouded deck, smoking a cigarette, he was greeted by a fragile, golden-haired woman. A foreign motion picture star, Steve suddenly realized; he and Randi had seen her only last week in a Henry the Eighth thing in which she played all six wives. So Irita Vallman was on board. The voyage would be glamorous, if nothing else. . . .

STEVE JOINED his wife amidst the mad hugging and kissing as the ship prepared to depart. With his arm around Randi, he waved at the family on the dock below.

As the ship headed out toward the unseen, fogbound Pacific and Randi's seasickness began to subside, Steve wondered about the two familiar faces he had seen on deck, wondered about what attraction the older man held for the golden Irita Vallman. Money? Power?

It was Randi who answered his question. "I saw Leo Prysing on the deck today. He's sailing too. Imagine!"

"Who, may I ask, is Leo Prysing?"

"The movie director. He made *Nomads of the Sahara* and *Time Before Man.* Wonderful pictures. I saw both of them with your mother. They showed them for her Bayside Beautification League."

"Are we to expect the Bayside to look like the Sahara now?"

She made as if to hit him and he laughed. "I wonder what he sees in an empty, vain creature like that wife of his?" she asked. Steve was surprised.

"Irita Vallman is his wife?" Good God! he thought. It must be money, or his professional influence—it couldn't be anything else.

Now that Randi was feeling herself again, and better still, looking it, Steve wanted to take her down to the dining room and show her off.

Randi was ready, as soon as one final worry could be cleared out of the way.

"Do you really think Tony will be all right? He looked so little down there on the dock."

He answered her with pride and amusement. "Did you see the way he was ordering his grandfather and Bridget around?"

"But not Alec. I'm relying on Alec to keep him in line."

"Our Tony will get by. Believe me, sweetheart, he'll always get by."

She hesitated, not liking the implication. "Good. Let's go," she said.

"First," he suggested, opening the big steamer trunk, "here's a little surprise I forgot to tell you about. Remember, this is strictly illegal, so don't open this drawer in front of anyone else."

While she watched, he took out the bottom drawer and reached behind it. She could see the bottoms of several bottles, anchored between the backs of the drawers and the trunk's heavy wall. He pulled a bottle down to show her.

"What will it be, sweetheart? Rum? Cognac? Real British gin? Not the kind Eb Stanley makes in his bathtub."

"Do we have to? It's illegal." She must have sensed his impatience and she gave in. "Anything. Just so it has lots of water. I don't want to get queasy again."

"Maybe you're pregnant. How about giving Tony a little sister? Any chance?"

She threw a lime at him from one of the fruit baskets. He ducked but caught it, sliced it open with his pocket knife and announced that he would have his version of a Singapore sling. She went around examining the cards on all the flowers and then made an investigation of the cabin.

He wondered if she would be disappointed. It was not a luxurious stateroom, just an upper and lower berth that looked extremely shipshape, with a chair, wash basin, folding table, a bureau under the porthole, and a tiny bathroom with no bath, but a real flush toilet and the first wall shower she had ever used.

"I love it! It's like being on a real ship."

He laughed at that. "You *are* on a real ship. Here. Next time I'll make you a fruit mess like this concoction of mine. You'll like it. But just now you ought to have Cuban rum. It will keep your stomach settled."

She took the plain water glass, sipped, said "Ugh!" and then surprised him by drinking down the inch of rum.

"Sweetheart, you are a lady of infinite variety." With her glass and his and her leis between them, he leaned over their hands and kissed her. He was in great spirits and her nervousness began to fade.

He fingered the flower leis around her neck, removing several while the heel of his hand caressed her neck. He loved the graceful lines of her neck and throat, and had often wished he could sculpt them in clay.

"Don't ever leave me, Randi. Promise."

It was so odd, so unexpected a thing to say, that he realized she was wondering what had prompted it.

"How could I leave the man who seduced me in a romantic ship's cabin?" she teased.

His fingers remained caressing her throat. For an instant his smile did not reach his eyes; then, belatedly, he laughed and let her go.

"Better wear just one lei to dinner. It's the custom."

"Far be it from me to go against custom." She peeled off all but a cinnamon carnation lei and they went out of their cabin and down the staircase to the brightly lit dining room.

"Some day," he promised her as the little bellboy opened the two doors for them, "they'll have ships on the Pacific like the *Aquitania* and the *Leviathan,* all those Atlantic beauties."

It did not seem unlikely, for this little liner, the two-hundred-passenger *Mahala,* was crowded and the Hawaiian Islands were discussed everywhere on the Pacific Coast nowadays . . . In the back of Steve's mind, the germ of an idea grew . . . Why not invest in some of those lush green valleys and build some livable houses, tear out all the useless jungle growth? Perhaps one day the whole set of islands could be as prosperous as Florida's land boom. There was only one hotel of any reputation on the beach, the venerable Moana. Although Steve hadn't seen the islands since the time his family made the voyage to celebrate his college graduation, he had a mental picture of hotels dotted along Waikiki Beach. They would be even fancier than the Moana, which was right out of Somerset Maugham . . .

"Not that I'll build them," he thought, ushering his wife through the dining room toward one of the center tables. "But I'll see to it that the housing situation keeps pace. It has worked out so far."

The ship's dining room sparkled with starched white linens, crystal and overhead lights. The choppy seas had cut down the attendance and many of those diners already seated were looking a trifle green.

"Are we to be at the captain's table?" Randi whispered.

He hoped she wouldn't be disappointed. "No. He will be on the bridge tonight. He seldom comes down anyway and he's a bit of an old fogy. The purser's table is much livelier. Besides, I played against the purser in college. He was on the Stanford team, our deadly rival."

"Good heavens! That should be cozy."

"And a good friend, I forgot to say. He's a Shriner too, member of Islam Temple, San Francisco."

"Oh. That's very important. I know LeMass is a member of the Knights of Columbus."

"Catholic. You have to be Catholic for that one."

"Naturally."

He looked at her, wondering if she was making fun of him. He decided not to risk calling her on it. Her light streak of sarcasm sometimes made him edgy.

Then he set his jaw muscles and straightened his tie. He had seen the golden creature at the purser's table. She looked like a cool sort, but he was not interested in her. He would bet on his wife against any competition. Nevertheless, he felt a desire to impress the actress.

"THERE WE are, in the middle of the room. Purser's table," Steve announced with satisfaction. Randi noted that the elegant headwaiter thawed at the sight of Steve.

"Mr. Lombard. How very good to have you aboard! Just like the old days. And this lady, of course, must be the lovely Mrs. Lombard. Time flies. The last time we saw your husband, Mrs. Lombard, he was only a tyke."

"Come off it, Albert. I had just graduated from Cal."

The headwaiter sighed. "Before the war. It all seems a very long time ago. But let me present your tablemates." His voice lowered impressively. "Hollywood persons. But not entirely undesirable."

Randi, who had encountered snobbery in her childhood, wondered what he had told the Prysings about the Lombards. In any case, she was thrilled with the idea of sharing a table with the director of *Time Before Man*.

The headwaiter showed Randi to her seat on the left of the purser's vacant chair. On her right was the blonde actress, Irita Vallman, whom Steve had admired on the deck. On Irita's right, the movie director stood up, came around and shook hands with both Randi and Steve.

Randi found him as impressive as she had expected. His shock of black hair was already threaded with gray, although she had read that he was only in his early thirties. She saw that he was about her own height, five feet six. She thought he could probably be severe and abrupt, for his thin mouth was hard. But she had never seen eyes so keen, so penetrating. She wondered what he thought of her, but it seemed as if he looked at everything in much the same way.

Randi's first impression of Leo Prysing's wife was reinforced by the evening. The woman accepted introductions with a deliberate inclination of the head, and gave Steve a wan smile; Irita Vallman expected tribute to be paid to her beauty and to her screen image. Whenever the conversation wandered, she brought it back to the subject of herself, often with considerable skill. Randi knew that Steve's excellent manners could be counted on to encourage Irita Vallman's chief interest.

And he did so that evening, giving Randi time to ask the director numerous questions about his films, questions which he answered abruptly, sometimes impatiently. But when she turned to speak to someone else, Prysing continued to prod her on whatever subject they had been discussing. It was not an easy conversation, for they sat on opposite sides of the table.

The dinner party became more genial when the purser bustled in, apologizing and making a big scene out of his reunion with Steve, his old college rival. Donald Chapplain, called "Dinks" by Steve, was a jolly, talkative, flirtatious man, perfect for his job which involved a good deal of contact with the public. He was heavyset and balding, though like Leo Prysing, still a young man.

Dinks and Steve shared reminiscences of their college games, which obviously bored the movie actress, and she came at last to Randi for her audience.

Listening to her and obligingly throwing in an interested "Really?" and "Yes, I remember," Randi was distracted by the director's behavior. He seemed to be drawing figures on the tablecloth with his butter knife. When she caught him at it he looked guilty and smiled unexpectedly. It was an attractive smile, Randi thought.

"I am always at work," he explained. "It is my pleasure. I am lucky. With my brother in Germany, it is the same, but not so pleasant. He is a physician."

"Is it very bad there nowadays?"

He spoke flatly. "When Josef, my brother, is paid, his patients drop two handfuls of paper marks in his hands. And that is payment for the simplest matters. The removal of a microscopic blemish or what-have-you. Yes. It is very bad." He glanced at his wife, who was basking in the glow of sudden attention by Dinks and Steve. "We are lucky. Irita made a successful film at Ufa. You have heard of our studios?"

Randi, who had been baffled and then fascinated by the great Wiene film *The Cabinet of Dr. Caligari,* agreed enthusiastically.

"And then I received an offer from Hollywood. I asked Irita to marry me, and we came to America on our honeymoon. Now I am on my way to film my first American picture, with island settings. Irita has already finished her first film. A life of Theodora, the empress of Byzantium. Not much history, I am afraid. But it will be popular. She is remarkably photogenic."

"Yes, indeed!" There I go again, Randi thought. I would be perfect in Hollywood—I'm such a yes-man. "And you sit here planning great scenes while we chatter away."

"What else can I do? My secretary has been seasick since she came aboard."

When dinner ended and the table conversation broke up Randi expressed the hope that Prysing's secretary would recover by morning. Steve had meanwhile invited Irita Vallman and her husband to join him and Randi in the lounge for an hour or two of dancing. To Randi's surprise the woman refused. Her husband, she said, would be working on a breakdown of location shots in his script and he needed her advice.

"Curious. She certainly is loyal to that guy," Steve remarked to Randi as they crowded into the tiny elevator and rode up to the lounge where the small jazz band struggled valiantly with "Sheik of Araby" to a listless audience.

Remembering a magic afternoon in a Market Street movie house, Randi asked, "Do you suppose Mr. Prysing knows Valentino?"

Steve ignored this. "Let's show them a fast fox-trot."

The comfortable, old-fashioned room held a number of overstuffed chairs and two leather divans, one on either side of the deck-wide room under the big windows. Tiffany lamps were scattered around the big room. The dance floor was simply an area in the center with the furniture removed.

Only a handful of sturdy travelers were sticking it out in the lounge and of these, only one pair was dancing. Disappointed by the desolation of the room, Randi accepted Steve's challenge. "We'll show them!"

Tonight they seemed to flow together beautifully. Even the incomparable grace of Rudolph Valentino faded from her mind.

Some minutes later, Steve spun around. "Good Lord! She said she was going to their cabin to help her husband. Now look out there."

The golden Irita was leaning against the rail on the passenger deck outside the lounge, locked in an embrace with an unknown male passenger.

Steve laughed. "You can't trust those Hollywood babies."

Randi wondered if Leo Prysing knew about his wife's dalliances. However, she soon forgot about the director's problems as she surrendered herself to the music and to Steve's strong arms.

Randi felt less romantic but considerably more tender when she was awakened on that rough first night by Steve knocking over a vase of flowers.

"Damn!" Steve's voice was hushed yet furious.

Startled, Randi sat straight up, fumbled for the light but couldn't remember where the press-buttons were. She put her bare foot over the side of the bunk and then gasped.

"Water! Oh my God! Are we sinking?"

Steve found the bathroom light and pressed the button. In the middle of the cabin, water trickled across the worn carpet. The big glass vase lay on the floor and a half dozen red roses were scattered in the water. Brushing the table aside, Steve surveyed the damage.

"Sorry, sweetheart. Where did you put the damned box of Mothersill's?"

She was careful not to laugh. No one knew better than she how unpleasant seasickness was. She got out of the bunk, stepped around the puddle and found the remedy for him.

When he returned to the bunk he explained nonchalantly. "It was that crab cocktail I had for dinner. Probably spoiled or something."

"Very likely," she agreed, trying hard to stifle a laugh.

They returned to their bunk and lay close in each other's arms. "You know, honey, I'd much rather be married to you than that movie star. You can't count on women like that," Steve murmured.

Lying in the dark with Steve fast asleep, she wondered what the relationship really was between Leo Prysing and Irita Vallman. She had a good notion to volunteer as his secretary if the seasick assistant was still incapacitated in the morning. He might even let her think up some titles, those intriguing lines on the screen that explained what was going on in the pantomime of the silent movies.

It would be a fascinating job.

# *Chapter Five*

IT began on that simple whim: the career, the fame, the work which came to occupy Randi's mind only slightly less than her love for her family.

Leo Prysing was out in his deck chair early every morning. Randi was also an early riser, whereas Steve was in the habit of sleeping late. Only the closing of an important deal would get him out of bed before Randi was up.

Randi found the director without trouble. He had brought out a cup of coffee and a jelly doughnut that he called a "Bismarck." While he ate he scribbled what appeared to Randi to be strange hieroglyphics in columns on a big note pad.

"Still no secretary?" Randi asked, pretending to move on.

He scowled. His olive-skinned complexion and forbidding features made her wonder if she had made a mistake. He didn't look like a man who needed anything, not even a secretary.

"Claims she will never get out of her bunk until this little canoe reaches Los Angeles."

"Los Angeles!"

"Return trip."

She laughed at that. The ship rolled and she fell against his outstretched legs on the chair. He put a hand out but she was already on her feet again, pulling her coat collar up.

"So long. I have to make ten laps around the deck."

He nodded and went back to his curious columns.

When she came by the second time, brisk and indifferent, with a nod and a mere flicker of a smile, he called to her. She hesitated, then turned around as if she were pausing briefly in the midst of important business.

"Mrs. Lombard, you're a woman."

"Granted." What the devil? Randi wondered.

"Favor me, please. I need a title."

"Like *Time Before Man?*"

He waved this away impatiently. "Linking cards. Writing on the screen, so we can know what they are saying. Dialogue, in this case. A prince of the islands who—"

"A chief."

"A princely chief who falls in love with a missionary's wife. In the early tease scenes she asks him to promise he will take no native wives. He is proud. He answers proudly . . . What?"

She was momentarily confused and sat down abruptly in the next deck chair. "I'd have to know the scene, the reactions, the way your chief feels. And the woman, is she honest? Simple? Sexy or plain?"

"Very sensuous. There have been other men, and the chief knows it. But she sincerely loves the chief. She asks a promise of him and he says—"

Her face lit up at a memory. *"It all depends."*

"On what?"

"No. He says, 'It all depends' or 'That would depend.' And she says, 'On what?' He says, 'On whether pleasing you is worth it to me.' "

He sat there frowning at the big European pad of graph paper in his lap.

"Hardly romantic."

"But challenging."

Something in her voice caused him to raise his head. His eyes, with their powerful concentration, made her self-conscious.

"How do you know this?"

"Because I said it to my husband and it made him notice me."

He laughed. It was an abrupt, harsh laugh, but he seemed satisfied and she felt a small triumph when he agreed. "I'll use it. They tell me I am unorthodox. Well then, so be it. I wish a few of these other lines were equally unorthodox. I don't suppose you would consider rewriting some of the more sugarcoated titles."

"Why not?" she said, feigning flippancy before she could remind herself that this was a time-consuming job for a man who was obviously a hard taskmaster.

By the time Steve came along, looking especially handsome in a blue turtleneck sweater that matched his eyes, and trailing drops of coffee from a full mug he brought her, she was well into her new work. She was loving every minute of it, and tried to interest Steve in the director's mysterious charts.

"Those are camera cues opposite the action. And that column is for the sets. And the last is miscellaneous. The actors needed. The unusual costumes. Things like that."

"Looks like a diagram for a fourth quarter round-end run," Steve remarked. "By the way, Prysing, your wife is in the lounge. I think she's looking for you. Randi, Dinks wants us in his cabin before lunch. Want to go and change?"

"I think that's a hint," she joked, but got up and went away with him. She looked back once but the director had his head buried in his work. He probably didn't even know she and Steve had gone, she thought, and was amused without quite knowing why. The knowledge, however, made it easier for her to go to work with Prysing again that afternoon.

STEVE BEGAN to pray for the calm, incredibly blue seas he remembered from his last Pacific voyage. Unfortunately, when calm seas arrived two days later, with the voyage more than half over, Randi was so entrenched in her job for the brusque movie genius that she didn't realize it was work. She seemed to think she had somehow become indispensable to him . . .

Steve pointed out that the severe and hatchet-faced Miss Angerstein had handled Prysing's secretarial work before this voyage and could do so again, with the waters calm.

"You don't understand a thing about it," Randi insisted. "I'm rewriting the script, a kind of play Leo is using. He shoots his pictures from a script, like the one I'm working on."

Steve curbed his impatience and chucked her under the chin, playfully. "This is your vacation, sweetheart. You're supposed to be resting, not scribbling all day. Pretty soon, he'll have you working nights —for nothing."

Since he had brought up the matter, Randi felt free to pursue it.

"He says I've earned ten dollars a day already, but I wasn't sure you would approve of my taking it, considering it isn't exactly a regular advertised job, you know."

"I don't! My wife getting paid for running around picking up after some Hollywood character! You know what everyone would think. Well, of course, they know you. But they're bound to talk. No, thank you." He studied her face. The firmness was there, but it was now softened by her disappointment and doubt. He hated to see that.

"If you really feel that strongly about it. But I love doing it. It's got nothing to do with Leo Prysing. He hardly knows I'm alive," she said in a low voice.

My God! he thought. She thinks I'm jealous of that ugly foreign genius. He had to convince her otherwise.

"Look, sweetheart, if it makes you happy, I don't mind you doing a little of this kind of thing every now and then. But I want to show you around the islands. Show you off. Give you a good time. So you'll have to forget dear old Prysing and his ten-dollar jobs when we land."

"Whatever you say," she agreed. Her seemingly willing acceptance made him uneasy. Yet he knew there was nothing to be jealous about —Randi would never betray him. But it was still annoying to think that every time he wanted to do something, go somewhere with her, even on the ship, she was locked into this script business with Leo Prysing, leaving Steve vulnerable to the director's wife. He hadn't gotten rid of an old friend like Alma Cortlandt in order to fall into the rapacious clutches of Irita Vallman . . . His fear of Randi learning about the affair, knowing that she was proud enough to destroy their marriage, still gave him cold chills . . .

At first Steve had been interested in observing the beauty of the German actress, but it soon became clear to him why she was constantly changing partners on board ship. Even in his brief encounters with her over the dining table or on deck, he had been bored by her single subject of conversation, herself.

It was, therefore, no thrill to enter the purser's cabin and find Irita Vallman seated there all in white, looking Randi up and down with an appraising and critical eye. The muscular fellow who presented himself as Irita's male counterpart made even less of an impression on Steve, who caught him eyeing his own reflection in Dinks's shaving mirror. Steve wasn't surprised to find him introduced as Kurt Friedrich, the leading man, who spoke only German.

*I must have shot at a few who looked just like him,* Steve told himself as the actor ignored his extended hand and instead bowed. He paid some attention to Randi, making several remarks in German which Irita translated, to the amusement of the purser.

"Frau Lombard is a well set-up woman of her type. One does not see a form like that in Europe."

Steve expected Randi would bristle at this. Its condescension was insulting, but to his surprise—and to his annoyance—Randi instead went over to talk to him about his role in the film. The director's wife did not appear pleased when Friedrich turned to her to translate. Not once did Randi ask him the question Steve was aching to ask: "Just how does a Nordic blonde like you fit into the role of a Hawaiian prince? . . ."

Leo Prysing arrived, clearly in a businesslike mood. Dinks furnished beer, probably to oblige his German guests, and Prysing sat down on the arm of the leather divan. With a beer stein in his hand he announced calmly, "I think a better opening would be aboard this ship. A schooner, perhaps with the lookout sighting a landfall."

Irita raised her golden head. "Commonplace, my love. But if there is treasure here in the islands from the Orient . . . precious, precious little packets . . . it could be a reason for the stopover. Perhaps the schooner's captain is carrying a very small cargo. You understand." She clapped her hands. "This missionary husband, he does not know his wife or her needs. But those needs could be drugs, as it is today in the world."

Whatever she meant Randi didn't seem to understand—that was clear to Steve. But Steve began to realize how far-reaching was the free and easy attitude these movie people had toward drugs. Dinks quickly changed the subject.

"I say. Do you suppose we seafarers are going to be sunk and forced to swallow the anchor, so to speak? I hear that a flier just made it from coast to coast, Florida to San Diego, in less than twelve hours. Fellow name of Doolittle. Next thing you know, they'll be making it from Frisco to Diamond Head."

"Interesting," Prysing remarked, obviously not interested at all in what the purser was saying.

Steve was still dwelling on the Vallman–Prysing arrangement. Perhaps Irita Vallman depended on drugs for her thrills, Steve thought, and recalled last year's brawl in San Francisco's select St. Francis Hotel which resulted in the death of an actress and the scandalous trial of the film star Fatty Arbuckle.

Steve studied the actress, thinking that her emaciation, her nervous moods and her glittering quality were hardly typical of the wholesome American stars of the day. It was for this reason alone, he told himself, that he objected to his wife's becoming involved with the Prysings . . .

Prysing interrupted his wife's prattle about her most recent role. He moved around the room and propped himself against a bulkhead behind Randi, which did not escape Steve . . . Not that he was jealous, he thought. The man obviously was using Randi, but only as cheap labor. And in defense of his wife, Steve quickly developed a dislike for the whole Hollywood crew.

Leo Prysing gave his beer stein to Dinks and asked if he had any whiskey. Dinks poured him two inches of bonded scotch.

"No opium smugglers will appear in *Prince of the Golden Isles.* No doubt a great disappointment to Hollywood," Prysing said flatly.

"Is it that bad in Hollywood?" Steve asked, hoping Randi would take the hint that this was an unhealthy environment for her. " 'Dope fiends,' they called them when I was a boy," he added with a smile.

Dinks waved the scotch bottle. "Guess that makes us liquor fiends."

Everyone laughed politely except Randi. As Steve knew, she was not enthusiastic about breaking the liquor law, however unpopular Prohibition was. Leo Prysing answered Steve's question.

"I have found this use of drugs in what you call spots. Like a cancer, it is here, there. A dot in the center. Then it spreads out from the center. One man is capable of infecting the circle. In any case, it is not permitted on my sets. Nor are the men responsible."

He sounded bitter, perhaps with cause. He did not look at his wife. While everyone jumped in to change the subject, the director leaned over Randi.

"I am having trouble with the titles for the seduction scene. Are you free this afternoon?"

While Steve seethed, Randi began eagerly, "I'd love to—" She stopped, gave Steve a guilty half-smile. "That is, I don't quite know yet. Are we doing anything, darling?"

Prysing added, "And I might as well get your opinion on the script as a whole. It may not be worth much—your opinion—but I have been having second thoughts about the captain. If I cut the role, point up his—"

"Oh, no! You've got a great character there." Randi set her glass down, turned around to him. Steve had never seen her more animated. "You'll destroy him. The wholeness of the film demands him. In fact—Steve, do you mind?"

They were all looking at him. He waved his glass. "Far be it from me to stand in the captain's way. Your movie captain, I mean. You go and save him, sweetheart."

NOBODY WAS happier than Steve Lombard to see the faint streak of Makapuu Point on the horizon as dawn broke. It was the first landfall on the island of Oahu; Honolulu waited around the rugged coastline, past Koko Head and Diamond Head. His elation was diminished, however, when he saw how let down his wife seemed to be.

She had worked late the night before with Prysing, and now, leaning on the rail with Steve, she kept yawning. "He's going to cut the ship captain's role, sure as shooting. He thinks it's superfluous. Superfluous! What does he know about women's taste? The missionary is weak. If the young chief dies in the volcano, who's left for the female audience?"

Steve couldn't think of a single subject in which he had less interest. Randi sensed his boredom and changed the subject.

"I'll be glad to see Brooke again," she remarked. "Do you think she will be happy with this doctor?"

"I think she enjoys the life in the islands. When she forces him to follow her back home, that's another matter. Wonder what kind of doctor he is. Can he even practice in California? But she'd better marry him. She's been living in that beach place of his for two months now."

"Don't be so old-fashioned, darling. Besides, they're well chaperoned," she said, referring to Dr. Ware's young daughter and his houseful of servants.

Steve wasn't reassured, however, until he saw his sister in the crowd on the dock beside the landing sheds. He thought that Brooke looked older and though she didn't appear to be behaving like a starry-eyed lover she nevertheless looked suntanned and relaxed. The gray-haired man who held her by the arm was tall and thin and looked every day of his fifty years. At first glance, Dr. Nigel Ware seemed to Steve to be an unlikely attraction for his vital, mercurial sister.

A young red-haired girl about ten years old held the doctor's other hand. She must be his daughter, Eden Ware, Steve thought. She seemed to be watching everything, the dockworkers, the lines being pulled taut from the ship, the churning green waters between liner and dock, as well as every face at the rail of the *Mahala.* When she spotted Irita Vallman and her blonde leading man, she yelled and pointed, quieting herself only after a nudge from her father. Then she made out Steve and Randi, waved to them and nudged a petite Oriental girl on her other side.

"It's them. Right there."

Fifteen minutes later the families had met. Steve and Randi were draped with leis in a rainbow of colors. Even Steve felt the romance of the flower wreaths and the warm, light kisses of the exquisite females who dropped them around his neck.

The group was divided into two cars for the ride to Dr. Ware's estate on the windward coast. In one car, an old Model T Ford, a shy, attractive Japanese woman was introduced as Dr. Ware's housekeeper,

Tamiko. Riding with her were her very pretty daughter, Chiye—the only unfriendly member of the party—and young Eden Ware.

Noting Chiye's side-glances at Brooke as well as Dr. Ware's gentle familiarity toward the housekeeper, Steve quickly figured out the reason for young Chiye's resentment. She must feel that the doctor belonged to her mother, he thought, and now her mother was being shunted off into the second car . . . He worried about Brooke's marriage within this curious menage. . . .

In the other car, the doctor pointed out the various faces in the streets of the small tropical city. "Every nationality. Notice? A few pure Hawaiians. But very few. There's two Chinese. That's a Japanese girl. The boy with her is probably Filipino. Maybe with some Portuguese blood."

Brooke joined the conversation. "The Japanese children are the only ones I've ever seen that study as hard as my Alec. Would you believe it? They go to our schools in the morning and their own Japanese classes in the afternoon," she said with pride.

"Fine people," the doctor put in. "All that melting pot makes these Pacific people the best folks in the world."

Randi agreed. "The most hospitable I've ever met."

"Should be." Brooke hugged her fiancé. "That's why I'm marrying one. I was so miserable when I arrived here. That ridiculous Russian calling himself a prince really did me in. The Whitcombs—mama's friends, you know—were staying at the Moana Hotel. Well, one night under that huge banyan tree they introduced my dearest doc to me. He was so cheerful and uplifting. Why, daddy himself couldn't have been sweeter. But then, one thing led to another and here I am, adoring him."

"Good for you," Steve said and Randi echoed. "It's so wonderful! We're delighted for you both."

As they neared the sharp, cloud-wreathed Koolau Range behind the city, and then the incredible greenery lining the road to Waikiki Beach, Randi gasped in admiration.

"Looks like rain," Brooke called out knowledgeably from the front seat. "But on the other side of the street the sun will be shining. Ever see anything as bright as that blue water out there, and those dark, wet mountains on the other side? That's *mauka* direction. The sea is *makai.*"

"Show-off," her brother teased.

Dr. Ware laughed. While driving he pointed out the various kinds of flowers that grew wild everywhere, often obscuring the view of small dwellings that occasionally dotted the area.

"I never knew there were jungles between Honolulu and Waikiki. Flower jungles," Randi said.

"Not precisely, Randi." The doctor explained that a great deal of this lush green beauty was made up of brush and coco palms and a thousand varieties of flowers.

"Now you see why the Hollywood people are using our island for their movie," Brooke boasted.

"We met them on board. Are they filming near you?" Randi's excitement did not go unnoticed by her husband.

"Next estate," the doctor said proudly. "All around Crouching Tiger Point. Probably a darned nuisance. But my little girl Eden is so thrilled I couldn't possibly have made trouble for the movie company."

"She is a darling. You'll love Eden," Brooke put in, patting the doctor's shirt collar affectionately.

"What a wonderful coincidence!" Randi exclaimed and settled back. She glanced at Steve. "Don't worry. I won't make a pest of myself with them. We don't even have to go near them. Except maybe a day or so when—if—they let us watch them shoot."

"Great," he said quickly. "You haven't heard, Brooke. This girl of mine has been rewriting their script for them. And doing a hell of a job, I might add. If the picture turns out to be anything at all, they can thank Randi."

Randi reached out and took his hand. His palm was moist with sweat . . . Must be the climate, she told herself.

# *Chapter Six*

RED Lombard decided that if his son could go halfway across the Pacific, he himself must take Alicia somewhere, preferably to Washington again. It was obviously worth his while to keep in touch with his cronies who now controlled the country, he thought. But as his wife reminded him, he chose a time when San Francisco had opened the first season of a sensational opera company which Alicia Lombard herself was promoting. Red had been in Washington, D.C. the previous year, where he and Alicia were invited to attend the dedication of the Lincoln Memorial and afterward were received by President and Mrs. Harding. "Rather common persons, but they mean well," was Alicia's summing up. She wasn't keen to go back to Washington, or even to visit Hawaii, though she missed her family and kept asking why there were no letters from them.

Alec explained carefully to both grandmothers.

"The folks have got to get to Honolulu. That's five days if it's a fast ship. Then their mail is put on the first coastwise steamer and that's another five days if it leaves the day they arrive. Then it's got to be delivered here on the Coast."

"Well," Bridget said, studying the bottom of her empty coffee cup, "I s'pose I knew it. But I'll be telling you this. I don't like it."

A few minutes later Bridget was winding up the Victrola in the parlor and offering to teach Tony the Charleston for the benefit of his slightly shocked Grandma Alicia.

"My dear," the older lady ventured in her wisp of a voice, "You have remarkably fine limbs for a female your age."

The subtle hint went over Bridget's head. Her knees were busier than ever and her still-abundant hair bounced out of its precisely marcelled waves. Even Alec was amused to see the four-year-old Tony imitating her with a certain coltish grace. Alicia, though, was still bothered by the display.

"You must be dead tired, my dear. Why don't we get Stella Burkett down to help you teach Tony. I understand she is very good at it."

"Can't!" Tony announced. "Stella's sick."

Alicia motioned Alec nearer. "My boy, why don't you go and see if she needs anything. I suppose it is nothing serious or she would have told us. Tell her to lie down a while. She may use my hot water bottle if she likes. The little Bellini girl can do her work this morning."

Alec knew the other maid had her own tasks to perform and things were liable to get a bit messed up. Hoping that Stella had merely overslept he knocked on the door of her little back room.

She didn't answer so he tried the doorknob. The door opened just in time for him to see Stella in her flannel nightgown bending over her china washbowl, throwing up. Horrified, he started to back out but was stopped by the desperation in her choked voice.

"Holy Mother of God!"

He didn't know what to do. "Shall I get—" Who could help her? "I'll find someone."

"No." Stella wiped her face on a towel and swallowed hard. "Come here, kiddo." Alec received this with one eyebrow raised. "Look here, boy, you got to promise me something."

"Well, what?"

She stood with the morning sunlight behind her body's silhouette. To Alec's astonishment she was perhaps four or five months pregnant.

Stella knew by the look on his face that he had guessed. She dug her fingers into his shoulder blades like a stern teacher. "I mean it, kid. Just forget it."

Her face looked bloated and pale. He wanted to spare her the embarrassment he himself felt.

"It's just that I didn't know you were married," he said nervously.

She startled him when she threw back her head and gave out a deep, throaty chuckle.

"You'll be the death of me, kid. That you will. I been livin' in this house the last year. Be your age. Don't need a husband to get pregnant in this house."

He felt the blush spread over his face. He had hoped he was too old to let his feelings show, yet here he was, acting like a child . . . Who was the father of her baby? he wondered. Not the old handyman. Or Grandpa Red. The only other possibility that came to Alec was so calamitous he couldn't even voice it. He backed away.

"If you're all right, I'll—I'll go."

He remembered when Alma Cortlandt told Uncle Steve she wouldn't get married if he told her not to. It had been obvious to Alec at the time that there was something between them . . . So why not with the maid? Uncle Steve could visit her room any time of the day or night without anyone knowing . . . It was Uncle Steve, all right.

He needed time to think, to figure out what to do, but before he got out of the room Stella Burkett called to him. "You gonna keep quiet? Or you going to get me in trouble? I'll beat it soon's I get paid for taking care of things while Randi—*Miss* Randi's gone."

All Alec could think of were Aunt Randi and Uncle Steve, so happy over there in the Hawaiian Islands, never dreaming of the shock that would be waiting for them when they came home.

"I don't think anybody should say anything." He surprised himself. His voice sounded as mature as he could have wished. "In fact, Stella, you ought to go somewhere for a while."

Hearing Alicia Lombard coming down the hall, Alec burst out of the room to divert her.

"Grandma! Don't tell me you've lost interest in Grandma Bridget's Charleston. She's really good, you know." He tried to take her arm, to turn her around and head her back down the stairs. But frail Alicia Lombard was indomitable when she wanted to be.

"No, dear. Bridget is lying down. She has a bit of a headache. Too much exertion. I must see how Burkett is getting along."

"She's fine, grandma. Getting dressed—I mean—she just overslept a little. We don't want to keep her from her work."

"Very true, dear. You are in my way. Be a good boy and go and look after your cousin Tony. He is probably annoying poor Bridget about now."

"Yes, but—where are you going?"

"To see Burkett, of course. Really, Alec, I wonder if you aren't getting hard of hearing."

"Now, wait, grandma. She's coming. She's fine."

But he was too late. Alicia Lombard walked right into Stella Burkett's room and caught her as she was lacing up her old-fashioned whalebone corset.

"Burkett, what seems to be the trouble?"

"Feeling better, ma'am. Just a little headache."

But Alicia had seen the washbasin. Alec watched, frozen. He saw his grandmother watching Stella try to lace up her torso-length corset.

"You are gaining weight, Burkett."

"Yes, ma'am."

Alicia circled around the maid, and Stella dropped the laces and licked her lips nervously. Alec could see that she was scared. The word of a Lombard would be taken long before anyone would believe Stella. Alicia moved toward her, put her fingers in between the laces while Stella remained like a statue, permitting this indignity.

By now Alec was certain his grandmother perfectly understood Stella's condition.

"Who is the father, my dear?" Alicia asked in her whispery voice.

Stella pulled herself together. "I reckon you know, ma'am. My bedroom being here, and all. And him being in and out of the house so much. It was the temptation, you see . . . You'll be wanting me to quit, I guess."

Alec started to speak but was surprised, as was Stella, by the quiet power in his grandmother's voice.

"How long has the affair been going on?"

"Off and on, ma'am. I never meant it to go this far."

Alicia's fingers shook and she covered her eyes briefly. "Does he know?"

"Not yet, ma'am, though he might suspect. I always thought that was why he wanted to go away."

Alicia stifled a groan. "Yes. Though he is not usually a coward."

"I hoped you wouldn't be having to know, ma'am, if I made the money to go away, get another job."

"Thank you. I thought he was so faithful since his marriage. He seemed happy." Stella's mouth dropped open when she realized what Alicia was thinking.

"Does his wife suspect?"

Stella looked down. "No, ma'am. I'm sure of it."

"Well, that's one blessing. He does love her, despite this affair. I would swear he loves her. You are right, however. You will have to leave here."

"Yes, ma'am. But I got no money. What I make goes to keep pa and the boys. I need a job. References. It's going to cost me. That's why I was hoping to make a little taking care of young Mr. Tony."

Alicia moved slowly back and forth.

"Burkett, I cannot let you leave us entirely. We are a tightly knit family. I will want to know about the child. Perhaps even keep an eye on it, from a distance. I'll find a place for you. But you must be gone from this house before my son comes home."

"Yes, ma'am. I'll do that," Stella said eagerly. "I'd thought of asking Mr. Red—Mr. Lombard—about that big place he owns in Southern California after the baby's born. I could be real handy there, cleaning and all. And Mrs. Lombard—" She reached out and tried to touch Alicia, who withdrew almost imperceptibly just beyond her reach.

"Mrs. Lombard, I swear on my mother's grave, I'll never make any trouble for you and yours. I'll never knowingly be seeing Mr. Steve, nor pay him any mind. That what you want to hear?"

Alicia kept pacing the little room while Alec held his breath. "It would be so easy to send you far away, never see or hear from you again. But the child is a Lombard. I'll see to it that you have the proper references. If—*if,* mind you, there is never any contact between you and my son."

"I swear it. I'll never be contacting Mr. Steve. Better: I'll never have words with him if he happens to look me up for any reason. I never lied to you, Mrs. Lombard. As God is my witness."

Alicia sighed and looked as if she were going to faint. Alec ran to her, catching her just as Stella Burkett reached her. Alicia smiled at her grandson, patting his hand. "You heard?"

He nodded.

"Well, you must be our witness. You are a good boy, and discreet. I trust you." She looked up onto Stella's wide eyes. "Send me a photograph of the child when there is some character in the face. No words, except some triviality. You are married, or divorced, or widowed, whatever you wish. Send the child's name, and your own married name."

"I get you, ma'am."

"And the photograph. I want to see what my third grandchild looks like. If you keep your word—"

"I will."

"If the child is as you say, you will always be taken care of in a small way. Alec, you are my witness. There must be no blackmail from this woman. If I am gone, I trust you to arrange everything as you know I would want it."

Stella drew herself up. "If there was blackmail on my mind, ma'am, you'd be hearing it before this. But fair is fair. I gave my word, and I don't need your charity. I do want a job. If you're willing to send me something for the child, that's your business. I'll put it by. But I swore by oath. I'll be leaving soon's you get me a replacement."

Alicia stroked Alec's hair absently while she stared out the window at the windy November day.

"I never thought he would be so foolish. And with a fine, capable wife, too. What will the future bring? God knows. I'm afraid my daughter-in-law is going to be upset when you leave. It means more work for her, breaking in a new maid; but it must be done." She considered. "I don't want my husband to know about this. He and Stephen never did get along too well, and he would certainly use this against Steve and poor Randi. Yes," she made her decision. "It must be our secret. Alec, would you mind helping me? I feel a little weak. I think I will just lie down for a few minutes. I'm getting too old for this sort of shock."

Taking one small step at a time, she and Alec moved along the upper hall toward her sun-filled front bedroom.

"You know, Alec, I would like to have known my other grandchild," she said unexpectedly, then waited until Alec tucked her in with the comforter, pulling it up to her thin shoulders. "Alec?"

"Yes, grandma?"

"The child could be your cousin. Like Tony. If ever you have the occasion, be kind to Stella's child. But no one must know."

"I'll remember, grandma."

They broke off their conversation when young Tony tore into the room, wanting his grandma to come down and watch him do the Charleston.

Alec caught his grandmother's gesture, her forefinger against her lips, reminding him that no one, not even Stella's child, must know their secret. Alec nodded and turned to order Tony out of the room.

"On your way, kid. I'm coming."

"I want to stay with gran," Tony insisted.

"Well, you can't, so go on. I'll be with you later."

Tony dug his heels into the thick carpet. "I don't want you. I want gran."

Alec wondered how his grandmother could want any more grandchildren, especially one like this. And the more he thought of what Stella and Uncle Steve had done, the more he resented them for hurting the family. His disappointment in his uncle was enormous, but at that moment he despised Stella Burkett. He would not forget that she had almost wrecked the family . . .

Alicia raised her head with an effort. "Now, Tony, be a good boy. Go on. Alec will play with you."

Tony's sunny face fell and his small fists clenched.

"Don't want Alec. Alec can't play. Alec's a cripple."

Alec's back grew rigid. His grandmother read something in his eyes, and she reminded him, "I depend on you, my boy. Remember."

He had spent fifteen years learning restraint. He also had the example before him of a woman who found that her son had sired a child no one could claim.

"Don't worry, grandma. It doesn't bother me."

It was probably the biggest lie he would ever utter to his grandmother.

# *Chapter Seven*

SEPARATE letters from both Alicia and Red went out to Steve, Brooke and Randi in Hawaii, with the news that Stella Burkett was leaving.

*My dearest children,*

*Little Tony is getting more beautiful every day. A precious jewel. Perhaps we spoil him a wee bit. But such a lovable child! Alec too is a treasure. And helpful to me in ways that I cannot even count.*

*I am sure you know my heart will be with you on the occasion of my little girl's marriage. We received the latest snapshots of Brooke, the good doctor and his delightful little daughter. What an attractive group! We do so look forward to meeting our new son-in-law. You must come to the Coast very soon.*

*Mary-Randal, you will be put out by the news that Burkett is leaving. I believe there is a fiancé in Southern California. Since the young woman obviously feels the need to advance herself, as they say, I feel it would be uncharitable to stand in her way. Then again, her faults were considerable and I am sure we will find a suitable replacement.*

*Brooke, my dear, I trust you and the dear doctor received the little wedding remembrance. I am afraid Redmon has just plunged (as he puts it) more deeply into his oil land in Wyoming. Something about Teakettle Domes, or some such. As a result, money is not as easily come by for the moment as it might be.*

*My best love to you all.*

*Your mother,*
*ALICIA CALDWELL LOMBARD*

Arriving on the same steamer was a letter from Red to his daughter. Brooke offered it to Steve, who read it aloud.

*My little girl,*

*May you have a great wedding day with all the trimmings. Miss you like the devil, baby. When are you bringing that doctor of yours home to Nob Hill? San Francisco could use a good G.P.*

*I wanted to go to Washington, maybe even Europe. But Alicia won't go, so that's out. But they say a good old U.S. dollar will buy a whole country over there. Last month a newspaperman named Benito Mussolini got together a bunch of dagos and marched them down to Rome and demanded law and order and jobs in that benighted country. Their little king put him in charge. So now they've got a newsboy running things, but only for a year. I'll bet Benito gets thrown out by Christmas of 1923.*

*Germany's even worse off. We'd be billionaires over there right now.*

*I guess your mother told you Stella Burkett's got her walking papers. She got too ambitious. Wanted more money, the way I hear it. And there's a husband in the wings. Something none of us guessed. Your mother says he lives in L.A. He would.*

*More gossip. This time about money and things that count. A fellow I knew in my Comstock youth, Harry Macondray, is a contact between the attorney general's office and the Department of the Interior. He told me why the attorney general's assistant committed suicide. Something about Elk Hills naval oil reserves in California and the Teapot Dome land in Wyoming, or that's the rumor. That meddling old buzzard from Montana, Senator Walsh, is investigating and causing more trouble. Calls it graft just because a few enterprising oil men were given drilling rights in the area the navy was letting go to waste. I got hold of Macondray and he said to forget it. Walsh has nothing. Just being nosy. And Macondray said we should plunge. The Teapot Dome is better than ever. The rumors were spread to get the leases cheap for other grabby guys. Clever?*

*But I've plunged as deep as I can go on it.*

*Can't think of any more gossip. You come on home, you and the good doctor, and give my best to Randi and Steve.*

*Love,*
*DADDY*

Steve set the two letters side by side on the table. "I hope father knows what he is doing with those Washington friends of his. I tell you, I don't like the smell of it. If Senator Walsh is on their trail, I'm inclined to believe there is evidence. He isn't a stupid man." He looked at Randi and smiled. "But you don't care two beans about oil and government land, do you? You're worried about what the Stella business means."

Randi shook her head and picked up the letters. "Not a word about ma. Leo—Mr. Prysing is driving into Honolulu today. I think I'll send ma a letter again. Ask her to write a line or so. I've written three and she hasn't answered one of them."

But Steve wasn't listening. He had the contents of the letters on his mind. "Well, honey, this means more work for you when you get home. Otherwise, I can't say I'm sorry the girl is gone. She did always seem kind of fresh."

Randi agreed but was sorry to lose her. She couldn't forget how helpful Stella had been during Mrs. Lombard's illness. "She was capable, though. And I never dreamed she planned to marry."

Steve shrugged. "I'm sorry on your account. That's all. Shall we go swimming, sweetheart?"

"Oh, Steve, could you wait just an hour? That tiresome Mr. Prysing wants to stop by and get my ideas on the first meeting between the leads . . . that means the hero and heroine."

"I gathered that."

"And I want to send a letter to ma. The *Sonora* is in today from the South Seas. Prysing said he would take me to the dock to get it off. He has to drive into Honolulu about a new secretary."

"I'm quite capable of driving you."

"I know, dear, and I'd rather go with you any time. But will it bore you if he goes along? He wants to get my ideas, as I said, on the meeting between the chief and the missionary's wife."

Steve turned his face away. "Okay. You let him take you. I'll be out on the beach. Meet you there in an hour or so."

With a prick of guilt, she watched him go . . .

Randi felt reborn since she had begun working for Leo Prysing. It seemed to her an act of fate when she discovered the day of their arrival in Honolulu that the Prysing company would be working on *Prince of the Golden Isles* practically next door. In her excitement, Randi thought that fate had brought her here, and the conceit of the idea even persuaded her that Steve was happy. She did notice that he watched her now more than usual, though, and took care never to give him cause for jealousy. . . .

When Dr. Ware drove the Lombards up to the famous Pali and showed off the sheer cliffside, with its treacherous drop masked by incredibly green jungle growth, he chose the very morning Prysing was filming the death plunge of the prince's army. Prysing had chosen to duplicate the real-life mass suicide of the defending army, pursued by the great conqueror King Kamehameha the First. Half the island of Oahu seemed to be gathered in the parking area, hoping to catch a glimpse of Kurt Friedrich and Irita Vallman saying their tender farewells before the battle.

The director sent his assistant over to ask Randi for a final farewell to be uttered by Friedrich. With fifty pair of eyes on her, Randi came up with one triumphant and all-inclusive "Aloha!"

The simplicity of it struck everyone as brilliant and she received enthusiastic applause from Leo Prysing's local audience that rippled through the windy Pali air.

"They say 'aloha' means everything," she explained. "Hello. Good-bye. I love you. So it could be a simple, tender farewell."

Dr. Ware beamed at her. "How right you are! And what says my lovely bride-to-be?"

Sheltered by his arm from the wind that whistled through this famous cut in the mountains, Brooke giggled, repeated "Aloha, honey" to her fiancé and got good-natured cheers from the audience.

Brooke lowered her voice as she turned to speak to Steve and Randi. "You'd think I'd never been married before. But I'm nervous as a kitten over the ceremony tomorrow."

"You'll do beautifully," Randi reassured her.

Steve laughed. "Any time my sister won't be at her best at a wedding! You'd steal the show from the great Vallman any day in the week."

Unfortunately, Irita Vallman was nearby and heard this remark. She gave him a smouldering look, batting her darkened lashes, and pouted. Steve grinned. As Randi could plainly see, he was enjoying himself.

"That woman is on something," he whispered to Randi. "Notice how her right cheek twitches? And her throat? She's on it or she needs it."

Randi hushed him but she did wonder uneasily. She was relieved when the wind proved too much for Brooke, and they all piled into the car and drove back down through warm, humid fern valleys and past Diamond Head to the doctor's house. There they changed to bathing suits and Steve shocked the other mainlanders present by wearing swimming trunks with no tank top.

Randi would never forget her first sight of the beach from the windows of Dr. Nigel Ware's large bungalow. The house was old and comfortable, with the sultry smell of the trade winds and the moist plantings filling the air. Tall coco palms marked the boundary of the estate from the roadside, and close to the house were exotic bushes and flowers.

Striding down to the wet sand, Steve looked impressive enough to appear in one of Prysing's movies, and everyone admired him. Eden Ware and Chiye Akina followed him into the warm waves and back onto the white sand. Randi was delighted that Steve was enjoying all this attention. They lay on the sand together, his bare, sandy foot rubbing the back of her leg.

"Do you know something, Mr. Lombard? I love you more than ever."

He tickled her neck under her bathing cap. "Do you, sweetheart? More than the day we were married?"

"Much more. I think it gets better with age, don't you?"

He studied a long strand of her hair which he had pulled out from under her cap. "If you say so."

It was an odd thing to say, and sounded rather flat. She looked around, hoping to find a change of conversation.

"I do hope Brooke is happy. Dr. Ware is such a nice man. Do you suppose he will actually move to the mainland? He hasn't said a word about it."

"Why not? People usually marry Lombards for their money, don't they?"

Randi gave him a startled look.

"Except you, of course," he said, and pulled her hair.

She pretended to accept that, but there was a special note in his reply that made her acutely uncomfortable . . .

They were still lying close, each locked in silent thoughts, trying to imagine what thread of trust had been ripped out of their marriage, when Eden came over.

"Daddy says we're going to have a *luau* tonight instead of a—a—"

"Bachelor party," Chiye put in. She added proudly, "Mama and some Hawaiian boys are going to do it."

"And guess what?" Eden demanded, her lively eyes sparkling. "They're inviting those movie folks. Irita Vallman and Kurt Friedrich are coming right here on the beach where the *emu*—the oven—will be. They're going to eat with us."

Together, the girls explained that a *luau* was something quite splendid in Hawaiian feasts, featuring a succulent pig roasted in the ground with coals and *taro* leaves.

"Like spinach," Chiye put in. "But it tastes better than spinach."

"And *poi,* and *lomi-lomi* salmon—"

Chiye added, "Raw fish. We rub it in salt water with bits of tomatoes and onions. Mmmmm."

Randi couldn't imagine how raw fish could be as delicious as they all claimed.

"And squid. It's quite good. Kind of rubbery." Steve was grinning at Chiye's description. "And all kinds of surprises," she added.

Randi smiled weakly. "I'll just bet they are."

Randi wasn't too anxious for the promised *luau,* but much to her surprise, the food turned out to be delicious. The ground was prepared late in the morning, and the porker, smothered in greens and vegetables, was placed over the glowing coals. Endless other good things had been prepared inside the house.

"Wait 'til you taste the coconut pudding," Eden promised Steve and Randi.

"Wait 'til you taste another dram of *okolehau,*" Brooke put in. "How do you like yours? Think our Hawaiian alcohol will ever take the place of good old bathtub gin?"

"It could peel the skin right off your tongue. But I think I'm used to it now. I'll have my usual," Steve said.

Chiye's mother, Tamiko, her unlined face wearing a shy smile, brought Steve his cocktail. In Japanese, she ordered the two maids to serve taller glasses adorned with long strips of pineapple to Randi and Brooke.

"Just to make you happy," Brooke promised Randi, "we've asked the movie people to join us."

Randi saw Steve's grimace, and didn't know what she could do to improve his dark mood, what even to talk about.

It was Leo Prysing himself who plunged into a discussion of desert property around Los Angeles, pointing out the expansion of the city and the value of land beyond the city limits.

"It was so in Germany. And in Austria where my brother now lives."

Steve responded, "Recently, I had an offer from a fellow who wants a beachfront income property in Strand. He's retiring and wants to invest. But he'd like to trade me twenty-five acres of rabbit holes somewhere between L.A. and the Pacific. Unfortunately, not close enough to the ocean. Do you know Culver City at all?"

"Take his rabbit holes, my friend. They will be worth something if you can wait, will be especially handy for my profession. Do you know where the Ince Studios are? Culver City. Then there is the Metro Studio further west. They are consolidating, growing bigger."

Steve was impressed . . . .

Brooke ran over to Randi in panic. "We forgot about Mr. Prysing. His wife and that good-looking actor are able to eat our *luau* feast. I've even seen them sampling the fish and crabmeat already. But Mr. Prysing is Jewish. How can he eat tonight? What can we do?"

"Tell him," Randi said promptly, "the cooking is being handled out here, so send him into the kitchen with Tamiko. Or me. He may think it's fun."

Prysing took the problem very well. He spoke to Randi with unaccustomed cheerfulness while she tied an apron around his waist.

"I am not an Orthodox Jew. I have traveled too far from my beginnings. With pork and shellfish, however, I seem to hear my father's shocked outcry and I must refuse. I cannot eat the pig out there."

While he arranged vegetables and Tamiko brought a huge slab of steak from the icebox, Brooke apologized for the meat. "Not kosher, I'm afraid."

"I will think of the cow as kosher," the director said, wishing to cause no further upset on his account.

Tamiko turned to Brooke. "It is the same with us, Miss Lombard. We come to another country. We must make peace with our new diet. It is possible. I have made peace like others."

Prysing commended her. "Very intelligent. You are a survivor, Mrs. Akina." She blushed at his praise. He added, "My people too are survivors. I married out of my faith. My wife is pure Aryan, or so she reminds me when she is angry. Possibly because Heinz—you know him as Kurt—seems very much an Aryan."

"Your wife is very beautiful," Randi said.

Prysing agreed, and his hard gaze seemed to take on a gentleness unlike him. "When I met Irita she was a bit player at UFA, our great cinema company in Berlin. Enchanting creature. Full of self. But that is necessary to an actress. I flatter myself to believe I saw in her the qualities of a star. Not a Pola Negri, nor a Lil Dagover, but light and charming. Fame, though, changes people and it has changed my wife."

Tamiko avoided his eyes, not wanting to embarrass him, but Randi and Brooke were too interested to bother with politeness. They hung on his every word.

"One must survive at all costs," he said. "My wife understands that very well. We were on the edge of divorce when I was invited to Hollywood and the Famous Players studio. Irita joined me in that journey." He laughed, shook the pan over the flames. "I regard myself as a passport to America. Nothing more."

Noisy laughter and shrieks of delight and alarm reached the kitchen. Randi went to the doorway, looked across the long living room whose windows faced the beach.

"They are having a swim before dinner—your wife and some young neighbors with surfboards."

"Not my Chiye. I have told her not to swim when surfboards are out. This is dangerous," Tamiko said, and hurried outside. Eden and Chiye were both in bathing suits but they huddled over the steamy pit, the *emu,* where two Hawaiian boys of about fifteen had removed the golden-brown pig and were now lifting out all the parcels of seafood and vegetables wrapped in *taro* leaves.

With the help of Steve and several neighbors, Dr. Ware was arranging the mats with utensils for those who did not wish to follow the custom of eating with the fingers. As he set down the last mat in the wide semicircle around the *emu,* he stuck his finger into one of the *poi* bowls and licked his finger, winking at the children.

"Best kind. One-finger *poi.* Sissies use two or even three fingers. But one is enough if the *poi* is the right consistency. And Kaneohe there knows the secret."

The Hawaiian boy smiled, but he went on slicing pork while the steam enveloped him.

Steve made the traditional claim that the *poi* tasted like putty, but he was corrected by his prospective brother-in-law.

"The correct comparison is wallpaper paste. But honestly, how many people know what wallpaper paste tastes like? Let's call in the swimmers, and especially those surfers. Time for *kau-kau.*"

Steve assumed *kau-kau* was the Hawaiian word for "chow," and went to call the swimmers. As he waded out, waving to Irita Vallman, Friedrich and some young boys he didn't know, he wondered to himself what Randi was doing all this time in the kitchen with Prysing.

No one seemed to be behaving sensibly today, he thought . . . The golden Irita and her boy friend were out there risking their lives so close to the surfboards, and Randi was inside the house huddled with that damned movie director. He splashed angrily through the water.

# *Chapter Eight*

STEVE was not entirely reassured to see Brooke and Tamiko come out of the house with Prysing and Randi; as usual, they were arguing about titles.

What neither Steve nor Brooke was aware of was the effort of Dr. Ware and Eden to have Tamiko join the other diners. With head averted, Tamiko replied that it would not be suitable. She would eat in the dinette with the others who had prepared the lavish feast.

Steve watched Chiye curiously. She was obviously contemptuous of her mother's strict sense of protocol and she saw to it that she herself sat beside Eden Ware, in an honored position. Bravo for her! Steve thought with amusement.

He made room for Randi beside him and then saw that the director had stopped with Randi, as if he expected her to kneel on the mat beside him. To Steve's great relief, she said something to him and went around the circle to join her husband.

It was Steve, mollified by her conduct, who proposed the toast to the future bride and groom. Everyone joined in with good will, except young Chiye who put her glass of fruit punch to her lips but did not drink.

Halfway through the feast, with the sun gone down behind the great jungle range behind them, Randi confessed her feelings to Steve. "I love it. All of it. Even the squid." She leaned against Steve's shoulder.

"Darling, I do hope they'll be happy."

He guessed she was worrying about Brooke and Dr. Ware. "Why not? They certainly like each other."

"But is that enough?"

He had his arm around her, holding her close. "*We* like each other."

"Don't be silly. We're in love. There *is* a difference. I know how she felt over André. A passion. Not like this."

Steve was impatient. "She's better off. André is burned out from all his losses. I doubt if any single woman could replace a wife, a mother, a sister, everything he loved. Even his home. This fellow is better for Brooke."

She knew it was so, but she still wondered whether Brooke really wanted a man who was almost her father's age and, though certainly a good man, nevertheless lacked the excitement of her former lovers . . .

Something new, Randi thought—that's all Brooke is trying to find —a new sensation. As yet she hadn't heard a single word about where they would live or how they would reconcile their very different lifestyles. . . .

"Those surfers are pretty close to the swimmers. Did you notice?" Steve had sat up and was frowning at the great waves rolling in toward the long shoreline.

She turned in his arms and followed the breakers with her eyes. Evening shadows made it difficult to see Irita Vallman and her actor friend, but they were out there, yelling at each other in German, bouncing out and into the waves while the boys on the surfboards rode the waves in toward them, avoiding the swimmers by about fifty yards.

"Maybe we should do something," Randi suggested. She glanced around, but Leo Prysing was at a window in the long living room of the house, discussing some problem of tomorrow's shooting with his lanky cameraman.

Steve called out to Nigel Ware. "What do you think? Shouldn't someone separate those swimmers from the surfers?"

"Quite right. I'll call them in." Dr. Ware got to his feet, and Brooke watched him with a tender, almost motherly expression. The doctor strolled down to the wet sand, cupped his hands to his mouth and called Irita Vallman.

"Better come in, ma'am. That long, easy surf can fool you."

The actress waved. Bobbing up and down in the water, she cried out something in German.

Dr. Ware looked around helplessly. "What is she saying?"

Nobody knew. A short distance up the beach a boy rode his board in, tumbled off close to the shore, and Dr. Ware strode over to him, his sandaled feet sinking deep in the wet sand. The boy, a *haoli,* or Caucasian, dragged his board up on the beach, listened politely to the doctor and nodded. The boy got his board up to the dry white sand, then turned and beckoned to his three friends out beyond the breakers. One of them saw the boy's arms raised in a crisscross and began to swim in toward shore. The other two, a Hawaiian and a *haoli,* were already on their boards, racing in on a wave.

Everything happened all at once. Irita Vallman's head and body surfaced above the green water and foam, and the two boys racing toward shore swerved to avoid her. The Hawaiian boy kept his balance and rode the wave, missing a collision by several yards. The *haoli* boy, however, had panicked and toppled over. The surfboard went slamming into the golden creature borne above the wave.

Around the *luau's* semicircle, everyone jumped up and dashed along the sand to the water. The boys dove in, but Steve and Dr. Ware were the first to swim out beyond the long stretch of shallow water, Steve still in bathing trunks and a sweater, the doctor in a shirt and trousers. The boy who had fallen off the board grabbed Irita Vallman under the chin and tried to keep her afloat.

Steve reached the actress first. She seemed to be in shock. He took over from the exhausted boy and with Dr. Ware's help got her ashore. Minutes later, shivering a little, he was grateful for the robe Randi threw around his shoulders. Along with the *luau* party he watched Leo Prysing and Dr. Ware carefully wrap blankets around the chilled body of Irita Vallman.

Steve felt Randi's hand on his shoulder. He had a sudden horrifying vision of Randi lying there, rigid and stiff . . . He put his lips to her hand and kissed it.

Even in this moment of tragedy for the Prysings, he thought of how lucky he was.

BROOKE DIDN'T like the idea of postponing the wedding.

"It's going to be bad luck, and I'm going to need all the good luck I can get, Randi. It isn't as if the woman was a friend of ours. We hardly know her."

It might all be true, Randi thought, and Irita Vallman had scarcely made many friends, but she was Leo Prysing's wife, and Randi regarded Prysing both as an employer and as a friend.

"Are you really afraid? About your marriage, I mean? Everybody loves Nigel."

Brooke grew pale. "Sure, Nigel's wonderful. Every day I feel lucky that he's my friend, my dearest, most understanding friend. And that's better than some fly-by-night like André, or that phony prince I almost married. But . . ."

"But you wonder how long it will last."

"No. I wonder where we will live. You know me. Over here the beauties are all homegrown. Even the orchids grow wild. Whereas I'm strictly the hothouse variety." She flashed Randi her mischievous little-girl look. "Anyway, I always was a gambler, so here goes. We're going to have a quiet wedding right here in the house on Saturday. Who knows? Maybe by then Prysing's wife will be up and walking. I hope so, for my sake as well as hers."

The actress was not up, much less walking. Her spinal injuries were severe, though no one knew the actual extent of them. A specialist who practiced at Hilo on the big island of Hawaii was brought in by a fast boat. He joined the physicians of Oahu as they worked on Irita Vallman at the big Honolulu Hospital.

Considerably subdued, the ceremony took place. Randi stood with Steve, behind the groom, while Eden Ware, with her pale red hair neatly brushed and braided, stood behind the glamorous bride.

Randi glanced at Steve several times during the ceremony. He caught her at it and seemed to like her attention. She looked around at the wedding guests. Even young Chiye had perked up and stood with her mother, proud and half-smiling. To Randi, there was great devotion in the older woman's eyes as she watched Dr. Ware speak, giving his vows clearly and warmly.

When the rest of the little group crowded around to congratulate the bride and groom, Randi heard the great, roaring surf beyond the windows of the long living room and looked out.

She saw Leo Prysing striding along the beach from the house he had rented beyond the point. It was obvious to Randi that he hoped to avoid making his presence a damper on the wedding party. One of the serving girls went out to the steps, then came back inside where Randi met her.

"Movie man say very quick see you. *Wiki-wiki.* Nobody else."

"I understand." The news must be bad . . . She had thought about him a good deal since the accident, imagining the pain and regret he must be suffering because of the lost years, the estrangement between him and his wife. But no matter how little sympathy there had been between Randi and the beautiful actress, she couldn't help identifying with her as another young woman in the prime of life. Randi tried to imagine her own life shattered before she was thirty years old, and the thought was hard to shake . . .

Leo Prysing looked older than she remembered. He hadn't shaved and his face was exhausted.

"Please," he said softly as soon as she joined him. "May we speak without being seen? They look so happy in there."

"They are. Brooke is lucky. The doctor is a fine man."

They moved beyond the kitchen walls of the house.

He blurted out, "The spinal cord is severed."

"Oh, no! Are they sure?"

"We have not given up. She has movement to her waist. We are sending for specialists from the mainland and one my brother recommends from Vienna. But five days to wait for the California doctors. And endless time for Dr. Fassman. And then—I have seen the X-rays. The cord was severed."

There were no words of comfort she could offer.

He cleared his throat. "All of this costs money," he said briskly, "so I must do what I can to rescue the film. Kurt, that weak jellyfish of a man, wants to stay as far away from my poor Irita as he can. He claims that deformity—deformity, my God!—repulses him." He paced up and down the sand below the pantry steps, his fists clenched tightly.

Randi felt a painful sympathy for him. "You still love her, don't you?"

He was impatient with what he apparently regarded as her stupidity.

"Never! I suppose I once loved her beauty. She was the most enchanting creature to look at! But she was always obsessed with that beauty, and nothing else mattered. She was not capable of any emotion beyond her own comfort and self-love. But seeing her lying there like a china doll broken in pieces—I am sickened. I would also be sickened with loss if someone broke an exquisite Ming vase of mine, so I deserve no credit for what I suffer now."

Though his motives, his concern, were in essence as selfish as Irita's, Randi felt for him all the same. She found herself pitying him more than she pitied his unfortunate wife . . .

"Then you will continue working on *Golden Isles?*"

"I must. I would go mad doing nothing, dwelling on old days, on things as they might have been. And there is the money. It must be earned."

She hesitated over what was an extremely awkward subject. "And Miss Vallman's role?"

He shrugged. "I haven't thought it through. A double perhaps, for long shots. I don't know. You are sailing home soon?"

"The next coastal sailing is on Friday. We haven't seen our little boy for almost a month, and there is a great deal to take care of at home. Domestic matters."

"I understand. It is natural." He shook hands with her. "Make my apologies to the others." He turned and started away across the sand, then looked back just as she heard Steve call her from the beachfront of the house.

"Randi? We need you. Bride and groom are ready to leave."

"Coming, Steve," she called.

Prysing had walked back over to her. "May I get your opinion on a title or two when I am in trouble?" He must have a thousand writers who could do better, Randi thought. But it was good of him to think of her, even though she knew it would be impossible. Household and family problems would take up her time, for a while at least. Still, it was a nice thought for the future . . .

"I'm afraid once I get home my mind will be on a hundred things, all domestic and uninteresting to an outsider, but they will take up my time. I'm sorry. I wish it might have been different. You know that I'll be praying for your wife's recovery. We all will."

"Thank you."

She watched his departing figure a moment, then went to join Steve and the wedding party.

Two days later, Irita Vallman died of a blood clot, and Randi thought the saddest thing was the fact that neither her lover, Kurt Friedrich, nor her husband had been able to weep when the appalling extent of her injuries first became known. That lovely creature had left no real mourners . . . .

Despite the brief time in which Leo Prysing had opened up and confided some of his troubles to her, Randi decided that he was a hard man and a dangerous one to love.

# *Chapter Nine*

IT grew harder and harder for Randi to concentrate on the problems of faraway Hollywood when there were problems enough at home in San Francisco to keep her busy.

A big problem had been the replacement of Stella Burkett by two girls and then, when one proved wholly incompetent and the other drunk, two others. This time Bridget helped her out by recommending a middle-aged woman named Hilda Thorgerson, who had lived in Bridget's rooming house and had been unfortunate witness to Bridget's noisier quarrels with LeMass, who wanted to move to the San Pedro docks for more work in Southern California.

LeMass had finally left, quite suddenly. "Got the wanderlust," Bridget said. But she confided to Randi. "He'd been carrying on, the spalpeen! And that I won't put up with. Asked me for money. But he ain't getting it from me, just to entertain his floozies. I sent him off to Pedro with a flea in his ear, I can tell you. Let the Los Angeles women take him up."

Not that Bridget was strapped for money. She still received a monthly income from Steve though she remained living in her rooming house on Sutter Street. "When the price is right," she would say, "I might just buy it. Who knows? I could be another Red Lombard before I'm through."

Randi could only mutter, "God forbid!"

But Randi felt confident of Hilda Thorgerson, whose many assets included the ability to handle Tony Lombard. No small trick, Randi thought . . .

Randi and Steve had been met at the docks on their return from the Hawaiian Islands by young Tony with hugs, kisses and tears of delight.

Tony had a series of complaints that were barely covered by the lavish holiday season of 1922–23 that stretched well into Valentine's Day. Grandma Bridget got sick on some "bad water" and couldn't take him to Golden Gate Park to feed the birds; Grandma Alicia got sick when Stella left and was still too weak to buy him the toy auto she promised him; and Alec wouldn't read *The Voyages of Dr. Doolittle* to him, also as promised.

Alec had an excuse. He had been studying for midterms and moreover, according to his story, had read Tony two chapters the subsequent night. There was an unpleasant disagreement about this, since Tony insisted it was only one chapter. Randi was inclined to believe Alec but Steve defended his son. The quarrel left a bad taste in everyone's mouth . . .

Tony later claimed that Alec has also neglected to give him his penny allowance all Thanksgiving week. Alec swore that he had.

Randi told Steve, "The plain truth is that Tony has learned to tell fibs, and you and Red encourage him by laughing. It isn't at all funny."

Steve refused to believe it. "Don't tell me any son of mine is a thief."

"Not a thief, dear. To a child of four it isn't thievery. But he does tell fibs."

Steve found even the facts ridiculous, and became angry whenever Randi hinted at some imperfection in his son, who gazed up at him with wistful wonder and wanted to be "jus' like daddy."

Red Lombard likewise adored his younger grandson. He seemed a little in awe of Alec, but Tony, with his whimsical, big-eyed charm and his way of wheedling chocolates and chewing gum out of "my very own Grandpa Red" won him over every time.

And yet, the old father-son relationship between Steve and Alec seemed to have disappeared. Even Randi noticed the boy's abruptness toward Steve when they were together, and Alec seemed to go out of his way to avoid Steve's company. She knew that this was likely due to Steve's favoritism toward his own son, but Randi could see that Alec's behavior hurt and baffled his uncle.

THAT SPRING Alec became the youngest sophomore in his class at Cal. He was a young man who seemed to know exactly where he was going. When Berkeley got a radio station he spent every free period and most afternoons hanging around listening to announcers, acquiring a certain brisk, clear style that was curiously unlike the Alec Huntington they all knew. When once he was allowed to report Cal's spring track meet against its powerful rival St. Mary's, he electrified the fans by the excitement he was able to convey. . . .

By the time President Warren G. Harding began a speaking tour and cruise to Alaska, intending to return to Washington by train from San Francisco, an aide, Colonel Harry Macondray, wrote to Red Lombard assuring him that the president was hoping for a good poker game with "old Red" during his stopover in San Francisco.

*The madame isn't to know about the little poker meet. How about making it that suite I remember seeing in your Monarch Building, right opposite the Palace presidential suite? He can slip across in my suit and hat, or someone else's. But it's got to be when Florence is otherwise occupied. She's keeping a tight rein on poor Warren since she heard about a certain "lady-bird."*

*A word to the wise, Red. Don't listen to all the foul gossip being spread by Warren's political foes. Men like Borah and LaFollette and Walsh are looking to next year's elections. All that talk of graft in the Vet's Bureau is about as sound as the talk about the Teapot and Elk Hills oil belonging to "the people." Hell, aren't we people too?*

*Take my advice. Forget the gossip. Just remember who your friends are. And no matter what happens, as long as old Warren is in office, your investments are perfectly safe. The president is our shield. This talk of running V-P Coolidge instead of old Warren next year is dirty politics at a low level. Never in a million years would Coolidge ever cooperate with us the way Warren Harding has.*

It was the last paragraph that really impressed Red, and he showed it proudly to Randi and Steve.

*The president heard about your nephew recently through a U. of C. alumnus. Isn't Alec the U. of C. boy who made radio reports on sports, entertaining the alumni clear across the bay in Frisco? The president expressed an interest in meeting the boy when he's in your town. "Might go far in Republican politics," is how Warren put it precisely.*

*And, by the way, burn this letter.*

*With the best wishes of your old Comstock buddy, temporarily living high on the hog in Washington,*

*HARRY MACONDRAY*

Thanks to the paper value of Red's oil leases, he had left Steve far behind in the rating of most financial experts on Montgomery Street, popularly referred to as the Wall Street of the West. Buck Cortlandt had gotten in on the fringe of the Elk Hills leases, investing in the oil company whose officials were presidential cronies. Randi heard through the grapevine that he had even invested some of his son-in-law's money.

Only Sam Liversedge, with a typical banker's caution, held out, and Steve decided to follow suit, partly through a contrary streak, and partly because he shared Sam's belief that too much rested on the power and good will of one man, Warren Gamaliel Harding, who was himself in the power of so many others.

Randi knew that if her father-in-law was to save the fortune he had poured into his oil leases in Wyoming and thus protect the entire family's investment, she must help him. She was a little afraid of Steve's reaction. Much to her relief, however, Steve realized how important Red's investment was to their financial position. The failure of the Wyoming oil leases would have repercussions through the entire family.

"Go to it," Steve told Randi. "Old Warren, as Red calls him, may help to pay Red's share of our property taxes this year."

The president was due in San Francisco at the end of July. . . .

Unexpectedly, Dr. and Mrs. Nigel Ware and Eden, who had just turned twelve, arrived the week before President and Mrs. Harding were expected. Brooke and her family were bound for Europe and a belated honeymoon. Randi was anxious, knowing the poker party between Harding, Red, Harry Macondray and several others was to be secret, but fortunately the Wares were totally uninterested in the president's visit.

To Randi, Brooke's marriage appeared to be working out. Steve, knowing his sister all too well, was of a more cynical opinion.

"She's bored stiff. Wait and see. I only hope she doesn't run off with some Latin gigolo. Maybe I should write André to look out for the pair of them. He's sure to like Nigel. And young Eden is a likable kid. Even Alec looked twice at her. Too bad he's so stuffy around girls. Wait 'til Tony is a few years older. He'll be stealing girls right out from under Alec's nose."

"I certainly hope not," Randi said. Although Alec had made little effort to befriend Eden, Randi felt that Alec seemed more outgoing with Eden than with any girl his own age. Eden was surprisingly adult for a child of twelve, and Randi thought that except for her sense of humor, she was very much like Alec when he was her age.

Randi's thoughts turned to the idea of Brooke meeting André again.

"What if she still finds André attractive?" she asked Steve.

"André respects us all too much to let that happen. Besides, he made no moves when she was in Paris and practically alone. But he could certainly amuse Eden, and he's just soft-hearted enough about children to do it, too."

Randi said no more when Steve wrote André, but she had her doubts about the wisdom of bringing André and Brooke together again . . .

Meanwhile, Red Lombard had never been so popular. The governor, the mayor, the board of supervisors and almost every Republican in the predominantly Democratic city hovered around him, begging for an introduction to the president. The telephone in the Lombard house hardly ever stopped ringing.

The senior Mrs. Lombard had weakened shockingly during Steve and Randi's month in the islands. Her heart was not strong, and she complained of palpitations, but the doctors could do nothing beyond advising quiet and bed rest. The frail woman seemed deeply troubled but for some reason was kinder than ever to Randi and Bridget. Her relationship with her grandson Alec had become extraordinarily close.

One evening, while Randi was tucking her into bed, she said a curious thing. "My dear, we owe you so much. We can never repay you for the deep—"

Alec came in abruptly, cutting her off. He was there to give his grandmother her nightly kiss and Alicia held out her hands, one to the boy, one to Randi.

"Take care of the others, won't you? They are all strong in their way—Redmon, Stephen, Brooke and Tony—but they can break. You won't. Promise me you will never let them down."

Troubled and uncomfortable with this morbid talk, Randi was brusque. "Alicia dear, you are being silly. You know perfectly well there is no one stronger than Red. Unless it's Steve."

She caught Alec looking at her from across the bed.

"We promise, grandma," he said.

"And promise you will forgive them when they are weak or if they hurt you. They love you both very much."

"Well, of course we promise," Randi said and kissed Alicia's forehead.

Alec took the toy truck off the end of the bed where Tony had left it and examined the wooden wheels. He was obviously stalling.

"Alec?"

It seemed to Randi a long time before he looked down into his grandmother's faded eyes and spoke with great seriousness.

"I give you my word, grandmother. No matter what." Then he kissed her cheek.

Randi awoke several times that night and tiptoed into her mother-in-law's bedroom, but Alicia appeared to be sleeping comfortably, her face serene.

Randi couldn't shake her own peculiar dread, the sense of something hanging over the family, until her thoughts were occupied with quite different subjects.

Hilda Thorgerson stomped in to find her the next evening while Randi was discussing the menu for the president's private poker party with Colonel Harry Macondray.

"A telephone call, ma'am, from Hollywood. For you. I told him it was late. But he insisted. He's a real insisting man."

"Don't worry, Hilda. I'm not being discovered for movies. It's probably some friends we met in the islands." Randi felt flustered, but covered her nervousness with a smile. Ashamed of her own excitement, she took her time going downstairs. Though she was not aware of any personal affection toward the director with his one-track mind, she felt guilty without quite knowing why, and she took her time reaching for the phone.

As she had known all along, it was Leo Prysing.

"Mrs. Lombard? You sound tired."

"I don't know what time it is in Los Angeles, but here in San Francisco it's close to midnight."

"You are working too hard. You should have taken my advice. Write for Famous Players, and hire a housekeeper."

"I am quite happy with my job here, thank you."

He seemed determined to ignore her rebuff. "I would have called before, but I haven't had any news."

"Louella Parsons says you finished the picture," she ventured, hoping to sound professional.

"Far be it from me to contradict Lollipop. I finished. The *Golden Isles* has been cut, your titles remaining, and it was previewed this evening down in Strand. To resounding applause, I add with suitable modesty."

She felt breathless at the achievement . . . *Her* words would appear on the screen . . .

"I owe that to you, Leo."

"Quite true, and I am glad you perceive it. When are you coming back to your job?"

"Back? I've never been to Hollywood in my life."

"Who knows? The grapevine tells me your husband recently traded a lot and a building in Strand for thirty acres in Culver City. Perhaps he will take you down to inspect the rabbit holes and you can then come and visit the studio."

She laughed. "I'm afraid I have to refuse. You see, we will be rather busy entertaining President Harding."

"That should keep you occupied. Enjoy yourself. And take notes. I may want them later when I make a film about a private visit by the president of the United States." She heard his wicked chuckle. He added, "I'll pay you twenty-five dollars a title. Or—well, I might even buy the storyline. Whip one up in your spare time. Let your protagonist—"

"My what?"

"Your heroine fall in love with the president."

"What?"

"But being a loyal creature, she remains with her charming, totty-headed husband."

She slammed the receiver down and went upstairs to complete the menu with Colonel Macondray . . .

By the time Steve returned home from a lodge meeting, Randi was especially glad to see him. She could neither forget Leo Prysing's contemptuous remark nor could she forgive it—especially once Steve told her his news. "I traded one of the Strand properties. Did I tell you? I got to thinking about that Culver City thing, with the studios coming in there and all, and it looked like it might have a future. My God, I've been besieged all evening by this president business. Wait 'til I tell you."

Bridget, who was visiting Alicia Lombard to discuss a tatting and knitting sale for the benefit of San Francisco's proud new Opera Association, did not please either Red or Steve when she got her Irish dander up.

"You and your politics! It's glad I'll be when your precious president is on his way back to Washington."

"Ma, that's because you're a Democrat. You'd feel different if it was Governor Al Smith visiting the city."

Bridget admitted there was much truth in what Randi said. "So I will. And comes '24 I vote for the Wet candidate again. Anyway, I'm taking up Alicia's mail to her. Meanwhile, you Republicans run off and count the poker chips for your precious crony."

Downstairs Alec came in through the kitchen door and started up the back stairs. To Randi's surprise, Alec had changed courses at Cal, allowing him to take the Berkeley ferry at noon so that he could read to his grandmother in the afternoon. Randi was touched by his devotion, though she couldn't understand the depth of the bond between them.

Alec came running into the room.

"Aunt Randi, I missed the mailman. I usually get here in time. I—I like to read grandmother's mail to her."

"That's all right. Bridget brought up her letters. She's with her now."

He rushed upstairs to Alicia's room. Dumbfounded by his inexplicable behavior, Randi stared after him in wonder. What was the link between Alicia Lombard and Alec? Steve merely laughed at Randi's suspicions and teased that she was afraid Alec would get Tony's inheritance.

Her fears, though, had nothing to do with money.

ALEC CAME into his grandmother's bedroom just as Bridget was reading off the return addresses on Alicia's mail.

"A Lit-Lit'ry Digest . . . a *Saturday Evening Post,* a letter from the Opera Guild. Bet you they want money. As I live! A foreign stamp. Must be Brooke. Here's a funny one from L.A. The envelope's bigger. They wrote in pencil. They write as bad as me; so they do. What'll you have first?"

Alicia's fingers poked nervously at one of the letters in Bridget's hand. "You'll be wanting the fine, fancy foreign one, a'course," Bridget teased.

"No! Alec, the letter."

Her feelings hurt, Bridget surrendered the mail to Alec's outstretched hand. "I'm sure I didn't mean no harm."

"Gran—Bridget, I've been writing letters for grandmother since she's been feeling poorly. Could you come back in about half an hour?"

Bridget pulled her emerald green cloche hat further down around her face, and stalked out of the room. In the doorway she stopped briefly to fling back a startling challenge.

"Red says I can write real good. He says I could be real useful here helping Alicia. But if you don't want me seeing your mail, well—ta-ta." And she was gone.

Alicia Lombard nipped at the letters in his fist. "Is it from her? Is it about the child?"

Usually he opened the mail with care, using her ivory-handled letter opener, but today he ripped open the envelope. An enclosure fell out on the bedspread. Alicia picked up the postcard-sized Kodak snapshot as Alec began to read the penciled note.

"I can't make out the face. My glasses, dear."

He took the glasses from their case and helped her arrange the thin gold wires over her small ears. Then he bent his head over her shoulder and together they studied the photograph of Stella Burkett, looking a trifle older and neater, her black hair bobbed and crimped in a marcel wave. She looked handsome. Astonishingly enough, the baby had been set in an upturned tuba in front of Stella, apparently on a padding of baby blankets. She had her hands behind the baby's back, and the baby, grinning with delight and waving her small hands, did not look much like her mother. Alec thought her the prettiest child he had ever seen. She reminded him vaguely of someone, but he couldn't place the resemblance. He resented the threat this child posed to the family he loved, but tempered his hostility with the recognition that she was his cousin, related to him by blood. She was, after all, a Lombard. Her future would have to be his concern.

Alicia squinted at the snapshot. "These glasses are so unsatisfactory. I can't see it clearly. What do you think?"

"Looks like a regular baby, but I don't see uncle's—I don't see anyone else's features at all."

"Read the note to me." Alicia said.

The letter was simple.

*Dear Mrs. Lombard,*

*You said send you a snap of my baby, and here it is. The tuba means it was taken by my friend in the band at the new Alexandria Hotel where he works. This is real style here, let me tell you. Baby Heather and me, we got a little room at the back of the hotel. I'm maiding here temporary.*

*Hoping this finds you all well,*

*I remain,*
*Yours truly,*
*Stella Burkett*

They were silent for a moment or so. Alicia asked finally, "Well, what do you think? Isn't it strange that Burkett never hints at any connection with us?"

"She promised she wouldn't. And grandmother, the two hundred dollars you sent her away with would cover her medical expenses and then some. Maybe she is grateful."

She sighed. "It appears to be something we will never know. Alec?" He had been studying the letter as if he hoped to find something written between the lines of her childlike script.

"Yes, grandma."

"Will you think it odd if I tell you I am a little disappointed? A girl grandchild . . . and such a very pretty little girl . . . Heather Burkett . . . Heather Lombard . . ." She smiled weakly. "Well, let's have the rest of the mail."

# *Chapter Ten*

ONLY days before the Sunday that the presidential party's special train was due in the city from Seattle, the first rumors reached San Francisco. The president had suffered a severe "digestive upset," as the newspapers called it, the month before he set out on his strenuous tour. Then, on the way down from Alaska to Seattle, the president fell ill again.

"He's in bad shape," Steve told everyone. "They say he weighs fifty pounds too much. His blood pressure is high. He should be in a hospital, not in San Francisco playing poker."

Red waved aside all he heard as mere idle speculation.

"Propaganda. Colonel Macondray says he's never been better. Matter of fact, it's Florence. That damned wife of his is responsible. He wants to get free of the chains for just a few hours. Harry says he's looking forward to our little get-together in San Francisco."

Steve looked at Randi and shrugged.

Aware of Steve's deep-rooted jealousy of his father, Randi was inclined to think Steve had perhaps exaggerated the extent of the president's problems. Moreover, she had spent so much time preparing for both the poker game and the elegant Palace Hotel reception that she very much wanted to believe in the reality of the president's visit.

Matters took a turn for the worse, however, on that Sunday in July when President and Mrs. Harding arrived at the Palace Hotel on Market Street. They were surrounded instantly by those seeking to protect them, to ask favors or merely to catch a glimpse.

Mr. and Mrs. Stephen Lombard were introduced to the president and Mrs. Harding by Colonel Macondray in the busy lobby of the hotel. Warren Harding's jovial, handsome face—"the handsomest president in seventy-five years," he had been called—was sagging with weariness, and his familiar ruddy complexion had lost all its color. Randi noted how Florence Harding kept a worried eye on her husband during this draining public session.

Steve took pride in the fact that the president kept Red talking in the lobby long after the rest of the hangers-on had been shooed away.

"How do you like that, honey?" he said to Randi. "They're talking about making time for the poker game. The old man really is thick as thieves with the president of the United States."

"Thick as thieves," Randi repeated ironically. "Better not say that too loud. Not in this crowd of thieves."

She wasn't surprised to see Steve's shift of affection for his father. The Lombard men might be bitter rivals but they did stick together against the rest of the world. Besides, the pride of Red's Washington connections reflected on all the Lombards . . .

Steven frowned. He took her arm and piloted her out of the crowd. "We don't know anything for sure."

"We know the secretary of the interior resigned six months ago. We know the attorney general's assistant killed himself. And we know there is a senatorial investigation—"

One of the Secret Service men looked carefully at her as she and Steve passed, and she immediately shut up.

They crossed Market Street toward a basement German restaurant where they were to meet Bridget for lunch to tell her all about the president and his wife. Both of them were relieved to escape the tense atmosphere of the hotel.

"He does look sick, doesn't he? All these betrayals by his so-called friends have really torn him to pieces."

But Randi had something else in mind. "Is it true about the woman they call Nan Britton, his mistress, and the illegitimate child?"

He shrugged. "Who knows? Probably. It's just another sordid sidelight on the whole mess."

"Mrs. Harding looks rather formidable, but I'd bet she loves him. She really cares—I just know she does. It must kill her to know about that disgusting mistress. I'd divorce him so quick it would make his head spin."

"Would you?" He gave her a strange look.

She squeezed his hand and grinned. "Why not? You'd do the same to me."

He laughed nervously and, holding hands, they hustled down the steps to the *hofbrau.*

Bridget Gallegher held a table for them. With her was Alma Cortlandt Gault, who looked remarkably well, even to Randi's rather critical eye. Beautifully dressed in summer pongee and a straw hat, she gave Steve a warm smile and held out her cheek close enough for him to take the hint and kiss her. She coolly extended her hand to Randi.

"Now," Alma said quickly, "we're dying to hear about the president and Mrs. Harding. Is he as handsome as they say? And old Florence—does she really look like the side of a barn? Father and Edwin have an appointment with Red and that Colonel Macondray. I couldn't wait for them, so I just barged in here and joined dear Bridget to wait for *you.*" This last word was uttered with her eyes fixed on Steve, and Randi's hackles were further raised.

Steve was seated between Alma and Bridget and they immediately assailed him with questions about the First Family. He waved them off, diverting all their questions to Randi. Alma wasn't content with this, and persisted in her line of inquiry.

Randi turned and spoke to her mother.

"I hope Tony wasn't still pouting when you left."

"No. Behaving like the angel he is. Playing with his building blocks and his new gold wristwatch. Surely you'll not be finding a sweeter lamb than my little Tony." She lowered her voice. "You want some home-truths, my girl?"

Randi didn't but she held still anyway.

"Mary-Randal, if you was to spend more time with the boy he might behave himself."

"He is with me every day and most every evening. When he is six and goes to school he will learn the piano. Meanwhile, I'm teaching him to read 'Over the Garden Wall' and something called 'The Robber Kitten.' Naturally, he prefers 'The Robber Kitten.' "

"That's my grandson, so it is. But you'd ought to cater to him more. He's going to be a big, rich Lombard someday, what with no other children coming along but Alec."

"Heaven knows Alec will deserve his inheritance. He works hard enough at college, and even at home. I don't know what we'd do without him."

"You bet." Bridget put her head close to her daughter's. "He's got that sharp nose of his in everything. Trying to get poor little Tony's share of Alicia's money. Wait and see."

"Ma, I don't even know that Alicia has any money. Neither Steve nor Red ever mentions it."

"Mark me, she's got it. It just keeps building. They're thick as thieves, her and young Alec, wouldn't even let me read her mail to her. Threw me out the other day so's they could talk about secrets. In the mail."

Randi spoke brusquely. "Ma, you're an incurable gossip. Your imagination runs away with you sometimes."

"Don't you be saying I didn't warn you. And what's all this going on between you two, Stephen me boy? You and this colleen."

Alma blushed prettily. "You've found us out, Mrs. Gallegher. We had a wicked conversation about the worth of daddy's oil leases."

Everyone laughed.

They were joined half an hour later by Buck Cortlandt and his bland son-in-law and junior partner, Edwin Gault. Cortlandt was bound and determined to be invited to the presidential poker party and objected loudly when his son-in-law brought up the unwelcome subject of the president's health.

"He didn't look very spry to me, Buck. What did you think, Steve? Any chance this whole thing will collapse?"

The men looked at him angrily. "You mean the oil leases?" Cortlandt asked.

"No, no. The poker game."

"Oh, that. Possibly. But as long as old Warren is running things, we're safe. You saw them swarming around him today. They know who's still boss."

Randi gave Steve a side-glance. He was playing with his fork. Alma pursued him again. "What do you think, Stevie?"

He threw the fork down. "I wish I knew. Red is mortgaged to the hilt because he tied in with this administration."

"Who didn't?" Cortlandt put in. "And I'm not about to leave my little girl here penniless. I'll tell you that for sure."

RED LOMBARD came home early that evening with the bad news.

"Nobody's to see the president tonight. He's all tuckered out and went to bed. Something about his blood pressure being too high. That alongside of his weight. But old Warren will fool them. The colonel says he'll be sneaking out under his own steam by tomorrow night. Or next night for sure. We've got to be ready, no matter what night it is."

Randi sighed. This meant putting off the caterers, warning the bootlegger and making a new date for the hiring of a barman. Each plan had to be subject to change at the last minute. They had taken a police captain into their confidence and he promised that the Secret Service would not be informed until the very last minute so that the poker party could at least get started before they knew.

What made everything especially hard was the fact of Alicia Lombard's weakness. She seemed to be slipping away. Each day her fragility became more apparent, and now it seemed that she was just hanging on. Every breath became an effort and yet no one could do more than give her spoonfuls of liquid and beg her to eat the meager meals put before her on a cheerful tray. Yet Alicia did not seem unhappy. She appeared to live for the mail, and for Alec to read it to her.

Randi told Steve of her misgivings, and he agreed.

"I don't intend to go to this damned poker party. Not while mother is feeling so poorly."

Red too was upset, especially after Alicia told him she wanted him to go downtown and entertain the president.

It was nerve-wracking to set up the party every night and then have to cancel it. After the third postponement came the sudden alarming information that the president had developed pneumonia. While everyone sweated out the terror of a critically ill president, Red came home from the Palace Hotel to report that the first words the president spoke when he made his astonishing rally only hours later were, "Oh, I'm so tired," and then, "Tell Red—tomorrow. Certain."

Mrs. Harding, from whom the secret of the poker party had been kept, wasn't at all sure that the word "Red" was spoken but the story circulated anyway. By morning, Red and half of San Francisco were convinced. After waiting all night with Steve and Buck Cortlandt in the big, comfortable offices of the Monarch Building, the proposed setting of the infamous poker party, he was able to report that the sick president's words were "Tell Red—tomorrow. Certain."

Steve was the only one who seemed to find it preposterous to plan on a poker game with the president only just recovering from pneumonia.

"Don't you see, old boy?" Buck Cortlandt told Steve. "It doesn't matter whether we play or not. It's the fact that we're ready. His friends. He can trust us when everyone else he knows is hightailing it out of sight. When he gets back to D.C. he'll remember us. Because he can count on us, whether he gets over here to play or not."

Three days later, with the president still recovering, Colonel Macondray hurried across the street to the Monarch Building and reported to his friends. "He's sitting up. Swears he'll be on his feet tomorrow. Gave me a sly wink, and you know what that means. It's set for tomorrow night. Maybe not a party, but we'll see him somehow."

Once more, Randi arranged with caterers, barmen, police and the building superintendent. Since she would be the only woman present, she planned on inspecting the arrangements and then quietly vanishing into an adjoining room. There, with the door securely closed, she decided she would spend the time working on a tentative screen synopsis for Leo Prysing.

At the last minute that afternoon, however, she changed her mind. Despite Dr. Humphreys's reassurance, she did not like the way Alicia's pulse fluttered. Though the older woman insisted that she had suffered from palpitations all her life, Randi was haunted by a vision of her mother-in-law dying with only the servants around her.

"No problem that I can see," Alec said calmly. "I'm staying. I'll be in grandmother's room."

"Me too," Tony insisted. "I want to stay with gran."

Alicia ran her fingers along young Tony's profile.

"Let the boy stay. Alec will send him to bed when the time comes. And Thorgerson can sit with him." She smiled into Steve's troubled eyes. "My gossipy friend Bridget will be here. I had the nurse call her. She has a report on the stitchery sale. Now, will you take Mary-Randal off to meet the president of the United States?"

Steve's grin wavered but he finally gave in.

"I wouldn't go without her. Good night, dearest." He kissed her cheek, stroking her hand. "You will be all right?"

"Don't worry, my dear. Now, Randi—how stunning you look in russet taffeta. It won't wear well, but you musn't care about that. Speaking of which, you must wear my topaz set. The necklace and earrings, at least. Stephen, in my jewel case. Yes, they look lovely on you . . . Good night, daughter. Take care of them all."

Randi thanked and kissed her, hiding her tenderness and her fear for her mother-in-law's condition. She supposed that Alicia's words referred to the jewelry, or perhaps even to the poker party: "Take care of them," and promised that she would do so. Then she lifted Tony, who clung to her, pleading.

"Don't leave me, mommy. Take me with you." Great tears welled up in his eyes and trailed slowly down his cheeks.

"I'm coming back, sweetheart. Maybe sooner than you think, if grandpa's game doesn't come off."

Tony's tears stopped in mid-journey. "Grandpa says it will!" He made small fists. "It will, 'cause grandpa says so!"

They were all amused at that and none more so than Red himself, who had arrived to tell his wife all about the evening before him. "He's been sitting up for hours," he announced proudly. "We may have to go over to the Palace, but he's looking forward to seeing us tonight. The colonel says it will lift his spirits. Even old Florence may be let in on it."

Steve didn't like the sound of this, as he confided to Randi a few minutes later. "It's clear the original plan is off. All this stuff about meeting Harding in his suite. Nobody's going to stand for *that.*"

"But it certainly won't hurt your father's credit in Washington. The president will remember how Red Lombard tried to ease the pressure on him."

Red wanted to hire a limousine to drive them down to the Monarch Building in secret, but fortunately Steve talked him out of it, and drove them downtown himself. They made their way up to Red's suite across from the Palace Hotel.

Although Randi was convinced that it would be useless to order the preparations carried out, Red tramped back and forth, insisting they must be ready for any contingency. When Buck Cortlandt, Edwin Gault, a supervisor and the captain of detectives arrived, they reported that the Secret Service knew all their identities and were keeping a close watch on their windows.

And so Red gave up his last hope for the poker party. When the caterers' iced trays arrived, the group began to nibble, and Randi watched the whole fiasco with barely concealed amusement. Even if the president did arrive now, the food was a mess. All the patés and meringued delicacies had been attacked, including the mayonnaise on aspic that spelled out *Harding in '24*.

No one would have time to get drunk, but by seven o'clock the alcohol was brought out to cheer up the disappointed men. Suddenly, a knock on the outer office door surprised everyone. Colonel Macondray rushed in breathlessly, and they could see a stony-faced man in plainclothes peering in at them from the hall.

"Secret Service," the colonel hissed. "I came over with a little message from The Man. Can't see you tonight." A groan went up. "But he's rallied wonderfully and the missus thinks he might like seeing Red for a few minutes. I gave her that new *Saturday Evening Post* article by Sam Blythe, the political analyst. Praises Warren to the skies. Florence is going to read it to him, and if that don't get him going, nothing will. Steve, you and your missus get your coats on and come over with Red. You'll have to wait in an anteroom but at least Red will be able to have a few minutes' talk with the president."

Well aware that the others were scowling, the colonel's pink face turned redder in his excitement. "Warren's going to reassure Red that all your investments are secure. Soon as Warren gets back to Washington we're going to go to work and squash those damned investigations. A little pressure on some sensitive spots ought to do it."

Disappointed as they were, the men who were not invited over to the Palace Hotel knew that Red spoke for them all, that if the president promised Red things would come out all right, they would all make a killing on their oil investments.

Cortlandt reached up and slapped Red on the back, but his eyes were cold.

"You'll probably get some kind of promise from him, old man. Something so we'll know he's using the weight of his office for the men that put him in there. He owes us that."

"He knows, gentlemen, the president knows," Colonel Macondray said rather severely.

Everyone tensed with the awareness of the seriousness of what was at hand—millions of dollars of private income—and wished Red Lombard good luck. Led by Colonel Macondray, he left the building accompanied by Steve and Randi.

As they strolled through the long hotel concourse, with hundreds of eyes upon them, Steve whispered, "They're staring at you, sweetheart. You never looked better."

Randi managed to keep a cool smile on her lips but she felt like jelly inside. There was something eerie about this whole business, she thought, something about the idea that they were hounding a sick man in order to save the illegal investments of a few rich men . . . She murmured her doubts to Steve.

"You miss the point, Randi. They all had a chance to get in on the ground floor. Red and Buck were just more willing to take a chance. They invested their own money, didn't they?"

It seemed to make sense, and for a few minutes she almost believed it . . . .

An elevator had been specially held for them. Nearby she could hear the clatter of china, silver and stemmed glasses, the voices of diners in the spacious Palm Court. She wished she and Steve were in there instead.

Getting out of the elevator, they were escorted to a large sitting room overlooking the busy evening traffic of Market Street. Randi remembered her honeymoon night with Steve, and she turned to him with her eyes sparkling.

"What are you thinking about, Steve?"

He shook his head, tapped his fingertips on the long window. "I wonder how much that little fellow has invested in the leases and the drilling plans."

"Who?" The conversation wasn't turning out quite as she had hoped.

"Eddie Gault. Do you suppose that it is really a happy marriage? He doesn't seem her type at all."

This time she didn't have to ask whom he was talking about. "Maybe she loves him."

"Ha!" It was an eloquent answer to her cool remark.

The door to the next room was ajar. A man was softly singing "Ain't Gonna Rain No Mo'." Long afterward, whenever Randi heard the song, she would always be overwhelmed by a sense of foreboding and dread . . .

They could hear Red Lombard in the hall, evidently being escorted into or out of the room next door, where Mrs. Harding was reading to the President the *Post* article, "A Calm View of a Calm Man."

Randi took a deep breath and looked down at her new birthday wristwatch, a beautiful little hexagon engraved with lines like tendrils of gold. It was 7:35. Soon the evening would be over and they could return home. She was uneasy about Alicia.

Just then a door slammed down the hall. A woman's voice, shrill with terror, reached them two rooms away.

"Call a doctor! Call Dr. Boone!"

Steve threw the hall door open with Randi looking over his shoulder. His face went white.

"That's Mrs. Harding's voice. Something has happened."

Men and women filled the hall, and a Secret Service man reached over and slammed the door in Steve's face. Seconds later Steve opened it again, and Randi noticed that his hands shook. She put her hand on his.

"He must have had a relapse. I hope Red hadn't already gone in."

He shook his head. "He's still down the hall."

"Thank God for that."

It seemed an eternity before order was established. Randi heard a loud voice in the next room talking on the phone.

"Well, find him and get him up here. Dr. Ray Lyman Wilbur. And especially the surgeon general. My God, what a disaster!"

Colonel Macondray came to the door with Red and left him there with Steve and Randi. Red had never seemed so unraveled.

"I wasn't going—going in. Just waiting outside the door like they said 'til she finished reading. She ran right past me—didn't know me. She—" He stumbled to a chair and covered his face with both hands.

The colonel spoke quietly to Steve.

"The president has been stricken. It happened like a bolt of lightning. I want you to promise me you will say nothing when you leave here."

"Certainly. Tell us what to do." Randi was proud of Steve's cool-headed response.

"Leave by the regular elevators. Mingle with the diners and the others down in the lobby. And for God's sake, don't speak to the press. Or anyone else."

"Very well. Can you tell me one thing?"

"His heart has stopped. All the vital signs . . ." For the first time the colonel's voice failed him. "My old friend is gone."

Red raised his head. "I don't believe it. He can't be *dead.* What will I say to all those friends of mine who invested on my word? On *your* word, Harry."

Randi was astonished at Red's callousness, but the colonel merely waved the words away.

"Maybe the next administration."

"Not old Calvin Coolidge. If he gets in, we're all sunk."

Steve spoke. "Colonel, with your permission, we will leave by a rear exit with my father. We will not see anyone."

The colonel nodded, wiped his forehead and hurried back into the now-crowded room off the president's suite. Steve startled Randi when he grabbed his father's lapels in both hands.

"Father, we say nothing. To anyone. If you have any hope of saving anything from all this, you'll keep quiet."

Red drew back, resenting Steve's admonishment. But he knew he was beaten and, wordlessly, he agreed.

There was so much activity going on around the hotel that no one paid any attention to the Lombards making their way out past the pantries and storerooms.

They drove home with very little discussion. Red was stunned. Steve and Randi were both alarmed about what was in store . . . The whole country would soon be in mourning, with Red Lombard grieving perhaps more than the rest. Three-quarters of his fortune went down the drain with President Harding's death. . . .

The minute they got inside the house on Nob Hill they heard the phone ringing.

"Nothing but ring-ring-ring, the last hour. They all want Mr. Red," Hilda Thorgerson muttered.

"You take it, Steve. Tell them—God knows what."

Randi was removing her gloves as she went up the stairs with Hilda. "How is my mother-in-law?"

"Been dozing off, that nurse-woman says. Mrs. Gallegher went home a few minutes ago. Said Mrs. Lombard was feeling fine but a mite tired. Mr. Alec is doing his homework in Mrs. Lombard's room."

"And Tony?"

"Little rascal wouldn't stay in bed 'til I told him I'd swat him good and proper." She chuckled. "So we made a deal. I told him all about me and my sisters when we were kids on the farm in Minnesota. That put the little rascal to sleep."

Tony turned over in bed and, seeing his mother, gave her his angelic smile.

"I was a good boy all night. Alec was nasty. Alec wouldn't let me get on gran's bed."

"And he was very right, darling. If you got on her bed you might disturb grandma."

He ignored this as his eyes closed. She kissed him, straightened the covers and left the room with the door ajar so she might hear him if he called out.

She found Steve outside his mother's door. The tension of the evening showed in his face.

"How is she? Have you told her?" Randi asked.

"God, no! I warned father not to. He's in with her now." He removed his topcoat and loosened his stiff collar. "Randi, it's going to be bad. I remember when McKinley died, the awful panic. The depression of spirit everyone felt."

"The president is definitely dead then?"

"I'm afraid so. That was the mayor on the phone. Seems to have been very sudden. A blood clot, Dr. Wilbur thinks. The surgeon general agrees."

"But darling, this is different from McKinley. President Harding wasn't murdered, and besides—" She saw his face. "Steve! Surely there is no question!"

He threw down his bow tie. "Actually, no. But some of the doctors are asking for an autopsy." She gasped. "Only to find out the exact cause of death."

She felt weak. As if to recover her common sense she began to pick up after Steve.

"Anyway the autopsy should satisfy them," she said. "Tony is fine, by the way. He says he's been a good boy."

"I should go and say good night to him. Sweetheart, could you stick your head in mother's room after a few minutes—I don't want father upsetting her."

He started down the hall, and she looked after him anxiously.

"Steve, the autopsy *will* satisfy any gossip, won't it?"

He gave her a quick look over his shoulder.

"We'll never know. Mrs. Harding is refusing permission."

Well, she thought, all those doctors must know what had happened . . . She peeked in at Alicia Lombard lying against her pillows, smiling at her husband. Alicia saw Randi and with an effort, raised her voice.

"Quite all right, dear. Alec is going to bed too. Yes, you are, Alec. Our little talk. Remember."

Alec understood. He kissed her with a gentleness he saved for her only.

"Run along, child. The nurse will be in and out all night. And . . . Mary-Randal?"

Randi looked in again.

Alicia tapped one finger on her husband's grizzled head. "Take this dear boy and put him to bed. Good night, my daughter."

"Good night, dearest," Randi said. "Sleep well. Red? Alec? Are you coming?"

They followed her, obedient and tired.

THE WORLD knew that night as the evening President Harding died, but for the Lombard family it was the night Alicia Caldwell Lombard slipped quietly away in her sleep.

# *Chapter Eleven*

BROOKE Lombard Ware grieved deeply over her mother's death, regretting that she hadn't been there to make things easier for her. Eden Ware and her father did their best to comfort Brooke when the cablegram came that August morning announcing Alicia Lombard's death. Brooke wanted to take the first ship home to New York, but she would not be able to make it home until after the burial. She chose Paris instead . . . .

Eden always suspected that it was Mrs. Lombard's will which made Brooke decide not to return to San Francisco to pay tribute at her mother's grave. Eden didn't blame her—it sounded awfully unfair.

Mrs. Lombard's husband Red received only five thousand dollars "because he has so magnificently earned his own way through his life." He had expected and badly needed the small fortune she had built up since receiving Red's ten-thousand-dollar dowry on their wedding day thirty-three years ago. She had wisely invested through the years, never telling anyone and never making any loans. No one ever suspected she was so well-off. Now her children Steve and Brooke received two thousand dollars each "and all her love." Randi received a similar amount and the injunction to "take care of my loved ones."

But the munificent sum of twenty thousand dollars was divided between her two grandchildren, Alexander and Anthony, with Steve as guardian of Tony's trust. Alec was to handle his own inheritance on his eighteenth birthday.

Most mysterious of all, Mrs. Lombard's remaining ten thousand dollars in stocks and municipal bonds was also left to Alec with the proviso that "he shall administer it to certain charities we have discussed, as he sees fit."

Whatever that meant, they all wondered.

Brooke summed it up to her husband neatly. "I'd sue to be made Alec's guardian if I weren't afraid he knows more than I do about handling whatever he gets."

Red Lombard talked wildly of contesting the will. Then he threatened to move out of the house on Nob Hill because Steve refused to let him mortgage it again to pay for his enormous losses in the Teapot Dome fiasco. The government had now clamped down on the oil leases and Red had only one other way out . . .

He had always professed to despise Southern California, but several months after his wife's death he began to talk of going to live in Strand at the one property he still fully owned, the Monte Carlo Arms.

Hurt by her mother's will, Brooke stayed in Europe. In the end, as she wrote to Steve, there was nothing she could do. The tragedy was much greater for herself than for Steve, she said, because she had seen her mother so seldom the past year. She would light candles for her mother's soul, she promised.

Dr. Nigel Ware was perfectly willing to be shown postwar Europe, especially the Paris that Brooke knew so well. A man of independent means and vast Hawaiian territorial properties inherited from missionary ancestors, he could afford to pay their way deluxe—and Brooke expected it.

But it was clear to his wife and daughter when the new president came into office in Washington that Dr. Ware was relieved to find an excuse for returning to the Pacific a month early. His roots and his work on the island of Oahu constantly occupied his thoughts. His daughter, though, was more venturesome. She had loved Paris from the minute she and Brooke and her father arrived in the overdue boat train early one morning and walked out of the dark St. Lazare station to see Paris come alive with produce wagons and street sweepers in a golden summer dawn.

Twelve-year-old Eden listened with anticipation while her father and stepmother discussed whether she and Brooke might stay on for a month after he left, as the three of them had originally planned.

"I haven't taken your little girl to Switzerland, and we had such a short time in Germany last week," Brooke reminded her husband. "We owe it to Leo Prysing to at least visit his brother in Austria. Vienna, I think."

"No use going back to Germany. It's worse than Italy was. I'd rather we didn't get involved in all that misery. If they're not starving, they're rioting. And if they're not rioting, they're marching. We had enough of that in Rome." Dr. Ware was firm.

Seeing that things were going badly for her stepmother's argument, Eden worried that if they all sailed home they might never come back . . . How many people visited Europe twice in a lifetime? she asked herself. How many people got to meet a real French count as handsome as a movie star? . . . Meeting André de Grasse had been the greatest thrill in all of Europe. André had even shared their grief over the death of Brooke's mother.

Eden pleaded, "Daddy, could we stay just a little longer? I have heaps of places to see. All the theaters here, and in Berlin and Vienna and London. Daddy, I want to be an actress. A real live actress."

"Yes, honey, I know all about that. You wanted to be a movie star last year when you met poor Mrs. Prysing."

"Not a movie star, daddy. A legitimate actress."

"You'd be back to movies again if you met Lil Dagover or Pola Negri, or that smooth fellow you adored those three days in London."

"Herbert Marshall," Brooke put in, suddenly enlivened. "The London theater is so inspiring. Nigel, I do think Eden should be encouraged in her love of the arts. There isn't a great deal of that in Honolulu, you must admit. No one but Leo Prysing would be foolish enough to film in Hawaii, what with all the difficulties."

Dr. Ware had been on the verge of giving in, but all the talk about acting began to bother him.

"I suppose I've spoiled you, Eden honey. God knows, I want you to be happy. But no daughter of mine is going to be an actress. You're coming home with me on the *Aquitania.* A new administration in Washington means a lot of new rules and red tape in the islands."

"Why, for heaven's sake?" Brooke was very quick to ask. She and Eden exchanged anxious glances. Brooke fussed over the doctor's collar. "Darling, you talked me out of going home after mother died, so now, less than a month later, you want to rush us home. We haven't seen *any* of the museums yet."

Picking up her cue instantly, Eden clapped her hands.

"Daddy! I can't go home before I see the Rembrandt things and those lovely fat lady paintings in Belgium somewhere. And Spain. Daddy, you know you wanted me to see your beloved El Grecos and Goyas and stuff."

"We don't talk about Goyas as stuff." But as they left for Italy, he began to give in . . .

The family had barely arrived in Rome when street fighting broke out between Communist sympathizers and Mussolini's own black-shirted Fascisti. Dr. Ware publicly denounced them as "a bunch of chuckleheaded bullyboys."

Unfortunately, the concierge at their hotel, a fascist sympathizer, overheard their remark and it became necessary to leave town on the first train north. Their taxicab was delayed while they watched the new dictator march up the palace steps to an interview with Italy's diminutive King Victor Emmanuel III.

They barely arrived at the station in time to make the Paris Express. The porters had gone on a sympathy strike and the three were forced to trudge back and forth through the old station before they got their luggage loaded in the *forgon* of the train. After that, they couldn't get out of Italy fast enough.

By the time sailing day arrived, Dr. Ware had given in. His two ladies saw him off at the Gare St. Lazare, sorry to see him go and promising to be on the boat train in one month.

Two days later the Comte de Grasse arrived at their hotel suite facing the magnificent place de la Concorde to show them around Paris.

"I think Mademoiselle Eden will remember all her life that she once saw where the great Gertrude Stein lives. She is the patroness of young artists in many fields."

Brooke rolled her eyes, but Eden was thrilled.

"Could we go? Could we?" Her eyes shone with delight.

André looked at her with a warmth and tenderness not often seen in his face. But even young Eden could detect the tinge of melancholy behind the smile . . .

For Eden's benefit, they drove all over Paris on their way to the rue de Fleurus. Then the count crossed the river by the Concorde bridge, and was pointing out the silent, shuttered preserve of the St. Germain district. "It is the enclave of the oldest aristocracy. The Bourbonists. They despise the Orleanists. The Orleanists despise the Bonapartists. The Bonapartists despise the Bourbonists. Back to checkmate."

Eden giggled. It was so grown-up, she thought, to hear sophisticated conversation like this. But Brooke seemed bored and, apparently finding the weather unseasonably cool, huddled nearer André de Grasse.

The vast, impressive Luxembourg Gardens loomed up. Eden leaned out the back window and pointed to the row of aging dark statues of the queens of France. All around the statues were children playing. Pigeons strutted along the pebbled paths.

"They wish they were us," Eden cried.

"Who?" André asked.

"All those statues, those queens. They want to be alive, like us. Living and feeling things."

André reached back and patted Eden's shoulder. "You are a profound young lady. I shall call you Wise One."

Eden blushed with pleasure. Being admired was delightful, she thought.

"Aren't we near Gertrude Stein's atelier by this time?" Brooke asked. "We might as well get it over with. We aren't going in, are we?"

"We are not, *chèrie*. We are not invited."

He started the car again. They drove around the big park while Eden marveled at the sights. However, she insisted that the long, gray palace of the Luxembourg looked just like a prison.

"So it was, during the revolution. Now it is merely a prison for the lawgivers while they are promulgating their great laws."

The car stopped in a small, unfriendly looking street. Brooke looked over the view.

"I must say, I find Barbizon a lot prettier."

André winked at Eden. "Artists come here. And then they become famous. Madame Stein has the touch. She is lucky for them. It is the same with writers. You know the Englishman, Ford Madox Ford. The young Americans. A Spaniard, Pablo Picasso—a painter. There. Two young men coming out. Who knows? Another Scott Fitzgerald. I understand he is the rage in America now. They could be anybody. But one thing I do know. They will be famous."

Leaving the atelier as they watched was a tall, powerful-looking fellow with a dark mustache and abundant dark hair. The man opened the gates and, with a nod in Brooke's direction, walked away. . . .

Five years later, when he was the talk of Paris, Eden would always insist that it was Ernest Hemingway she had seen before he was famous.

# *Chapter Twelve*

TWO weeks later, Brooke went out one night to the Folies Bergère with some friends, leaving Eden to order her dinner from room service. It was the first time Eden had been left completely alone in Paris, and she was both scared and thrilled. Tonight, she decided, she would have a real adventure . . .

She put on her most grown-up dress, a georgette blouse with a box-pleated, plaid taffeta skirt, and a velveteen jacket of a bluish green that matched one of the colors in her skirt. Fortunately, her braids had been cut short so that her hair curled in a halo around her head. It wasn't quite a movie star's look, but it would have to do, she told herself.

She took a deep breath as she walked out of the hotel's elegant glass doors and found the fountains, the obelisque, the grandeur of the place de la Concorde lying before her. On the far left the Tuileries gardens lay in shadow, and on the right were the first great trees of the Champs-Elysées.

A movie star would certainly take a taxi, she thought, so with ten sous in her hand she airily told the doorman, "I'd like a taxi, *s'il vous plaît.*"

The doorman helped her into the high-roofed black cab, accepted his tip and saluted her. She felt much more sure of herself after that.

"I would like to go to Montmartre, *s'il vous plaît.*"

The driver didn't understand, and she had to repeat herself. He finally got the drift but asked if she wanted the "butte" or the "rue de Montmartre."

After a failed attempt to make themselves understood, the driver said, *"Eh bien, la butte,"* and off they chugged.

Eventually, they drove past the place de Clichy where, long after dark, people were buying one silver fish, a small cardboard boat of mayonnaise, slices of ham so thin you could almost see through them. She was still looking back at the little shops of the place de Clichy when the taxi climbed another unknown street and she saw on the horizon for the first time the highest white dome of Sacré-Coeur Cathedral.

She tapped on the cabdriver's shoulder. "Let me out," she said and opened her handbag. She took out the change purse her father had given her and handed him the silver francs one at a time.

Eden saw at once that all the cafés on this curving street were open to passersby. Most of the men, usually seated out on the *terrasses* in front of the cafés, had now moved inside. The autumn night was cool, but a few remained, still drinking pretty colored drinks, thick, sweet and strong, as Eden knew, having sampled them. These men, and an occasional woman, watched her walk past.

She found the great white dome of Sacré-Coeur looming up behind the noisy cafés, then walked out of a narrow street into a bright square full of lights. There was a sidewalk café in the middle of the square, and everyone seemed to be having a marvelous time.

Eden hitched up her skirt, cleared her throat and marched into the center of the café tables. Then she saw a man with an Adolphe Menjou mustache staring at her and hesitated. He said something to another elderly man and both turned to look as she retreated toward a small table for two at the edge of the café area. She was beginning to regret having come, but it was too late now, and so she must be brave.

As she sat down in a chair which she thought was rather like an ice-cream parlor chair back home, it slid along the cobblestones and she barely recovered the chair—and her poise—before the waiter came up and flicked a wine-stained towel over the dusty little table. He asked her something in a bored voice.

Taking care not to look up at him, she said haughtily, *"Citron pressé, s'il vous plaît."*

The waiter seemed to think this an odd order for eight o'clock at night, but he left her alone. A trifle relieved, Eden settled in her chair, assuming a sophisticated pose, and watched the strollers passing near her table. Most of them were in pairs, which didn't impress her very much.

"I'd as soon be alone," she thought. "Then I could pretend to be

Norma Talmadge, aloof and sad, having given up my love to save my kingdom."

She became aware of someone breathing heavily at her shoulder. She glanced up and was startled to see the man with the Menjou mustache. He rattled off a lot of French in a hushed whisper.

In her nervousness she stammered "P-please, I can't understand you. Talk English." She started to get up. He went on rattling, shaking his head. Panic-stricken, she contradicted herself. "No. Don't talk English. Don't talk to me. I don't speak to strangers. Go away."

Adding to her terror, the man's stout companion arrived. The two stood there, blocking her means of escape. They poured forth another torrent of French. She turned away, thinking she might jump up and join all those strollers passing so close to her.

Then she saw him across the square . . . The Comte de Grasse. He was about to enter a restaurant with a lady companion. She was blonde, with an extraordinary amount of makeup, and seemed to Eden to be overdressed for a comfortable district like this. Eden had never seen such high heels. The woman *must* be an actress, she thought.

Eden leaped up and yelled, waving her arm.

"André!"

She had to call him twice before he turned, left the lady and ran over to Eden, who stepped over the low barrier and ran to him. With eyebrows raised, he received her embrace.

"May one ask what you are doing up here, Wise One? And where is the *belle-mere?*"

"Belle—?"

"Stepmother."

"She and some friends went to the Follies."

"Do you tell me you are up in Montmartre completely alone? She does not know, surely?"

He seemed as shocked as her father would have been, and it took some of the romance away from her adventure.

"No. I came in a taxicab. I didn't have the least trouble. Until those two—oh, golly! They're coming!"

Sure enough, the two men huffed and puffed up to André and began to babble in French again. When they finished they marched off indignantly.

André burst out laughing. "Your seducers were a Sorbonne professor with a daughter your age, and a highly respectable banker with seven children. They were trying to send you home to your parents where you should be, they said. And they were right."

She had never been so humiliated.

He must have guessed it. He looked into her face with a winning and all too rare smile.

"Have you eaten dinner?"

She shook her head. She was determined not to cry but couldn't trust her voice.

"Well then, you will be my guest at dinner. Now, you must stop frowning. It will give you many wrinkles and then you will truly be the old wise one."

She laughed, then reminded him that he already had a date. The woman stood beside the restaurant's glass-and-timber door, tapping her foot impatiently, throwing unfriendly glances at Eden.

"True," André agreed. He looked at Eden, then at the lady, then back again. He sighed. "No. I would never be forgiven . . . Wait here."

He walked over to the blonde woman. They spoke first in low tones, and then the woman's voice grew louder. André slipped something to her. She stuck the money into her beaded bag, gave Eden a final unpleasant look and tottered off in her high heels.

She watched the blonde walk away until she vanished among the strollers. *I think I could imitate that walk,* she told herself. There was a little of Brooke's walk in the woman's hips.

Eden looked up at André admiringly. "You *are* sophisticated. Was she a real harlot?"

Andrew almost tripped over a cobblestone.

"My dear child, never use that word. It doesn't become a young lady."

"I'm sorry, André. Really I am," she said, admonished.

They ate dinner in a café with an accordionist, and while Eden ate her onion soup and *vol au vent,* he questioned her about her life at home.

"Stephen is a good friend. It is strange that we do not see each other very often. But we remain friends. He is prospering, though his father, unfortunately, has had a severe loss. Something to do with oil land that did not properly belong to the drillers. It is a tragedy, because I think he needed his wife very much—and now she is gone."

Eden put her fork down. "It's awfully sad."

"I hope Stephen takes good care of his own wife. She is a rare woman."

"Randi? I like her, but she's hard to get to know. I never felt as if I knew her well." She broke off another piece of bread and buttered it thickly. "Do you?"

"Do I what?" His thoughts were far away.

"Really know Randi Lombard."

"Oh." He came out of his reverie. "Yes. I think I knew . . . She is a beautiful woman. Exciting in her way."

"Randi?" She would never have thought of Randi Lombard as exciting. She was kind and awfully capable, but she didn't need anyone. Eden found it intriguing that André de Grasse should make such claims for Uncle Steve's wife . . . Randi didn't seem André's type at all.

She changed the subject, but throughout the evening, while the accordion played haunting, romantic music, Eden kept bringing up the subject of Randi Lombard, just for the fun of it, to see if André really was interested in his friend's wife. It was hard to tell, she thought . . .

He behaved like a perfect gentleman to Eden, flirting with her when the woman who waited on them came around and asked if "Mademoiselle had everything she wished," and Eden wondered if the woman thought André was her sweetheart. What fun if she did!

He asked a lot of questions about the islands and about Eden's ambitions. He said he once had a little sister like her and his little sister wanted to be an actress, too. He was the only grown-up Eden had ever known who seemed to believe it was possible that Eden Ware, with her carrot-colored hair and plain face, could actually become an actress.

"Personality is everything," he reminded her. "Looks are unimportant. In the movies, it is pantomime, of course, and there must be grace. But you will have that. Indeed, I believe you have it now."

When he took her home to the hotel, he kissed Eden's hand with a sincerity that made her think he had truly enjoyed himself tonight.

André started to leave, then changed his mind. He took her hand again and brought her out to the sidewalk. Paris was before them, the river, the dark blue night.

"There you are," he said. "Think hard that one day it may all be yours. All those people walking, and those others in the automobiles going so fast to the theater. Will they know Eden Ware? You must make it happen. Then I will proudly boast that I was the first to discover Mademoiselle Eden Ware."

Several men and women in evening clothes turned to stare at them. André ignored them all, kissed the palm of her hand and walked rapidly away under the arches.

# *Chapter Thirteen*

ONCE Alicia Lombard's will had been probated and the contents distributed, with Tony's inheritance held in trust for his eighteenth birthday, Steve was willing to raise money on his Pacific Dunes properties in order to bail Red out in the Monarch Building and the Seattle warehouses. But Red, who never knew when to let well enough alone, pointed out that he needed a new mortgage on the Nob Hill house. In a fit of anger, Steve called off the entire deal.

Steve had never really believed that his father would ever walk out on the family. He had never quite stopped admiring the rugged man who saw his own father's fortunes ebb and flow, and who, during his youth, came up from the deep mines of the Comstock to buy choice properties along the Pacific Coast.

Steve knew that Randi did not hold Red's lifestyle or his business methods in high esteem. She was not comfortable with much of what Red stood for.

Red and Randi had almost nothing in common, except drive; yet Red could talk to Randi by the hour, reliving the old days of his youthful triumphs, boasting of the way he had laid them all at Alicia's feet. And Randi seemed to be the only one able to comfort him during those lost weeks after Alicia's death . . .

Unexpectedly one day, Steve came on the two of them in Alicia's room and was baffled by a side of his father he had never before seen.

Red was in a confessional mood. "It was the biggest surprise in my life when a girl like Alicia said she'd marry me. Her family were among the genuine First Families of Virginia. You know the type. It might have been the money I settled on her, but you see, I was getting something beautiful that I'd always wanted. And she came to love me. She was kind of delicate, you know, especially the last few years. And me being a lusty fellow—well, there was another woman once or twice back in the old days, but . . . You know how it is."

Randi's reaction took Steve by surprise. "Yes. I do understand. But you haven't seen these women lately?"

"Oh, Christ, no! To tell the truth, I'm not up to it. Used to rather enjoy that Burkett wench fussing over me. That's the extent of it." He buried his head in his hands, laughing a little at himself. "More mental than physical, if you want the truth. A bit of harmless flirting . . . Well, I won't go into it. But it's just as well it wasn't more than that. I wouldn't like that on my soul now with Alicia gone."

"What will you do now?"

Suddenly, Red became himself again. "Show up that son of mine in the market. In real estate. Politics. Whatever pops up. You know, girl, it's not the money. I'm broke now. But I'll get out of the hole. It's the winning. Winning is the one word I understand. Does it shock you that I can talk about profits with my Alicia gone?"

"I don't think so. Maybe because I know you so well."

He laughed. "I'll take that for a compliment. Hey, here's old Steve. Didn't mean to hold down the fort with your wife. I'll be on my way. Sam Liversedge doesn't think I can pull off another mortgage on the Guerneville property, so I'm going to prove him wrong. . . ."

Steve was not too surprised, then, when Randi stopped Red in the hallway the day he left for good. She kissed him and asked him to change his mind.

But Red continued to carry his three shabbiest suitcases out the front door. Flashes went off blindingly as a photographer from the Hearst *Examiner* got his picture.

"NOB HILL LOSES MOST COLORFUL DENIZEN" was the caption that later appeared. Red had milked his departure of all the pathos he could.

In the doorway little Tony had clung to his trouser legs sobbing. "Don't leave me, grandpa. Don't go! Gran went and never came back."

Randi tried to comfort Tony, but tears had started in her own eyes at his words.

Steve looked at his son and thought that if they had another child, Tony might not be so spoiled and so lonely. He and Randi had been trying for a long time now, but with no success. Alec, who might have been a help, had turned away . . .

Steve walked out to the big gates and opened them for his father.

"Red, you don't have to do this."

Red puffed himself up. "Since Alicia's death. I've known I was unwanted in this house. Please, boy, no apologies. The old build for the young. It was only—just for a minute there—I remembered the day I carried your mother across the threshold of that house. I built every inch of it to please her."

Steve lost all patience at that, knowing as he did that the Lombard house had been built by Mad Tony Lombard long before anyone had ever heard of Alicia Caldwell. He threw up his hands and without a good-bye or even a pat on the shoulder, he stalked back to the house.

Tony's fears had not lessened, and for the rest of the day he would follow either Randi or Steve around the house, terrified that they might disappear too. When Steve told Randi that Tony was too old to be carrying on like this, he was surprised to find that Randi, usually the strict disciplinarian, understood the boy's fears.

"I felt like that when pa died. I kept holding onto ma's skirts until she nearly tripped over me. She wasn't in too good a condition herself. But when she licked me, I figured things were back to normal."

Steve was not used to hearing her talk about her childhood. Caught by both pity and tenderness, he pulled her to him and held her close.

"Well, sweetheart, there's nothing like that ever coming your way again."

IT DID not promise to be a happy Christmas in the Lombard house that year. The family had hoped to coax Red back home for the occasion but he had either found friends to entertain him or was just being stubborn. Fortunately, Brooke and Eden came to San Francisco in mid-December to buy Christmas gifts, though they would be returning home by Christmas Eve to be with Dr. Ware.

So the Lombard family celebrated early that year.

It soon became clear to Steve that for the first time Alec was opening up to a girl. But he certainly didn't want the boy seducing a child of thirteen, as he warned him after Alec brought Eden home from a museum one day. Alec's response took him aback.

"I don't seduce children, Uncle Steve. Neither children nor servant girls."

"Good God! I hope not."

"As a matter of fact, Eden's quite intelligent in her own way. She wants to learn everything she can. She thinks it may help her in her career. She wants to be an actress."

Steve laughed. "Well, don't worry. She'll get over it."

"I don't think so," Alec said stiffly.

The family went down to the pier five days before Christmas to see the Wares off on their voyage home. Alec and Eden were so deep in a passionate argument over the relative merits of a new ballet which Eden had seen the year before in Paris, that they had to be forcibly separated, still arguing.

"How does he know so much?" Eden demanded while being marched up the gangplank by her amused stepmother. "He never even saw the dumb thing. He's only going by what some dumb critic said."

"But my dear boy is very bright," Brooke remarked with a sigh. "It's such a shame he doesn't want to come over for a visit. I see him so seldom. It worries me."

Eden explained. "He doesn't want to leave his classes or his radio. He does the university news five days a week."

"Which he prefers to his mother's company."

Steve and Randi spoke of the ties between the two children.

"Eden thinks she knows her own mind. But she is just the sort of girl who will have her heart broken by someone unsuitable," Randi said.

"Unsuitable! That's a snobbish word for you to use. It doesn't sound like you, Randi."

"I don't mean socially unsuitable. Suppose she falls into the hands of a man who makes her believe that nothing matters except pleasing him. A little sex appeal would do it. It's only human. And I don't want her to sacrifice that wonderful belief in herself that she has."

Steve laughed to cover his own uncertainty.

RED LOMBARD was lonely, and now that he was back on his feet, he was thinking more about his family. He had bought into a new radio concern, sold it at a three-hundred-percent profit and had then plunged into a new method of freezing vegetables. He invited the family down, ostensibly to visit him on his sixty-fourth birthday, but actually to discuss letting Steve in on the ground floor of a new deal which involved abandoned oil wells in Strand.

With the knowledge that most of his own properties were still wholly owned and that his portfolio was worth twice that of his father's, Steve agreed to go. He decided he would stop off in Los Angeles to see Leo Prysing about a land deal Prysing wanted to discuss with him.

Brooke and Eden were on their way to Paris for the Exposition, and would join Red's party. Steve and Randi had agreed to visit Leo Prysing's studio in Culver City as Leo's guests. Only Alec objected to the Los Angeles part of the trip.

"It's as if he didn't want us going near Los Angeles," Steve grumbled.

But when the family took the night train down to Southern California, ordering a drawing room plus a lower berth for Alec, he reluctantly went along.

The Alexandria Hotel on Spring Street in Los Angeles affected Randi the way Paris had affected Eden Ware. Its exterior did not have the solemn grandeur of San Francisco's hotels, but it was exciting, she thought, to walk into the plush lobby and see all the movie stars milling around.

Leo Prysing called on them in their two-bedroom suite only minutes after they settled in. But before Steve could express his annoyance, the director pulled out a map and pointed out the property he was interested in.

"It's mine, all right," Steve agreed. He hadn't liked the look of Prysing when he came in, all that unabashed power in his square, rough face, his knotted hands. It was hard to figure out what any woman would see in him, Steve thought, and wished Randi would not hang on Prysing's every word as if it were gospel.

"That's the land Leo told you about in Hawaii, Steve. The least you can do is sell it to him now," Randi said.

"At a suitable profit," Prysing's voice was brusque. "But that is up to our land baron here."

The door between the bedrooms opened, and Alec stuck his head in.

"Thought I'd look around downstairs."

"Don't go far," Randi called. "We're ordering up breakfast any minute. Maybe Leo will have a bite with us."

"I can't make it." Alec stopped. He seemed nervous. "I just remembered somebody who used to be in English class with me. She—he works in the hotel."

"Aha!" Leo observed when Alec had gone. "That young man has a mistress here."

Randi laughed. "Not Alec. He's very studious."

"Don't forget he's come into his money," Steve pointed out. "Gentlemen of eighteen may have interests we know nothing about."

Randi and the director laughed, but their interest was clearly on the business at hand.

"When are we going to visit your studio?" Randi asked.

"At once, if you like. As soon as you have eaten. Have we a deal, Stephen?"

Steve hesitated before answering. "We'll see. These are times to hold on. You said yourself that this Culver City is on the move."

"I've got to have that acreage. I've an option on a Washington Boulevard studio. We're going there now. Been closed for a year or two. The old owner died. You'd probably know him."

Steve brushed the remark aside. "Not me. I don't keep up with movie gossip."

"Well, I do," Randi said. "I think it's wonderful, your own studio. Are you going to produce your own pictures?"

Steve listened to them chatter away.

"Modest budget films, you understand, to absorb the overhead. And one very special film per year. My own. I am hiring good men to handle the others. But the special is mine . . . Would you like to write some of the storylines for the budget films? From scratch, as you say? Get your hand in?"

Before Randi could answer, Steve cut in. "Couldn't do that, Leo. My wife and I have made up our minds to enlarge the family. Tony is getting entirely too spoiled. Aren't you, old man? You need some responsibility."

The boy was delighted to be the center of attention and climbed into his father's lap.

"Will this affect the lines you are working on for *The Last Rifle?*" Prysing asked.

Randi looked at Steve oddly before she corrected the impression he had given.

"I'm not pregnant yet, for heaven's sake! We've just been thinking about it. Certainly, I'll finish *Last Rifle.* I think it's marvelous. If they had a Pulitzer Prize for movies, you would win it."

They rushed through breakfast and, with Alec in tow, were driven out to Leo Prysing's new studio.

It was a gray day and the approach to the heart of Culver City, a tiny enclave surrounded by Los Angeles, was an uninspiring sight. As they drove along Washington Boulevard, past vacant lots and general desolation, Steve wasn't too keen on the worth of his own property.

They turned in past the big iron gates which opened at the approach of Leo's Pierce-Arrow. Leo, sitting beside the chauffeur, saluted the old gateman and then began to point out two long buildings.

"Most of our shooting is done in the open. On any of these so-called streets," Leo explained. "But the westerns need those hills behind the back lot there. And that is where you come in, Stephen. A great part of that is your property."

The more excited Randi became, the more Steve determined not to sell.

"It's going to grow. It will be worth ten times the present price in ten years," Steve said.

"Then what about a lease giving me first right of refusal when you sell?"

Steve could make no objection to that. But he was uncomfortable with the idea of being tied to Leo Prysing through business. A lease would mean keeping up some kind of relationship between the two families, just when Steve would have liked to break those ties.

"I'M AFRAID we never divulge the addresses of our employees, sir," the hotel housekeeper told Alec.

Alec thought it probably wouldn't be too difficult to wheedle the information out of the old battle-ax. He raised his chin and looked down at her.

"Will you be so good as to contact Mrs. Burkett immediately and tell her Mr. Huntington must speak to her about the legacy?" He tossed one of his cards on the desk where she had been counting double damask napkins.

Obviously impressed, the housekeeper tried to save face by asking if he would step into the next room while she called Mrs. Burkett.

"Ask Mrs. Burkett to see me in my suite on the fifth floor."

"Certainly, Mr. Huntington. I'm sure she won't keep you waiting long. She is a very efficient young woman. We are thinking of promoting her to an assistant. Of course, any question of legacy—are we in danger of losing her?"

Alec turned and went back upstairs, relieved that the movie director had left with his guests, and considered his moves so far. He should have rented another room, he thought, for this all-important talk. But that seemed like a waste of money, considering the broadcasting salary he had lived on since Grandmother Alicia died. After the contents of the will were made known, he had returned the modest allowance Brooke had always provided him with, and it had been a tight squeeze until his eighteenth birthday . . .

Still, his ten thousand dollars in securities remained secure. He had not yet touched them, and when he did it would be to make wise investments. No buying on margin, like his grandfather, who had just written that he was picking up an unlisted company, Keester Radio, on margin. Alec had thought the old man was crazy but Red sold out at a profit. Still, Alec thought, it was too risky.

He didn't yet know why it was important to him to save his own money. He wanted only one thing in life, to be a broadcaster for a big-city station, talking about national affairs. But he sensed that his family's respect would come only from his following in the Lombards' footsteps . . .

A brisk, no-nonsense knock on the hall door jarred him. Nervous and trying not to show it, he strolled to the door.

She looked much the way she always had, in a green and white uniform with a black skirt, her dark hair piled high off her neck. She didn't look eager.

"You've grown some, Mr. Alec. You turned out real nice-looking. I never thought you would, somehow."

He ignored the dubious compliment. "I guess you know why I'm here."

"I kind of thought you would be looking me up. You being of age and all."

He made a little gesture, stepping aside for her to enter the room. She came in, not smiling, though he couldn't help feeling she was amused in her own strange way.

"Well, Mr. Alec, you're an honest boy. I figured that charity thing in your grandma's will was my Heather. My pa read about it in the *Chronicle* and let me know. He would've really turned handsprings if he'd known *who* that charity was."

"You've never told your folks?"

She looked surprised. "I give my word. They think Heather's daddy was Dobbie Yoast, my friend in the orchestra here."

"And he supports you now?"

"Who? Dobbie? Hell, no! Me and Heather, we're alone. He high-tailed it off to Arkansas with his orchestra. It's not easy, what I'm doing here. Six days a week of real elbow grease."

"I take it my grandmother's two hundred dollars went long ago."

"Some of it went for hospital expenses. My Heather was born in a real hospital. She was kind of special, I figured." She shrugged, and then looked at him hard. "I might as well tell you. Being honest and all. A longshoreman friend in Pedro gave me a hundred dollars last winter when Heather got the whooping cough and I was laid off for two months. Wouldn't you know? Everything piles up at once."

He was surprised by her apparent honesty. She sat down carefully on the couch. Her dark eyes studied his face so intently he felt uncomfortable.

"There may be a legacy for your daughter. You understand the importance of blood tests? It is somewhat new, but the courts rely upon matching types for matters of this kind." If the child was not actually a Lombard, this would tie up the woman's schemes for a while, he thought.

But she was ready. From her apron pocket she drew out two cards, slightly frayed but nevertheless official, from the Queen of Angels Hospital. He glanced at them. The official blood type of Heather Burkett: O-positive. The blood type of Stella Burkett: AB-negative.

Alec had hoped for more time. The San Francisco hospitals had told him that O-type blood was the most common. But he couldn't deny that Steve Lombard was the O-type, like his mother. Red and Brooke were A-positive. Alec tried to figure out how to stall for time so he could check this out more thoroughly.

"All the family still at the old house? Seems to me my pa said Mr. Lombard was thrown out, or something."

"Uncle Steve is still very much at home," he answered impatiently.

She had opened her mouth to say something, but stopped and smiled instead. Her expression made him uneasy.

"Glad to hear it. Must've been the senior Lombard that went. Where'd he go? I can't picture him straying far from the old house."

Alec knew better than to tell her. Though he believed her story of the struggle and the child's sickness, she might try to blackmail Red, he thought.

"After I've seen the child, I can make a better judgment. I have to go down to Strand for a week or so, but I can get away and come up to Los Angeles for an hour, maybe this week. Can you have the child here then?"

She grinned. "Say no more. She's right outside the door."

"Good God! You mean a two-year-old child is out there in the hall?"

"No. In the empty single next door. Right handy." She went to the door, came back almost before he could catch his breath, and in her arms was an enchanting girl-child, with large blue eyes of a shade Alec had heard Grandma Bridget call "Irish blue," whatever that meant. Heather's hair was a wheat color not too far off from Steve Lombard's hair.

He had one more card to play.

"You understand I've got to check the hospital and a few other places. Just to be sure you aren't bringing in some child on us."

She was patient to the end. "Sure. I'd be the same way. But honey-boy, you're going to find out that whatever I've said, I've never out-and-out lied to you or to your grandmother. Whatever you and Mrs. Lombard thought, it's your business. I never told you different. I'll be here at the hotel, me and my little Heather, hoping you'll help us."

She walked to the door, and the child looked over her shoulder at Alec. No getting around it—Heather Burkett had the Lombard charm. She held her tiny arms out to Alec, and it was all he could do to keep from hugging her.

In the doorway Stella Burkett stopped. "So you're going down to Strand. You folks have property down there, don't you?"

"My grandfather used to, but not any more," he answered, not wanting her to remember that Uncle Steve also owned seaside courts in the beach city. Then he realized he shouldn't have mentioned Strand at all.

Stella appeared to be uninterested. "Well, have a good time. 'Bye now."

He wasn't sure why, but he felt that in some way Stella Burkett had her own code of honor. She had never made trouble for Uncle Steve and Aunt Randi. He would turn over one-tenth of the money for Heather, with the proviso that the rest would be paid over a period of ten years if Stella Burkett signed a statement disclaiming any blood connection with the Lombards. That ought to scotch any possibility of her blackmailing the family.

Still, he wished he hadn't mentioned Strand to her.

# *BOOK THREE*

# 1926-1933

# *Chapter One*

FOR Randi Lombard, 1926 was the year in which her name appeared for the first time on the screen.

Leo Prysing was thoughtful enough to preview his first budget film, *Ashes of Desire,* in San Francisco at the small Casino Theater. Steve couldn't make it, because Leo Prysing had chosen to hold it the same night that Steve was to address the new officers in his Shrine order.

"It works out fine," Randi said after expressing her disappointment that Steve couldn't be there. "Now I won't have to spend the evening alone."

"With Tony and Alec?" Steve was edgy.

"Alec is practicing with his door locked. He's due for a tryout here in town at KHO. It's the biggest thing in his life."

"Funny kid. You notice how he avoids me?"

She denied it, but she had noticed. Alec had become a strange, solitary young man, and the only one who could break through his shell these days was little Eden Ware on her infrequent visits with Brooke.

"All I can say is, I wish to God I knew what I've done to put him off. Well, sweetheart, have a nice time. Don't let those Hollywood sheiks keep you and Tony out too late."

They kissed and he left her. He looked back from the hall to give her one of his flip salutes but she was anxiously trying to decide what to wear and didn't see him.

By the time she and Bridget escorted Tony to his first motion picture, Randi was shaking with nerves.

"I'm scared to death. Does it show?" she whispered.

"Not with that black lace outfit. Holy Mary! Is that your bare skin underneath?"

"Flesh-colored silk, ma. Makes me feel a little conspicuous." The August night was chilly, and she pulled her velvet coat close around her. But though the coat's big roll collar concealed the four-strand crystal necklace Steve had given her last Christmas, it did not conceal the sparkle of her crystal earrings. Scared or not, she couldn't help feeling that she was living up to Hollywood's image tonight.

Tony squeezed her gloved hand confidingly. "You're pretty, mommy."

Randi's cheeks were flushed with excitement.

"Thank you, sweetheart."

Customers were being turned away from the box office where a Sold Out sign had been hastily printed in pencil.

"See how popular you are?" Bridget pointed out. She was feeling like "Mrs. Astor herself" in her new, full-length squirrel fur coat and perky little hat with a quill stuck through it.

"They don't know I'm alive," Randi said. "It's the word 'Hollywood' that gets them. It will always be magic."

The theater manager proved her point by barring their entrance with a pompous flourish. "Afraid not, ladies. Every single seat is gone."

"Surely not every seat." Randi's voice purred with light irony. She took Leo Prysing's card from her black beaded evening bag. At the same time Tony chirped up proudly, "It's my mommy's show."

Whether it was Prysing's words on the card or Tony's boast, which made them all smile, the manager changed his tone at once and personally ushered them to their seats among the roped off rows in the center of the little theater.

Bridget whispered, "I sat right here watching the old Will King show. And that's legitimate."

The theater went dark. The audience buzzed and then hushed as the Leo Prysing logo blazed across the screen. A trickle of applause rose from the audience.

Randi suspected this was generated by the Prysing employees present, but it spread, and she almost laughed when Bridget and young Tony joined the applause. Prysing's name appeared almost continuously: "Leo Prysing Presents . . . a Leo Prysing Production . . . Producer, Leo Prysing . . ."

But three-quarters of the way down the credits came the line she had been waiting to see: "From a story and adaptation by M. R. Lombard" and then "Titles by M. R. Lombard."

To her embarrassment, Bridget and Tony applauded in the expectant hush. Randi wanted to sink through the floor, but she recovered when the film opened on a scene she had so often envisioned as she wrote it in the faded comfort of the back sunroom. While the actors pantomimed, Randi thought back to her first sight of Steve in the sunroom on the day the Great War ended. They had come a long way since then, she thought.

The scenes progressed, always punctuated by her careful, deeply thought-out lines that illustrated a disintegrating marriage. She began to feel extremely self-conscious and was relieved when an elegantly scrolled *Finis* flashed on the screen. The applause surprised and shook her out of her thoughts. Tony had fallen asleep during one of the love scenes and was still half-asleep when Randi led him out to the aisle after Bridget.

Public opinion seemed to be favorable. Almost all of them concerned the handsome leading man, but Randi told herself that he couldn't have won the audience without her story. She half-expected some flattering comments in the lobby, where the audience was gathered in clusters, buzzing about something. She had never seen such grim faces.

A stout, middle-aged woman in furs shrieked, "Oh, my God, no!"

An usherette moaned and swayed, barely caught by the ticket-taker before she collapsed.

There was pandemonium outside the theater. Bewildered, Bridget grabbed Randi's arm, and Randi was so relieved to see Leo Prysing standing in front of her that she threw her arms around him.

"Leo! Was it good? Did they like it? They're acting so funny."

He accepted her brief embrace with a tolerant smile.

"Come along. You three won't want to remain here. The place will soon be awash in tears and I do not swim well."

Mystified and somewhat troubled, Randi picked up Tony and followed Bridget and Prysing out to the street. He managed to hail a taxicab and herd them all into it within moments.

Bridget got in first, and took Tony on her lap while Randi stepped up on the running board after her. Taken by surprise, she found Leo's arms around her hips, boosting her into the car and then onto his lap.

"What—? Leo, can't you sit with the driver?"

"I thought you wanted me to tell you what the opinion of your script was, and why the public is plunged into mourning."

"Oh yes, of course." Randi found herself more anxious about the opinion of her work than the cause of the calamity. She tried to settle on the producer's lap.

"Tell us whichever you want, but don't keep us in suspense."

"Very well. Your film was a great success in its budgetary category. I have a contract somewhere in my topcoat. Two more stories. The price will escalate. If you sign."

Randi hugged him again. "I'll sign!"

But Bridget wanted to know, "What the hell does that mean, escalate?"

"Up, Mrs. Gallegher. Your daughter's price rises. Two hundred and fifty for the second storyline and three hundred for the third."

"We're rich!" Randi cried, dazed by her success. "Wait 'til I tell Steve."

Prysing's legs shifted under her. She started to rise but he pulled her back. "Only a leg cramp. There. Comfortable?"

"What was the crisis in there?" His question had made her uneasy.

"He is dead."

"Who?"

"Rudolph Valentino. Died in the hospital today. In New York. Complications from an appendicitis operation."

"Oh, my sainted mother!" Bridget cried. "Oh, that poor dear man! And so young, so handsome."

By the time the taxi reached Bridget's rooming house, Prysing had given them the details of the Valentino tragedy and Bridget tearfully made her way up to her rooms. Prysing then gave Randi's address to the cabdriver as Randi slid over into Bridget's place on the back seat.

"Turn the boy over to your servants," he ordered her as the cab ground its way up Nob Hill. "Remain in the cab."

"Why?" Resenting the idea, she was furious with herself for expecting it.

"I want to get your signature on that contract and I haven't much time. Must make my plane."

"Plane?"

She hadn't been in a plane since her terrifying flight on her honeymoon with André de Grasse, but Prysing took the whole thing calmly.

"Private flight by a friend of mine."

"At night?"

"Midnight." He laughed. "Life is full of danger. My brother Josef tells me he and Sarah were crossing the Kartnerstrasse the other day and almost got trampled by fifty fascists who were marching illegally in protest of something or other."

She was relieved he had changed the subject. "Good heavens! Were they hurt?"

"No, no. Nothing like that. The hoodlums—all in dead-black and jackboots, mind you—were jailed. But you see, we are all in danger every minute. Even crossing the street."

She took Tony into the house, delivering the sleepy boy to Hilda Thorgerson and returning to the cab. The cabbie unfolded a newspaper and began to read.

Randi got into the back seat. Prysing was businesslike, with a briefcase on his knees and several blue-backed, legal-sized pages fanned out for her signature. He handed her his heavy fountain pen.

"Read first," he directed her. "Never sign without reading first."

She held the original two pages up to the streetlight, pretended to skim through them, then initialed and signed at the lines he pointed out. He rolled the papers up, slipped a rubber band around them and stuck the roll in his briefcase.

"Now, then, that is out of the way."

She reached around to open the door but his hand closed hard on hers. He pulled her to him. Her angry and agitated "No!" was stifled by the brutal directness of his kiss. He had one hand behind the back of her head, holding her in a vise. She squirmed, hoping she wouldn't have to kick him.

His kiss was very much as she had imagined it would be, harsh, devouring, utterly sensual. She felt that she was being drawn into him, and when he abruptly let her go, she fell back against the door.

The cabbie's innocent concern was a perfect climax to the ridiculous scene.

"Hurt yourself, lady?"

"Certainly not," she said haughtily. She reached behind her for the door handle but Prysing moved past her and opened it. Before getting out, she spoke. "You've ruined everything. I can't work for you after this."

He leaned toward her with a light in his eyes.

"Don't be silly. We've only begun our partnership. Remember?" He waved the briefcase. "Anyway, I've wanted to kiss you since the day I first saw you on the deck of the *Mahala.* At the risk of sounding like one of your titles, I've been in love with you almost that long." Before she could protest he held up his free hand. "All right. I promise not to misbehave again until you give me your permission. How is that? Meanwhile, I have your signature and I mean to hold you to it. Again, congratulations on *Ashes of Desire.* Not bad for a first attempt. Driver, let's go."

Randi stamped up the walk, then stopped to pull herself together. She was a Lombard, she told herself, and not Bridget Gallegher's sensuous daughter.

# *Chapter Two*

EARLY the following morning Alec sat up, punched his pillow and gave up the fight. The nightmare was too near the surface. The minute he closed his eyes, it returned: his voice was scratchy, lumpy and far too boyish. He was trying too hard in his audition.

Relax, he told himself. There will be other tryouts. And I will be older. Next year I'll be twenty . . . When father was twenty he had only six more years to live . . . Six years. Where will I be then? . . .

He imagined his voice being heard over the airwaves from San Francisco to Los Angeles; Chicago to New York. But time was slipping by . . .

He got up, disgusted at his own weakness, and went out in the hall toward the bathroom, almost bumping into Uncle Steve. His top hat was perched on the back of his head and his white scarf dangled from one shoulder.

"So! Another night owl. You're growing up, boy."

"I was thirsty," Alec said gruffly.

Steve had been about to go into the bedroom, but he stopped and studied Alec with a look of sympathy which Alec resented.

"Worried about tomorrow's tryout? You needn't be. You'll do well."

"Thanks. I expect to. Good night, sir."

Steve laughed. "How old that makes me feel! Well, good night.

Maybe I'll go with you tomorrow. A word in the right direction can do wonders."

"Yes, sir." Alec resolved to be gone tomorrow morning long before Steve could come along and play the gallant hero.

Behind him he heard Steve open the door. "Still awake, sweetheart?"

"Come to bed, you noble Shriner, and tell me all about your evening."

"It went well, sweetheart. How was your movie? My God! Here I am yawning and it's only 3.00 A.M. I'm not as young as I once was."

"Come to bed, old man."

Alec shivered and went on to the bathroom. Returning to bed, he slept badly, dreaming about a beautiful woman who fell in love with him but seemed to float away out of reach, still stretching her arms out to him . . . He woke up sweating and angry, and not quite sure why.

It was after eight, and he had overslept. He left the house quickly and walked down Market Street to the Embarcadero, watching the ferryboats, smelling the roasted peanuts and the delicious local chowder served in great clam shells. He tried hard to think about anything but where he was going.

When Alec finally started walking up Mission Street toward the radio station he had convinced himself that he had nothing to lose. Braced for failure, he intended to give the audition everything he had. He got off the elevator on the third floor, found himself expected when he arrived in the dark room, its worn carpeting pockmarked with cigarette burns.

He glanced around at the complicated panels against the far wall and saw two faces staring at him behind a glass. So this was big-city broadcasting, he thought. When he was broadcasting the university news in Berkeley he had been surrounded by more glamor than this. Alec began to relax, and his confidence returned.

He kept one eye on the standing microphone across the room, nodded to the scrawny, bored fellow who asked, "You Huntington?" and walked over to the mike. Alec had expected the technicians' indifference so it didn't put him off. As he held the loose pages of his two scripts his hand was steady. But just as he stood in front of the big mike he heard a low-voiced exchange between two men at the back of the room. Alec squinted through the shadows to make out their faces. The men moved into his view and Alec felt as if ice water had been showered over him. Uncle Steve stood there, grinning encouragement.

"Okay." Steve's friend gave Alec the go-ahead.

Instantly, Alec became self-conscious.

He pulled himself together, and started out quickly, reading the eyewitness report he had made on the 1926 Rose Bowl game. As he read he tried not to see Uncle Steve, whose hands were raised, palms down, telling him to slow down. But it was a moment of triumph when the station manager beside Steve gave Alec the "okay" signal.

"Not bad. You pump up enthusiasm with that fast delivery. What else d'you have?"

Alec hesitated. He had recently taken all the information he could get from the press and the news magazines, and wove it into a piece about Gertrude Ederle's conquest of the English Channel. He began at a fast, clipped pace.

"All right, now. Remember, we've got to understand you. Or a lot of little old ladies out in radioland are going to be asking 'what'd he say?' "

Alec began again, hearing his voice clear and distinct but still with a note of excitement.

Before the mike was turned off, Steve applauded.

"What do you say, Hoot? Does he get the job or doesn't he?"

Alec groaned. But Hooter Baccagalupi came into the pool of light surrounding the mike and shook Alec's hand.

"Nice work. Let me show you something. Drop each sheet when you finish. The hell with where it goes. I heard a bit of a rattle here and there. Carry 'em loose, like you do, then let 'em go. And for God's sake, don't watch where they fall."

"Yes, sir."

"We can use you Saturdays on sports and who knows? There may be fifteen minutes you can fill now and then, after you get your feet wet. Start after Admission Day next month. What do you say? Write your own material?"

"Yes, sir. Or I ad-lib."

"Good." Baccagalupi grinned. "Incidentally, my alma mater was Stanford, so I wasn't too happy with the Notre Dame victory you rubbed my nose in." He nudged Steve. "Why couldn't he give me last year's big game when we finally trounced you Cal guys?"

Alec felt so good and so relieved after the tensions of the last twenty-four hours that he even welcomed his Uncle Steve's company as they drove back home.

"Wait 'til Red hears about this," Steve boasted. "He's going to be damned impressed. With radio growing so fast, he may hear your voice on a Coast hookup one of these days."

"Yeah . . ." Alec sank down in euphoria. "I guess grandpa must be pretty lonesome down there all by himself. I wish we could get him back home."

Steve laughed. "Not Red. The Monte Carlo Arms seems to be his home away from home. He talked to Randi on the phone this morning. Guess who he's hired as housekeeper to run that white elephant? An old acquaintance of ours."

Alec sat up. "Who?"

"Good old Stella Burkett. Remember her? Has a child with her, by the way. Stella seems to have been busy since she left us."

Alec was shocked at the callous indifference of a man who could talk this flippantly about his own daughter. "Is that all you can say?"

"I don't know. I didn't take the call. Red told Randi there had been a tuba player involved. Gone now. Anyway, Red is crazy about the baby. 'Little Heather,' he calls her. Says she's another Brooke. God forbid!" He remembered then that he was talking to Brooke's son and apologized. "Sorry, I didn't mean that the way it sounded. But he certainly spoiled Brooke, so we can expect the same for little Heather."

Alec caught his breath, remembering the enchanting little girl. "You can wash her out of your life like that? An innocent child, your own flesh and blood?"

"My *what?*"

"Watch out. You almost hit that jaywalker."

"The hell with the jaywalker! What's this about my flesh and blood? Is there something you know about Burkett's child?"

Alec couldn't believe his own ears. Rage and confusion tore at him. "Your child! Burkett said so." He was trying to think back . . . What exactly had Stella Burkett told him and Grandma Alicia? . . .

Steve's fingers tightened on the wheel but it was his incredulous laugh that made Alec wonder for the first time if they could have been wrong.

"Where the hell did you get that idea? I didn't even like the woman. I mean—not my type at all. Wait 'til I tell Randi. She'll have a fit."

"You can't tell Aunt Randi. She might divorce you."

"Not over Stella Burkett. My lad, you're dreaming. I never even touched the woman. I remember LeMass and I were discussing it one time. I caught them loving it up in the hall and LeMass asked me to keep quiet. Afraid he'd lose Bridget, of course."

"LeMass!"

"Could be."

The pieces began to fit. LeMass needed money from Grandma Bridget. He went off to Southern California—San Pedro, in fact. And

Stella went to Los Angeles. What had she said in the Alexandria Hotel?

*"I got money from a friend in Pedro when the baby had whooping cough."*

Steve was less angry than Alec might have expected. He seemed to find the whole story more ridiculous than offensive. "Well, Alec? What are you thinking?"

"I wish I knew LeMass's blood type."

"Bridget might know. He's been injured any number of times on the docks." Steve chuckled and shook his head. "So LeMass sired a daughter. Red says she's a beauty."

"She is."

It was a day of surprises for both of them. "You've seen her?" Steve asked with interest.

"At the Alexandria Hotel the day you and Aunt Randi went out to Mr. Prysing's new studio. Stella brought her to me."

"Well, I'll be damned!" A new idea banished some of Steve's humor. "Don't tell me she accused me. I'll bet she played on your sympathy. Got some money out of you."

With a sinking feeling Alec admitted the truth. "Yes. You could say that." Stella Burkett had already collected almost three thousand dollars, with another thousand on the way soon if he didn't stop it.

"Uncle, would you let me off at Grandma Bridget's?"

"Not only will I let you off, I'll personally go with you. I'd like to know if Bridget had any inkling of this, making me the heavy of the piece."

Bridget did not know, and was a good deal angrier than Steve had been. They caught her at home just as she was expecting a visit.

"From Mr. Liversedge, my banker. He has some idea of changing my portfolio."

Alec and Steve exchanged glances. Bridget Gallegher was doing very well these days. They were delighted, but they couldn't help being amused.

"Now then," she said, sweeping papers and a gin bottle off the round center table. "What's this about LeMass fathering a baby at his age? Blasted fool! I kicked him out for playing around, but I sure as hell didn't think it would be that Burkett wench. It all fits, though."

"About the blood type," Alec put in anxiously. Every minute he felt more guilty.

"That I couldn't say. He stuck his foot in a broken box of caustic soda once, but you don't need blood for that. What you need is a lot of new flesh. On the other hand . . ." She reached for the gin bottle, thought better of it and gave it to Alec to put in the china closet.

"Honest to God! You can't trust the best of 'em. LeMass come near losing his arm when some lumber slipped out of a sling back in '09. Laid up in Letterman Hospital for months on end . . . or on his back, as it happens."

She had an idea and went into the bedroom to rummage through her old keepsakes. She returned in triumph about five minutes later with a card from Letterman Hospital.

"Yep. I paid for the blood. Zero-plus, it was."

Steve looked at Alec. "That's Heather," he said. "She could've belonged to LeMass."

"Could have?" Steve asked. "Believe me boy, she does belong to LeMass. Don't get me involved with somebody like Stella Burkett. I've got to tell this to Randi."

Bridget looked up, and Alec noticed that her face looked suddenly tired. "Take my advice, Steve. Don't you be telling her. Matter of fact, I wish I didn't know. I used to love that man!"

# *Chapter Three*

LOOKING after her beautiful stepmother had become a full-time occupation for Eden Ware—and one that suited her own dreams of making her way in the great, unexplored world that waited for her.

As far as Eden could tell, Brooke had never been unfaithful to her husband, though she suspected it had been a near thing with André de Grasse. She liked to think it was his indifference that had prevented an affair. So Dr. Ware's betrayal came as a great shock.

"You can't run off to the Coast or New York or Europe every year and expect daddy to live alone," Eden explained to her outraged stepmother. "Not with a nice-looking woman like Tamiko in the house."

"But it's so humiliating," Brooke wailed. Two days later she sailed for the mainland to be comforted by her father while she considered a second divorce. "To find them together in Nigel's bed like that—well, I could see what they were doing. At their age, too!"

"I guess maybe it seems natural for the two of them because they're so used to each other after all these years."

Eden had been with Brooke that afternoon when they returned home from Honolulu earlier than they were expected, and she at first shared her stepmother's shock and disgust at the revelation of her father and Tamiko. Later, though, her father's straightforward, unembarrassed explanation had satisfied Eden . . . Dr. Ware loved Tamiko. He had realized his love for her many months ago, but he considered

Brooke helpless without the protection of a husband. He had known from the first that the marriage was a mistake; yet he had done nothing. Then, recently, his feelings and Tamiko's overcame their good intentions. Now that it was out in the open, he asked for a divorce so he could marry Tamiko. She was, he said, the kind of wife he had always needed . . .

Eden had one regret. "The difficulty is that Brooke is a perfect travel companion," she explained to Chiye, who wanted the divorce but nevertheless resented the shame brought upon her mother.

"How can you like her? She never thinks of anybody but herself. The only time she talks to me is to give me orders. Like I was a servant."

"That's because she's what they call new-rich," Eden explained from the height of her fifteen-plus years. "Daddy's family made their money almost a hundred years ago. It's different with us."

Chiye had been helping her friend pack for a trip to the Coast where Brooke hoped her father would talk her out of granting Nigel a divorce. Chiye stopped and looked at herself in Eden's mirror.

"I'm as good as that so-bright son of hers. I'm a lot prettier. And I'm just as smart. I'm no servant. She brags up her famous Alexander all the time, but I'll be teaching Japanese next year. Can he say that?"

"No, Chiye, but let's not be mean about Alec. I like him."

Chiye looked back at her own reflection. She wrinkled her nose at Eden's reflection beside her. "After all our talk about going out and capturing the world, you'll go and get married."

"To Alec? Don't be silly. He's my friend. I'm going to have lovers—wonderful Frenchmen, or whoever turns up—and never get married. Great actresses don't have to."

"You're as selfish as she is. You go traveling with that woman and she'll steal all your lovers."

Eden brushed this aside. "We don't attract the same kind of men." She considered. "Although, once in Paris, when I was twelve, I have a sneaky feeling I might have stolen somebody she had a crush on. So there!"

"At twelve?"

"It wasn't love, silly. He just kind of protected me. He said I'd be famous some day."

"Doesn't sound very romantic to me."

Eden smiled at the memory . . .

Two days later she and Brooke sailed for Los Angeles.

At breakfast, they walked in on Red Lombard being waited on by Stella Burkett. He announced that Burkett was now official housekeeper of the Monte Carlo Arms.

"I took her in, poor creature. She has a baby. Cute little girl. Her lover must have deserted her, the bastard!"

"And of course you took her in, pa. It doesn't sound like you, somehow, you old dear." But he embraced his daughter and was not at all offended by her remark.

"Now, you don't mean that. I've got a heart as big as all outdoors."

Brooke laughed in disbelief and nodded cordially at her onetime housemaid. But later, she complained to Eden as they were unpacking. "Pa is never going to see my side of things when he's doing the same thing with his housekeeper."

"We don't know he is, Brooke. Your father is awfully old for—things like that."

As it happened, Red supported his daughter.

"Divorce him, little girl. And get all you can. Anybody that makes a monkey of my kid deserves to be taken. Sorry, Eden. But you've got to admit your pa didn't behave like any gentleman."

Brooke wept a little, careful not to let her mascara run. She reached for Eden's hand.

"I'm filing for divorce as soon as I return to the islands. But Eden and I are good friends. If she didn't have to go back to high school next month, I'd take her to Europe with me."

"I don't want to finish high school. Going to Europe made me lose a whole semester. I can't even graduate with Chiye."

"My Alec thinks education is the most important thing in the world," Brooke reminded her, then added, "Poor Alec."

Stella Burkett served them luncheon on starched linen placemats. She asked if they wanted cream of mushroom soup, and they were impressed at her new abilities, but she waved aside their compliments.

"Comes in cans now," she said, and left the three of them alone in the penthouse alcove overlooking the sunlit Pacific Ocean.

"It's not what you think, girl," Red said quickly. "It's like raising you again. Those were good years. I like the feeling when I see that little Heather Burkett. Like it was with me taking you around, pointing out places, words, people. Being your pa."

To Eden's surprise, Brooke softened. She took her father's hand across the table.

"I remember those days, papa. They were nice. I felt that way about Nigel for a while." She sighed, "It's over. I see now. He and that Tamiko have been making eyes at each other for ages. Well, I wish them luck. I'll get a divorce, for his sake, so he can make an honest woman out of his old—Tamiko."

Red took in hand his three girls, as he called them, Brooke, Eden and little Heather. He showed them all over the Monte Carlo Arms, carrying Heather most of the way. Both Brooke and Eden were impressed by the marble and glass lobby, as well as the apartments with their extraordinary view.

Red's tenants, however, troubled Eden. "They all look so temporary. Some of them don't look married, either," she whispered to Brooke.

A broad-shouldered man in a neat gray suit rode up the elevator with them as far as the sixth floor, where he held the elevator and its operator in order to speak to Red. "I hope you did something about that tip I gave you, Lombard. United Sealanes is on its way. Get in on the ground floor. It can't miss."

"You know it, Cavanaugh. I plunged in the first of the month. A hundred shares at eighty-seven. The *Morning Sun* quotes it today at just under one-five. How about that?"

"You're a shrewd one, Lombard. I always said so. We must get together for lunch one day at the Yacht Club. How is that good-looking housekeeper we've acquired? Told me last month she had come into an annuity or something. Asked my advice about putting it to work. I promised her I'd give it some thought."

Brooke and Eden stared at the two men. Even Heather's big, unblinking blue eyes were fixed on Red, who merely shrugged.

"All taken care of. A dab of Keester Radio and a wee dram of United Sealanes. We'll see later, after her next payment comes in."

The crucial moment came soon and from an entirely unsuspected source. Red was preparing swordfish steaks from an old Barbary Coast recipe. He had made friends on the police force and managed to keep a store of liquor on hand, he told them as he chipped off ice from the block in the icebox and poured a Mexican "whiskey" for himself and his daughter. Between sips he shifted the fish around in its big iron pan, checked the gas ring and finished slicing tomatoes, cucumbers and onions for a salad.

"Father, for heaven's sake! Our Hawaiian *okolehau* may burn the skin off your tongue, but at least it's liquor. This stuff is rotgut."

"Next election," Red promised, "we'll get in Al Smith and repeal. Wait and see. Old Al's our boy."

Eden mused thoughtfully over her soft drink. "Daddy says it will be Herbert Hoover. He did such great things in Europe, feeding millions daddy says. And he's a very honest man."

Red snorted. "Give you odds it'll be Governor Al Smith. Prohibition is dead and no Republican can win with it."

"I know lots of people who don't drink."

Brooke rolled her eyes.

Then the doorbell rang. Stella Burkett was in her tiny one-and-a-half room apartment on the other end of the floor, so Brooke got up to open the hall door. Eden heard Brooke's sharp gasp, followed by the sound of sobbing. Eden ran to the foyer, and found Brooke weeping in the arms of an obviously baffled young man. It took Eden a minute or two before she recognized Brooke's son, Alexander Huntington. He had grown into quite a handsome fellow, and Eden thought that the gray eyes looked less forbidding than usual as he considered his mother.

Eden went to them and released Alec from his mother's grip. She explained the situation to Alec.

"She and daddy are divorcing and she's upset about it."

Alec sighed. "It was only a matter of time. What did she do?"

"What did I do!" Brooke sobbed. Eden felt for her as she would have felt for a child.

"He doesn't know. That's all." Over Brooke's tousled auburn head she explained briefly to the bewildered Alec. "It was daddy. He fell in love with my friend Chiye's mother."

Alec's face softened, and he reached out one hand tentatively as if he didn't know what to say.

"I'm sorry, mother. I didn't mean anything. I came to see grandfather. I never dreamed you were here."

Brooke was comforted by her son's kindness, and pulled herself together at the sight of her father coming out of the little utility kitchen. Red Lombard appeared to Eden curiously uneasy at the sight of his grandson.

"Well now, Brooke, here's your boy, come to comfort you. Who says you're not loved?"

Alec had no baggage, which surprised Eden, and she wondered what he was doing here so unexpectedly. She stepped aside while Brooke brought Alec to sit down in the big living room where blinding sunset light poured through the long southwest windows.

Alec looked up at Eden, seemed glad to see her and held out his hand. She shook it in the manner of a good friend. But he was so worried about his mother that Eden felt she owed him some reassurance.

"She'll be all right, Alec. Just give her a few minutes. Brooke can be free to travel and not have to run home to daddy just when she's having fun."

"Fun?" Alec's light eyebrows raised. "Maybe she loves your father."

Brooke blinked away tears. "I did, darling. He was so good to me. Like being warm and safe with papa here. I liked him better than all the others—I mean, my other friends, I mean—of course, he was more than a friend."

Alec stroked his mother's beautiful hair as he spoke to Eden over her head.

"I think I understand. It was good of you to come over with her."

Eden was easy about it. "I hated returning to high school anyway. I lost a semester back in '23, and everybody I know has gone ahead of me. Chiye is already well up in her Japanese courses. She does that besides all her regular senior classes, if you can imagine."

Having rescued his fish from the stove, Red stuck his head around the kitchenette wall. "What the hell is she going to do that for? Teach Jap talk."

Eden didn't want to be rude, so she was pleased when Alec spoke up.

"Excuse me, sir. I think the more we learn about our Pacific neighbors the better off we'll be. Japan is pretty new to our Western ways, and yet we're ignorant about Japan."

"Besides," Eden put in, "Chiye's always talking about Japanese culture, and art and poetry. She thinks it's a crime that the kids in Hawaii don't appreciate what their ancestors did. A lot of families in the islands send their children to Japanese class after regular school hours. I'm glad I'm not Japanese. There would be too much studying to suit me."

Red applauded her. "That's my girl."

When Red invited Alec to dinner, he refused, to everyone's surprise.

"I have to get back home. But I want to straighten out something first. Can I talk to you in private, grandpa?"

ALEC HADN'T wanted his mother and Eden to become involved in all the sordidness, but he was too angry now to care . . . He had been made to appear a fool, and even worse, he had betrayed Grandma Alicia's trust by his stupidity.

Red had seen the way everybody looked at him after Alec's question.

"I've got no secrets from my little girls. Spill it, laddie."

Alec didn't hesitate.

"You hired Stella Burkett as housekeeper for this place."

"Well, don't act like it's a crime. She's real capable. She's got the cutest little girl. Kind of reminds me of my little Brooke here." He waved everybody to the table. Stella Burkett had set it for three an hour before. Eden watched as Alec pulled up a chair absently, still looking at Red. He ate nothing. Somehow, he was sure Eden had guessed at his tension.

"Grandpa, Stella Burkett has been taking Lombard money under false pretenses and we have to get it back."

Brooke dropped her fork. "How could she get our money?"

But Alec was still watching Red. "You don't seem very surprised, grandpa."

"I am. Lordy, I am," Red said hastily. "It's just that I kind of figured she might have a little money. She dresses the kid so well."

"I'll have to see her."

"I don't understand," Brooke interrupted. "Why is Alec involved?"

Alec's eyes narrowed. "Grandpa, you're the one who should have asked that."

Red licked his lips. Before he could think of an answer Brooke broke into her teasing laugh. They all stared at her.

"I knew it. Oh, pa, you *are* an old fox, like Steve always says. Telling us about how you took in poor, poverty-stricken Stella Burkett. You and your 'heart as big as all outdoors.' It was Stella's money that won your soft heart."

Everybody looked at Red again. His stricken face was a giveaway.

"I'll say one thing. It's not her sex appeal, the way all my smart-aleck friends think. I wouldn't do that to my Alicia's memory. But the little one, she's different. Like I said. Puts me in mind of when you were that age. Makes me feel I'm young, with my life ahead of me, like when I took you around, showed you the world." He turned to Alec. "I won't say the money didn't matter. But all I did was invest it. It's sound as a dollar."

Alec got up. "I believe the money doesn't belong to Stella Burkett; it should be returned to the fund. Where is she?"

"Across the hall. Other side of the elevator." Then Red called after him angrily. "How come you were appointed the guardian of all that money? I'm Alicia's closest heir. I should have had charge."

In the doorway Alec replied without expression. "I suppose you know the child's father, too. Or were you responsible?"

Brooke and Eden gasped at Alec's accusation.

"If I was, you wouldn't be questioning my right to the money. But I'm not taking the rap for that Irish rapscallion," Red blurted out.

Alec smiled. "Then you know LeMass was the father."

"Good Lord, boy, I pried that out of Stella first thing. I'm not taking a pig in a poke. Just look at that little girl. You'll see old Paddy's merry eyes looking back at you."

"Then, of course Burkett has no grounds for keeping the money."

"But why?" Brooke wanted to know. "Why was Stella to get it in the first place? What connection would she have—"

Alex left them to their speculation. He could have kicked himself for not seeing the resemblance when he first saw Heather. Where was LeMass now? he wondered. He obviously knew nothing about the money Stella had acquired by palming off their child as a Lombard.

He knocked on Burkett's door. However angry he felt, he didn't like the idea of shaming a woman. He had to make himself remember the way she had humiliated him, playing him for a fool.

When Stella opened the door, she knew at once that he knew. Without even saying hello she stood aside. He walked into her apartment, noting that a couch and a child's crib were the chief articles of furniture. The room had an alcove with long windows and a view of the oil wells north of the city. A small folding table and two chairs occupied the alcove. There was a tiny kitchen and another door that must be the bathroom.

"You should have settled for a better apartment," he said coolly. "You could have afforded it."

"Yeah? Rents are high in these fancy joints. And from the look of it, my annuity has just collapsed."

Heather scuffed her way in from the kitchenette eating an apple. She beamed at Alec.

"Want'n apple?"

He wasn't going to let himself get sidetracked by the enchantments of baby talk. He pretended not to see the child's lovely eyes following him, and got back to the subject.

"You lied to my grandmother, Miss Burkett. I can't ever forgive you for that."

"No, Mr. Alec. I never lied. I never said it. Mrs. Lombard just figured it out herself."

"You let her think she had a granddaughter. She wanted one so much, and you did that to a dying woman."

Stella looked at him in the straightforward way that both annoyed and impressed him.

"I never come out and lied. She was an old lady and she jumped to conclusions. And like you said, she wanted a granddaughter." She called to Heather, took the little girl's hand. Alec was shaken by her sudden vehemence. "I haven't had the best life. I wasn't shrewd as Randi, marrying into money. But by God, Mr. Alec! This kid isn't going to grow up like I did, lowest pickle in the barrel. She's going to have things. And I'd do worse than this to get 'em for her. But I never lied."

Alec's stubborn streak would not allow him to yield, no matter how much sympathy he felt. He turned away.

"You have received three thousand dollars by fraud. I'll have to ask you to return it or I'll put the matter in the hands of legal counsel."

He heard the door open and Heather broke from her mother. She tottered happily to Red Lombard who grabbed her up and set her on his shoulder. Stella had started to say something but Red shut her up.

"Hush, Burkett. This has nothing to do with you any more. Alec, my lad, tell me. Suppose I scraped up three thousand and returned it to you. What would you do with it?"

"Add it to the fund. It's already earned over seven hundred from the dividends and two hundred from the bond coupons I've clipped. But now—" Alec considered. He hadn't thought that far ahead. "It belongs to the family. Not Tony and me. But mother, and Uncle Steve and—"

"And me," Red finished.

Alec's legs felt shaky, and he sat down on one of the little chairs at the alcove table. Feeling like a child, and not knowing what to do, he tried to shift the subject.

"I think the market has peaked. The money shouldn't remain with those stocks. It can't go up forever. By next year—by '27, you'll see, it's going to taper off the way it did after the war."

Red was not fooled. "Alec, you're evadin' the issue. We got a right to lose our own money any way we like. Just suppose you did sue Burkett. Everybody in California's going to know you thought my boy Steve was the father, and the shame won't rub off."

Alec groaned. He was feeling younger and younger . . .

He had to face facts, but he wasn't going to let this woman steal Lombard money. He stood up with knees shaking but managed to keep his voice cool.

"As far as I can see, grandpa, you've got your share. The rest belongs to mother and Uncle Steve."

"Does my boy Steve know he's entitled to some of that money you're hoarding?" Red corrected himself with a toothy smile. "I mean handling?"

"No. Not until they need it. Do you mean to tell him? And mother?"

Red considered the matter. Again came his foxy grin. "It's all accumulating under the management of a child like you? If it's taken out, divided, there goes a passel of interest, dividends and the rest. Keep it safe, boy. The more that's in the trust, the better the profit when it's split. That is, so long as you won't let me invest the whole thing myself, right now."

"No chance, sir."

Red looked at Stella. "You hear that? We're not telling my kid Brooke about it. Or Steve. Not yet."

It seemed to Alec that he heard an implied threat, but he would deal with that when it happened. He tried, however, to get some kind of commitment.

"Can I count on your word, sir?"

Red offered his hand, and they shook.

"It's a deal, laddie. I'll look on Alicia's money as rainy day stuff, not for now. But I want a third share in all the interest that accrues. It should be considerable."

"Agreed. Burkett can keep what has been paid out. But no more of grandma's money."

"You're hard, Mr. Alec," Stella Burkett said. "You expect Mr. Red to support me and Heather?"

"I expect grandfather to give you a salary. What does he give you for handling the job here, by the way?"

Red cleared his throat. "Now, see here."

Stella was looking at him so intently he became uncomfortable. Still watching Red, she told Alec. "He promised to take care of Heather and me. And I get half the dividends on my—his investments in Sealanes and Keester Radio."

"Get a salary, Miss Burkett."

Alec started for the door while he still had the upper hand. Heather reached out to him from Red's shoulder.

"Go?" she asked. "Bye-bye, Alec."

He couldn't keep himself from shaking her little hand.

"Good-bye, Miss Heather."

Red moved to get between Alec and the door.

"Alec, lad, one more thing. I've been—we've counted on that money coming in for seven more years. Not to mention the dividends it would privately accumulate for us. I could go to court and get myself appointed your guardian. Overturn Alicia's will."

Alec called his bluff. "Are you going to, sir?"

Red shrugged. "I don't want scandal any more than you do. Besides, it would put Steve and Brooke against me and I need them. We'll go along the way you lined it up, while things are booming. If you're right and if next year or so things go to pot, we'll talk about this again."

"Good. Let's let it ride a while, collecting sizable dividends on the whole sum, before we make any decisions. Good-bye, Miss Burkett. Grandpa."

Red opened the door for him. Alec went out with his grandfather's compliment ringing hollowly in his ears.

"Alec, she's right. You're hard. But you're a chip off the old block. You'll go far."

# *Chapter Four*

IN the election year of 1928, shortly after Dr. Ware and Tamiko Akina were married, the Lombards sailed to the islands, still friendly with their former in-laws. They stayed at the palatial new Royal Hawaiian Hotel, but spent much of their time swimming at Dr. Ware's beach. Their conversation bored Eden who spent her time inside the house with Alec Huntington, rehearsing what she had learned at her drama classes at the university. She liked his serious approach to her ambition. He never made fun of her, as Steve Lombard did, and she appreciated that.

In her turn, Eden learned more than she wanted to know about the future of broadcasting and about Alec's own program called "By the Bay." He was also the only member of the family who thought her job as an usherette and cashier in a local movie house would get her anywhere. What he alone seemed to understand was that if she was to earn her own living—and she certainly couldn't live off her father forever—she had to earn it by being close to the things she cared about.

With the Lombards' arrival in Hawaii that year came Eden's big opportunity for a movie connection. Unfortunately, the consequences were devastating . . .

Eden and her family had gone to the opening of the new Royal Hotel in Waikiki in the territorial governor's party. They found it breathtaking enough to recommend to the Lombards when they came, though it was not quite so romantic as the old white Moana Hotel with its South Seas feeling . . .

One thing above all about the Royal had impressed Eden; movie stars came. One of them just might be the key to her future if she could make a suitable impression, she thought. She had read in the *Star-Bulletin* that two movie names were on the passenger list of the S.S. *President Fillmore,* the sexy siren, Olga Rey, and the idol of German films, Kurt Friedrich.

She had met Mr. Friedrich years ago as her father's guest, and hoped to get in to see him now. She would not mention the late Irita Vallman, and only prayed that he would remember her . . .

The movie house where she worked was within walking distance of the Royal's vast grounds. Chiye and her boy friend, Jimmy Nagumo, a promising young cartoonist, shared night classes in art at the university. Dr. Ware had allowed his daughter to work at the movie house only if she returned home every night with Jimmy and Chiye.

The second night of Kurt Friedrich's stay was Eden's night off. She arranged with Chiye that she and Jimmy would pick her up at ten o'clock on Kalakaua Avenue outside the Royal's parking entrance.

After studying the movie magazines covering the last four years, Eden had found two interviews with Kurt Friedrich. Apparently, he was not at the top of anyone's popularity poll. He and Leo Prysing had split up after Irita Vallman's death and he had done only one other American film, though he had appeared in a couple of critically acclaimed UFA films distributed in the United States.

Still, he must know someone, she thought. He was the only actor of her acquaintance within her reach.

She unearthed one nugget from the magazines which would help her. Friedrich was quoted as saying that Paramount's Clara Bow was "so *peppy.* Is that the word? Quite unlike our European women. I find her young appeal irresistible. She conquers us all. A man would do anything for a peppy little redhead like Miss Bow."

*A man would do anything for her.* Magic words, Eden thought . . .

Eden had imitated Clara Bow in her drama class. She tried hard to straighten her hair, parted it on the side, slicked it down and stuck a barrette in it. She wore her new peach-colored rayon dress with the low-slung sash, stuffed her brassiere with handkerchiefs, and fastened on her high-heeled, T-strap shoes.

She strolled through the grounds of the Royal, sniffing the luxuriant tropic growth. By the time she stepped into the subdued elegance of the hotel concourse she saw her profile reflected in a long showcase and stopped swinging her hips. No matter what Clara Bow got away with, it looked vulgar to her.

She got Friedrich's suite number from the desk clerk who thought she was delivering an invitation from her well-known father. But as she came closer to the actor's door in the third-floor corridor, she began to lose her nerve. She knocked on the door so lightly she was forced to do it again.

She had convinced herself that Kurt Friedrich had all the charm and mysterious quality of the one man she considered ideal—André de Grasse. So it jarred her a little when Friedrich opened the door with his pale yellow hair tousled and his eyes slightly bloodshot. He was in a floor-length dressing gown embroidered with gold dragons, wearing slippers to match.

"Well, what do you want? My autograph, eh?" He now spoke English, though with a heavy accent.

She nodded and swallowed. She could see he was drunk.

"Why stand there like the silly child you are? Come. I write on a picture. You like that?"

"Very much, sir." Since he was holding the door open, she walked in.

"Always the kids," he complained, closing the door. *"Kinder.* Where are the tropic beauties, I ask you?"

Resenting his comment, Eden gave him her Clara Bow hip-sway as she crossed the parlor of the suite. On the kidney-shaped desk he had laid a stack of nine-by-twelve-inch glossies of himself, a veritable sun god, she thought, with no red flecks in his eyes and the golden column of his throat romantically revealed by his sport shirt. She still thought André de Grasse would beat him in a looks contest. His lascivious mouth made her think of raw blubber, but she held one picture out.

"I'd love one of these."

Something about her, perhaps the hip movement, had finally attracted his attention. He took the photo, fumbled and found the pen and the glass inkwell on the desk.

"You don't remember me, do you? Out at my father's house in 1922. You and the Prysings stayed there at the Point, next to us."

He stopped writing, squinted, and finally placed her. He glanced at her hips.

"You have grown up, *Liebchen.*" He continued to look her over, especially what he supposed were her extremely well-endowed breasts. He reached for her hands.

"But this is pleasant. Olga is gone. Invited without me, the bitch! One of those native feasts. Like your father held."

*"Luau,"* she put in quickly. Now, she wanted to get his attention away from her body. "I'm an actress, Mr. Friedrich. Can you tell me how I go about getting in the movies?"

For an instant she imagined she saw contempt in his eyes, but the look vanished. "Come. This so-big ambition of yours, you will tell me."

He led her to the couch flanked by Tiffany glass lamps which seemed out of place. He pointed to them.

"Olga thinks they flatter her. Nothing flatters that wrinkled crone. But you, *Liebchen,* such young flesh, soft and yielding, still supple."

She tried to force his hands away.

"I was unhappy," he complained. "Alone. I needed someone, and here you are." The liquor had roughened his voice which scared her, though not as much as his next move. He opened his dragon robe wide and displayed his nakedness.

She snapped her eyes shut and averted her face, which only amused him. He forced her closer. "I told you, I needed a girl tonight. Now, now, don't playact. I saw your walk. That figure."

She tried to pull away, but his grip was firm. She raised her foot with its sharp-heeled shoe to kick him, but he caught her ankle and yanked her down flat on the couch.

She screamed and struggled. He stifled her screams with his hand and she bit at him but all the time she was aware of her clothes being stripped away, his flesh touching hers.

She put all her strength into one effort to pull herself out from under his weight. She never would have succeeded . . . The hall door opened, and the well-known husky voice of Olga Rey boomed out.

"Where are you, kraut? Still sulking? Come on, behave and I'll let you—What's all this?"

What it was seemed obvious. "By Christ, now you're picking up babies!" She crossed the room, shedding a Chinese silk jacket, and helped Eden pull herself together.

Kurt Friedrich stumbled up, dragging his robe around him, trying in his drunkenness to assume some kind of dignity.

"Threw herself at me. Damned swinging hips . . ."

Olga Rey fussed over Eden.

"Look, kid, this won't go any further, will it? We can't afford a scandal. No harm done. He didn't hurt you, did he?"

Through her tears, Eden shook her head. She had never experienced such a close call sexually. The struggle had been bad enough, but what burned it on her consciousness was the fear that after this, she wasn't going to ever enjoy being with a man. Would it always be so ugly and so ridiculous? . . .

Olga Rey got her smoothed out. The handkerchiefs had fallen out of her brassiere and Olga picked them up. Her painted mouth spread in a grin.

"Honey, you're in luck. Look at me. No padding. Just plain udders."

If anyone else had said it, it would sound disgusting, Eden thought, but this big, blowsy, overage "vamp" in her slinky beaded gown had become her rescuer—like the Comte de Grasse had been in Paris long ago . . .

Eden laughed through her tears, sniffing and accepting one of her own handkerchiefs to wipe her eyes.

"Thank you. I'll go. I have to meet my friends."

She didn't look around, but she heard Kurt Friedrich storm out of the room.

"Tell you what," Olga said, taking her arm. "I'll show you out. You're taking this very well. No hysterics. You're a born actress, kid."

"How did you know? I really am an actress. I mean, I will be."

Olga swept her out into the hall and toward the elevators.

"So that's it! You came to see my kraut hoping you could get in the movies. You poor dumb kid!"

Eden's body was too stiff with nerves to ache yet. Would she feel this revulsion forever?

"You're going to be all right now? I know you are. Sure?"

"Sure."

Olga hesitated. "Look here, Enid—"

"Eden."

"He's really quite likable when he doesn't get carried off by his own inadequacy."

"Inadequacy? But he seems so bossy. Conceited."

"Not Kurt. Poor boy. He's not much of an actor, and that accent—well, he's on his way out, along with silent movies. But he's good in bed. When he's not drinking. 'Bye, kid."

When Jimmy and Chiye drove up minutes later she was almost her old self. It was a good act and Jimmy bought it, though Chiye wasn't so sure.

But it was one secret Eden kept. She didn't want to talk about it, and knew that, somehow, if she never thought about it, the memory would have to vanish, like so many pangs of childhood . . .

Now she wanted to get away, go somewhere far off from the memory of the scene. The lovely islands had lost their romance for her.

# *Chapter Five*

DR. Ware had been in a good humor since the 1928 election and the victory of his candidate, Mr. Hoover. His export business was prospering under the new administration, and he regarded the shipment of fruit grown on Ware lands successful enough to allow him to cut down his medical practice. Dr. Ware now spent far more time walking, sometimes driving, along the acres left him by his acquisitive missionary ancestors.

In the summer of 1929 Eden received Brooke's magical letter from France. It came just at the right time.

*Eden honey,*

*Such a good time we had when I looked after you in '23! Now you are near eighteen you deserve a reward. I know dear Nigel will understand when I ask you to stay with me in Paris for a month to celebrate this important year of your life. My stocks have been booming sky-high in spite of the gloomy pessimism of my boy; so let me give you this fall in Europe as a birthday present.*

*You will like Dr. and Mrs. Josef Preysing who would certainly be your chaperones if dear Nigel does not trust me. The doctor is the brother of the film producer, though they spell their names differently. They are a very decent, respectable pair, and were helpful in Vienna during my visit.*

*I was in Berlin recently. It is still bright and gay at night. Not like parts of Germany, with factories closed, crops rotting in the field, riots between the Communists and Socialists, and the government does nothing. The government is hopeless.*

*In those adorable Viennese coffee houses they furnish newspapers every day and people explain to me when I don't understand all of the language. That's how I learned about Germany. There is the Socialist party (these are troublemakers like the Communists) and then there is the* National Socialist Party (Nazis for short) *and this party is for order and for a revival of the old national spirit. They, at least, have a plan written out in a book someone gave me. Very dull, I'm afraid. But it does outline a new order in Germany, and written by an Austrian, of all things. A plan is more than the Weimar Republic offers. It's definitely on its last legs.*

*I might have taken you to London to see the theaters there. But they haven't come out of the depression caused by their general strike; so it isn't very jolly.*

*Nigel dear, I am dreadfully lonesome. Do let Eden come. She will be surrounded by highly respectable people like the Preysings and others, including the Comte de Grasse who has asked when she is due to arrive. André makes quite a nuisance of himself inquiring about her. He is Steve's friend, as you may know, and thoroughly trustworthy.*

*Affectionately,*
*BROOKE LOMBARD WARE*

Chiye thought Eden was crazy.

"Who wants to go clear across to Europe when everything is happening in the Pacific? If it was me, I'd go to Japan and China and maybe the Dutch East Indies. Or French Indochina where everything is supposed to be quaint and fascinating, though it's in ferment too. Japanese culture and art are being felt everywhere in Asia these days."

"I'd just as soon they didn't move quite so fast with their culture," Eden's father put in dryly. "China is so torn up, its government so erratic, bandits everywhere—Mark my words, there's more than art and culture being shipped to Asia."

Chiye remained adamant. "Everybody knows the Chinese are in shreds. There isn't one central government in the whole country."

Tamiko surprised them all in her timid voice.

"Once it was good in Japan. When it became bad, my father came away to Hawaii. There are men who do not wish Yamaguchi and the

Western powers to succeed in their talk of peace on the sea."

"Treaties about naval parity," Dr. Ware explained to Eden, who had never heard of Yamaguchi.

"Mother, half the progress on Oahu is due to us Nisei." Chiye saw Eden watching her in surprise and continued defensively. "I don't like militarism any better than you do. And I really have heard of Yamaguchi. As prime minister he will be a great force for peace."

"He is only one man," Dr. Ware reminded her gently. "Though I agree, we will all sleep better with Yamaguchi in power."

"That isn't what Jimmy Nagumo says," Eden teased. "He doesn't think anything in Japan is good these days."

"What does he know?"

"He's crazy about you."

"Crazy, you mean. A cartoonist, and not very funny."

They all laughed. Though Jim Nagumo shared three of Chiye's classes at the University of Hawaii, they argued constantly. Passionately pro-American, he resented anything that implied the superiority of another nation, which managed to get on Chiye's nerves.

When Chiye saw Eden off on the white Matson liner that day, Jimmy went along. Chiye felt that even Jimmy was a better companion than the long, lonely Pacific rollers washing along the sand.

AFTER ENDLESS coaxing and promises, Eden started off to Paris at the end of September with Dr. Ware, who insisted on escorting her as far as New York. They stopped over in San Francisco, where Eden felt that Alec Huntington's success as KHO's best-known announcer was a good omen for her own fame. Alec had twice invited Steve to appear on his program. On the first occasion, Steve had described the death of President Harding at first hand, and the second time he discussed with Alec "what it takes to be a land baron." Alec seemed to be trying hard to make a friend of his uncle.

His young cousin, Tony, ten years old and a stunningly handsome boy, had much of his dark Irish grandmother's charm. Tony had stayed with his grandfather while Randi rewrote her first talkie script for Leo Prysing in his now-famous studio in Culver City. Steve teased Randi because she insisted that he go with her to the Prysing studio whenever she had night conferences with Prysing.

During their Southern California visit, young Tony apparently had the time of his life bossing around both his grandfather Red and the housekeeper's little six-year-old daughter, who adored him.

One night in the house on Nob Hill, Eden felt that she had caught the imperturbable Alec in a display of jealousy. He called down his cousin Tony in front of the family and the Wares.

"Can't you talk about anything but Heather? She's only a baby. Grown-ups aren't interested in spoiled brats."

"She's not that spoiled," Tony boasted airily.

"I mean you."

This began a "Yeah? Yeah!" match which made Steve laugh, but which Randi broke up. "Alec, you're not very courteous. Tony, if you haven't a bigger vocabulary than that, you'd better go up and study your parts of speech. We are expecting you to do a little better than a C this year."

Tony was finally sent off to bed, despite his Grandma Bridget's coaxing, and Alec said no more about the child Heather.

DR. WARE came aboard the *Ile de France* to see Eden off on her romantic midnight sailing. It was the most beautiful ship either of them had ever seen, but still Dr. Ware shook his head.

"We live in paradise. Do you think you can find something better in that tired, bloody old European continent? Do you know what people call the *Ile?* 'The longest bar in the world,' because they can get liquor from New York to France. I call that disgusting."

"Father! For heaven's sake! They might hear you."

Now that the "all ashore" was being called, she suddenly realized how far she would be from her father and Chiye and Tamiko, and her stomach fluttered.

Dr. Ware seemed nervous too. "I only wish someone were sailing with you tonight. When you get off the boat train in Paris, wait right there until Brooke finds you. Don't you wander around the city alone."

"I won't, daddy," she promised demurely. She couldn't explain to him—he would never understand—that wandering around a city like Paris was one of the great thrills of travel.

He kept at it. "At least, it's a big relief to know Dr. and Mrs. Osterman will be sailing home with you next month. They'll take care of you here in New York and put you on the train the next day. In San Francisco Steve and Randi will be waiting. Send me a cable from New York and San Francisco. And don't leave the Dearborn station between trains when you get to Chicago."

"Yes, daddy—I mean, no, daddy."

"The Atlantic can be pretty rough in November. But I'm sure the ship will have seasickness pills."

That was the least of her worries. "After having crossed the Maui

Channel in a hurricane, I'm not afraid of the Atlantic." Her own plans did not include a return in November and she added guiltily, "Daddy, take care of yourself."

His lean face softened. "Don't you worry. Tamiko will do that for me . . . That reminds me. Give my best to Brooke." He sighed. "It all seems a long time ago. Marriage to Brooke was like raising another child. I'm too old for that nonsense. Though I will say, she was the prettiest thing I ever did see."

"She still is fond of you, in her way."

"Do you know, Eden, she is the only woman whose giggle didn't sound like chalk scraping on a blackboard?"

"I know." Eden felt she was going to cry, but was determined to hold up until he had gone ashore.

As if he sensed this, he changed the subject and became very much the stern parent.

"I don't want Brooke taking you into Italy. I don't like what I hear of those fascist-type governments where they rule with the boot and the uniform. Stick to Northern Europe. Austria. Holland. Possibly Germany."

Eden teased him. "Will Rogers says Mussolini is the greatest man in the world today because he got that treaty with the Vatican. Our own government says Il Duce is the greatest man since Garibaldi and Bismarck."

"A likely couple to be paired, I must say. I don't care how many princes and presidents and comics get on the bandwagon, I don't want you there. That whole pack is nothing but gangsters."

"Really, daddy!"

He got down to basics. "I want you to promise me something. No hard liquor until you are twenty-one. An aperitif, maybe, the way they do it in those sidewalk cafés. A little wine with dinner. That's civilized. But don't get onto the liquor trail."

"I promise, daddy. And I'll be wary of dictators. Does that include Marshal Hindenburg in Germany? And maybe General Ludendorff? Brooke says her friend, Mr. Friedrich, might take her to meet the marshal."

"Don't be disrespectful. They are both decent soldiers. I'm talking about riffraff."

"Brooke says General Ludendorff backed a fascist *putsch* headed by a Viennese painter in Munich a few years ago. So much for your innocent soldiers, daddy."

"Impertinent!" But he smiled. He was not interested in General

Ludendorff's little games, or in Viennese artists making abortive *putsches.*

The last "all ashore" sounded . . . "*Messieurs et mesdames,* ladies and gentlemen, this is the last call."

She hugged her father's slight frame. He held her close and kissed her, then turned away abruptly. She hurried along the deck after him. He sniffed. "Got to go," he said, and mingled with the others leaving.

It was an especially painful departure for Eden. She had decided she did not want to return home to "paradise" until she could return as a star, making a private resolution based on Brooke's remarks about Dr. and Mrs. Preysing . . . Eden would offer to carry messages back to Leo Prysing in Hollywood. Once she met him she would at least have her foot in the door . . .

"The difference between Brooke and me," Eden told herself, "is that I'm going to pay my own way. Somehow."

As long as her money held out, Brooke would enjoy the nomadic life of the rich American expatriate, moving to Paris for the collections and the Longchamps season, to London for the theater, to St. Moritz for the winter sports, to Venice for the balls in crumbling palazzos and of course, Vienna and Berlin for the music and for what Brooke called "the fun."

Eden's optimism crept back. Some day, everything she wanted would come to her. Not the marriage and children and dull home life that most women wanted, but a world of romance and glamor and fame . . . .

As if the first of her fantasies had come true, the Comte de Grasse was waiting for her in the cavernous Gare St. Lazare when her boat train pulled in one evening late in October of 1929. And he was alone.

# *Chapter Six*

ON Monday, October 23, 1929, Steve Lombard received a call from Sam Liversedge who had, as he put it, "something of importance to discuss."

"If you mean the market," Steve assured him, "I know how jittery it is. I didn't like its behavior in September and I like it even less now. But as soon as we get our own interest rates back up to compete with the Continent and Britain, we'll stop the drain of foreign investors. Hoover is a businessman. He knows that."

"Hoover doesn't make the laws. Congress does and most of those asses don't have the slightest head for business. Anyway, that isn't what I want to discuss with you. It has to do with your family. One member in particular."

His curiosity aroused, along with a slight uneasiness, Steve agreed to meet him at the Olympic Club.

Liversedge had gained weight and found it difficult pulling himself up to the table in a corner of the room. He tucked the napkin into his stiff, starched collar and leaned toward Steve. The room was almost deserted but he was taking no chances.

"Steve, my boy, are you holding steel?"

Steve was surprised at this opening. It had nothing in particular to do with the family.

"Something under a hundred shares of U.S. I sold out last month when I heard how the production figures had plunged. Why?" He grinned. "Are we about to be wiped out?"

"It's bad. You have any interest in radio stocks? RCA, for instance?"

"No. That's my nephew's department. Alec is all wrapped up in wireless."

The banker hesitated, patted his mouth with his napkin.

"Alec. Hmm. Yes. Very talented boy."

Steve's uneasiness grew with the banker's odd behavior. "Look here. Do you have some inside information? Tell me, for God's sake! And I'll relay it to my father. I know he's heavily into the market."

"And Alec?"

Steve hesitated, surprised. "I doubt it. He's a cautious kid. He had those charity bequests from mother but he told me that was taken care of. I suggested the Red Cross and the Salvation Army, which was damned good to us in France. A lot of people don't know that. But that would be gone by now. He can't have more than a few thousand of his own money. Shall we order?"

Sam Liversedge looked around the room and lowered his voice. "It's about Alec Huntington. I had occasion to spend an evening with Red—I mean, your father—about three weeks ago in Strand. I thought I'd be impressed by that Monte Carlo Arms of his. For looks, I am impressed. After all, I did tout you onto it in the first place. It's just that I'm not happy with all that stucco over brick. You wonder what's being covered up. The place was rushed through pretty fast. But then, I'm a San Franciscan. We learned in 1906, eh, Steve?"

From the moment the Monte Carlo Arms was mentioned Steve froze. He made a slashing motion, which scared the very proper waiter who was setting oysters on the half shell before him.

"If that's the family matter you wanted to discuss, Sam, you might as well forget it. I lost all interest in the Monte Carlo a long time ago."

"No. Lord, no. Red is into a million things."

"Much of it bought on margin. There ought to be a law to protect fools."

Sam nodded. "I agree absolutely. We had a nice time. Dinner prepared by that housekeeper he has running the building. Not a bad cook. And the cutest little kid. Heather Burkett. Apparently—er, not quite legitimate."

Steve was amused by his fussiness. "A bastard, in fact, Sam. The father was my mother-in-law's old gentleman friend, Pat LeMass. Remember him? He's a longshoreman over on the Wilmington docks, I believe."

"Apparently not interested in the child. Red told me Miss Burkett supports Heather." He paused. "On her own salary and judicious investments."

Steve scoffed at the idea. "Don't tell me my father has turned generous in his old age." He studied the bank officer's face. "But that isn't it, is it? Well, then, where the—not LeMass."

"Your nephew." Steve was left speechless while Liversedge rambled on hurriedly. "Not that there was ever any connection between the boy and Miss Burkett, according to Red. Red was drinking a bit. He may not have intended to tell me, but it came out over cigars and some excellent brandy he had acquired, heaven knows where. He claims the money came from Mrs. Lombard originally."

"Randi?"

"Mrs. Redmon Lombard. Your mother. There never was any charity bequest. Red claims the boy has been holding onto the money that actually belongs to Red, you and Brooke. I thought you should know. It has more than doubled in these boom years but who knows where it would have gone if you three had had the handling of it?"

"None of this makes sense. I saw mother's will myself. She clearly bequeathed ten thousand to charity and left it in Alec's care. Alec is an exceptionally bright kid. A hell of a lot brighter than my father."

"Well, that's Red's story. And I've made it my business to check on it. I'm afraid there is something to it. I agree with you, though. Alec is one smart kid."

Steve began to wish Liversedge had kept his mouth shut. There were some things he would rather not know. He pushed away his plate.

"I've lost my appetite. Look, do you mind if I walk out on you? As you can imagine, I've got a lot to think about."

Sam was sweating. "Don't you want to hear the rest of what I found out?"

He didn't, but—"Well, how devious was he?"

It came out then. Three thousand dollars had been paid out of the trust fund during a period between 1923 and 1926. Alec had signed for the cash and his signature was witnessed by a bank official. After that, nobody knew for sure what happened to it.

"According to Red, it went to Stella Burkett in postal orders. She in turn was persuaded to turn most of it over to Red, who invested it. I suspect she hopes eventually to get Red to marry her. Her plan hasn't worked yet and I doubt if it will. But Red claims—drunkenly, I admit—that he is entitled to all the rest of that so-called charity fund as your mother's closest relative. Either that, or he will settle for one-third of it, 'if there's trouble.' I quote him."

"Having already gotten rid of three thousand from Stella. That's Red for you."

"What are you going to do? Confront the boy?"

Steve didn't know. The whole thing had rotten timing, he thought. Dr. Ware, on his way home from New York, was a guest in the house and Alec was devoting more time than usual to showing him around KHO where he made his broadcasts. Last night Dr. Ware had been an amused bystander while Alec announced and talked up "The Sweet Sounds of Ed Sexty" for the entire Pacific Coast. There was talk today of Alec picking up Alma Gault in Oakland and driving with her and Dr. Ware to the Greek Theater in Berkeley.

*How will I get onto the subject?* Steven wondered. *Do I wait until Ware is gone?*

He had often noted Randi's ability to face unpleasantness with almost brash courage. Steve, on the other hand, wanted to avoid confrontations. He knew that Alec would never forget or forgive an accusation as serious as this, even if it were true.

*I wish Sam had never told me, damn it! It isn't as if we needed the money. The world isn't coming to an end.*

He crossed the dining room. Near the doorway he was shaken out of his thoughts by the panic-stricken voice of Buck Cortlandt. He was lunching with his son-in-law, Edwin Gault, and both men looked gloomy. Gault's hands were so nervous he could scarcely hold the fork to his oysters.

"Sealanes is down sixty-three points in less than four trading days, and you know that's a trend. It began with the damned foreigners offering better interest rates. Then all these up-and-down whirlings of radio stocks. Like a jack-in-the-box." Cortlandt's voice was shrill.

"But Sealanes was underfinanced, sir. As near as I can find out, Ponsonby, who lives in Strand, California, and a couple of fellows from back East, got hold of a string of run-out freighters. They tried to buck the big cargo carriers like the Matson and President lines. They put out paper and got a lot of suckers . . . er, sorry, sir."

"When I got in, Sealanes was New Orleans and Galveston. The Pacific run was just an adjunct. I knew. But if we could have had two years more. Just two measly years . . ."

They looked up and saw Steve standing nearby. Edwin Gault's prim mouth sealed tight. He had never liked Steve, even in college, and Steve couldn't help wondering how much Gault knew about him and his wife.

"Pull up a chair, Steve. This is a bad business." Buck Cortlandt looked pale and unhealthy.

"Nothing alarming." Gault waved away panic. "Buck just had a little problem with one of his investments."

Buck ruined his effort. "I'm in deep, Steve. No use in Ned covering up for me. After I lost that bundle on the Wyoming oil deal—the way the government reneged on backing our play—I had to recoup in a hurry. I mortgaged what I could, the Triangle Building in Oakland and those new lots in Oakland Hills. But worse luck, I kept my stocks."

"At least you didn't follow Red. He's gone heavy on margin. The stocks have gone up. He was on easy street, but he kept investing. Now, with the market so edgy, he'd be better off with property. I never have much cash, but I'm land rich and I like it that way."

Buck shook his head. "Not if it's mortgaged to the hilt. I've got paper out on everything I own."

He leaned toward Steve, nearly ignoring his son-in-law. "I've got to make a payment on the Triangle loan. The interest alone is eating me up. How would you feel about going on a note for me? I can redeem it as soon as Dynamic Radio merges with Keester. And I've got my steel and a few glamor stocks as backup."

Considering the panic Sam Liversedge seemed to be in, Steve was not enthusiastic about any of the market's so-called glamor stocks, but he couldn't bring himself to refuse an old friend.

"How much will you need?"

"A hundred would save Triangle and leave a payment on the Joaquin tract in the East Oakland Hills." He saw Steve's startled look. "But fifty . . . say forty thousand . . . would be a real help. Steel is bound to turn around in a few weeks. It's all a matter of higher production, and selling abroad. Wait 'til the market stops these jitters. You'll see."

Buck had not once reminded Steve of what Steve owed him. His beginnings in the Pacific Dunes tract. Everything stemmed from that. And Steve had known Buck since his childhood when Buck and Red went into a couple of deals together. Steve felt that the present erratic market was only temporary. With all the wealth of the United States, and so much concentrated in production and industry, it was impossible to lose, he thought. Today it was down. Tomorrow it would go up. It always had. The big thing was to count on solid issues, solid unglamorous stocks.

He got up. "I'll meet you at Wells, Fargo in an hour. That suit you?"

Buck's gaze shifted to the tablecloth. "Switched my trade to the S.F.-Comstock. I got a little irked at Wells, Fargo a while back."

Steve understood. They had refused him a loan.

"Great. See you in Averback's office."

Buck rose and shook his hand so hard Steve winced. The market's flutterings had made everyone edgy, but it was the wrong reaction, Steve thought. It merely added to the problems of the market. Confidence was what was needed now.

But it was hard to feel confident himself when he might soon be signing away fifty thousand dollars. Until the recent boom it had been enough to satisfy a man for a lifetime and then some . . . He went out and walked down the street, then remembered his nephew . . .

The rest of the day was not much better. He tried to put on an easy front when he cosigned Buck Cortlandt's note for forty-five thousand dollars, but it did give him some qualms, especially when his San Fernando Valley property was politely turned down as collateral. The bank was happy, however, to accept a deed on a section of the Pacific Dunes district.

Afterward, sounding more confident than he felt, Steve reassured Buck. "It's only fair. You backed me on the Dunes in the first place."

"I'll never forget this, my boy. If you were my own son-in-law I couldn't feel for you more than I do. I'd die before I'd let you take a bad fall with this."

There had been anguish in the older man's puffy face before their bank meeting, and it seemed to Steve that Buck was still desperate. But as painful as this business had been, Steve dreaded even more the prospect of going home to accuse his nephew of misappropriating family funds . . .

He didn't get a chance for the showdown that night. Alec was out late with his broadcasting friends. Dr. Ware confided his own worries to Steve and Randi.

"I'm not a gambler, but I have everything the family left me tied up in my fields. The shipping is all-important, our being five days away from the Coast. Maybe I was crazy, but I'd be nowhere if I couldn't ship at decent rates."

"That makes sense," Randi said. "I wouldn't call it gambling, would you, Steve?"

But Steve could predict what was coming. He tried to be noncommittal. "And you put everything into—I hope it was Matson. Or . . ."

"United Sealanes. It seems to have plunged since we left Honolulu. Frankly, what I want to know is, will it settle somewhere?"

Steve would like to have consoled him with some hogwash that would save the evening, but the matter was too important.

"Nigel, try and sell the minute the Exchange opens. I don't care if it's the crack of dawn."

Dr. Ware took it well. A muscle in his cheek seemed to quiver but he smiled. "That bad, eh?"

"I'm afraid so. I had some inside dope today. My father has been notified, too. He was heavily into Sealanes. In fact, the chairman of the board of Sealanes leases an apartment in my father's building. For a girl friend, I'm told."

"Then your tip comes right from the horse's mouth. Or should I say—the mare's mouth."

They all laughed. "I'll have to get Eden home as soon as possible if I lose heavily. Can't afford all this gadding about."

"If she wants to act, maybe I could talk to Mr. Prysing," Randi suggested. "You knew him quite well in Hawaii that time. Remember? There might be something for Eden in Hollywood. Bit parts, or whatever they are called. I mean, to start with."

"I'd rather not. Hollywood isn't my idea of a safe place for a girl Eden's age."

Steve was amused. "My wife has managed to do several scripts for Prysing without getting herself ravaged."

"But my daughter isn't married to an ex-football star."

That ended the subject of Eden—as far as Dr. Ware was concerned, she was safe in Europe, but not in Hollywood . . .

The next morning Steve and Randi were awakened by Alec who knocked at 6:15 A.M. and stuck his head in. He was fully dressed.

"Morning, folks. You told Miss Thorgerson you wanted to see me first thing."

"Damn!" Steve sighed, propped himself up on his elbows, then remembered the subject at hand. He cleared his throat. This would be bad enough between the two of them, and for Alec's sake he didn't want Randi to get an inkling of it until it was straightened out.

"I'll be with you in a minute, Alec." Steve put on his robe, kissed Randi and explained. "It's about the market, honey. Boring stuff."

He was uncharacteristically cool to Alec as they went down the hall to the sunroom.

"The new furnishings. Are they what Aunt Randi bought with her movie money?" Alec asked.

Steve wanted to get this over as soon as possible. "This is Randi's room. That's how she wanted to spend her money. But that's not what I wanted to talk to you about." Abruptly, he added, "What have you done about mother's charity bequest? Is there anything left of it?" He was watching Alec.

No question about it, Steve thought. The boy looked guilty, or at least unusually pale. "Sure, there is. It's more than doubled. I got rid of Hupmobile and that old foundry stock and put it in solid futures."

"Such as?"

"RCA, for one. And Atwater Kent Radio. And General Motors. Some airline stock. I thought I'd ask Mr. Liversedge if I shouldn't sell while it's high and stick it in the bank."

The telephone began to ring in the upstairs hall, but Steve ignored it. He sat on the edge of the couch, still eyeing Alec. "What do you intend to do with all this wealth?"

"I want it to go where it's needed, when it's needed." He waited for Steve to speak. Someone had answered the phone. Alec burst out, "You know it's yours, don't you? Yours and Grandpa Red's and mother's."

"All right. You kept it because you figured your grandfather and your imbecilic old uncle couldn't handle it. What I want to know is why you gave away three thousand of it."

Alec's quiet answer baffled him.

"Grandmother thought she knew all about that girl."

"Alma? What has she to do with it?" The minute he spoke the name he knew it was a mistake, but the Cortlandts were still on his mind. The worst of it was, Randi had come to the doorway.

"Telephone for you, Steve." She glanced at Alec. "What's all this about Alma?"

"Stella Burkett," Alec corrected her. He bit his lip. "It was all a mistake. Grandmother thought that because Uncle Steve was popular with girls in college and in France, he was Heather's father."

Randi stared at them in silence for a few long seconds and then burst into laughter. "But you have only to look at a photo to see she is Paddy LeMass's daughter. Even the nose. The forehead. Her Irish ways. Besides, if any Lombard had been the father, it would have been Red. They were thick as thieves."

Steve relaxed, hoping his wife had not overheard his idiotic mention of Alma Gault. "You are the limit, sweetheart. I wouldn't put it past dad."

"It was LeMass, all right," Alec admitted. "Gran Bridget knew LeMass needed money for a girl who was going to have a baby. But nobody told Grandmother Alicia, and Burkett let her believe you were the father. Grandmother was so anxious to have a granddaughter, I guess she wanted to believe it. Anyway, Stella got three thousand dollars from me before I found out the truth. Stella admitted the truth to me at grandpa's apartment house."

"And you kept the rest of the money?"

"Now, Steve," Randi began. "Alec is the last boy in the world to—"

Alec raised his voice indignantly. "I never touched it except to build it for the family. I didn't want you and Aunt Randi to know what grandmother and I suspected. I knew there'd come a time you'd all be glad to get the money. I was kind of a caretaker. But I'll sign it over today. The certificates are all down at Wells, Fargo. The monthly reports are in the trust department."

"Oh, my Lord!" Randi cried, startling them both. "I forgot. That phone call was for you, Steve. Sam Liversedge. He sounded as though he had asthma."

Although few businesses were open at this early hour, the Pacific Coast Stock Exchange was cued into Wall Street time. There must be some important news breaking down on Montgomery Street, Steve thought as he ran for the phone.

# *Chapter Seven*

AS Steve made a grab for the telephone, the recent events kept running through his head. He wanted to believe Alec. It fitted both his mother's ideas and Alec's character. And above all, he thought, no one had ever presented evidence that Alec had spent even a penny of the bequest on himself . . .

Sam Liversedge did not come on the phone at once. Steve could hear Sam's harried voice speaking on other phones and then apparently to men around him. Steve called out to him several times.

"Sam? Are you there? Sam? What's this all about? You know what time it is?"

The banker got back to him. "Steve, things are happening. I've been getting calls from my man at the Exchange. New York opened wild. It's a selling wave. The rest of the trust department are all here in my office. Cavelli thinks the big boys on Wall Street will put a stop to it. Maybe it's only a little distress selling. What do you have on margin?"

"Nothing. You know me. I seldom have cash to play with." He then thought of his father. "But Red is up to his ears in stocks he's bought on margin."

"I know. I called him before I called you. He's got about an hour to get up every cent he can beg, borrow or steal. He's probably trying to call you now. Would you believe it? He not only has all this on margin, but he's deep into United Sealanes and Keester Radio, and they've kept right on tumbling. Sealanes finished yesterday at sixty-three points down. It'll go through the floor today unless something—or somebody—puts a stopper in this thing. " 'Scuse me, Steve. I've got a lot of troubles here. Have to go now."

The click in Steve's ear was definitive. What to do first? he wondered. Red had been warned. But there was Buck Cortlandt—Sealanes! Right here in this house another friend would suffer. Dr. Nigel Ware. And Alec had the Lombard money tied up in God knew what "safe" stocks.

The phone was ringing again. It was bound to be Red, asking to be bailed out. Steve knew that if he put up almost fifty thousand dollars' worth of property to save a mere friend like Buck Cortlandt, he couldn't turn down his own father. But Red would have to wait.

Miss Thorgerson was calling from the ground floor extension. "It's your paw on long distance, Mr. Lombard. Would you please take it on your phone? He says it's life and death."

Steve leaned over the upstairs bannister. "Tell him I'll call back. No. He'll insist. Tell him I'm out. I'll call him in a few minutes when I get back."

At the foot of the stairs Thorgerson bellowed, "He sounds real excited. Couldn't you . . . ?"

"Tell him!"

In the hall Steve barely caught Randi by the shoulders before running into her. "Sweetheart, this may be something big. Just don't ask questions until I get all the bases covered."

"A run on the bank?"

"Worse. A whole lot worse. Where is Alec? And wake up Nigel."

The phone was ringing again. "Take the call, Thorgy!"

"Never mind," Randi said calmly. "I'll handle the calls. I'll give you a list from time to time. You tell me who you want to talk to."

"Sweetheart, you're an angel."

"It's Mrs. Gallegher," Thorgerson yelled.

"I'll take the phone."

Steve watched Randi go off to handle her mother, her back straight, her figure in the wheat-gold dressing gown as slim and proud as it had been at their wedding eleven years ago . . .

Alec had heard the commotion and awakened Dr. Ware.

"Alec says it's about the stock market. How bad is it, Steve?" the doctor asked sleepily.

"We don't know yet, sir. But get rid of your Sealanes stock. Maybe you can still salvage something."

"My God! I'll have to call Hawaii. Tamiko has my power of attorney."

"Go right ahead, doctor. Alec, Sam Liversedge told me yesterday that RCA was tumbling. Probably priced over the market. Hadn't you better get rid of it?"

Alec was looking desperate. "But Uncle Steve, it's radio and communications. Those stocks are a sure thing, even if they go down now."

"Do you have Keester, too?"

Alec nodded.

"Well, it's gone already. Through the floor. Dump it if you can."

Somebody else also had Keester. His father—and poor old Buck.

But the crash hadn't happened yet. The great Wall Street bankers wouldn't let it happen. Somebody had said recently that Morgan was in Europe. Why the devil didn't he stay at home where he could oversee things and prevent this kind of mess?

The phone stopped ringing only long enough for a few quiet words from Randi. Then it rang again. The kitchen had a separate phone, which Dr. Ware used to try to call his broker in Honolulu. It wasn't easy, but at last he got through.

Alec left the house, and Steve supposed he had gone to get the Lombard legacy he had tended for six years and doubtless lost today with some of his other idiotic stock buys.

By the time Steve took Red's call he should have been prepared but it still came as a shock. Red's panic had now reached the quiet certainty of despair . . .

"I need every cent I can scrape together, lad. Every single cent. I'll have to ask you to go on my notes, right away. Got to get it all up to pay off the margin stocks."

"What about the stocks you own?"

"Gone, Steve. I can't think how it could have happened. It's gone in less than a week. United Sealanes. Keester Radio. Even the sure ones. General Motors. Well . . . get down to the Exchange. Read the tapes, hear the reports. You can't believe it. I've put up everything. I've offered a mortgage on the Monte Carlo Arms. No takers yet, but I'm expecting something. The Seattle property is a sacrifice, but I can raise seventy-five there. And maybe close to thirty on the Wilshire ground in L.A. It's got a future."

"The La Brea Tar Pits?"

"Them too. Don't kid me, Steve. I need everything. I need what I can raise on the Nob Hill house, too."

"Impossible. You only own one-third."

"Steve, this is not some family joke. I know you've always tried to compete with me. That's the tradition. Forget it now. I've always opened up the horizons for this family. The oil concessions we got through Harry Macondray—"

"Red, don't bring that up. You broke Buck Cortlandt and a lot of others with that one."

"But it was me that did it, Steve. Like Strand here. I took this white elephant off your hands, this Monte Carlo thing. I saved you a bundle of cash and years of loans." He went on and on . . .

Steve kept seeing his own honeymoon with Randi, taking her and André de Grasse through the building, showing if off as if it were his. And then, what Steve always thought of as the end of his innocence—the awful moment when he discovered, with Randi looking on, that his own father had undercut him. According to what Red said now, it had been deliberate. *"I saved you a bundle of cash."*

But Steve thought differently. Red had deliberately bought the Monte Carlo out from under him . . .

"I'll see what I can do, Red. You put up the Monte Carlo to me and I'll see what can be salvaged for your other properties. You have some in the Hollywood Hills now, don't you? Las Feliz? Near the DeMille property."

"Yes, but Steve, this is fast money I need. Today. Before the market pitches lower."

Steve was adding numbers in his head. He drew lines on the doily someone had placed under the telephone's green felt pad.

"All right, Red. I'll have the credit on the wire to L.A. inside the hour. But I want security."

"Sure, lad. It's all in the family, anyway."

"Just what your father would have said."

Steve knew what Red had thought of his own father. It had been one long struggle to rise above Mad Tony. Perhaps Red was thinking of the days of his boyhood, during one of Mad Tony's periods of failure, when Red went to work in Nevada's Comstock lode. The one thing Steve admired about his father was the period in which Red Lombard had struggled for his life and his future in the silver lode deep in the bowels of Sun Mountain . . .

The story of his father's dogged boyhood courage now clashed with Steve's bitter memory of his own first great failure, the Monte Carlo Arms, the dream Red Lombard had destroyed.

"Are you with your broker now, Red?"

"You bet. In L.A. We've an open line to Sam Liversedge. You give him the go-ahead sign, and they'll go along with me here for everything but the margin stocks. I'll need everything you can raise, or I'll go under."

"I can't guarantee to go that far, but I'll do what I can."

BY THE time Steve reached the crowded offices of Sam Liversedge he had a pretty good idea of what he could afford to put up without destroying his own base. Even so, it would be touch and go to pay off the interest on the loans, let alone the principal. He had taken note of Randi's parting words.

"Steve, I know how important it is, the Lombards against the world, and all that. But you do know better than to trust Red in money matters."

He had given her what was perhaps a patronizing answer. "I may not know movie scripts, but I do know my business, sweetheart. You leave the market to me."

All the same, he was appalled at the losses his father had already sustained. Red couldn't possibly rescue anything he had bought on margin, and would be lucky to keep some of his solid stocks. Steve began to get the eerie feeling that there was no stopping today's slide. Like a capsized ship, the market had turned over and was now plunging downward . . .

Alec Huntington came into the office an hour later. He ignored Steve, speaking directly to the bank officials.

"We ought to be buying solid stocks right now. Not running scared."

They looked at him as if he were insane, but Steve wondered if the boy didn't make good sense. Steve tried speaking to him, but Alec merely laid a thick manila envelope on Sam's desk.

"It's all there, sir. The stock certificates, the bonds, the trust department reports, carbon copies of all correspondence in regard to sales and purchases."

Sam glanced at Steve, who tried to play it lightly. "No hurry now, Alec. We'll see what's left after today's debacle." Alec reddened, and Steve realized he had made it sound as if he were blaming Alec for the market's bad day. "Anyway, we're all in the same boat," he added, but Alec rattled on in his businesslike way.

"I realize that with today's market I owe the trust several thousand. I've put up my own stocks to cover the difference. There is a little under sixteen thousand there."

"Alec, that's not necessary."

Alec looked up at Steve for the first time. "I'll be out of the house before you come home, sir."

"Now, just a—"

Alec walked out past the startled trust department executives.

Steve had one hope. Randi would probably talk the boy out of leaving home in this mood.

The phones in the outer office had been ringing constantly. Sam's young clerk rushed in.

"Sir? Gentlemen. There's been a big conference at the House of Morgan. It's still going on. But they're buying! The big men, like Mr. Whitney and Mr. Rockefeller and the other leaders are buying up stocks. Otto Kahn and Mr. Rockefeller say the market is still solid. The problem was with the glamor stocks."

Sam's voice quavered. He shared the doubts of the others in the room. "Are you sure?"

"Sir, these men are all optimistic. They're pouring in millions. That's what I'm told. Millions!"

Sam took courage. "Then the key stocks are saved. The market is firm."

Alec's proud departure was forgotten. There was more hugging, more yelling than Steve had ever heard in Sam's offices. He could imagine Red's relief. He had lost most of the stocks he bought on margin, and his Seattle properties were gone, but he still owned the Wilshire property, though it was heavily mortgaged. So was the Monte Carlo Arms. Steve himself now exclusively held the mortgage on the Monte Carlo . . . It was within his grasp at last.

FOR THREE days the financial world held its breath. The small investors began to follow the lead of the big plungers, nibbling again on the "sensible" stocks, ceasing their desperate nightly prayers. Things would work out, they said. America's great balloon couldn't burst . . .

It burst on October 28.

Steve explained to Randi. "The big boys bailed us out on Tuesday. They won't this time. God knows how long it will take the market to climb back up, but it will. In the meantime, we'll have to tighten our belts. People like Red and Buck Cortlandt and Sam Liversedge are suffering more than we are."

Randi spoke quietly.

"They were fools. And they've pulled you in to sink with them."

For a minute Steve didn't know what to say. It was like getting hit in the stomach, a blow that took his breath away. Her words reminded him vividly of the wager she had made . . . Was this in her mind now at the prospect of the financial burden ahead of them? . . .

He watched her sit down to her rattling typewriter. She straightened out the blue pages of copy work which she had once explained were the third draft of a script. The green came next, for the fourth draft. She rolled two green sheets and a carbon into the typewriter.

He spread his fingers over the keys. "Randi?"

She looked up with a little frown. He lost his nerve and brought up another subject instead.

"Is Alec still at Bridget's rooming house?"

"Bridget asked him and he agreed. I brought Tony over after school today. He was delighted, and wanted to know all about Alec's work. You know, Steve, we may have another broadcaster in the family."

"I thought the two always quarreled."

She shrugged as she began to type. "They didn't today. He followed Alec around the studio like a little puppy."

"But Alec still won't come back home?"

"You know Alec. He's always kept his feelings bottled up. He'll come around, eventually."

"All too true, damn it. But it isn't as if I was in the wrong."

She looked up at him with her warm smile. "Darling, the fact that he was wrong hurts him more than anything else . . . Well, here goes. Another Prysing low-budgeter. Three geniuses worked on it before it got to me. I've got a notion to tear up their masterpiece and start my own."

"I'll let you get on with your work." He started for the door of the sunroom, but suddenly remembered something and turned back. "Do you know, the first time I saw you, Randi, was in that doorway. How I went for you!" He laughed. "Still do."

But she was busy typing. "Thank you, darling, and I went for you, too." Then she added a curious thing. "Of course, it wasn't really the first time."

The telephone rang and he took the call. It was Edwin Gault, and he sounded stiff and pompous as usual, until he got the message out. Then his voice cracked.

"I thought his creditors should know, since you stood on one of his notes. Buck is dead."

The shock jarred Steve. "Good God! What happened? His heart? Or a stroke?"

"He jumped off the roof of the Triangle Building here in Oakland.

About an hour ago. I guess it's pretty clear why he did it. He's lost everything." The phone went dead.

Randi's voice, close by, was unexpected. She rested her hand on his shoulder.

"Darling, I know you have to help the others, and I love you for it. I was afraid when you told me the house was mortgaged again. But all we have to do is pay it off. We can do it and I can help. Mrs. Schultz wants to stay on. We're about the only family she's got. I thought we could give her some kind of note, indicating what we owe her on the salary cut, and pay it off when we get on our feet. Thorgy, the same. We certainly don't need the parlormaid. She's not very efficient anyway."

Though he suffered deeply the terrible loss of his old friend, Buck Cortlandt, Steve was comforted by Randi's unexpected approach and by her touch . . . Things were all right between them, he thought. Hadn't eleven years taught him that?

# *Chapter Eight*

INCREDIBLY, the European continent seemed pleased by Wall Street's disaster. The stock market plunge may have shaken the Americans, but Eden learned about it three days after her arrival, and then only as a sort of joke played on the richest nation in the world.

She overheard the news by accident, a small matter of gossip not intended to interfere with the winter festivities planned for Eden in France and Austria.

But at her arrival at the Gare St. Lazare, Eden would not have been interested in such matters as the stock market. She was looking in vain for Brooke, and was beginning to feel a twinge of panic as amid all the confused sounds around her it was difficult to understand anything.

She lowered her train window but could not see her glamorous ex-stepmother anywhere in the crowd that stood outside the windows of the train.

At last Eden made out her first familiar face in the crowd . . . André de Grasse! At that moment she thought his was the most beautiful face in the world. The tall Frenchman was trying to make her out among all the boisterous people gretting the train.

André looked very much as he always had, with a slight stoop and the fine brown eyes that always seemed a little melancholy. But he was glad to see her; she was sure of it. She ran through the corridor and jumped off the platform, calling his name.

He kissed her on each cheek, which thrilled her, then looked her over approvingly.

"You are all grown up, *chèrie*. I am quite afraid of you."

But he didn't look afraid, she thought. There was unusual excitement in his splendid eyes and she took a deep breath of the smoky October air.

"I'm home again. Let's go."

"Precisely." He signaled the tough little porter in dusty blue who already had Eden's biggest pullman case lashed over his back and then picked up her smaller bags, one in each hand. Eden looked through the scattering crowd.

"Where is Brooke?"

He cupped her elbow in his hand and escorted her out to the street.

"Brooke could not make it, I'm afraid. A migraine. Very unpleasant."

"I didn't know she was subject to migraines. Some people say it's all in the mind. Like Coué with his 'every day in every way I'm getting better and better.' But I don't suppose that would work with Brooke. Daddy says the pressure of a migraine is real. Poor Brooke."

He said without expression, "Poor Brooke? She is suffering in Vienna. A very grand hotel in the Inner Ring. You will like it."

She was shocked by André's apparent indifference, but at the same time her excitement increased. She was on her own—in Paris.

"I am to put you on the train for Vienna."

Eden's heart sank.

It was evening, and Paris was ablaze with white lights on the Right Bank.

"But why? What's so good about Vienna?"

"Some actor," he explained lightly. "I have not seen Brooke in some time. I received my instructions by long distance telephone."

Their porter found a taxi and they piled in after her baggage. Eden settled back, enjoying his nearness . . .

"I don't understand why you obeyed her. You don't owe Brooke anything. You weren't even interested in her when we were here in '23. Were you?"

He smiled. "No. I certainly was not. Maybe I wanted to see what Eden Ware, the international celebrity, had grown into."

"I haven't got there yet. I didn't have a devastating romance on shipboard, either. I graduated last year with a C-plus average, except in French and German, in which I got a B-plus. And I've never even had a professional stage engagement." He was watching her with interest. She raised her voice. "But I've had a lot of amateur experience."

"Bravo." He touched her hand playfully, then, almost before she could enjoy it, he said, "I beg your pardon. I sometimes forget how young you are."

"Don't apologize. I've thought about you so much. You can't imagine."

Sneaking a side-glance at him, she suspected he was pleased. She knew she had to get him over the idea that she was too young.

Either he or Brooke had chosen an elegant old hotel on the rue St. Honoré for Eden's single night in Paris. She wanted him to stay with her. What a glorious introduction to her new life that would be! The Comte de Grasse was the very man to teach her real passion, she thought, and Paris was the city.

She tried to convince him to stay. But after helping her with the desk formalities, picking up her mail and assuring her it was safe to leave her passport, he left her at the door of her romantically old-fashioned bedroom whose two windows looked out on the Tuileries across the wide rue de Rivoli.

He gave her one reprieve before leaving. "Brooke tells me you may remain in Paris two nights, and if you like, I have planned to show you my France tomorrow."

Her eyes sparkled. "I would."

"Let me drive you out for a true French picnic at what is left of the Grasse family chateau."

"I'd love it!"

Her face shone with delight as he kissed her, cheek-to-cheek. "Tomorrow, early," he reminded her and went off to the elevator.

Eden did not wait to unpack. She ran water, climbed into the tub and read her mail. The letters from her father and Chiye both harped on what a romantic time she must have had on shipboard and in Paris. If they only knew, she thought happily.

Alec Huntington had written as well. His letter, dated October 21, was extremely businesslike.

*I'll bet you're having a great time, but would you do me a favor? Mother sent me a card from Austria, saying she might be there for some time. Typical of mother—she didn't give me an address.*

*I have been watching the market lately. I warned mother two years ago that the market was too high. But it went higher, so I was evidently wrong. However, it is now behaving oddly. I want her to give Liversedge and the trust department the order to protect her assets. Sell the glamor stocks, put the profits into a bank, as I am going to do pretty soon with certain assets of grandma's that I am holding for the family.*

*Have a good time, Eden. Lots of luck in your career.*

*Yours,*
*ALEC*

That night Eden dreamed about André de Grasse . . .

He picked her up early the next morning for the long drive he had promised her. He waved a big wicker basket at her before chucking it in the rumble seat of his Isotta Fraschini coupe. "Lunch," he promised. She could tell that he was trying hard to act like her father.

They had breakfasted on mushroom omelets and coffee at a café in the outskirts of Paris. In the early afternoon André slowed down as they drove through the Marne valley town of Rogier-Grasse. Here, André had spent many happy days of his childhood as young lord of the local chateau.

"My father went off to fight the Boche in 1870. A German cannonball took his left foot but he came home to run the chateau and the vineyards. He did not marry until he was nearing fifty. By the time the Boches marched again in 1914 he was seventy-seven. Sad to say, they would not take him when he tried to join the colors. He said to me, 'Go to Berlin. On your way, bring back my foot.' "

"What happened to him?" She sat close, nearly touching the rough leather patch on the sleeve of his hacking jacket.

"He died of bronchitis in the second week of the war. It is no wonder. He smoked like a chimney stack. But he went out happily. I thank God he did not know the first great battle of the war would sweep straight through his lands."

"How sad!"

"Not for my father. For my mother. For Lisalotte, my wife. Lisa got my mother out before the bombardment, but they both died in the retreat. Mother first, then Lisa. The town was shelled. You can see the signs of the shelling there in the fields. Those gray stones are what remain of the *mairie,* the town hall, you would call it. It had been there since the days of the first Napoleon. Beyond was the manor house of Lisa's brother. He died a prisoner in a Boche camp."

Eden felt an overwhelming tenderness toward him, and she knew she had to let him know . . .

They passed the outskirts of Rogier-Grasse, a charming gray stone village with winding roads parallel to the misty river. Eden pointed out the high chalk cliffs against the serpentine curves of the river.

"All those sticks in rows, are they grapes?"

"Chardonnay. Our Rogier-Grasse grows the Chardonnay, though I personally prefer the Moselle, further east."

She was exhilarated by the October wind, brisk and musky.

"You must have very good crops here. Everything seems to grow so well."

André agreed. "Ironic, isn't it? A great battle was fought near here. The blood of thousands soaked those fields. And now—"

She suddenly remembered something. "André! I heard it in school a long time ago: *'I sometimes think that nowhere blows so red the rose as where some buried Caesar bled.'* "

He didn't look at her for a few minutes. When he finally spoke it was to say something flippant, almost cruel.

"Omar Khayyam was always the favorite of adolescents."

He must have guessed that he hurt her. He slowed the car suddenly and before she could look around and see what was so important in the lovely autumn landscape, he leaned over and kissed her, this time on the lips. Her green eyes were wide as she stared at him.

"Why?"

"I did not mean to hurt your feelings. You are very right to enjoy Omar Khayyam."

She wanted to resent his patronizing tone, but it was hard to resent anything that inspired his warm kiss. It had in it more tenderness than passion. But tenderness suited the moment, she told herself.

The landscape was beautiful through this valley with its yellow, red and brown colors against the fading greenery. By comparison, her first sight of André's chateau was a distinct disappointment. André pointed out a lopsided pile of gray stones about forty feet high. Grass grew in tufts between the chunks scattered over the ground under the shadow of the rubble.

"You wouldn't know a chateau had ever stood on this ground."

There were roped off areas with *Defendu* signs everywhere. Andre parked the car in the pebbled clearing at a right angle to the pile of stones. Beyond the car was a grove of poplars that acted as a windbreak.

"It's like a private room inside those stones and the car and the trees," Eden cried. "All it needs is a roof."

André was more prosaic. "And a floor. I would not like to sleep on those stones. Or those tufts of grass between the stones. They look cold and wet. Still, it is a warm day for October. He lifted out the picnic basket and they strolled over the area.

"You see the signs? The cellars are below there. And there. We found Stephen Lombard and his men at the far end. The north wall had collapsed on them."

"How horrible!"

"But we are not to think of war today. We already fought 'the war to end all wars.' I will never fight another. What do you say to this place for our picnic? Not too much sun, but it is protected from the wind."

"I love it."

"You must help me unpack."

She had never seen such a picnic . . . A red and white checkered tablecloth was spread over a large, flat stone block. Then came a dusty bottle of Moselle. "My choice," he said. "And this from our Chardonnay grapes, which you may like." He produced another bottle. Then came sandwiches with Ardennes ham piled high between halves of crusty rolls. There was a ripe Brie that melted in the mouth, a little wire-sealed pot of *foie gras,* and pastries, apples and grapes.

"If I ate all those, I'd be fat as one of those pigs we saw up the road," she protested.

"Very well. I will eat one." With his somber eyes smiling as they watched her face, he ate one small lemon-filled square. "Now. It is done. Let us begin our picnic."

The autumn winds, rustling through the poplar leaves, affected them as much as the wine did. By the time they had finished their picnic and jokingly fought over the crumbs along the tablecloth, they were feeling the effects of almost two bottles of wine. André made a grab for a crumb of Brie. Eden's hand leaped onto his. When he boasted triumphantly, "Mine!" and ate it, she pushed him over backward and fell on top of him. They were both laughing.

André groaned. "I am sick. I cannot, as you say, cope with the younger generation."

She pounded his shoulders. "Don't say that. You are just the right age. So am I. And I'm ready. I came prepared. Do you know what I mean?"

He grabbed her wrists and looked deeply into her excited eyes.

"I am older than this century. Ten years older. Next year I will be forty."

She saw the faint rays of lines at the corners of his eyes and loved them all. She shook her head, breathless from laughing. "I won't listen to you. See?" She dropped against him, pressed her lips as hard as she could on his and kept pressing with what she supposed must be desperate ardor. His hands moved to her face, cupping it while he raised it from him.

"Don't you like me? Am I too young?" she asked uncertainly.

"I love you, my sweet girl. You are not too young. You are precisely the right age. But you are not kissing me. You are fighting me."

With a tenderness she had never known before, he lowered her face to his, touched her mouth with his. She was surprised by the feel of his soft, warm lips. She had always thought passion was violent. Not with André . . . .

From his first, almost hesitant touch, she enjoyed the delicious union with him, her first love. His gentle command over her body and her senses would always bring her memories of joy. No one had ever made her feel like this; she was unable to think, only to feel his mouth, his tongue, his gradual possession of her body . . .

"You know you may be hurt, my sweet girl," he murmured, but his hands continued to mesmerize her so that she wanted him never to stop.

"I know all about it. Go ahead." Through half-closed eyes she saw his tender smile.

"You know all about it, do you?"

When he entered her she felt that she had been pierced by an exquisite sword, the pain shrouded in a curious joy. The pleasure was that of a deep merging, almost a clasp of friendship. While she and André clung together, she heard herself repeating, "I love you. I do love you so." And in some way she knew she would always love him. Not as she had expected, but warmly and tenderly.

"You love me now."

"Always. And always."

She was sure she could have prolonged this closeness forever, and when he withdrew she said, "Oh, no!" which made him laugh.

She dressed hurriedly, embarrassed under his attentive gaze.

"You have grace, my young love. It is an enchantment to watch you. Do you know that?"

"Don't be silly. I'm an actress. I only pretend to be graceful."

He reached for her hand. "If I were beginning my life as you are . . . if there had been no war . . . if—well, *if*."

"Tell me. If."

"We might have been the greatest lovers since Heloise and Abelard." He thought that over. "No. Poor Abelard. I hope I am not quite in his state. Let us say, Romeo and Juliet."

She helped him wrap the picnic items in paper and then pack them in the hamper.

"I'll never forget today as long as I live," she said firmly.

"That is as it should be."

"And I'll love you 'til I die."

His laughter was light, warm and teasing. "Not that long, I hope. Come along. We still have the evening before us. The Left Bank, I think. An old place I know on the rue de la Harpe. Not far from the rue du Chat-qui-Pêche."

That made her laugh, too. " 'Street of the Cat Who Fishes.' No matter what you say, I'll love you 'til I die."

"Make it until *I* die. That should give you a little more time to love someone else."

She hit his shoulder with her fist and got into the car.

# *Chapter Nine*

EDEN Ware left Paris a wiser and happier girl. André had offered to go with her on the long day journey across the continent to Vienna, but she knew she couldn't hang onto him forever, no matter how much she loved him. He should remain a free man, she knew, because in that way he might always think of her as special.

Watching the still-green, lush fields of France pass swiftly by the train window, she thought about André and the pile of stones at Rogier-Grasse, the only memorial to a family that had lived there almost a thousand years. She saw something of André's spirit in the tall poplar windbreaks in the distance and the meadows mottled with haystacks that huddled against the coming winter. André was like his native soil, a land that had become worn and cynical after its bloody history and yet stubbornly retained its beauty . . .

At the Gare du Nord, she said good-bye to André. He had given her a little bouquet of Parma violets. "What will you do today?" she asked.

His reply jarred her. "I think I will drive out again to Rogier and visit the cemetery this time. Lisa was fond of Parma violets." He smiled. "Do I shock you? I assure you, we French are not sentimental. We often go to cemeteries and think about the earth renewing itself."

"I hope I renewed you." Though she was not usually shy, her words now sounded wistful.

"You have, Eden," he said quietly. "For me, you will always be *primavera.* The bright springtime."

They kissed and she felt his heartbeat and her own as he held her close. A man in the blue uniform of the Orient Express company tapped André's shoulder.

*"Monsieur, attention!"* But he was most polite, doubtless influenced by the sight of lovers parting, Eden thought, and she felt like a true heroine.

She climbed up the steps and found her compartment with its window seat. Under the cold gaze of her fellow travelers, she waved to André until she lost sight of the station platform.

Aware of her companions, three traveling businessmen with satchels and one elegant woman in an ermine-trimmed black suit, Eden smiled. She assumed that someone would remark her romantic departure, but no one did. The woman, obviously French, simply raised her eyebrows and shifted her gaze. One of the men appeared ready to smile but his frosty companion pointed out someone passing along the corridor outside the compartment. Both men got up, slid the door open and engaged in a long conversation in the corridor, all in German. Eden found their subject boring, but she understood the language well enough to pick up what they were talking about.

The Germans were discussing the dependability of the powerful *Kreditanstalt* bank of Vienna. For some reason another privately owned bank in Munich had failed, and this, it seemed, affected small businesses and factory workers.

"Communists!" the German in the corridor insisted loudly. "These business failures, the blame is communism."

The other man waved his hands as his face reddened with anger. "Perfect grounds for those crazies who met for the celebration of the good marshal's birthday. National Socialists? Where is the difference—Socialist . . . Communist . . . National Socialist?"

"Not the same," the tall man contradicted him. "The Communists, you say. The National Socialists—Nazis, we call them—they promise to give. Back comes our pride. Back comes the Saar. The Rhineland. *Lebensraum.* The breathing room we need. Do you know what Herr Hitler says in his book? Much read, this book."

"Yes. *The Struggle.*"

*"My Struggle,* it is called. My plan. My dream. *Mein Kampf.* Truly, you will be impressed. And no more little banks failing. I will lend you my copy of *Mein Kampf.* You will not forget it, I guarantee."

"They are all the same to me," the fat man insisted. "Communist Lenin. Fascist Mussolini. And this *Kampf* fellow."

"Hitler. *Kampf* is the book."

The man in the corridor wasn't impressed. "My friend, I have too many reports to write, too many papers to read. Keep your *Kampf.* Come and tell me about it when these National Socialists prevent the factories from closing, the banks from collapsing, the harvest from failing. Do you know that my sister's husband—his crops rotted in the fields this fall. He could not get fertilizer early. Now, he cannot get even his cabbages to the market. His team was poisoned by tramps. Out of work. Hating the world. He tried to borrow from the *Nürnberg und National* bank. Refused."

"It is no surprise," the tall man aid. "Examine the board of *Nürnberg und National.* Meier. Salomon. Kreismann."

"True enough," the man put in. "But Jews do not go about poisoning animals."

"No, no. Not there. Gypsies. Pouring in from Hungary and the new regime there."

The men fell silent, each thinking that someone else was to blame for his misfortunes.

Eden could never recall hearing anyone in the islands speak about such things. She took out her copy of Shakespeare, intending to rehearse silently the role of Juliet.

The three German-speaking men got together later when the man from the corridor stuck his head in again.

"Ulrich, have you heard the news? For the second time in a week. A sweep of Wall Street. The market is down. Millions in dollars lost. For the moment I would say, caution. Still, it is not all bad. Certainly it is good for us. The reparations payments."

The lean man chuckled dryly. "But this is good. I have already made the move to London for the lower interest rates. This will let the air out of these prosperous Americans."

Eden looked at the Frenchwoman, whose thin lips curved faintly upward. She too found the American disaster something to smile about.

Eden wasn't at all sure she wanted to stay even a month in Europe.

The Lombards would be hit, she thought with dismay—and so many others. But at least her father would be safe . . .

As the hours dragged by, she regretted having taken such a dislike to her companions. She would have liked to ask about the fuss at the border. The train crossed the wide gray-green waters of the Rhine before Eden was aware that they were moving into another country.

She had seen the German border guards only once, with her father and Brooke at a time when Germany was floundering in defeat, starvation and the destruction of its currency. Today the customs and passport control men were more harassed than ever. Tension was everywhere. The customs men were quickly finished, but the security man examining passports asked their destination.

"Augsburg," the Frenchwoman said crisply.

"Good." He saluted.

"München," the two Germans said.

The official hesitated. "A problem exists in München. It may be necessary that you leave the train by an outer station."

The men exchanged glances. "What is the problem?"

"A riot centered near the Münchener Bahnhof."

The first man said, "Aha! Communists."

The official slapped the passport into the man's hand. "Two parties insist on marching. They threaten a clash near the Bahnhof. The Communists and the National Socialists."

The other man began to look nervous.

The security man examined Eden's passport, then gave Eden a brief smile. "Fräulein? American? Your destination?"

"Vienna, Austria."

His smile faded. "From München east, there are difficulties. If our München station is taken, the Austrians may close the border. We can promise nothing. I regret, fräulein."

ONCE THE officials left the compartment, the German passengers, with occasional glances at the Frenchwoman, discussed the troubles in Munich, joining in a condemnation of the Communist troublemakers.

But when the Frenchwoman left the train at Stuttgart, the men united in blaming "outsiders" for the Munich riot . . .

In the dining car Eden met an American family of three. She asked how far they were going. The woman spoke. "To Vienna, if we ever get there. How serious is this Munich riot?"

Eden returned to her compartment suffering feelings of uneasiness such as she had never known before. Her anxiety increased with every German town that the Orient Express roared through. She noticed that not many passengers got on the train and many got off at Augsburg.

Late in the day the two men opposite Eden began to gather their luggage. Eden looked out her window . . . *We must be getting toward Munich,* she thought, as her nerves tightened . . .

The train had passed through a green countryside full of carefully cultivated fields, cows, geese, white ducks, and picturesque villages. It was hard to see the poverty-stricken land that the international press spoke of with such pessimism.

But the speeding train slowed to a stop, and Eden's two male companions in the compartment got up and headed along the corridor.

The train pulled on and as they approached the heart of the railroad area in the next city, the side streets and the tracks were littered with paper, placards and torn banners.

The long train stopped, and Eden saw marching along the opposite track under the train windows what looked like a platoon of soldiers. Their boots shone in the evening light, but they wore an assortment of uniforms from the Great War, some field gray, some green. Their leader, strutting along and turning to march backward several times as he faced his company, was dressed in black.

Passengers crowded around Eden's window, looking out and commenting on the youth of the little group. Surely these young people were not responsible for the riot, they all said. Just then a handful of rocks, followed by undersized cabbages, pelted the window. Everyone dodged back.

Eden sat back and watched the young commander in black. He didn't look to her like a casual youth led by a sudden fit of resentment at the occupants of the famed Orient Express. He had rehearsed all this, she realized, his strut, his authority, his sharp commands in tight, guttural German.

Eden began to wonder what she would do if everyone was ordered off the train. What concerned her most was that she had no Deutschemarks, and she wondered if her Austrian or French money would be accepted if she had to spend the night here.

A conference seemed to be taking place toward the front of the train. Two local policemen in bucket helmets and belted coats climbed aboard, cheered on by the marchers. Eden got up nervously and stood by the open door, trying to hear what was said as the policemen, trailed by two of the train's obviously worried conductors, slid open each compartment door.

"Deutsches?" they demanded, then examined passports. They squinted to see that each passport matched the face, then slapped it back into the passenger's hand.

Those that had declared they were German were left alone. All others were questioned as to their party affiliation.

"By the lord Harry!" one of the Americans exclaimed as he watched outside the next compartment. "Now they want to know our political party. Well, they'll get it."

The city policeman reached his compartment. The American spoke in a ringing voice. "You know you Müncheners have no right on this train. It's an international express."

"Passport. Name."

"Von Eck is the name. Harvey von Eck."

"Ah," said the first policeman. Then he saw the passport. "Amerikaner!"

Von Eck winked broadly at Eden. "And my politics? Like Will Rogers says, I don't belong to an organized party. I'm a Democrat."

The policeman saluted and went on to the others in the compartment, one of whom carried a German passport.

While Eden watched, her throat dry with fear, the German made a quiet reply. Whatever it was, the policeman waved the man's passport at the uniformed crowd outside who cheered. Orders were given. The German was hustled out of the compartment protesting and motioning for his baggage. The second policeman lowered the window, threw out the man's old blue cardboard suitcase which landed on the track and split open. Among shirts and underwear, books poured out. The marchers surrounded the books, holding up several in triumph.

"Karl Marx! Engels! Lenin!"

"Must be German Communists they were after," von Eck remarked good-naturedly. "Whatever the ruckus is about, you can say one thing. They've got no use for a Red. Look at that. They've got a couple of others down the line. They're beating up the poor guys."

Eden made her way back to her seat. She didn't look out again. The sounds were clear enough . . . shouts, muffled screams and the thud of blows. But worst of all were the laughter and jeers of those on the track who watched cheering.

One of the Americans in Eden's compartment said, "Well, we know who won that riot they promised us. It sure wasn't the Commies."

The policemen now stood in the compartment doorway with the train conductor behind them.

"In this compartment, Americans. All Americans."

"So?" asked the policeman. Every passport, including Eden's, was held out to him. He waved them away and went on with the other policeman.

Later, one of the American men complained as had von Eck. "Those fellows had no authority there. They're nothing but local ward heelers."

"You want to argue with them?" asked one of his companions. "They were both wearing sidearms, if you noticed."

Everyone shut up after that . . .

Twenty minutes later the train began to move quietly into München Bahnhof. It did not remain long but sailed out of both station and city with all its celebrated speed, arriving at the Austrian border only twelve minutes late.

OSTERREICH said the sign over the passport control office as the passengers filed through, had their passports checked and climbed back on the train inside Austria. Eden still felt shaky. For the first time in her life she had discovered what it was to be rendered helpless while senseless brutality took place within a few feet of her.

"How do we know that professor deserved to be beaten up?" she asked suddenly. "Had he done something terrible? Killed someone?"

Mr. von Eck heard her question and stuck his head inside the compartment. "I guess they figure books are more dangerous than guns. Maybe they are. Of course, the gang that pulled this will be in jail tonight, but that won't help that little Commie."

"I think we'd all better say nothing until we are safely back in Western Europe," one of the other Americans suggested. "This is no place to argue about other people's laws. It's their country, after all."

"Not now. We're in Austria," von Eck reminded him with a grin. "Or Osterreich, as they call it." He went back to his compartment.

Eden looked out the window, trying to make out the outlying areas of Salzburg in the twilight. But she kept hearing the sounds of that badly uniformed crowd of hooligans, their shiny boots stamping the professor's hands, crushing his ribs in . . .

She closed her eyes and was asleep when the train attendant came through calling, "Wien! Wien!" She knew she had reached the end of the interminable and horrifying train ride.

AS THEY pulled into the station, the Westbahnhof was crowded, but no one could mistake Brooke Lombard Huntington Ware for anyone else. Her laughing voice rang out as she ran along the platform to the window where Eden was standing. Eden pushed her way out to the platform where her stepmother hugged and kissed her. "It was awful. You can't imagine. They beat up some men who—"

"Was it bad? You poor lamb! They say there were riots. We thought we might have to rescue you from those Communist rioters."

"There were two groups. The other side won. Two policemen came on board. They took—"

"I'm sure it was dreadful . . . I have a divine surprise for you. You will never guess. Come along. Someone you haven't seen in years, since you were a child." She was waving to the porter who loaded up Eden's cases and followed the two women.

Realizing that Brooke was always more interested in her own

schemes, Eden tried to simulate some enthusiasm as they walked the length of the Westbahnhof.

"So you've found friends here. I'll bet they're good-looking."

Brooke grinned. "One of them certainly is. Wait 'til you see. He'll be as surprised as you are. I just told him we were meeting someone he knew ten years ago. I exaggerated a little. But I wanted to make it a real surprise. You'd never recognize each other after all this time. Oh! There he is. Come and meet a very young fan of yours, Kurt. All the way back to Hawaii, 1922. Do you remember my stepdaughter, Eden Ware?"

Eden's own astonishment was eased by the ludicrous expression on Kurt Friedrich's face, and she could barely keep herself from laughing. He was afraid of her, she knew at once, afraid of what she might tell Brooke about that evening at the Royal Hawaiian . . .

He offered his hand tentatively.

"I would never have known the young lady. So grown up she is."

"Grown up indeed. But very sweet and inexperienced, Kurt. So none of your naughty flirtations to break her heart, or I'll have to scold you. Now, Eden, you remember Kurt's old boss, Leo Prysing? His brother, Dr. Josef Preysing, is a friend of the famous composer, Franz Lehar. The one who wrote "The Blue Danube" and all those pretty pieces."

"You refer to *The Merry Widow,* I think," Kurt corrected her politely.

"Yes. One of those Viennese operettas. Anyway, dear Josef got Kurt a job in a revival at Mr. Lehar's favorite theater. You'll love Kurt. He started out in a smaller part, but here he is playing the prince who dances the Blue Danube Waltz."

It would have been pointless to correct her again, so Eden merely said, "I didn't know Mr. Friedrich sang."

The actor's smile did not come fast enough to hide the narrow-eyed look he gave Eden. "The range is not impossible. I am a very good beer hall singer, so I am told."

Stepping out into the chilly Vienna night, they crossed the semicircle where cabs were all being snapped up. Brooke took Eden's hand, pressing it hard.

"Like the old days, traveling together. I was so lonely when I wrote to you. Of course, that was before Kurt and I met in the lobby of the Ambassade Hotel. Would you believe, a Viennese paper had actually mentioned my name as one of those attending *Der Rosenkavalier* at the Opera."

They headed for a large black European touring car. A middle-aged man with curling gray hair stood beside the front car door. He took his hat off and kissed Brooke's hand.

"Eden, these are Leo's family, the Preysings. Sarah?"

A comfortably stout woman with a warm, pink-cheeked face looked out. She spoke English surprisingly well. "Welcome to Vienna, Miss Ware. A pleasure to know Leo's young friend."

Dr. Josef took Eden's hand in his friendly way. "Not so good a welcome for you, I think. The radio says the Express was in a riot at Munich."

"How did it turn out, doctor?" Kurt asked.

"Some Communists beaten up. Two Munich police have been jailed. They seem to be members of the Nazis, a splinter party."

Brooke shrugged. "Fortunately, nobody was hurt." She urged Eden into the back seat of the car and then followed with Kurt.

"But some Communists were beaten up. Dr. Preysing says so himself," Eden said. No one spoke for a moment. Dr. Preysing was starting the engine, but Eden sensed in the darkness the actor's gaze.

When they were driving toward the great, gloomy Hofburg Palace, Dr. Preysing pointed it out. "Our Emperor Franz Josef lived there. I was named for him."

Out of nowhere Kurt Friedrich said to Brooke, "You know, *Liebchen,* it is a pity I did not know Eden was coming. If she wishes to be an actress, Paris is a wonderful opportunity. There are men in the cinema industry who could use an unusual voice like Eden's to dub in for the French actresses."

No matter how much the man revolted her, Eden would never turn down such a marvelous opportunity. Besides, she thought, it would mean being with André for a while. She forgot all about the events of the Orient Express.

"How did you know Eden wanted to be an actress?" Brooke asked sharply.

Kurt and Eden spoke up together. "When she was a child she said—"

"I told everyone even back in those days."

Brooke was satisfied.

The Preysings dropped them off in front of the dignified Hotel Ambassade.

*"Liebchen,* was it not lucky to think of my friend Raymond Zelle in Paris? The very man who needs American voices to make his speaking films understood in the United States."

"But why don't *you* get a job like that, Mr. Friedrich?" Eden asked.

He gazed at Brooke before waving away the idea. "Not for me. My accent, you know. And—shall we tell her?"

"She has to know sooner or later," Brooke said. "Darling, it's been an absolute whirlwind. Less than three weeks, and Kurt and I are engaged."

Eden stared at them, dumbfounded. She now understood the real reason for Kurt Friedrich's sudden generosity with the Paris job . . . He wanted to get rid of her, fast . . . She wondered if she should tell Brooke, after all.

But then Eden realized that Brooke probably wouldn't care. And there was Paris. André. Above all, she would return to the United States with a movie background of sorts . . .

"Congratulations, both of you. It's very romantic, I must say. Mr. Friedrich, you are giving up a chance in Paris to be with Brooke. I think it's noble of you."

"Well, we *could* live in France," Brooke started to say, but Kurt cut in.

"You forget, my darling, my world is here. I am German."

"Silly," Brooke chided him. "This is Austria."

"Same thing," Kurt said and led them into the hotel lobby.

# *Chapter Ten*

BROOKE'S latest marriage was received with mixed feelings by her family. Randi marveled that she could marry a man who had behaved so indifferently when his mistress, Irita Vallman, died. Steve swore up and down that he would write Brooke and refuse her request to have the monthly payments from her trust doubled. Alec had heard from his mother on the same subject and came to Sam Liversedge to ask that the extra legacy from Alicia Lombard be sent to his mother.

"She needs protection. She is really quite helpless. I don't want her to be taken. You know what I mean," Alec told Sam.

Sam explained this to Steve and Randi at the Lombards' quiet Christmas Eve party at which he and Bridget were the only guests.

"The boy insists it must go to her, but like you, he knows the husband will get hold of it. Alec has letters from young Eden Ware in Paris. She seems to be doing some work, dubbing her voice in those movies no one ever understands. But according to Alec, she doesn't trust this Kurt Friedrich, either. Nothing definite. Alec says it just kind of creeps into the girl's correspondence."

Bridget spoke. "Alec is real fond of his mother. You'll excuse the liberty, but I never quite knew why. Anyways, if he wasn't so stubborn, he'd be here tonight with you folks."

"According to Brooke, the new husband hasn't asked for a cent."

"He wouldn't have to," Steve explained. "All he has to do is say they can't have this or that because of the money situation."

"Isn't that how Alma Gault handles her husband?" Randi asked.

Her faint stirrings of jealousy died down when Steve promptly agreed. "Alma is a problem, all right. I'm sorry for her. Damn it, we all are. Has she made much trouble for you, Sam?"

Sam sighed. "Poor old Buck. I think it was the way he hurt Alma financially that pushed him over the edge. He'd never have done the thing in his right mind."

"He hurt Steve pretty badly, too," Randi snapped. "Between Mr. Cortlandt and Steve's father, we're mortgaged to the hilt right now."

Bridget, though, was cheerful. After all, she had been poor before. "Well, me lads, we just tighten the belt and go on. Holy Mary, I daily give thanks I bought the rooming house with the profits you helped me to get, Steve. Buying it was the smartest thing I ever done. It's a roof over my head, and it brings in fifteen or twenty a month from each room when they're all taken."

They were taken now, Randi knew, but rental payments were getting slower. In two years Bridget would be fifty; her pert Irish beauty had finally begun to fade. Randi hated to see it go almost more than her mother did.

"The young laddie-boy is after telling his old gran she should hold onto her steady stocks, not throw them in a heap for loose change. What's your opinion, gentlemen?" Bridget asked.

Tony piped up. "Alec is dumb, but he sure knows about talking on the radio. I watch him a lot."

Bridget ruffled his hair fondly. "He does that. And you mark me, my lad here with his Irish eyes and his voice with the lilt of the Auld Sod is going to do big things in radio himself one day."

"I talk like you, granny."

"So you do, my precious. And I'll be immodest enough to say you're the better for it."

Randi was worried, though. "I just hope Alec doesn't mind Tony hanging around so much. He might get jealous. They used to quarrel a lot when they were young."

"I don't fight with Alec, ever," Tony said with the smile he inherited from Bridget. "Sure now, that'd be dumb."

The women smiled, but the men were still discussing Alec's stubborn refusal to make peace.

"I wish the damn fool would take the chip off his shoulder and come home," Steve said. "I think Alec was there in that room all the time I was knocking yesterday. Good God, it isn't as if I'd committed a crime or something."

AS FAR as Alec Huntington was concerned, Steve and Sam Liversedge had done worse than commit a crime—they had made *him* look like a crook.

He had behaved stupidly, he told himself, in holding onto the legacy, but he knew why he had done so. He had feared they would all spend it as lavishly and quickly as they always did—especially Red and Brooke. Now he had to turn over every cent the Lombard legacies were worth on the day before the first big market drop in October.

His own properties had dwindled down to nothing. And the market hadn't recovered yet.

Layoffs had begun. Alec's problem was symptomatic of trouble in other industries, but the fact interested him only slightly. The real terror came when the station manager and Baccagalupi, the program chief, talked to him about the lower revenues from the commercial messages. Baccagalupi didn't go as far as canceling his show. But he did cut Alec's salary twenty dollars a week.

All his plans to visit his mother and her new husband fell apart. He couldn't get enough money together.

From Brooke's occasional letters to him he had hoped that Brooke would return to San Francisco at least to show off her handsome husband. But given the reduced profits of her trust fund, she claimed she could not afford to make the trip.

So Alec had no real idea of how his mother's marriage was going. Though he didn't admit it to Bridget, his landlady and confidante, it was a big disappointment when another year went by without his being able to see his mother . . .

Alec began to consider new ideas for his broadcasts, pushing for a European visit as part of his job. The station owner wouldn't buy it, but Baccagalupi softened the blow.

"Fred says why not get some first-hand stuff from the Pacific, which is our bailiwick anyway. That Japanese prime minister they shot last winter right after the naval conference. Well, according to this bulletin that just came in, Yamaguchi finally died. That ends the peace movement in Tokyo. The war-and-expansion boys are already coming out of the woodwork."

But the station wanted Alec to fund the trip himself. A long round-trip sea voyage meant too much time lost from his job at the station, and the idea fell through . . .

Meanwhile, it became necessary to do what Alec dreaded; he had to go out and hustle up radio ads. He always felt that a job like selling time was like selling himself.

Maybe he wouldn't have to do it for long . . . By March the market was looking up. Dividends began to be paid. Things would soon climb back up to normal, Alec thought, and hoped that his climb up the ladder would continue with the market's rise.

RANDI KNEW what a blow it was to Steve when the market began to slide again after a brief upsurge. Five million unemployed in the United States alone, and the disease had spread to Europe, then to the rest of the world. She felt sorry for Eden Ware, who bravely refused to go home to be a burden on her father. She had remained in Paris working for little money dubbing films and otherwise "getting free meals from friends," as her letters said. She sounded happy, but Randi suspected she just might be putting it on . . .

The same week that Leo Prysing asked Randi to come down to Hollywood for a conference on his 1931–32 project, Red Lombard tried to wheedle thirty thousand dollars out of Steve to save his Wilshire ground.

"I can't make the mortgage date. There's the truth of it, son. If you want to see your old dad down sleeping in the fields off the flood control, like our old friend LeMass, just burn this letter."

"How the hell do I dig up thirty thousand?" Steve demanded, stalking up and down, waving his arms. "This morning it was Alma. This afternoon it's Red. Money, money. Everybody hanging around my neck like I was a—"

"What did Alma want?" Randi interrupted him coolly.

"Who knows? Complaining about that poor weakling husband. His company just folded. He's going to try and get a job, but it won't be anything like what he's used to. Alma is even threatening divorce. No loyalty in that girl."

Randi's hackles rose. "I suppose she will be hanging around here all the time, looking for sympathy."

Steve stubbornly defended the woman. "After all, Randi, she's used to money. She has never wanted for anything in her life."

With great difficulty, Randi refrained from a sarcastic remark. "I hope this won't interfere with our going south. This meeting involves the entire program for next year, and with studios like Warners and Paramount in trouble, it's a miracle that Leo keeps going."

"Look, sweetheart, you're a big girl now. You don't need me to chaperone you. It isn't as if he was trying to get fresh with you. I mean —has he ever tried anything?"

"Certainly not," she said. "He wouldn't dare." But her eyes were fixed on the floor.

"Well, then?"

"What would you be doing while I'm gone?" She didn't like the idea of their being separated. Their usual separations had been no longer than overnight and involved his business projects in some way. Only once, on a visit to Strand, had Steve ever spent more than one night away from home.

He laughed, "You sound mighty suspicious. If you're thinking of good old Alma, she's on her way to New York to buy clothes. She says that will ease the pangs of her coming divorce. That is, if she does divorce Gault."

So Alma really was going through with it, Randi thought. The idea didn't appeal to her at all. Alma would now have countless reasons for hanging around Steve's office . . .

Since Tony was now between grades, he had a week's recess and would spend the time of his mother's absence at Bridget's house, learning what he could from Alec at the radio station and giving Randi a chance to pay her mother some real money for Tony's care. Most of Bridget's roomers were at least a month behind in their rent.

By the time Randi had received all her instructions from Steve about the dangers of a woman traveling alone, she wondered at the sheer audacity of women like Brooke and Eden Ware, who had traveled like that for years.

To save money Randi took a single lower berth and on reaching Los Angeles took a room in a commercial hotel. She even took the bus to Culver City. She smiled to herself when she thought two years ago she would have hired a car and chauffeur or simply taken a taxi for the long trip across town . . .

From the bus window Randi tried to make out changes in the sprawling city of Los Angeles. She knew about the breadlines that were beginning to form during the past few months in San Francisco in front of charity kitchens and bakeries, and any place where food was advertised.

The difference between San Francisco and Los Angeles seemed to be the prices—things were cheaper here. Probably because San Francisco was a union town, she thought, and wondered what Paddy LeMass was doing these days. Things must be rough for him . . . Randi had written a storyline for an original movie based on what she imagined were the struggles these days of men like LeMass. She had read it to Bridget who gave her a few pointers on the personal habits of her old boy friend.

"I must look him up," she thought. "He could undoubtedly use a little help." If her story went over, he would be entitled to a fee.

She got off the bus, crossed the wide, almost deserted boulevard, and walked up to the sentry box where the ancient gateman guarded Prysing Productions, housed in the false front of a stately white Virginia mansion. Behind the facade were two sound stages which reached back toward acres of hills and flatland. It was the land Prysing leased from Steve Lombard.

A little wicket gate barred the walk. The gateman, who knew Randi and her husband from former visits, took his job seriously.

"How-do, Mrs. Lombard. Just a sec'. I'll get Mr. Prysing's secretary. I'm sure it'll be all right."

Leo Prysing himself came striding out across the gravel driveway and waved impatiently to the gateman.

"Mike, you know better than to keep Mrs. Lombard waiting."

"Sure thing, Mr. Prysing," the gateman said with a grin.

Leo took Randi's arm. "You are looking beautiful. But then, you always do. You trust me now, I see. No handsome blockhead of a husband to guard you. Or is it that you have decided to tempt me?"

"Keep talking like that and I'll tempt you with a jab from my hatpin. I'm here on business."

"And a pretty little confection it is." He pinched the pointed crown of the tiny hat that did not conceal her tawny hair coiled in a French twist, and walked up on the wide veranda with her.

"I wonder if you will ever tell me why you smile like that when you come to visit me," Leo said as he nodded to his secretary, a tall, striking blonde. She and Randi murmured greetings.

When Leo had seated his guest in the large, baronial chair opposite his cluttered desk, the secretary closed the door. Through the windows behind the producer's head, Randi could see the traffic passing along Washington Boulevard. She knew that she had been placed to receive the unflattering direct sunlight while Leo, with his back to the windows, was bathed in gentle shadows. It was not a plot against her, she thought, but against his visitors in general.

"Are all movie producers as obvious as you are?" she asked him suddenly. He raised his eyebrows, graying like his hair, innocently. She pointed out how her oversized chair made her seem small compared with the commanding presence of the man behind the desk.

He laughed and admitted, "It is expected of me."

"Where are your executives, stockholders, writers? All those people due for your conference?"

He got up, came around the desk, hooked one leg over the corner and sat there watching her. "That was settled yesterday. Now is the time for you to use that hatpin." But he did not touch her.

His nearness was disturbing. She forced herself not to draw back, but her pulse raced . . . She shifted to another subject that concerned her.

"I hear that my sister-in-law's marriage is one of those happily-ever-after things. What does Dr. Preysing think? He and Mrs. Preysing are Friedrich's friends, I believe."

Leo shrugged. "Maybe she enjoys being mistreated. Some women do." He saw that he had confirmed her worst suspicions and added quickly, "But from what I saw of Brooke Huntington that time in Hawaii she would put up with a good deal if she could be satisfied. And that Kurt can do. You know what a stud is?"

"Certainly," she said crisply.

"Kurt is insatiable. Ask Olga Rey. She's still talking about his prowess in bed. When your sister-in-law brought Kurt and my brother together, I suppose it seemed natural for Josef to help the fellow get a break. Franz Lehar has a Jewish wife and that probably is the tie between the Lehars and my family. But I knew Kurt's parents. They divorced shortly after Kurt was born. He was raised by his mother and horribly indulged. Still, he did attract a few females to my films."

And seduced your wife, Randi thought, but Prysing was off on a new tack. "What I can't figure out is how your sister-in-law ever happened to marry a decent, fatherly fellow like Nigel Ware."

"Because he *was* fatherly. Brooke is very fond of Red Lombard. He spoiled her, of course." She unwound the string closure of her pressboard envelope and pulled out a dozen typed sheets. She spoke quickly.

"Up to now, I've whipped up the stuff you asked for. But with business so bad—Steve says he's barely holding on—people like the tenants in the Dunes can't pay their rent and their bills. The tenants in Strand are the same. Nobody is buying property. In fact, nobody is spending money on anything but movies."

"True." Randi noted there was no smugness in his reply. "What's this to do with the script? What you have there isn't a script, is it? Too short."

"It's a storyline. About today. The suffering and the poverty and the breadlines."

Leo bit his lip as his manner subtly became more businesslike.

"Well, don't hold onto it all day. Let me see it."

Her hand wasn't steady. He closed his own fingers over hers, hard, not troubling to be gentle. He took the script and, still perched on the edge of the desk, scanned each page, dropping it to the floor as he finished. Randi followed each fluttering page with her eyes. Long before he finished she was discouraged, and fortified her fears with resentment. As she stooped to pick up all her laborious work, he put his foot on the pages.

"Well?" she urged him. "Well?"

He dropped the last page and it floated down to the carpet. He stood up, went around the desk and picked up a blue folder fastened with two brass brads.

"Now then, your next assignment. You've seen New York? Never mind. It's just an overgrown San Francisco. Girl is a waitress. The kind who wear those cutesy uniforms, all starched frills."

"Organdy." She was picking up her typed pages slowly.

"So. Feminine, but sassy. She works at some swank place. Say, the new Sherry Netherland. Or better yet, the Waldorf-Astoria. It opened this month. Topical."

"Speaking of topical—"

"She meets this fellow, all greasy and filthy. He's in the alley. She thinks he's starving but he's actually the prince of Ruritania. Looking for a hubcap he lost off his Dusenberg. Or something. So, we have—"

"I hope you don't call that really reading a script! You barely glanced at it." She could have slapped him.

"Of course I've read it. You just heard me reciting the essentials. Taylor Scott came up with them. What I want you to do is fill in the nonessentials."

"Don't be funny. You know what I mean. And furthermore, I produce just as many essentials as Taylor Scott does."

He sighed heavily. "They all get the big head eventually. All right. Dostoevski you are not. Your talent is small and pleasant and the ladies who go to my budget movies like all that guff about princes and waitresses. But that stuff there in your hands—men living on wharves, under piers, in the slums—these creatures are not your style, Mrs. Stephen Lombard."

"How about Mary-Randal Gallegher's style? I do know about poverty. Ask my mother."

"You do not know about men without women. What dock workers do you know? Not one, I'll bet. They wouldn't react like that. The very spine of the story is fake. An angel of hope among these creeps and no one does more than kiss the hem of her cloak?"

"She is in the Salvation Army?" Randi nearly shrieked.

He changed his tactics, became earnest. "Don't despise what you do so well. Shopgirl romance. It's the backbone of the movies. Leave all this gloom to characters who have lost their sense of romance. Take Scott's storyline and fill in the scenes. I'll up the ante. Give you a bonus to soothe your artistic conscience."

She got up and looked him in the eyes. "How much?"

After a flicker of surprise, he laughed. "Good girl. Business as usual. I'll add another fifty. That makes it two-fifty."

Like everyone involved in the industry she had taken a pay cut the year before. "Make it three hundred. I've got a lot of conscience to soothe."

The hard flippancy was unlike her, but he knew that it concealed the hurt to her pride.

"Good. Do we continue to send your checks to Mrs. Gallegher on Sutter Street?"

Until the first of the year, all Randi's earnings had been deposited to the Lombard accounts. But too many of these checks had gone to Brooke and Red. She didn't mind bailing them out once, but supporting them was out of the question. It annoyed her that Steve wouldn't spend her money on Tony or himself. He never said anything, but she felt that he had some secret pride about using her money, and Randi suspected that giving it to his sister or his father was his way of disposing of it. She resented especially that he had lent money to Edwin Gault. That money always went onto the back of Alma Gault, who had not stopped spending money since her father's suicide. Steve said spending consoled her for her unhappiness. But the unhappiness seemed disproportionate to her bank account . . .

"Yes. My mother doesn't know what it is, as long as you send it in those manila envelopes with the scripts or the storylines. Ma is a dear, but she is apt to talk at the wrong times."

"And what do you intend to do with all the treasure you've dug out of me?"

She ignored his humor. "When I get enough I'll tell Steve. I'll send mother to Hawaii first. She's never been any farther off the Coast than Catalina. Nigel Ware tried to get her to visit them when he was here last, but of course, she can't afford it, the way things are."

"Nothing being saved for the noble Stephen?"

"When I save enough, I want to see Europe with Steve and Tony. If Steve won't use the money that way, we could send Tony with some reliable friend."

"Send him with me. I'm reliable." She laughed, but for once he was serious. "I'd like to persuade Josef and Sarah to return with me. I haven't succeeded so far, but the German elections are going to mean trouble. If either the Nazi—"

"The what?"

"National Socialists. If either they or the Reds get control of the German Reichstag there may be trouble in Austria as well. Everyone seems to have been bitten by the Mussolini bug. Even Josef talks about how a powerful government may get Vienna out of the depression doldrums."

Randi hardly knew Austria from Germany. Steve had fought both countries in the war. Since everyone said America needed a strong leader, it wasn't surprising that Europe shared that view. She knew Eden wrote little jokes about one of the German parties and its leader, Adolf Hitler, but Eden was hardly twenty-one and her prejudices might pretty well be discounted. Only Steve seemed puzzled when he read her occasional letters.

Prysing shook off election talk. "We'll forget Mussolini, Roosevelt and these other would-be saviors. About your plans tonight, I'll take you to the Montmartre Café. Everybody who's anybody goes there, and they guarantee a fistfight each night. I understand the best fights go on in the ladies' room. Give me a storyline about that."

Fights in the ladies' room didn't exactly entice her, and in any case she wanted to call home to Steve before she took the train to Strand where she would spend the night with Red, Stella and little Heather. After this encounter with Leo she wanted more than ever to get to Strand and find out if Stella Burkett possibly knew where she could reach Pat LeMass. It would be worth everything to her if she could produce a storyline that Leo would accept.

She started for the door, noticed the big leather couch against the back wall.

"I see you have a casting couch. No wonder your walls are soundproof."

"Can't let the casting directors have all the fun."

He reached the door before her and kept his palm on it so she couldn't get it open.

"Some day, Mary-Randal Gallegher, your baser nature is going to take over, and when that happens I want to be there. You are going to love me yet. Want to get out the hatpin?"

"You conceited pig!"

"Please," he begged in mock horror. "Not pig. Porcupine. Rhinoceros. Ape. But not pig."

She hurried out, afraid he would guess she was on the verge of laughing herself into a good mood.

# *Chapter Eleven*

BY the time Randi reached Strand and the Monte Carlo Arms shortly after noon, her father-in-law was off "winning his future." According to Stella Burkett who always treated Randi with either excessive deference or conspiratorial familiarity, Red spent many of his nights out on the gambling ship *Danna Schimmer.* This freighter was stationed beyond the three-mile limit and reached by speedboat near the flood control.

This channel, often bone-dry, separated Strand from the swampy saltwater flats of Wilmington. The latter received all the larger ocean traffic from the Orient, the Antipodes and the Hawaiian territories.

In some respects, Randi was relieved. She had seen soon enough that Stella Burkett now shared Red's bedroom without any pretense. Heather, prettier and sweeter than ever, almost nine years old, slept in a little annex to the dining room. Her narrow folding bed reminded Randi of her own childhood in odd rooming houses here and there, wherever Bridget found cheap lodgings . . . Randi suspected that Stella had set her sights on Red and meant to have her way . . .

Stella claimed to have no current news of Heather's real father.

"LeMass loved your ma, Randi. I always knew that. But he was real nice and—you know he had an eye for me. Anyway, right after I got pregnant, boy, he ran! I figured he at least owed me the expense of the birth and all. He was getting together a couple hundred bucks. From your ma, I reckon. So I let Mr. Steve's mother think what she wanted. I thought—why not? You'd done all right for yourself. Why couldn't I get a little of that?"

"You did very well," Randi remarked, looking out at the silhouette of the distant gambling ship beyond the breakers shining in the hazy sunlight.

"So did you. But I don't mind any more. I just admire you for it. Maybe when this depression thing is over, I'll do better yet. Better than you."

Randi was jarred out of her reverie. "What does that mean?"

"Just talking. You asked about LeMass. He didn't care about Heather. I don't care about him. So he's hungry. Who cares? We all got our problems."

In the long run Randi knew only the longshoremen's local union office could tell her where Paddy LeMass might be. She inquired there, and they reported that he hadn't worked in four months.

"They show up at Pedro and Wilmington every day," the union man told her. "But you could show up a month before your turn comes. That's the way of it sometimes."

Knowing Bridget would want her to, she took the Pacific Electric train to Wilmington where the passenger ships used to come crowding in from the Pacific islands. She asked for LeMass on the docks, and then went on to San Pedro. Nobody could say where or when a man like LeMass would be called to a job.

She walked for blocks and could see only two ships, a tramp steamer and a freighter, rusting away and waiting for a load. Men stood around the pier head or squatted to shoot craps in front of an empty warehouse. They looked at her curiously, as if she were from another planet.

She found LeMass by accident while waiting for the train to Strand. Glancing in through the dirty front window of a lunch counter, she saw that the place was deserted except for one customer sitting at the end of the counter. A longshoreman, from the look of him. He huddled over a mug of coffee, his knotty hands cradling the heated mug. He sipped a little, then set it down again, still holding it as if it were a handful of diamonds . . .

Randi recognized LeMass at once, though he had changed. He was thinner, almost gaunt, and in his posture she could detect the uncharacteristic look of defeat about him. Paddy LeMass had always been full of plans and jokes and good nature. All that was gone now, Randi thought. She forgot the train that roared and rattled along toward her stop, and turned and went inside. A bell rattled over the door.

LeMass looked around, blinked and then set the coffee on the counter. He climbed off the stool and held out his arms.

"Sure, 'tis Mary-Randal Gallegher herself."

Remembering all the good moments with this man, the only father she had ever really known, Randi threw her arms around him.

"Paddy! I never knew how much I missed you. Here. You sit right down again and drink your coffee. I'll have some too."

A dark-haired woman bustled in at the sound of the bell over the door, wiping her wet hands on her apron.

"Presenting Mrs. Borges, the finest colleen that ever come from sunny old Portugal," LeMass said theatrically.

Mrs. Borges beamed at Randi. "I was born in Long Beach. On Anaheim Boulevard, I'll have you know. But this spalpeen'll have you think I just got off the boat. What'll you have?"

Randi looked above the counter, read the menu and remembered LeMass's old craving for ham.

"Let's have ham sandwiches. And more coffee, please."

Mrs. Borges gave them both a friendly look, and went off to the kitchen.

"That good woman just about saved me from—well—from getting a real good, thin figure." He studied his cup of coffee. "Honey, I'll be telling you straight out. I can't pay for it. The sandwiches, I mean."

She thought back. It wasn't the first time LeMass had been broke. Bridget had often supported him. On the other hand, when he had any money at all he was always bringing home treats for Bridget and Randi. She rapped his knuckles.

"Remember the ice cream you used to bring home and we ate it —I let mine melt—while we sat around the coal heater and warmed our toes?"

He grinned. "Fancy you thinkin' of that." She was touched by his emotion. "Long time ago, girl. Lots of water over the dam since then."

"And the delicatessen stuff you brought home. Remember those fresh shrimps? And the crab just off the boats? And the Christmas presents all those years? Eat your sandwich, LeMass."

While he was eating, she started to explain about the storyline she was writing, but then realized how insensitive it must sound and stopped. Maybe Leo had been right, she thought. Maybe her talent *was* for small, pleasant subjects.

"Paddy, ma asked me to give you what she owed you." She put her hand into her handbag, took out all the money from her purse and slipped it under his saucer. She didn't want to count it or even look at it, knowing that it might get his pride up.

"What's this? It's a liar she is, the blessed saint! She owes me not a cartwheel." But he took the bills and crushed them into a pocket of his reefer jacket. "Begod, it's enough to keep me 'til Governor Roosevelt gets in and then some!"

"How do you know he'll even run?" she teased. "You're as wild a Democrat as ma is."

Mrs. Borges had filled up their coffee mugs and departed again. Randi saw LeMass looking at the still uneaten sandwich on her plate. His was already half-gone.

"Would you do me a big favor and take this? I just had lunch and I couldn't possibly . . ."

He had no false pride. "Sure and it's done," he said, wrapping it in a paper napkin and jamming it into his other pocket.

She sipped the strong coffee. "Couldn't you come back to San Francisco now? I know ma would forgive and forget."

But he shook his head. "I've got seniority here. I'd have to start all over again up there." He added the proud boast, "Matson's bringing out a big new passenger boat, real class, all white hull, fancy little balconies for them as has money. I'll be top of the list to work her when she docks here inside a couple of months. Name of *Lorelei.*"

She hesitated. "Have you seen Heather? Your little girl?"

She was startled by his vehemence, almost fear. "No. Nor will I."

"She's the image of you, except her hair is lighter. Her eyes look huge, like the lakes of Killarney, as ma would say. And she's got your grin."

"So I've eyes like the lakes of Killarney, have I?" But he avoided the subject of his daughter and she finally gave up.

"Paddy, how about an address? After all, ma and I may want to send you a Christmas card."

He was unsure. "It's here and there. Depends. Send it care of Mrs. Borges here at the lunch stand. "Well, now, I'll be walking you to the train. Think I'll go get me a shirt with cuffs that ain't wore to pieces. Thanks to you and me dear Bridget."

"Will you be all right?"

"Surest thing you know. I been waiting for a little deal tonight. Private-like. They're bringing in some stuff from Mexico."

"Don't get yourself jailed, Paddy."

"What? Old LeMass in the hoosegow? You'll not be talking to no amateur." He grinned and winked.

When they parted and she rode back to Strand, she was filled with memories of the past. But remembering the days with Bridget and LeMass brought on an ache for the plight of her old friend and reminded her all too vividly of the suffering all around her.

On the train she jotted down some snappy dialogue for the waitress and her prince. It sickened her to think the big Irishman might have gone hungry, and for that reason she preferred to write Taylor Scott's silly film. It was an escape for her—maybe for the audience as well.

But she still wondered at LeMass's almost violent response to her question about his daughter. It was almost as if he feared something would happen if he saw Heather, she thought. Maybe he was afraid he would become attached to her . . .

When Randi arrived in Strand, Heather was already home from school and scurrying around peeling potatoes and carrots, washing lettuce and generally making herself useful to her mother.

Randi had brought Heather several presents. The one that thrilled Heather most was a dress of plaid taffeta and velvet. She preened in front of the living room mirror behind the sideboard.

"Mommy, I wish I was big."

"Why, for heaven's sake?" Stella asked.

Heather's lovely smile warmed Randi. "So I could do things and make money and get a tam. There's one in Baffon's store 'zactly the velvet color."

"How much is it, this marvelous matching tam?" Randi asked.

"Don't you encourage the kid," Stella warned her, but Randi suspected this was mere window dressing. Stella was waiting expectantly in the kitchen doorway with a potato masher in her hand.

"Ninety-nine cents," Heather said, tilting her head one way and then the other.

Randi knew she was being maneuvered, but the girl certainly was endearing. "I think you've earned the tam. You were such a good girl, helping your mother with supper."

"Oh, goody! I could wear it to the Saturday night movies."

Randi reached for her handbag and found only eighty-three cents in change. Stella saw her face.

"What's the matter? You been robbed?"

"No. I gave it to—a friend." Besides disappointing Heather, Randi found herself without money for the morning and for meals until the overnight pullman left for San Francisco. She had planned on cashing a check at the bank the next day before catching the train to Los Angeles. "Good heavens! Tomorrow is Sunday," she suddenly realized. Even Prysing's studio would be closed, and she had no intention of calling him at his apartment.

Stella laughed. "I know the feeling. Heather, go change."

"I want to show Daddy Red."

"Go change."

Heather pouted but obeyed.

Meanwhile, Red Lombard returned home in time for dinner, pleased to see his daughter-in-law but delighted to see Heather. He swept the child up into his arms, more or less ignoring Stella Burkett. Despite Heather's childish attentions, however—unlacing his shoes, getting his slippers, combing his hair—he was in a bad mood, which made things more difficult for Randi.

"Lost," was his succinct report to Stella who raised her eyebrows. "Those damned wheels are fixed. I'll bet on it. You know I doubled on simple fives. Right straight up to a couple of thousand. Don't tell me that five isn't looming up once in a dozen spins. I played a little poker but I didn't like the look of those boys. Hoods, all of them."

"I didn't know those ships ran their games in the daytime," Randi said.

"They'll favor a few special clients. They're honest enough. I was only kidding. But the odds are in their favor. Randi, you're looking awfully good. Classy, I guess you'd call it. But that's what goes with bigshots like Steve. Got to live up to him, I reckon."

"As a matter of fact, we've been cutting things pretty close to the bone. Things are bad everywhere. I read this morning that we've got twenty million unemployed, and another twenty or more who have *never* been able to get jobs. At least, we're better off than they are. *All* of us." She pointedly looked around his swank penthouse apartment which he still pretended to own.

"You needn't tell me. If I don't fork over the interest and a part of the principal in October, I'll lose the Wilshire ground."

"Again?"

"These things come up every three to six months. You know that. Young Alec holding up money that should have been mine was a dirty—"

"A drop in the bucket, Red. How soon was it gone? Maybe Alec should have doled out a few dollars a month to the three of you. At least you wouldn't starve." Her remark went completely over his head.

"Anyway, I told Steve I had to have the money by October 10. That gives me a few days' grace." Red leaned forward anxiously, "I hoped I could take care of the interest and principal if my luck turned. It was bound to turn soon. However, the *Danna Schimmer* wouldn't cooperate. So I'll do the best I can with Steve's thirty. Or even twenty-five thousand. That's why you're here, honey, isn't it? You have something for me?"

She had been about to ask *him* for a loan of twenty dollars, but stopped herself in time. She explained that he would have to discuss the money with Steve, and that she had come on a social visit to see him and Heather . . . and Stella.

"And to find LeMass," she added.

"That damned mick? He better not come whining around here getting his claws into my little Heather."

Heather came in at the right moment.

"Come here, little one."

Heather reached around his neck with her arms and hugged him, touching her cheek to his rough skin.

"My little girl's been crying. What's the matter? Who's been making my little girl cry?"

"It's nothing."

"Tell me!"

"It's bad of me. I've been so bad. Wanting a silly old tam when every—everybody's so p–poor."

He laughed, hugged her until she squealed.

"Not so poor you can't have your tam. How much?" He was reaching into his pants' pocket.

"T–two dollars. Oh, Daddy Red, I do love you!"

Randi glanced at Stella who looked away.

When she was leaving next morning, Randi realized she still hadn't asked Red for the twenty-dollar loan. Stella unexpectedly saved the day.

"Randi, you still thinking of getting your carfare from him? Don't bother. Be just like him to keep you dangling. Take it. I owe it to you."

Randi was ready to refuse. "Owe me? How?"

"You could have been catty about my kid last night. You know. 'Little Heather said the cap was only ninety-nine cents. What a little minx!' That kind of thing."

Randi was surprised but she took the money. She and Stella Burkett had a lot in common, she thought.

"I'll pay you back the minute I reach home. You know, Stella, your Heather and my Tony are both very good at getting what they want."

"I just hope life don't disappoint my kid," Stella said.

"Amen to that. Thanks again, Stella."

Stella shrugged. "Next time you come visiting, you may not be so keen on me and Heather."

Randi hoped this was Stella's peculiar form of humor, and tried to shake hands. But Stella had already turned away.

# *Chapter Twelve*

THE 1932 elections which swept the first Democratic administration into Washington since the Great War did not impress Europe. How could a crippled man bring America out of the depths of the Great Depression? they all asked.

"How could they vote him in?" Brooke wrote to Steve. She compared the American election with that of Austria's neighbor, Germany, where, she wrote, Adolf Hitler had led his party into power. "Herr Hitler is quite absurd to look at, Steve," her letter said. "But Kurt is enthralled. He says Austria's loss is Germany's gain. You see, this leader of the National Socialist party, the Nazis, as they call them, used to be an Austrian . . . Kurt says for America to vote in a Democrat like Governor Roosevelt—well, you'll see."

In Eden Ware's view, Europe's sufferings during the tiresome depression, which still dragged on, had turned into turmoil and riots, with new regimes taking over all the time. Not like the United States, she thought, preferring the American way.

But whenever she went over to visit Brooke in Austria, she heard Kurt Friedrich's sneers at the American system which had been tried and found wanting, as he put it. He believed in the importance of persistent propaganda stressing new solutions framed in strict German order. Even Chancellor Dollfuss, the tiny man who ruled Austria, clung to the idea that fascist power, properly used, would solve all problems.

Eden had only to look around the Friedrichs' luxurious suite in the Hotel Ambassade at their German friends to feel the tension, the excitement and optimism in the air. She had an uneasy feeling that there was more to this talk about a new German order, a kind of underlayer that she couldn't translate . . .

In her travels she noted how the old familiar newspapers seemed to disappear. She had never forgotten the beating of the little professor who had been taken off the Orient Express by the Nazis that day in 1929.

Kurt's popularity in German-speaking countries had increased, thanks to his occasional forays into German films, and he continued to be a favorite in Vienna.

When Eden returned to Paris and her comfortable little hotel on the forgotten Ile St. Louis in the middle of the Seine, she could hardly wait for André's arrival. She was dying to imitate for him Kurt's hero, the new chancellor of Germany.

André visited her often. Returning from Vienna that New Year's Eve she realized, however, that André had been right. The difference in their ages intruded now and then. She wanted to talk about politics, about Kurt Friedrich's influence over her stepmother, and especially to act out a joke about the new German chancellor going the rounds of Vienna's liberal set.

André had come from a convivial night with several Yankee members of the Lafayette Escadrille, and was obviously thinking about the days of the Great War. Eden wasn't too thrilled by the events twenty-five-years ago. "Why don't you take up flying again? You were so good at it."

"Never, *chèrie.*" It was one of the few things he was vehement about. "I flew for the last time when I took Randi to meet Steve in Southern California. It was their honeymoon. And I did that as a favor to Randi—Steve, that is. For me, when I am at the controls I am back in those bloody days of the war again. I see the burning of my home, my mother dying, Lisa dying. All of it. No war, *chèrie.*" He kissed her behind the ear. "No war. No planes. Let the world smash, but I will not go to war again."

"Okay. Nobody asked you to go to war. But you've got to watch this."

She jumped off the couch. He sat up, smiling.

"I am watching. Perform."

She gave him her pantomime which she had rehearsed before the slightly shocked Preysings and several actors from the *Volksoper* of Vienna. She swung her umbrella and teetered around the room, Chaplin-style.

"Who am I? I know. I know. It's obvious. All right. But I'm the strong-man chancellor of Germany, and the joke is, I think I'm Charlie Chaplin."

He did not laugh, and she jabbed him with her umbrella. "Don't tell me you like strong men. Everywhere we look they talk about strong men. Even Governor Roosevelt. I mean President Roosevelt. And in Austria, this Chancellor Dollfuss. All these would-be Mussolinis."

André looked out the window at the quay with its winter-bare trees and the slow-moving river beyond. The city, with all its domes and spires and mansard roofs, was shrouded in a soft gray mist.

"There are times which call for strong men, Eden. Britain, for instance. God knows, they have never recovered from their general strike in 1926. And I think France could use one too."

"A Hitler?"

"Maybe a Roosevelt. He might turn out to be stronger than your Chaplin friend. We'll see." He took her in his arms. "Let us leave politics to the great thinkers, like your stepmother."

Eden was willing. She enjoyed making love to André. His lovemaking had always made her feel wanted and feminine. There were moments, however, when she wondered if this was all there would ever be to sex. The passion seemed to be missing. Somewhere, she thought, there must be more to love . . .

TWO MORE California banks had closed their doors by the first of the year, and as if that wasn't bad enough, a man named Zangara had tried to assassinate President-elect Roosevelt during an motorcade in Miami.

"Nineteen-thirty-three has started out with a bang," Sam Liversedge told Steve from his hospital bed. He had just survived a touch-and-go operation for a bleeding ulcer. "Who do you think is responsible for this business?"

Steve, who was still thinking about the attempt to assassinate the president-elect, looked a little surprised. "The theory is that the guy is crazy. It's no conspiracy. Just one lone nut on a Miami street who tried to shoot Roosevelt and got Mayor Cermak instead."

"Oh, that. Very likely. Good man, Cermak. I hope he pulls through. But I'm concerned about a few German government bonds we're carrying. Do you think it was deliberate, that fire that wiped out their senate chamber, or whatever they call it?"

"The Reichstag. It's supposed to have been set by a Red. They're hot against Reds, you know. This gives them the perfect excuse to make a clean sweep."

"Reds aren't the only thing they're hot against. Someone I know has just come back from Berlin. Those boys in their fancy boots and their scary black uniforms—he thinks they're building up the German mentality for a pogrom. Wouldn't be the first time. Gene read this fellow Hitler's book. It's wildly anti-Semitic. Not that he can do what he talks about. You can't turn a decent, modern-day nation into a pack of screaming fanatics overnight. But Gene felt mighty uncomfortable. Couldn't wait to get out of Germany and into Austria, he says."

Steve remembered Eden's story of the policemen who came aboard the train and beat up a few passengers because of their politics.

"You might be right, Sam, to get rid of the bonds. There's a rumor around that the new German government, controlled by the Nazi party, as they are called, started the fire themselves. It's only a rumor," he apologized. "And you know a lot of this starts in France, where they hate all Germans."

With the inauguration of Franklin Delano Roosevelt came further unpleasant news. One of the new president's first official acts after the inaugural was to order the closing of all banks, giving the government time to assure itself and the country that the banking system was sound. But the idea was terrifying and after Alec Huntington's announcement on the radio news, the station was deluged by phone calls from panic-stricken listeners, among them his Uncle Steve.

When Steve suggested that Alec drop in for dinner sometime, Alec said he had too much to do. "Maybe later. But everything is happening now. We're living in exciting times."

Three days later, with the banks still closed, Steve got an offer for his Culver City property that he couldn't turn down. Prysing intended to build two new sound stages immediately on the acreage adjacent to his studio lot and would hold the rest for outdoor shooting and eventual development. The offer came at the right time.

There was one hitch to the money coming from the movie magnate. Prysing intended to leave for Europe the morning of March 11 and Steve would have to be in Prysing's office the afternoon of March 10. The trip would be a tight squeeze with the banks closed, but to his amazement, Randi came through with over four hundred dollars.

"You know ma. She always has money stuck away in some flour bin or cookie jar. She swears she won't need it until the banks are open."

"Well, we won't need more than a hundred at the most. Good old Bridget! We'll have to do something nice for her when we get back."

He reached his office half an hour later to find bad news quite unconnected with the government. It came in the well-curved shape of Alma Gault.

On this brisk March morning she was wearing a sable stole over her smart black suit and pink crêpe de chine blouse.

"I'm pretty busy, Alma. Could you make this brief?"

She waved a folded legal paper under his nose. "I'm free. My final decree. What shall I do first with my freedom?"

"Save your money."

"Not in the bank, I hope!"

Mrs. Midge, Steve's secretary, flashed a sour grin as she heard her boss's indifferent response to Alma.

"Shall I bring Mrs. Gault some coffee?"

"No, thank you, Mrs. Midge. Mrs. Gault just dropped in about a legal matter."

Mrs. Midge retreated, satisfied.

"Old gargoyle," Alma complained. "She'd love to get something on me. She'd run straight to Randi and tattle."

"Probably. But she's a loyal soul and I don't know what I'd do without her, so don't offend her. What do you want to discuss with me?"

She crossed her shapely legs. "I happen to know you're due in Los Angeles on March 10. Darling, don't be coy. Just tell me. I promise not to attack you bodily."

He had to laugh at that. "As a matter of fact, I've had an offer for thirty acres of ground I own in Culver City. Know where that is?"

"No. But I can find it."

"Very funny. But my deal happens to be with a friend of my wife's. Want to make a threesome with Randi and me?"

He made a pretense of straightening his desk. He had an uncomfortable fear that she was going to make a scene, especially when he heard the catch in her voice.

"Oh, Steve! Don't do this to us."

"Do what? Now, Alma, for God's sake, act grown-up for once." Afraid Mrs. Midge might overhear, he lowered his voice. "You keep forgetting, I'm a married man."

"I know, darling. It was tactless of me. But if I could see you on March 10, just one night without her—"

"Afraid not. Randi will be with me."

Fortunately, the phone rang at that minute and his receptionist buzzed him. "Mrs. Lombard, sir."

Randi never called him at the office, and it made him uneasy to have Alma Gault here, as if Randi might somehow sense the fact. "Just a second, Miss Blowers." He turned to Alma with badly concealed impatience. "We'll talk some other time. I have an important call. You'll have to excuse me."

"But Steve, if I'm at your hotel nobody can blame you for the coincidence."

"They'd blame me in a minute if some Biltmore clerk saw both your name and mine."

"I thought you used to stay at the Alexandria. I have some beautiful memories of the old Alex."

He waved her away, pressed a button and spoke to his wife. "Hello, sweetheart. What's going on?"

Alma took her time in leaving. With the receiver at his ear and the mouthpiece before him he nodded to her.

Randi was talking quickly. "Darling, I don't like to interrupt you at the office." She never had, though the formality was her idea, not his, and the significance now made him nervous.

"That doesn't matter, honey. What's happened? Is it—it's not Tony—"

"No, no. It's an invitation to Strand. Very fancy. Friday, March 10."

"That's the day I'm to see Prysing and his lawyers. Friday afternoon. What does Red want? Is he after the damned loan again?"

"Worse, I'm afraid. It's a formal invitation to his wedding. You can make it in the morning and still go up to Los Angeles in the afternoon. I'll stay and help Stella clean up, what with a buffet brunch and guests, and all."

"Good God!" Steve sat down abruptly. "He's actually going to marry Burkett?"

"She's made it at last. I think she always intended to." Randi went on quickly, considering all the problems. "It shouldn't matter too much to us, what with all the years they've been together. They'll still be over four hundred miles away from us. In a way, that makes everything respectable."

Steve had one big objection. "But it involves that woman and her girl in our inheritance."

But even here Randi was sensible. "Red owes you so much, he can never pay it back."

"Oh well, Heather is an innocent kid. And pretty as a picture . . . I guess it would help her in school and all if her mother was married. I don't like it, but it's too late now. I'll make an appearance at the ceremony and I can still get to Prysing by three the same afternoon. I want to pay off my next installment on the San Fernando Valley property while I'm down there, if I get the money from Prysing. Then I can meet you next morning at the—" He looked up. Alma blew him a kiss and left his office. He went on. "I'll meet you at the Biltmore the next morning. That'll be the eleventh."

# *Chapter Thirteen*

MARCH 10 did not dawn with Strand's familiar mild climate.

"Somehow I pictured a nicer day," Stella complained, pressing her cheek against one of the windows in the spare bedroom of Red's penthouse apartment. "I saw it as more like your wedding, Randi." She didn't look around but kept staring at the city's brick and stucco skyline, almost obliterated by the sultry haze that stifled the city.

"You sure smell it through the windows, so you do. And on my big day." Stella shivered and clutched her shoulders.

Randi understood something of her feelings but she tried to be cheerful. "What's all this? You're not cold."

Stella laughed shortly. "Just a plain shiver. Like somebody walked over my grave. Well, I'll be getting a hell of a lot out of my life before that happens, or I'll know the reason why, I can tell you! What do you think? How does the buffet look? Good enough to eat, I hope. Red is so stingy about the things that count. He wouldn't let me hire anybody to cater like he did when you and Steve were married. My Lord! I best finish dressing. Where's that girl of mine? Hope she hasn't spoiled her party dress. That salmon-colored georgette cost me plenty."

"She's showing off the vacant apartments in the building to Tony. I think they are quarreling over which of them will eventually own the Monte Carlo."

The two women looked at each other . . . Stella finally grinned.

"Time will tell."

The weather did not improve as the day progressed. Steve found it depressing for different reasons.

"Damn! If they don't hurry this thing up, I'm going to be late. How long do weddings take, anyway?"

"Ours took forever. Remember the fuss?"

"Afterwards was nice, though."

She felt his arm around her waist and moved her face to kiss him. How lucky she had been to win him, she thought. How handsome he would always be in her eyes. And in other women's eyes as well. She saw the way the female guests eyed Steve, and there was no mistaking their predatory interest in him.

Steve surprised her by his low-voiced comment. "Red always did have some pretty unattractive friends. Most of these people got him into his present fix. That fat fellow gorging at the buffet is the head of the late lamented United Sealanes. He keeps an apartment here for his girl friend, the brunette with all the teeth. And if I'm not mistaken, that polite little fellow holds the lease on a gambling ship somewhere off the coast here."

The thing that bothered Randi the most was how Tony, now fourteen years old, fawned over the bridesmaid, ten-year-old Heather. Randi could hardly blame him. Even Steve looked up when Heather walked slowly around the crowded apartment, a shy hostess welcoming her guests. Red Lombard discussed the girl with his son and Randi.

"That little kid's going to win back for her old Daddy Red all the things this gang of crooks has stolen from me."

"The gang of crooks can hear you," Steve reminded him. "But you never minded that, did you?"

"Hell, no! If you rob some poor sucker, you've got to expect a few nasty words."

Randi laughed, though she had her doubts.

"Are you happy, Red?" she asked.

"Well, I'm getting on. And there's no telling what would happen to the kid if I was to pop off. Not that I don't trust Stella. She's been a good worker. Loyal. No funny business. You should've heard the tongue lashing she give that LeMass when he came around a year ago. Asking to see his daughter, I'll have you know. I told him a thing or two. Said I'd throw his kid out in the street if he ever come around again. He skedaddled. Next thing I knew, he was sleeping in those overgrown fields beside the flood control west of town. A lot of company he's had out there, I'll say that."

Steve had heard about her visit with LeMass.

"Pa, you are an unmitigated bastard! That man has been starving to death. And a lot of others like him. I ought to know. We've been feeding and sheltering some of them in San Francisco."

One of the guests looked around. Randi nudged Steve. "We'd better discuss this later."

Before Steve could calm down, Red waved away the offense. "You don't have to worry about the big mick. Somebody gave him money last fall and he's been sleeping nights in the back room of a dump on Second Street. Place called the Phoenix Hotel. Cop on the night beat told me. I've been keeping tabs. Just in case LeMass tried to get hold of Heather. Anyway, he could have afforded to sleep indoors the last few months."

"It must have been the money I gave him," Randi murmured to Steve.

"Anyway, the least you could have done was let him see Heather," Steve said.

"He probably has. Wouldn't put it past him. But he's not going to get that little kid back." Red gave Randi a friendly hug. "Good of you to come down, both of you. Alicia would have liked that." He noticed Steve's scowl. "You do know, both of you. I'm not marrying that female to oblige myself. It's to help the kid. She's been getting some nasty remarks in school lately. I figured all this hocus-pocus might help."

Tony came over, looking as handsome as his father, to remind the bridegroom, "We're going to wind up the Victrola, grandpa. Then Heather comes in. And then Stella." Red went to see to things.

Tony said, "I don't know about Stella, but that Heather sure thinks she'll own the world after today. Is grandpa really going to leave her this building? She talks like it's hers already."

"Don't worry, it isn't. I hold the papers on it."

Tony was relieved, but then Randi took him aside. "You and Heather have been awfully friendly. I wish you wouldn't be so two-faced, Tony."

"You get more with honey than with vinegar," Tony said breezily. "She doesn't fool me any. Though, jeepers, she is one pretty thing!"

He went off to crank up the Victrola. The Bridal March from *Lohengrin* filled the dining and living rooms as the guests formed two lines with a narrow aisle between.

Judge Beesemeyer, a local crony of Red's, officiated with his back to the three dining room windows. The still, thick air outside seemed to crowd against the panes, blurring the view of the pale sea far below.

Randi nudged Steve, and he took his place beside Red, whose smile had suddenly faded. The guests, caught by the strange expression on the judge's face, began to buzz again. He was looking over their heads, and they turned around to follow his gaze as the bedroom door opened and Heather Burkett came out. Her light hair, brushed until it glistened even in this dim daylight, was crowned by a wreath of tiny tea roses.

Randi heard the murmurs everywhere. "That adorable child!" "Did you ever see anything so enchanting?"

They were probably right, she thought uneasily.

The bride, though attractive enough, was something of an anti-climax. Stella wore a brown wool dress with a tucked bodice, fur elbow cuffs and a two-tier, accordion-pleated skirt. It seemed to Randi as if she had gone out of her way to look subdued.

The ceremony was short. Red bestowed on his bride a quick brush of a kiss and went to embrace his daughter-in-law.

"Randi-girl," he confided, "I feel young again. Raising that kid's going to be like when we raised Brooke. Only, of course, then I wasn't alone."

"Alone!"

"Well, I'm getting a little old for these shenanigans with young women. This wedding was to help the kid. I wanted to adopt her but Stella wouldn't hold still for that. She wanted it this way."

Randi worried that Red might be taking on a lot more trouble than he had bargained for with this wedding. But right now the apartment and even the corridor in front of the elevator rang with laughter, drinking, toasts, gossip and whispers in corners. Steve brought her a champagne cocktail.

"This is the real stuff. Before the year is out we'll have repeal, wait and see."

She smiled, remembering the night long ago when Steve had been sure Prohibition would never last . . .

He raised his glass to hers. "I'm not going to waste this good stuff on that farce of a wedding. Here's to us, sweetheart."

They sipped the champagne together, then he moved her glass out of the way and kissed her lips.

"Ummm! Champagne flavor. I'm going to slip away in a few minutes. Can you handle things here?"

"I only hope I can handle Tony. Is he drinking over there?"

"That's lime soda. Stella furnished it for the kids."

Randi went down with Steve to the seventh-floor apartment where he picked up his valise, and walked him to the elevator.

"Why don't we pick up Tony and go on to Los Angeles," he suggested suddenly. "I don't want to spend the night alone. You can talk to Prysing in the meantime about scripts or whatever it is."

She very much wanted to be with Steve, but she didn't like discussing business with Leo in front of him, especially after her recent experience with the producer.

"I promised Stella I'd help her clean up. You come for us as early as possible tomorrow, darling. Then we can get an early start and be in our own bed tomorrow night."

"I like the sound of that. Meanwhile, I take it there's no honeymoon for the bride and groom?"

"What are you saying, my dear man? They are going to spend the evening on the *Danna Schimmer,* the gambling ship."

"So that's why Red wanted to borrow the extra money. I had to refuse him. I told him that the bank's closed, which it certainly is." Steve slapped the elevator door. "Remember that day on our honeymoon? How badly I wanted this place? I suggested these mirrors, by the way. Of course, with things so bad everywhere, the building is half-empty now, they tell me."

"Or half-full, depending on your outlook."

That tickled him. "Thanks, sweetheart. Anyway, it's mine at last. The Monte Carlo is scot-free of debt."

Neither of them mentioned the fact that Red Lombard still collected the rent and lease checks. She understood as well as Steve that his father had to live on something besides the handful of stocks remaining to him.

The elevator stopped in front of them and the little operator opened the door. Randi and Steve kissed briefly as he was stepping into the elevator, and she watched until the elevator started its descent. *I should have gone with him,* she thought . . .

She went back up the staircase to the penthouse floor, listened to the gossip, drank more champagne and joined the rest of the crowd in congratulating the bride and groom. Tony came to her later, wanting to go swimming.

"From your Sunday best to a bathing suit. Isn't that going a bit far?"

But Tony grinned. "You can watch me from all those windows if you don't trust me."

"Trust you?"

"Heather doesn't know how to swim. Grandpa doesn't trust her to go alone and she says no one else wants to teach her. I thought I'd give her a few lessons." He saw her doubt and grinned. "Mom, I know what I'm doing. Honest. I'm going to get her on our side. Wait and see. I'll twist her around my finger."

It angered Randi to see her son at his age adopting his grandfather's chicanery. "You're not going to twist anybody around anybody's finger, young man. I despise fake emotions. That's what you're doing. Faking with that child."

He looked hurt. "But she's faking with me. Why do you think she's tagging around after me? Her mother told her to. Mom, when it comes to conniving, that kid's ancient."

Randi studied Heather across the room. She had already enchanted two male admirers.

"We'll be back by five, mom. Then you and I can take the kid down to the zone for supper, after grandpa and Stella go out to the gambling boat. Heather says there's real neat hamburgers and hot dogs at a place called Queenie's."

Randi was reminded of her own childhood and the days of the Great War, and began to soften.

"We'll see. There used to be an old hotel up on Cedar Avenue. Your father and I went there on our honeymoon. We might eat there."

"Well, I'd like the zone. But—"

She made one last protest. "Your grandfather will be leaving at seven. You won't have much time."

"Feels perfect for swimming. Look, the sun's out. You may not see it, but it's up there." He kissed her quickly on the cheek. "We'll be back before grandpa and Stella leave."

With Heather and two bath towels, he went out to the elevator, singing off-key, *"Ain't gonna rain no more, no more . . . Ain't gonna rain no more . . ."*

Stella walked over to Randi. "Don't get that look on your face. I trust the boy. Well, here goes. Where do we start clearing, I wonder."

The children's swim seemed harmless enough, Randi thought as she stopped drying dishes long enough to glance out the high windows. She saw her tall son and the little girl wading out into the surf, Heather timid, holding her hands out to stop the waves as they broke into towering, white foam crests beyond her.

A minute later Randi was startled to see Red Lombard call to the children as he strode east along the cement walk above the sand.

"Good heavens! When did Red leave? I thought he was in the living room."

Stella shrugged. "He'll be back by six. He's off to borrow a few hundred for the gambling ship tonight. Guess he didn't get it from Mr.—from Steve. He got a certain fellow into the country from Ensenada along with a load of liquor. The guy owes him a favor."

Randi was sorry she had asked, and knew she would be relieved when her family was away from Red's shifty influence. Once more she realized that she should have gone up to Los Angeles with Steve. But now Stella was counting on her to look after Heather this evening.

By 5:20 Tony and Heather got back from their swim. "It's warm out," Tony said. "You wouldn't believe it, for March."

He washed and dressed quickly, and began to pound on the bedroom door, teasing Heather for "primping."

"They sure do get along, don't they?" Stella remarked with the complacency Randi was fast beginning to dislike. "You got a good head for heights? Somebody's got to stand on this chair and put that Haviland china on the top shelves. I never liked Haviland myself. That Royal Doulton you folks use on Nob Hill is real nice, though." Randi looked at her.

Tony came into the dining room. "It's ten to six. Grandpa better be getting back or he'll miss his own honeymoon."

Tony had shown up at the right time and Randi asked him to climb up on the chair and put back the china.

"Sure. You hold the chair, Stella. Mom, you hand me the dishes."

Pleased with the chance to show off his ability, Tony took two plates and reached high over his head to prop them up on the top shelf. As Randi handed him a platter and a covered casserole, and he stretched to grab them, the chair suddenly rattled and shifted under him.

"Hey! For crying out loud, Stella, hold still!" he yelled.

The threatening sway affected Randi like a wave of nausea. In vain she reached up to protect her son who teetered on the chair. Tony made a grab for the shelves to hold himself up. The casserole slipped out of Tony's fingers, but no one was aware of the noise as it broke.

The quake had begun.

After the first sickening sway came sharp jolts, shaking the penthouse back and forth. Tony lost his balance, tumbled off the chair against Randi. His eyes were wide with fright. "What's happening?"

Randi knew. She had lived through it all twenty-seven years before, on that April morning in San Francisco when the Great Earthquake came . . . But it was Stella who cried out in terror now.

"Holy Mother of God, save us! Holy Mary, Mother of God, save my little girl . . .'Tis the end of the world!"

And it did seem as if their world had begun to collapse. Between the sea view windows, one dining room wall screeched as it split away from the core of the building and buckled outward over the beachwalk far below.

Broken china and loosened shelves rained over the three in the dining room. Tony had fallen across his mother's body, knocking her down with him. Stella was scrambling to get to Heather's bedroom from the kitchen doorway into the hall.

For an instant the back and forth shaking subsided, but then the waves of rolling motion began. Randi and Tony staggered to their feet, holding onto each other. Then the swaying china closet, loosened by the jolting movement of the quake, pitched forward across the dining room floor.

Randi got to her feet again, and pulled Tony along a few feet into the doorway between the dining and living rooms. Her head was aching, and she saw fine threads of blood trickling down Tony's face.

"Is it over?" Tony mumbled.

He looked so young all of a sudden, so helpless, not at all like the cocky boy she knew.

"Mom, I can't stand still."

"Aftershock. It'll go away." She wasn't really sure. But she knew she had survived—so far—another killer quake. She prayed their luck would hold . . .

The rolling motion subsided to tremors. Yet the noise remained, the awful roar, the wind sweeping through broken windows and the missing dining room wall. Worst of all was the rip and shriek of timbers torn away, the endless fall of bricks, chunks of stucco and cement crashing to the street and the beachwalk below.

Another sound, closer now, finally registered on Randi's consciousness.

"Save her . . . please save her . . . Heather . . . Try, darlin' . . . pull the door open. Pull—oh, help me! Help me!"

Randi and Tony made their way shakily through the living room toward the bedroom. Another roll underfoot sent Randi to her knees. Tony tried to get her up but he was shaking badly.

"Don't die, mommy. Don't die . . ."

He hadn't called her mommy in years. The anguish in his voice gave her strength, made her realize that he needed her more now than perhaps he ever would.

"Don't be silly. Let's help poor Heather. She must be stuck in the bedroom."

They made their way into the hall. Another tremor rolled through, and they fell over Stella, huddled against the bedroom door.

She was sobbing, and they noticed she had a huge lump on her temple. Randi wondered how she herself must look.

"My baby's in there. And—oh, Randi—Red. Where is Red? He was due back at six."

Randi looked around for the clock that usually sat on the mantelpiece in the living room. It had been shattered, but the face lay within a few feet of her. It had stopped at 5:56. She glanced at her wristwatch . . . Six o'clock.

Less than four minutes had passed since the first tremor struck.

# *Chapter Fourteen*

AT four o'clock that afternoon Steve sat in Leo Prysing's leather-padded office and decided that the man must be doing pretty well for himself, not only from his movie racket, he thought, but also from the land deals. Anxious to get the last of the valley acreage paid off before 5:30 when the offices of the Marin City Title Company closed, Steve had politely refused dinner with Prysing.

Now Prysing suddenly brought up the subject of an added property "to sweeten the pot." He explained, "I'd like to get my hands on some small, money-making property where a man can also carry on a profession. I have a very stubborn brother, Lombard, who practices medicine in Vienna. A remarkable man. Far abler than I am."

"My sister is a good friend of the Preysings."

"Just so." Prysing's blunt fingertips met in a pyramid, his hard eyes drilling into Steve's. "I remember Mrs. Friedrich. Mrs. Huntington when I knew her. Has she mentioned the new atmosphere in that area since the German elections?"

Steve began to catch on. He remembered Eden Ware's letters about the cruelty and prejudices of the party which was now in power in Germany.

"Anti-Semitic, I suppose you mean."

"Yes. Then you see what I'm driving at. Josef has always been a loyal Viennese. I feel nothing for the city or my native country. I've been away too long. But he was born in Vienna. The Inner Ring, as a matter of fact. Next door to your brother-in-law."

"I see. And now you want your brother here and he won't come. But we're talking about two different countries. This Hitler is not running Austria."

Prysing seemed uncharacteristically unsure. "I don't know. It's a feeling. These diseases spread. Look how fascism has spread from Italy to Germany, not to mention the Balkans. And Chancellor Dollfuss—"

"That midget!"

"He is currently the master of Austria. Beginning this year his powers are dictatorial. Dictators must have successes to appeal to the crowd. Successes need scapegoats for their failures."

"We're back to anti-Semitism."

"Precisely. When *Kreditanstalt* of Vienna collapsed a year or so ago it took down with it several other banks, including German banks across the border. If you've read Herr Goebbels's garbage, you will see the scapegoat. I have also read Chancellor Hitler's *Mein Kampf.* I'll say one thing. He laid it out for the world to read. And my silly, patriotic brother must be made to see that we welcome him here. In short, Lombard, I want to settle him in some nice, quiet town like that place where you have what you call courts."

"Apartments with single walls between, on ground level, four and four facing each other. The rents won't make you rich, but I've never lost on them, once I owned them outright."

"One of the front apartments will be Josef's office. Sarah can supervise and collect the rents. Which is it to be? I'll make the thirty acres two-fifty each, a lot more than they are worth in this market if you throw in one of your courts for—say—ten thousand. Cash. Take it or leave it."

Steve tried not to show surprise. These days it was a good offer and would bring his remaining properties back into his hands.

While he was signing the deed which Prysing's secretary laid before him, Prysing asked casually, "Why didn't your wife come along? Afraid I'd put her to work?"

"She's in Strand, representing the family at my father's wedding."

Prysing was amused. "Your father must be quite a man."

"He's all of that."

They shook hands. Steve took the check from Prysing Films, Inc., and stuck it in his pocket without looking at it, not wanting Prysing to think he needed it . . .

Prysing escorted him out through the impressive colonial front of the building. "Tell Randi I'll be seeing her soon about a script I've got in mind. Rather a nice little thing. Her kind. She asked to do something special. You tell her."

"I'll do that." Steve was feeling generous . . .

It was almost five in the hazy afternoon when Steve reached the Marin City offices on Spring Street and made the final payment on his San Fernando Valley mortgage. It had been a day of small triumphs, he thought as he tucked the deeds into his briefcase and walked briskly back to the fashionable new Biltmore Hotel facing Pershing Square.

There was a message at the desk to call another room in the hotel. His pleasant mood vanished the minute he heard Alma Gault's voice.

"You caught me at a bad time, Alma. I warned you about this sort of thing. Business before pleasure. Sorry." She never learned, he thought.

"I know, darling. I didn't want to. I really fought with myself over it. But they said downstairs that you were alone."

"Good Lord! I suppose you registered."

"Well, I had to. But don't worry. I didn't give them my name. I take it that Randi isn't with you."

"Alma," he began calmly, feeling like a fool, "I told you I had a lot of business here." She started to interrupt him and he went on, his voice harsher now. "Randi is coming in tonight. If you'd like to join us—"

"Oh, Steve! Don't our memories mean anything to you?"

"Alma, I've honestly got to go. I'm meeting Randi and Tony at Lyle's Steak House. I'll barely make it. I told you how it would be."

When he hung up he had the unpleasant suspicion that he wasn't through with her yet . . . He left the hotel before he could possibly yield to any temptation.

He was crossing Olive Street at dusk before the evening lights came on when the paving beneath his feet began to rumble. His mind was in Strand with Randi. But he knew something was wrong and quickened his steps to the sidewalk, reaching the corner of Pershing Square just as the sharp jolting began.

From the open space of the square with its low shrubs and marble decor, he couldn't at once identify the low roar, like a wind whipping through the streets. It mingled with the sounds of cornice cracking and falling off buildings that lined the block around the square.

Steve had not heard a single scream, but saw people rushing out to the curb. Glass from windows was shattered along the streets, and dust rose from fallen bricks and cement along the sidewalks.

He knew that the quake had not centered here, or Los Angeles would have been harder hit. To find out what was going on, he ran back to the hotel. Another wave hit the building as he rushed across the lobby. Alma Gault was standing, panic-stricken, at the elevator.

"It's like the end of the world. Steve, let's get out of here."

He moved her aside. "Calm down, Alma. It was only a quake. Probably centered in the desert somewhere."

"I'm not waiting for the next one, I'll tell you that. I'm taking the first train out. Maybe I'll fly."

He didn't wait to wish her well. The elevator was working and the operator, somewhat pale, took him to his floor.

Steve was trembling as he walked into his room. He kept telling himself this was nothing compared to the San Francisco earthquake, but was in no way reassured when he grabbed up the phone and waited for the operator.

"Sorry, sir. The circuits to Strand seem to be busy."

"All of them?"

"There may be damage to the lines. We've just had an earthquake, sir." From her tone of reproof, he knew she was not being funny.

"Yes, but is the damage to the lines from our end or theirs?"

"I couldn't say, sir."

Not knowing what else to do, he hung up, hoping that Randi would be sure to call him as soon as she could get through. Someone must surely have told her about the earthquake, and she would be anxious about him, he thought.

He stood there staring at the phone, willing it to ring. Through the windows he could see people gathering in clusters on the sidewalks all around the square, milling about and discussing the damage all around them.

When the phone rang, he jumped nervously and grabbed it up before it quit ringing.

"Randi?"

"I take it you haven't heard from her." It was Leo Prysing.

Steve had been sure it would be Randi, and his heart sank. "The circuits are busy."

"They're not busy," Leo said crisply. "The lines are down. I heard it just now on the radio. The epicenter was in the Strand–Seal Beach area. It's still shaking."

"Christ! How bad?"

"Quite a few dead so far. A lot of casualties."

"I'm on my way."

"Use one of my cars. I'll go with you."

Steve said impatiently, "I can't wait. I'm leaving now."

"The radio says they are calling out the National Guard. You won't get into Strand. The place is a shambles. Even the train tracks are torn up. Maybe I could—"

"I'll get there if I have to walk."

"Good luck."

Steve was about to hang up when Leo's voice stopped him.

"Will you ask Mrs. Lombard to—Will you call me when you find her? I'll be by the phone."

Steve hung up without replying. There was something ominous about that request . . . *When you find her* . . .

He started down on a run to the hotel garage, trying to quiet his fears.

RANDI PULLED herself together and tried to instill confidence in Tony by her brisk orders.

"Don't go near the outside walls. Most of them are brick or stucco. That's what you hear falling. Stay here and talk to Heather . . . Stella, does the door give at all?"

Stella paid little attention, so Randi tried to push the door knob.

"The door doesn't seem to be jammed. There's something against it."

Tony called Heather's name in a quavering voice. After a moment of silence they could make out sounds like the mewing of a kitten behind the bedroom door.

"Dear God! She's alive!" Stella cried. "We're comin', baby."

"Heather, get away from the door," Randi said. "Can you walk? If you can't walk, crawl."

There were scrambling sounds, and then the door began to yield under the combined weight of Stella and Randi.

"Not too hard," Stella pleaded. "Don't hurt my baby."

Once the door was opened and they got inside, it became clear to Randi why the child had clung to the door for safety. Half the outside bedroom wall had been torn away along with the window and had dropped to the sidewalk of Ocean Avenue eight stories below.

Heather was curled up on the floor, still in her lace-trimmed rayon slip. Stella put her arms around her daughter while Randi grabbed a dress out of the closet and forced it over Heather's head and arms.

"Bring her along. I'll get my purse. Tony, get the coats. This is March, after all . . . Tony! Not across the room. Don't go near those outer walls."

Randi found her purse under the couch in the living room, then picked up the telephone. The line was dead.

Meanwhile, Tony stared out the open space through which he could see the distant oil derricks on the hillside and the city skyline itself. Shaking, he obeyed his mother, dragged out a shaggy gray sweater and two coats and followed the women. Heather was deathly pale and she was making little whimpering sounds against her mother's shoulder. Stella caressed the girl's hair.

"What d'you think? Can we get down before it all falls apart?" she asked.

Randi took Tony's ice-cold hand. "We're going to make one hell of a try."

The elevator wasn't working. They heard the creak of timbers and muffled cries from tenants trapped below.

"I'm takin' the stairs!" Stella yelled. With Heather in her arms, she ran down the stairs. Randi and Tony followed automatically, but Randi stumbled over broken cement as they reached the first landing. Tony helped her up, and they both saw the wide break in the cement wall.

"Don't look," she told Tony.

They hurried down to the seventh floor. Stella and Heather were already halfway down to the sixth floor. The breaks in the inner wall continued. The entire structure seemed to be doomed. Like murmuring ghosts, other tenants joined the procession. Between the second floor and the two-story-high lobby, the stairwell buckled out alarmingly.

Seventeen people reached the lobby. There they found an obstacle course paved with broken glass from the mirrored pillars and the frame of the elevator shaft. Tony peeked into the open elevator shaft and saw that the elevator cage was stuck just above the lobby. The twisting girders must have driven it into the stairwell, causing the terrible bulge.

All around Randi the other tenants were trampling over the broken glass and rushing out into the street. All of a sudden, another temblor rocked the building. Remembering the greatest danger at this point, Randi took charge.

"Don't walk under the front cornice. Go out the side door. Walk in the gutter and get to the park."

She saw that Tony could make his own way. His face was flushed with excitement now and he wiped away a trickle of blood on his cheek with a bold gesture. But Heather was still extremely weak. And Stella, who had supported her daughter down eight flights of steps, was losing strength. Randi noticed that the lump on her forehead had swelled to the size of an egg, and she called Tony.

Randi would never forget Tony's courage in this crisis. He supported Stella out the door and began to run with her along the gutter toward the city park three blocks down Ocean Avenue.

Randi took Heather's arm, drew it tight around her own neck, and started out the door. Just then, fresh debris, loosened by the last temblor, rained down. She turned and pushed her way out between the front doors.

Heather moaned as her dangling legs brushed against something on the sidewalk. A man was lying there, his body covered by dust and a huge slab of concrete. Randi felt faint with this final horror . . .

The man was Red Lombard.

# *Chapter Fifteen*

IT was almost dark now. There were lights here and there along the boulevard and a policeman was setting lanterns beside the largest piles of debris. Randi called to him desperately.

"It's my father. Could you please help us?"

The policeman set a lantern down near Red Lombard's head, and knelt to examine him. Randi sat down beside him, trying to dig Red out of the rubble.

She would never have believed that she would feel a deep, aching sense of loss over the old fox. But she could not imagine their life without the pinpricks and troublesome charm of Red Lombard.

Heather was stroking the dusty hair. "Daddy Red? Wake up."

The policeman finished his examination, watched Heather a moment and then looked at Randi. He shook his head. "No use, ma'am. I'd say your father's been dead maybe half an hour, since the quake started. If it's any comfort to you, he must have died instantly. He didn't suffer much."

Randi wanted to believe him. Tony had brought Stella back, and was on his knees in the debris beside the dead man. The shock had finally gotten to him and he burst into tears.

"Grandpa! Don't leave us, grandpa!"

The policeman got to his feet and glanced around at the chaos of people and cars.

"Ma'am, I've got a lot to do. Afraid I'll have to get going."

"But what can we do? His body—"

The policeman tried to reassure her but he was anxious to be on his way. "I'll give the word right away. Some bodies are being taken to Seaview Hospital. You can collect—you can identify him there. We've got over a hundred dead, they say. And lots of injured."

He started to walk away, but Randi stopped him.

"I've got to get these people to Los Angeles. Can we wait in the train station?"

"No ma'am. It's not safe. And the tracks are all galley-west. Best take the Huntington Park bus over there on Ocean at Pacific. It's still getting through, unless they stop it. You can transfer at the end of the line."

She couldn't get the children to leave Red. Finally, she threw her coat over him and Tony, still weeping silently, lifted Heather up. Stella hadn't said a word. She and Randi looked at each other in the glare of the lantern.

"We have to go," Randi said gently. "They may stop the buses if the roads are jammed."

Stella nodded, limping along. "He never loved me, you know. Never wanted me."

"Of course he did," Randi said.

"No. It was my kid. He was real good with kids. Like your boy. I'll say one thing. He didn't treat me bad." She startled Randi with her sudden laughter. "Hell of a note!"

"What is?"

"This happening on my wedding day. Red said that when it came to the family, our marriage would raise the roof. He wasn't just kiddin'."

Randi could barely restrain herself from joining the woman's hysterical laughter.

Few people were waiting for the bus when they arrived there, and they had no trouble getting seats. The bus driver was anxious to get out of town, but he waited for the passengers to board the bus. Soon the bus was filled, and the buzz of rumors started.

"Christ Almighty! Ain't it bad enough? They got to make it worse." Stella muttered angrily. "Some folks'll believe anything."

But it was harder to deny the remark made by a heavyset woman to the bus driver who was taking his seat. *"I heard there's a bigger one expected at eight tonight."*

The bus driver started off with a roar.

THE ARRIVAL of the two bedraggled women with their children aroused considerable interest in the Biltmore Hotel lobby in Los Angeles. Randi immediately went to the desk to register for Stella and Heather.

"I'd like a room for the lady and her little girl next to my husband's room."

The clerk on duty examined her signature. "Mrs. Lombard? But this isn't necessary. Your registry this afternoon is sufficient."

"That must have been another Mrs. Lombard. I was busy in Strand this afternoon."

"In Strand! You must have had quite a time of it. How bad is it down there?"

"Could someone take us up to my husband's room? We're all quite exhausted."

"Oh, certainly. Would you mind taking your old room? You left so late we haven't had time to make it up yet. Good thing we haven't removed your bags yet." He summoned the bellman.

Randi supposed he was hopelessly mixed up, and did not wonder . . . She asked the bellman to take them to Steve's room first, but his door was locked.

"Probably gone out to look for you, ma'am," the bellman suggested. "I saw him more than an hour ago running for the garage."

She felt badly let down. Though she dreaded telling him about his father, Randi had counted on Steve's comfort.

"All right. Take us to the other room."

The bellman opened the door. Surprised and confused, Randi, Stella and the children looked around the room at the unpacked luggage spread over the bed and hung in the closet. Randi picked up a pink chiffon negligée from the foot of the bed when she saw both Stella and Tony staring at it.

"Tony, call the bellman. All these things belong to someone."

Tony jumped to obey, but Heather only drifted around the room.

"Oh, it's pretty. Mama, look. Can I have this?"

Stella answered her daughter harshly. "No. Take your hands off. That's not yours. Sit down and behave."

Looking more perplexed than hurt, Heather sat down obediently on the bed. Stella turned to Randi, who headed for the luxurious black suitcase beside the closet, and tried to stop her.

"Look here, Randi, you been through a lot today. Don't think any crazy thoughts."

Randi picked up the suitcase with its initials in gold beneath the handle: A.C.G.

"Randi! Leave it be. Let's go wash our faces and set down." Stella shook her arm. "We're all tired, honey. So don't you go thinking things."

"I'm not thinking anything except that Alma Cortlandt Gault has been registered in this room as Mrs. Stephen Lombard."

"Steve probably knows nothing about it." But Stella's face was shocked.

Between the horrors of the day and this, Randi had an uncharacteristic urge to burst into tears, to throw things, to do *something.* But she was too tired.

"Stella, when he gets back—"

"Okay. Why don't I keep the kids in this room? You talk to him next door."

*Next door.* The words were another little stab, reminding her of what she had always suspected . . .

Randi looked at Stella and saw, for the first time since their arrival in the hotel, the bruise on her left temple which was beginning to turn a blue-black color. And there was Tony, whose cuts had stopped bleeding but who looked exhausted.

"I don't know what I was thinking of. We need a doctor."

Randi took the phone, spoke to the operator and explained the need for the house physician. When the doctor arrived Randi shook off his concern for her. "I wasn't hurt. They were. I've got to be downstairs. To meet my husband."

The doctor reminded her that she was limping. She hadn't been aware of it, but while he advised a poultice for Stella's bruise and applied iodine and adhesive tape to Tony's cuts, Randi removed her shoe and stocking. She discovered the sole of her foot was bleeding, probably from the broken glass on the floor of the Monte Carlo's lobby. She washed the cuts quickly, bound her foot in a cotton pad and adhesive tape, and hobbled out to the elevator just as another faint tremor made the building sway. The hall was empty.

She waited down in the lobby near the elevators. After a few minutes she saw Steve come rushing through the doors. He started for the desk, doubtlessly to ask if his family had arrived, but Randi headed him off. He caught her as she limped toward him. He was looking drawn, but she saw in his eyes what she herself must look like. He pulled her to him and helped her into the elevator.

"Sweetheart! I've been frantic. How did you get here? Is Tony okay? Sweetheart, you look awful." He kissed her face and hair.

"Tony's all right. And Stella and Heather. Red is gone. The cornice of the building hit him."

"I know. I couldn't believe it. Red never let anything get him. But

I went to Seaview Hospital. Poor old dad! His wedding day. They told me about him at the Monte Carlo. A few of the tenants are going back. I was afraid you and Tony might—Sweetheart, I was so afraid when I pulled up in front of the Monte Carlo and saw all that rubble. But they said you'd gotten out."

"How did you get into Strand?" she asked, feeling nothing but an aching weariness.

"Used Red's name. You know Red. Every cop in Strand owes him a favor." He realized that he had used the present tense and hugged her closer to him. "I can't believe he's gone. It doesn't seem possible. But all I can think of is you and Tony. I got an emergency line from the hospital. I called here and they told me you had arrived. But you didn't answer the phone. You were here in the lobby, I guess. Where are the others?"

"Down the hall."

He seemed to find nothing unnatural about this. The phone in his room was ringing as he unlocked the door. He sat her tenderly in the big plush chair and answered thc phone.

"Yes. She's here. But she's in no condition to talk tonight. Some other time." He covered the mouthpiece. "It's that Prysing. He hounded me after the quake hit. Now he's back again. Says he's been calling here for the last hour."

Randi roused herself. Every bone and muscle ached but this was her friend, she thought, the one man she could really trust. He at least never hid the women in his life . . .

"Let me talk to him."

"Sweetheart, you're too shaken up. You need rest."

*"Give me the phone."*

Startled by her voice, he obeyed.

"Yes. I'm safe. We lost my father-in-law during the first shake. Yes. The rest of us were lucky."

She had never heard Leo Prysing so concerned. He cared very much, she knew now.

"Can I see you before you leave tomorrow? I've put off my trip. I'll come down to the hotel. Just to see you, make sure you're really there."

She was surprised when she found herself teasing him. It was the first time in hours she had relaxed.

"I know. You want me to do an eyewitness shopgirl romance about an earthquake. Keeping it light, of course."

"It's so damned good to hear you laugh."

"But not tomorrow. I have to go home. Get my life settled." She looked at Steve, and he began to sense that the earthquake was not the only cause of her strange, cold manner. "All right, Leo. You make your trip. When you come back I promise you I'll come down to Hollywood and work with you on this great new script of yours."

"I don't care about the script. Randi, I want to see you. Soon. Tomorrow."

"Call me the minute you get back." She hung up. Her hands were trembling and ice-cold.

Steve knelt before her chair and tried to kiss her, but she turned her head away. "Sweetheart, don't take it out on me. I can guess what you've been through. But let me help you." He tried to take her head between his hands. "This is Steve, who loves you. I couldn't live if anything had happened to you and Tony. Don't you know that?" When she didn't move he waited, puzzled and nervous, then got up briskly.

"Let's get Tony and the others. Then something to warm you all up. Where is Tony?"

She raised her head, looking at him with a terrible coldness. "Tony is in Alma Gault's room. Next door." Steve was speechless. "You see, we know all about your affair with her."

"But that was years ago. Years! She—it meant nothing."

It was true then, Randi thought with an ache. The affair had begun long ago, and Alma Gault's presence today, one door down the hall, was hardly a coincidence.

"It meant something to me. Get Tony and the others. Do what you like. None of them have eaten since the wedding this afternoon. We can talk about our plans, yours and mine, tomorrow. I'm too tired to discuss anything legal tonight."

"Legal! Good God, Randi."

Randi could plainly see he still cared but she refused to be moved. She felt frozen inside.

# *Chapter Sixteen*

BROOKE Friedrich and her husband arrived home in record time for Red Lombard's funeral, and Steve was more than glad to see his sister.

In less than five days the Friedrichs had crossed the Atlantic on the new speed queen, the North German-Lloyd liner *Europa*, winner of the coveted Blue Ribband. During the days before the funeral, while the family waited for Brooke's dash across the Atlantic and her bold flight from New York to Chicago, Chicago to Denver and Denver to San Francisco, Steve felt the loss of his father sharply. All his ambition since childhood had been fueled by the passionate desire to beat his wily father. With Red gone, Steve's great drive seemed to be destroyed.

His fears about Randi, which kept him awake nights in that large bed alone, had become a deep-rooted pain that never quite went away. He hadn't yet been able to persuade her to share his bed. . . .

After Red's burial Alec walked over to him across the pebbled driveway outside the Masonic cemetery.

"May I get a ride back to town with you, Uncle Steve? Mother is taking Aunt Randi and Bridget and Stella in their car. Aunt Randi thought I might like to ride with you and Tony."

"Hop in. You're just the fellow I want to see. Your beautiful stepfather isn't likely to come along, is he?"

Alec, who had been feeling as gloomy as Steve, suddenly grinned. "Lord, no. I just can't figure out what mother sees in him."

Tony arrived on the run to join his father and cousin. "Heather's going to be scared, with nobody home but Schultz and old Thorgerson looking after her. Could you step on it, dad?"

Steve noticed the way Alec became suddenly attentive, even concerned, at the mention of the child's name, and it troubled him a little. As he pulled out into the highway and headed back toward San Francisco, Steve brought up the subject again.

"Do you two think Heather is a normal ten-year-old?"

"Normal?" Alec snapped. "Of course she's normal. After all she's been through—even Aunt Randi says it was hell. Well, ask Tony."

"Sure was," Tony agreed, then shrugged it off. "I think everything kind of stopped in her during the time she was stuck in her room. The wall falling out, and all that. It was enough to make anybody think the world was coming to an end. Even me." He brightened. "All Heather needs is a few months at the house with the rest of us cheering her on."

"Months?" Occupied with his own misery, it hadn't really occurred to Steve until now that the troublesome little beauty and her equally troublesome mother would be a part of the household from now on. Surely, he thought, some other provision could be made. But Alec put that thought out of his mind once and for all.

"Seems odd, doesn't it? As grandfather's widow, Stella Burkett owns a third of the Nob Hill house. And you won't be able to budge her out of it, if I know Burkett. I don't suppose anything else of grandfather's property will turn up. Isn't it all mortgaged?"

"Almost all of it. I think I can save the La Brea piece. That's in Los Angeles. If I can pay off the mortgage there, the two of them will have enough to support them when the property starts earning its keep. But meanwhile . . ." He wondered how Randi felt about Stella moving into the house that Randi had run for so long. Although Randi and Stella had been schoolgirls together, he had long suspected there was no love lost between them, and he knew that only one woman could rule a household.

Alec remarked, "Funny how nobody has talked about grandfather. I mean, except the preacher. It's hard to believe he's gone."

"He isn't gone from our house." The boys stared at him, but Tony understood.

"I know what you mean, dad. People like grandpa never really die. I keep thinking of the last time I saw him. In fact, I didn't even see him. I was teaching Heather to swim. We were fooling around and grandpa yelled to us. Heather saw him. She waved. But me, I was so cocky I just dove into a wave. Now, I wish—I sure wish I turned around." Tony looked at Alec. "I'm a real eyewitness. I'll bet your radio audience would like to hear me tell how it started, what it felt like. And how brave mom was."

To Steve's surprise, Alec refused.

"Underage, kid. It's a labor thing. Union rules and all."

Tony was quiet but threw his father a mischievous glance.

Two evenings later Steve found Randi on her knees beside the bed in the master bedroom; for an instant he thought—hoped—she was moving back in.

"I'll bet some of Red's ten-year-old collar buttons are still rolling around under there."

"Found it!" She waved a button triumphantly, not Red's but one of her own.

He reached over to help her up but she bounded to her feet as lithe as ever, and he heard with dismay his sister's voice behind him. He had hoped for a few minutes alone with Randi.

Brooke applauded her sister-in-law. "Eden herself couldn't have done it better. Nobody would ever think you were thirty-five, Randi."

"Hush up!" Randi called cheerfully. "Tell me, how is Eden doing these days?" She crossed the room, avoiding Steve.

Brooke's husband came down the hall. "We must be very respectful of the young lady. She is a genuine cinema star these days."

Brooke chided him. "Not a star, my love. She had a bit part in a Korda film in London."

"Really?" Randi was impressed. "How wonderful!"

Hoping to be included in the conversation, Steve joined them. "We'll all have to go and see the film, won't we, sweetheart?"

Randi did not respond. "What kind of a part is it?" she asked Brooke.

"It's all about Henry the Eighth. With Charles Laughton, didn't she say, Kurt?"

"I believe it is a bedroom scene."

"What!" Everyone looked at Kurt Friedrich who was amused.

"The ladies-in-waiting are changing the matrimonial bed for Henry's next occupant. One of the females in the background is our red-haired star."

Steve tried again. "Then she's on her way. She deserves it. She's had a long struggle, wouldn't you say, sweetheart?"

Someone came up the stairs, and Randi swung around. "Stella, can I help you?"

"Randi, we got to do something about that hag in the kitchen. She sure hates my guts. Always did. She'll have to go, Randi." Stella had added authority to her familiar directness.

"I'll see what can be done."

Steve noticed that Randi was looking tired and not like herself. He tried to make things a little easier for her.

"Stella, you can't mean to get rid of old Schultz. She was planted here with the cornerstone. Shall I go down and make peace?"

"I don't know, Steve." He was taken aback when she hooked her arm in his. "Anyway, you can try. I never knew a time when a good-looker like you couldn't settle between two females. Come along."

He found himself being drawn away from the others. But all he saw was Randi's face and the misery in her eyes. *Damn!* he thought. *Can't I do anything right?*

"Have we missed something, dear?" Brooke asked Randi. "Some problem between you and Steve? Everything's all right, I hope?" Her smile was full of mischief.

Steve went down to the kitchen with Stella. Heather ran to him and grabbed his hand. "Mr. Steve, I can hear him. He's coming out of the radio. My own Tony."

"Go listen to Tony, darlin'," Stella said to her. "Your ma's got business in the kitchen."

Heather ran back to the radio, where Tony's young voice came over the loudspeaker beside the radio in the living room. He was being interviewed by Baccagalupi, the program manager. Steve found himself genuinely impressed by his son's stirring description of the earthquake. He sounded modest, but Steve suspected that was carefully put on. At any rate, the boy made a wonderful guest, vivid and lively. The windup, in which the manager gently led Tony through the shock of seeing his dead grandfather in the rubble of the street, caught Steve by the throat.

Steve was not a patient man. He had endured a few shocks of his own during the last couple of weeks, and now felt hopeless about his wife's indifference. Walking back to the kitchen, he remembered the story of the wager. Something began to harden in him . . . Randi thought she married a rich man, and since the market crash, he had talked about nothing but his damned losses . . .

One thing sprang to his mind: if having a rich husband meant that much to her, she would have one.

RANDI HAD a splitting headache after the row in the kitchen. She went to find some aspirin but got no further than the front hall where she came upon Bridget and Steve. Bridget had been crying. She took her handkerchief out of her coat sleeve and blew her nose. Her every movement sent terror through Randi, and it was Steve who tried to calm her worst fears.

"Something's happened. Tell me! It's Tony. Where is Tony?" Randi demanded.

"No, sweetheart. Tony's fine. Matter of fact, he's cutting into Alec's territory. Didn't tell us a word about it but he's been on the radio tonight. Bridget came about your old friend LeMass."

She knew at once what had happened. "Ma, I'm so sorry. Was he hurt, or—"

"It was during the earthquake, sweetheart. The Phoenix Hotel, a little brick place. Two stories. It just fell apart. LeMass was in a back room. Bridget found his name here in the newspaper among the earthquake victims."

She and Steve fussed over Bridget and tried to comfort her. "Shall we go up and be comfortable in the sunroom?" Randi suggested.

But Bridget had her prejudices. "Not on your life, girl. I want to see as little as possible of that Burkett. She seduced my Paddy."

So they followed Steve into the darkened living room where he made drinks. Brooke and Kurt joined them within minutes. They drank and talked for hours, with Kurt making various unpleasant pronouncements about his admiration for the plans of the Third Reich.

"What do you think of your President Rosenfeld, by the way?" Kurt asked them.

"Roosevelt!" Bridget corrected him, then muttered into her gin, "Damn kraut."

But later, Steve remarked to Randi, "Friedrich meant that idiotic slip, you know."

"Which idiotic slip? Be specific."

He laughed. "Very true. The one about Rosenfeld."

"Oh, that. I don't think he meant anything special."

It might have been the alcohol, or the lively group, but despite her sorrow over the death of LeMass, Randi found herself going up the front stairs arm in arm with Steve . . . His warmth was beginning to thaw her bitter jealousy and hurt.

They got as far as the master bedroom. She felt the muscles of Steve's arm tighten around her waist, his lips lingering on the crown of her head. It was the moment for her to break away, to let him know that she couldn't sleep three in a bed . . . Alma Gault would always be there between them.

His touch excited her as it always had, but she resented his use of it to win her over, and abruptly pulled away.

All his hopes vanished with that sudden move, and disappointment quickly gave way to anger, then bitterness.

"I haven't told you what my plans are yet. You don't even know how much we'll have. You think because my father is dead that this ends the dynasty. Not by a long shot!"

"Please don't. Everyone will hear you." But he kept on hammering away with his business talk.

"You think because the Monte Carlo is in ruins that ends it for me? That property alone is worth a fortune. Those courts of mine—they were barely cracked. I'm a hell of a lot better off than I was when you married me. You'll be so rich you can swim in it before I'm done!"

He stalked off to the master bedroom and slammed the door shut behind him.

He must be drunk, Randi thought, and went to the other room.

They had lost their chance for a reconciliation.

# *BOOK FOUR*
# 1938-1941

# *Chapter One*

WHEN Eden Ware came home to the islands in January, 1938 for a short visit, her return was not quite the way she had pictured it. Her dreams of fame preceding her, of newspaper headlines announcing her return, were not fulfilled. No one would have to know how many bit parts and dubbed voices she had done in her career, she had thought.

Nevertheless, she knew she had a most loving turnout. Her father, who had last visited her a year ago, was there with the lovely Tamiko and Chiye. All of them were waving frantically and she fell into their arms, loaded down with leis.

Back home on the lanai of the house where she was born, Eden wondered how she could ever have made her home so far away. And yet, something in her vagabond nature told her that she was now only a visitor in "paradise."

Jim Nagumo, still a single man despite two engagements since he and Chiye broke up, was nevertheless a frequent visitor to the Ware house.

"He'll end by wearing Chiye down," the doctor confided to Eden. "She's been going with the nephew of the Japanese consul here, but Jim is going to get her. They quarrel so much that anyone can see they were born for marriage."

As usual, Chiye was defending the Japanese empire. She had done a superb job of teaching American-Japanese children the language, customs and heritage of their ancestors.

"Don't you see? It's only to equal things out. Every day the kids are filled with the American side of everything. It isn't fair. They should have a full ethnic education."

"Whatever that is," Eden teased. No use, she thought, in bringing up the Asian war between Japan and China, or the Anti-Comintern Pact the Japanese had signed a year or so before. "Self-protection," Chiye said, and for all Eden knew, she was right. But Eden had little to say about the other two Axis powers. She was accustomed to the silence that kept her friends from discussing the growing threat in Europe.

Jim Nagumo wanted to know all about what was going on. "Weren't you in the Stavisky riots in Paris?"

"Jim, that was years ago. I was just a kid. All I knew was that the public thought the government was in on the scandal about some stupid bonds. There was a riot in the place de la Concorde."

"And what were you doing there?"

"Just curious. I'm not curious any more. Jim, we want peace over there. And I think we'll go pretty far to keep it."

"And is the anti-Semitism as bad in Germany and Austria as they say? Shirer said that during the Olympic Games, anti-Jewish signs were torn down and then replaced after the visitors went home." She shrugged. She didn't want to get into all this, didn't want to be disturbed by war talk. But he persisted.

"I never heard anything like those Nuremberg Laws. It is now forbidden to marry a Jew. And they have taken away citizenship from the Jews? It can't be true. People won't stand for it. The Jews they took the citizenship from—are they foreigners, or Germans?"

"They were born in Germany. Look, Jim, I never travel through Germany any more when I visit Brooke and Kurt. I either fly or take the train through Zurich."

Like her European friends, Eden preferred not to discuss with "outsiders" what was going on in the Third Reich and in Austria. The Austrian chancellor had been murdered by Nazis who still failed to win power after their coup. And Britain and France were so terrified of starting a war that they watched helplessly while the Third Reich built up a conscription army.

"But Hitler has taken over the Rhineland," Jim reminded her. "Doesn't anyone ask what's next?"

She cut off more such questions. "Never mind Europe, Jim. What is this fixation Chiye has on Japan? Is that still what keeps you two from marrying?"

Jim grinned. "Nope. The real thing is, I keep teasing her about the charms of an old-fashioned wife and needling her every time she mentions Japan."

"Not very diplomatic."

"The truth is, I enjoy the give and take. She's too serious. Besides, if she really lived in Japan she'd have to be meek as Moses. No shooting off her mouth there. But Chiye loves me—even though we'll be old and gray before she admits it."

During the days that followed, Eden suspected he was right. She saw the way Chiye enjoyed Jim's slim grace as he surfed or walked the sand or played volleyball with the neighboring Hawaiian and Filipino children.

On the afternoon of her sailing, Eden spoke with her father about her return to Europe.

"Here you are, rushing off halfway around the world to live in a tiny attic among strangers when you might remain home here." Dr. Ware shook his head.

"I know. Paradise."

"Not at all. We've got racial problems here. You weren't here when we fought through the *Massie* case. And there have been others. We need bright, liberal young minds like yours."

"But daddy, I want the excitement that's in Paris while I'm young. It's a different kind. Not as grim as racial problems. It's the thrill of being part of history." She looked around at the crowd below her on the dock, heard the Royal Hawaiian band playing one after another of her favorite songs. She tried to explain what she couldn't understand herself.

"Daddy, here in the islands it's *pau, pau pilikia*—trouble all gone. It's as beautiful as heaven. But the thrill of danger and excitement is what I enjoy, and that's what I miss here. Hawaii is just too calm for me."

He gave in, looking a little sad, a little older. Kissing her cheek he said suddenly, "Give my best to the Count de Grasse."

Her startled eyes caught his gaze. He had seen André every time he visited her in Paris, though her relationship with André had become little more than a loyal friendship during recent years. As André got older, he turned more to his vineyards, to the rural life. She often thought he felt closer to his long-dead wife now than during the war and the months of his anguish.

Patting her on the arm, Dr. Ware added, "I like him. He's not bad. For an aristocrat."

Chiye and Tamiko joined them. Eden hugged Tamiko as she would have embraced the mother she had never known.

"You will be a good girl," Tamiko told her with great conviction. "When you come home Chiye is not so serious. She laughs more."

"You come with me, Chiye. Come to Paris. It's free and vital and alive. You'll love it."

Chiye smiled, "I think it is vital and free right here. In fact, I think we are more free than you and your Paris friends."

Before Eden could be offended, she went on. "We saw you in *The Private Life of Henry the Eighth* four times. What else have you done?"

Eden was grateful that her other two British films hadn't been shown in Honolulu. In one of them she played a streetwalker who got stabbed by a Jack-the-Ripper type in a scene displaying almost all of her bare breasts. In a French film made near Boulogne, her scene had been cut out and there was only one shot of her, swaying behind the leads in the crowded Métro.

Her voyage on the *Lorelei* took her to Wilmington, so she would not be able to stop over with the Lombards in San Francisco, though she didn't really mind. She had found her recent overnight visit with the Lombards disquieting. . . .

Alec had proudly showed her the newly opened Golden Gate Bridge, reported that the dock conditions were better and the long, dragged-out Depression really was going to end. But he was clearly besotted by the lovely Heather Burkett and kept bringing that tiresome girl, not yet sixteen, into all his conversations. Alec couldn't seem to see what was clear to an outsider like Eden, that the girl and her mother were determined to have handsome Tony Lombard instead.

Tony's feelings were hard for her to figure out. He might be attracted to Heather, but marriage? Eden was doubtful. Also, she wanted to think he had nothing permanent in mind. There was no doubt about his attractiveness. With his Irish blue eyes and dark hair, his impudent manner and his sweetness, he usually got what he wanted. And of course, he had the Lombard charm . . .

Stella Burkett Lombard, however, did not welcome Eden's presence. She watched Eden with a suspicious eye, especially when she was with Tony Lombard.

When Eden returned from her drive with Alec the first day she was there, Tony grabbed her.

"Hi, movie star. I've got a bone to pick with you. In private."

Stella, overhearing this, rushed over to them. "Heather was looking for you a minute ago, Tony. She wanted you to listen to that radio show with her. You know how scared she gets when she's alone." She explained to Eden, "Ever since that awful quake five years ago."

Tony waved Stella away. "I saw her and explained that I was busy.

Look here, Eden, how about walking over to the Fairmont with me?"

Stella knew him well enough not to argue. She went in to join her daughter, only to find Alec already there sitting with Heather.

After enjoying the view from the Fairmont Hotel at the top of Nob Hill, where the January night had already brought in the fog which shrouded the rest of the city, Eden and Tony walked into the hotel bar. Tony ordered Eden a Dubonnet and ginger ale for himself. He's still underage, Eden thought, with a smile.

"Now tell me," he said when they got their drinks. "Am I the only one in the family who's seen you in the raw?"

She almost dropped her glass. "What the devil do you mean?"

"That Jack-the-Ripper movie, of course." He grinned broadly. "Don't worry. It's our secret. I saw it the first time in a theater down on Market Street years ago, but they bring it back a lot. The other victims in the movie showed more than you did. But what you showed was the way I like a girl."

"Flat-chested?" she asked sarcastically, hoping he would think her warm flush was due to the drink and not his gaze, directed at the cleavage of her suit blouse.

"Not flat-chested. But not a fat cow, either. You know, some day, when you aren't behaving so much like my maiden aunt, I could show you a thing or two—"

"You've had too much ginger ale," she sputtered. "I think we'd better go."

He laughed. "I was only kidding. But I really have seen everything you've done. And I think you're going to be great. You're not pretty—"

"This is getting better and better."

"But neither is Katharine Hepburn. You're kind of—anyway, the guys in my frat house envied me when I told them I knew you."

He was brash, but he certainly had a way about him, she thought. "Careful, Tony. You'll get in trouble with the little beauty."

Tony knew exactly what she was talking about. "You know something? You're younger than Heather, in a lot of ways. She was born old. Six years ago, the day of the earthquake, she wanted the Monte Carlo Arms, dad's apartment house. Now she sees herself running our house on Nob Hill, taking mom's place. Believe me, I know little Heather down to her pretty little toenails."

"But you like her."

He shrugged. "I like a lot of things that aren't good for me. The difference between me and Alec is that I know what's the poison. He doesn't."

Yes, Eden decided when they returned to the house. It was a potentially explosive situation . . .

It seemed to Eden that Stella's presence in the house had managed to split the family in many ways. She discovered at dinner that Randi leased an apartment in Hollywood where she sometimes spent a month at a time working on her scripts for Leo Prysing . . . Steve was everywhere—in Washington, D.C., in New York, in Canada, even in rebuilt and recovered Strand, California—but never home. Nobody seemed to think there were women involved, just his insatiable ambition, like that of his father and grandfather. He was now on the East Coast somewhere giving a speech defending the Works Progress Administration.

At the dinner table that evening, Tony brought the situation to everyone's attention. "Hey! This is the first time in months we're all here together for dinner."

"Except your father," Randi reminded him.

"Oh, well, dad's out making a killing so we can all keep the old homestead," Tony explained to Eden. "Anyway, we've got mom and Heather and Stella and Grandma Bridget to entertain you, Eden." Bridget grinned at him and he took her hand. Tony had neglected to mention Alec, who was also at the table. Alec remained silent, but looked over his plate too often at Heather.

Randi turned to Eden. "That seems to be all my husband thinks of these days. He'll soon own half the country, the way he's going."

Heather Burkett put in softly, "Oh, Eden, I think Steve is ever so clever. Always off making money in romantic places. He told me he might go on over and buy his French friend's vineyards to add to what he owns in Sonoma County. Something about transplanting vines. It's so hard to understand when men talk business." Stella never took her eyes off her daughter.

Eden regretted she had missed Steve Lombard when he was in Paris, but hoped she might catch him before he finished his business with André. It would be nice, she thought, to find a friend like Steve. She was glad now that she would be making the direct trip to New York from Los Angeles, flying if she could get the connections . . . She didn't want to get mixed up in any more of that unhappiness and the intrigues of the Lombard house. . . .

Ahead lay Paris.

# *Chapter Two*

STEVE closed his deal with André de Grasse so quickly that he began to wonder if his French friend had gotten the better of him.

"I suppose you let me win this deal because we're calling it DeGrasse-California Wines. What are your feelings about Lombard-DeGrasse Wines?"

With his head thrown back, as if he were laughing, André finished off his vermouth cassis.

"DeGrasse-California has a splendid ring to it. Then, too, it appears on that legal contract you have signed."

Over the tiny round table of the Café de la Paix, André made a sweeping gesture. "How do you find Paris, my friend? I imagine you see changes." In the dark blue twilight, the city was coming alive for the night. "I myself see very few. It was the same when Lisa and I came here on our honeymoon."

Steve tried to be appreciative but he felt more at home in his native San Francisco, or New York, Chicago, even in Honolulu.

"The Nazis are threatening every day to grab off half the Continent, and these people stroll up and down as if they had all the time in the world. It was as bad in London. Peace at any price. 'Let Hitler stuff himself, he'll get indigestion.' "

André remained cool, uninterested. "We have the Maginot Line. It will stop any army."

"And any air force?"

"Be fair, Stephen. You Yanks do nothing to stop the Japanese. They have gobbled up Manchuria. Most of China. When they threaten the Philippines, will you act? I doubt it. We are the same. All of us. No more war, we say. Some think the paperhanger says it too."

All the same, the defeatist feeling on the Continent made Steve uneasy. As soon as he had visited Brooke and Kurt in Vienna, he was planning to return to the States on the next sailing of the *Normandie* and fly home to California. But this thought depressed him a little too.

"I'll probably find Stella ruling the roost and Randi down in Los Angeles working her head off for that damned movie fellow."

At last he had succeeded in alarming André. "Do you tell me there is something between them?"

Steve examined his glass with a frown. "I don't know. I've never known for sure. Physically, nothing is wrong between us, when we're home at the same time. But there is not much talking anymore, none of the great conversations that we used to enjoy. We don't even have anything in common to argue about. André, old fellow, it's my opinion she thought she was marrying a millionaire."

"Well, you are, are you not?"

"In the value of my land, considerably more. But I could never hold onto cash. It doesn't seem to intrigue me. But Brooke has always maintained there was—well, never mind. How about you making the flight with me to Vienna to celebrate Brooke's birthday? For old times' sake."

André smiled. "Sorry. The handsome Kurt's politics offend me."

Steve was anxious to leave, but André stopped him. He seemed to Steve to be worried about something.

"Do not go. Ask Brooke to come to Paris. Telephone her and say you have the tourist's trot, or whatever it is called."

"What the devil—Is the war on? Did I miss something?"

Andre took the folded copy of a newspaper out of his trench coat pocket. "I told you I do not fear war. I have reason to believe . . . There are underground sources sometimes that know things. The world will let Hitler march into Austria. The signs are everywhere, as you reminded me. If you do not take great care, you may find yourself greeting Adolf Hitler when you get to Vienna."

"You're a great one to talk. Ten minutes ago you were a regular pacifist."

"I remain so, my friend. But once in a millenium there may be worse things even than war. I would feel happier about you and Brooke if you were anywhere but in Vienna this week. Perhaps I am talking too much."

André obviously knew what he was talking about. Could he be in on official information? Steve wondered . . .

"Do as you like, my friend," André said finally. "You have your American passport. I believe you might be safe."

André made the excuse that it was a long drive back to the village. As they were parting, he asked Steve a disquieting question.

"Are you living freely now? Other women?"

"Once or twice. Nothing much. A widow in Washington. I also had a funny—I guess you'd call it a flirtation—on the *Queen Mary* coming over. Old-time actress named Olga Rey. Remember her?"

André smiled and gave him a slap with his newspaper. "There was always that friend of yours, Alma something, to fall back on. I met her at your wedding."

After five years Alma's name was still poison to Steve. "Married the head of Alliance Oil a year or so ago. She doesn't hang around San Francisco now. The fellow owns half the earth and he watches her like a hawk, thank God."

"Well then, remember what I said. Do your dallying in Paris, not Vienna. *Au revoir,* good friend."

Strolling up the Champs-Elysées after the long walk from the café, Steve was left with an empty feeling . . . Loneliness? He wondered. Or a sense that his friend knew a great many things he wasn't telling? . . . He walked into the lobby of the new Hotel George V, only blocks from the magnificent Arc de Triomphe. Standing in the crowded lobby, Steve thought back to the days of his youth in wartime Paris. Tonight he was going nowhere, and he was alone. He couldn't think of anyone he knew in Paris . . . except Brooke's stepdaughter, Eden. Paris was her home.

"Ile St. Louis," he read in his address book. "That's in the Seine. But if it's as crowded as the Ile de la Cité I'll never find her."

At the concierge's desk he asked about the island.

"Very small, monsieur. Its length is bisected by one street, the rue de l'Ile St. Louis. There are one or two short streets. And, naturally, it is surrounded by the quais. What address, monsieur?"

Steve had only the name of Eden's little hotel, Le Monarch. After taking a cab to the Pont Louis-Philippe, he walked across the bridge to the Ile St. Louis. There on the far quai was the narrow, three-hundred-year-old building, like all the others around it, with a mansard roof and dormer windows.

IN HER attic room, a hungry Eden Ware had found very little to inspire her in the closet cupboard near the window where her groceries were stored. She looked out the high window at the church domes of the Left Bank. The starlit March night was cold. She took a deep breath, reached for her gabardine coat and beret on the hook beside her sleeping couch.

The knocking on the door startled her. "Friend or foe?" she called out.

"Miss Ware?" The question was unexpected. Anyone who came to visit her knew her by her first name.

She opened the door hesitantly. In the darkness of the hall she could make out a tall man standing there only a foot or so from her. Then she recognized Steve Lombard. He looked relieved to see her.

"Eden? I've had a devil of a time finding this place. How are you?"

"Come in. Fine. As a matter of fact, I was in San Francisco, in your very own house less than ten days ago. I've just gotten back. Steve! It's good to see you."

He stepped inside her room and his height made the room look smaller than ever. She could tell that he thought it was awful. But he couldn't know the cozy feeling it gave her. Besides, the rent was only two dollars a week, which meant that she could live there and eat even when she couldn't get work.

He smiled at the way she looked with only one arm in her coat, the other fishing for the left sleeve. "You've got your coat on. Were you going out?" He helped her into the coat and straightened her collar. She liked the feeling of his hands against her neck. "I don't want to detain you."

All the same, she felt that he was disappointed and this encouraged her. "You're not detaining anything. The truth is, unless I want a meal of brandy and mayonnaise, my cupboard is bare. No point in buying anything this late in the day. I'm off to Vienna tomorrow for your sister's birthday."

His laugh was young, a boyish chuckle. At such a time he seemed younger even than his son.

"Look here, this is a coincidence. I'll be on my way to Brooke's celebration too. But meanwhile, I'm hungry. And I hate eating alone. Eden, be my guide. Lead me to some food. You know this town. What do you say?"

The chilly March night had begun to sparkle. "I'd love it. Follow me to nectar and ambrosia," Eden cried.

She gave some thought to a fancy Right Bank restaurant but suspected that he would perhaps enjoy a small café on the Ile. Halfway up the dimly lighted rue de l'Ile St. Louis they found the crowded Petit Mazarin, raised the latch and walked in.

They had to share a long table with four others, two plasterers just off work, with hands still stained chalk white, a young student and a lanky actress friend of Eden's who boasted happily that she had gotten a bit part in a new film. Eden was relieved when the girl finished her *mousse au chocolat* and rushed off to a late date with a casting director . . .

Mellowed by a bottle of cheap Beaujolais, Steve was beginning to feel more comfortable.

"What the devil did I order anyway?" he asked as he pushed his fork around. "Are these what we call innards?"

"Who knows? But it's good."

The place was noisy and they were sitting opposite each other at the center of the long table. But their companions ignored them and Steve soon got used to talking to Eden over the confusion around them.

"How do they do it? The flavor, I mean. It's great. I really enjoy it. And your life here. I can see why you want to remain here, even if it's so far from home."

After they finished dinner, they walked out to the street and looked up and down, wondering which was the shortest way back to her room. To Eden's delight Steve chose the longest way, first to the pointed end of the island where they stood looking at the bridge leading to the crowded Ile de la Cité and Notre-Dame. Then, under the bare, dry branches of a cluster of trees, they turned back along the quai facing the Left Bank and strolled very slowly toward her hotel.

Eden was thrilled by Steve Lombard's arm around her shoulders. The years that she had been André's mistress were almost forgotten . . . Nevertheless, she sensed somehow that Steve was still in love with his wife, and was using her tonight as some kind of replacement for what he missed . . . Randi's name came up often in his conversation.

Eden had never truly envied any woman until now. Here was Steve Lombard, so irresistible—and so unattainable. He never forgot that he was in love with his wife, mentioning Randi almost without being aware of it. But then came his compliment.

"You remind me a little of Randi when I first saw her. It was Armistice Day."

She laughed shortly. "Armistice. Seems a long way off from today. I don't even fly over Germany now when I visit Brooke. From what I've read it's getting to be an armed camp of fanatics."

They were leaning on the stone wall of the quai, watching a barge move silently downstream with its forward lights warm against the cold black waters.

"It always seemed an odd friendship," he said. "You and Brooke."

"Oh, no. We're so unalike we balance each other. Sometimes I feel as if she's my daughter. She's so innocent, really, as long as she gets enough loving from that pretty boy she married."

"You never did like him, did you?"

She shrugged, remembering that night long ago at the Royal Hawaiian on Waikiki. How naïve and silly she had been . . .

"I think somebody ought to prepare you, Steve. Your brother-in-law looks absolutely adorable in his Nazi uniform."

Steve slapped the stone parapet, hard. "I knew it! I wonder if that's what Brooke meant. She seemed scared. I'd written saying as long as I was so close and her birthday was March 12, I'd drop by. She told me I shouldn't make the detour just for that. Said she might visit the States soon. We could get together then. It wasn't like her at all."

Eden was surprised that Brooke was at least aware of the significance of her husband's politics. "I'm not supposed to know. I think his activities are secret, because his movies are shown in Western Europe and the Nazis aren't too popular with French and British exhibitors since the Nuremberg Laws against the Jews."

They said nothing for a moment, wanting to change the unpleasant subject. She shivered.

"Cold?"

"No. I'm enjoying this walk."

"So am I. Randi and I used to . . . sorry." He put his arm around her shoulder again. But she thought of Kurt Friedrich again. She didn't want a typically opinionated American like Steve to get into trouble in Austria, where the government was trying very hard not to upset their powerful Nazi neighbors.

"Jews, Gypsies, Freemasons, Catholics, and me—we're all a danger to the Third Reich."

"Why you?"

"I'm still an American citizen. I keep my passport up to date, thank God. But my politics are radical socialist. That would put me on the führer's little list."

They walked along the cobblestones, and Eden felt she didn't want this evening to end. But the world intruded on her thoughts again.

"Brooke keeps her American passport up to date. I can take a bow for that. Had quite a row with Kurt over it. But he's afraid of me. He gave in."

"Good for you. I suppose Brooke's panic has something to do with his politics. That and the Preysings. She said Dr. Preysing wasn't permitted to practice medicine now. I didn't know the Nuremberg laws affected Austria."

"I certainly hope the Preysings aren't still in Vienna. Anyway, as far as the laws go, it's all good Aryans together." Seeing his concern she reassured him. "But Hitler isn't in Austria yet. Well, here we are. My home sweet home."

"I've enjoyed this evening more than I can tell you. I wish it didn't have to end."

They looked at each other in the moonlight. Eden wasn't sure what she read in his face. She knew it was not passion, but something more like warmth and need. And loneliness . . .

"How about escorting me to my door? The elevator works, going up."

"Good. Will we be on the same plane tomorrow? Like you, I'm flying Swiss. I prefer not to fly over the Reich."

"Wonderful, I'll be on the same flight."

They squeezed into the tiny elevator, closed the gate and started up, accompanied by shrieks of protest from the machinery. The concierge rushed out of her ground-floor cave and bellowed up after them, but the elevator noises drowned her out.

Neither of them was sure what the other had in mind when they stepped out of the elevator, laughing over their ride, but Eden's laugh was cut off abruptly. A man was standing outside her apartment, watching them.

In the dim glow of the hallway they recognized him. It was Leo Prysing.

"Your concierge at the George V mentioned this dump. When I got here the old hag downstairs gave me your name, Miss Ware. Said Lombard had visited you."

"What are you trying to insinuate? Eden happens to be my sister's stepdaughter. We are both going to my sister's birthday celebration. I came by to—"

"Hold it!" Prysing put up both hands. "All this has nothing to do with me. I've got a favor to ask of you . . . Can we go inside, Miss Ware?"

"Of course. I'm so sorry." She fumbled to unlock the door and pushed it open. "There. Help yourself to the brandy and tell us what the favor is."

Steve, still out of sorts, followed Prysing inside and went to the cupboard to get the brandy.

"You look awfully serious, Mr. Prysing. Is it a secret?"

Prysing took out two thin booklets, and she could see they were

Swiss passports. "It's about these," he said. "I want one of you to deliver them to my brother. There are tickets inside. Two for the night flight out of Vienna to Zurich on March 11. Two for the International Express to Paris via Zurich, same night. In case the airport is socked in. Or something prevents the plane from taking off."

Steve was staring at the passports, and Eden thought: he doesn't realize that we in Europe hear about this kind of thing every day. We live on the edge of the volcano and some have already fallen in.

Steve finally took them. "They're for Dr. Josef and his wife, I take it? I thought they would be in your Strand court by this time. They certainly ought to be out of Austria."

"My brother thinks he is irreplaceable," Prysing said drily. "He is the chairman of the Social Democratic party of Austria. They are the last hope of democracy winning in the election Sunday. But after Sunday there will be no Social Democratic party. Hitler has given an ultimatum. Either the Austrians take the Nazis into their government, or the Germans march. It's my last chance. I had intended to go in myself and get them out, but it seems I'm too well-known. They certainly know I am a Jew. And then there are those two anti-Nazi films I have in release. If Josef is in danger they will connect him with me instantly. So it's false passports and I've got to stay behind."

"It's true that you would be a great danger to them," Eden said excitedly. "I'll take the passports to Dr. Josef. I'll do better. I'll take the flight out with your family."

Steve forced himself to forget his hostility toward the producer. "No, you won't. This is a man's job."

Prysing agreed. "You're pretty well-known yourself, Lombard, but in a safer way. Your name and reputation could make a good cover. They wouldn't want to offend you by questioning you."

Steve fingered the passports again. Eden looked over his shoulder. "Franz Hofer," she read. "Hilda Hofer."

"Swiss identities," Leo explained.

Steve examined and refolded the tickets inside the passports. "All the more reason for me to handle it. Makes it awkward, though. Brooke's birthday is the twelfth. I suppose I could make some excuse and fly out with the—er—the Hofers."

"Definitely not," Leo snapped. "You two are to have no part in it. If Josef and Sarah get out Friday night the eleventh, they are safe. They can get out alone. I'll be at the Zurich airport. Or at the Bahnhof for the train. A friend in Vienna will send me a coded telegram in Zurich mentioning his own apparent arrival so I will know where to pick them up."

Steve was still trying to unravel the mystery.

"How did you find out about your brother's danger?"

"It seems Hitler's favorite operetta is *The Merry Widow.* The composer, Franz Lehar, hears things from high Austrian Nazis. Herr Lehar's wife is a Jew. So we can count on his information. He says all Social Democrats are to be jailed Sunday before the voting. Josef is their main target. There will be an accident. He will never leave the questioning alive."

"But how will we find Dr. Josef? He may be in hiding already."

"You, Miss Ware, are not to do anything as long as Lombard is capable of handling this. One of Lehar's violinists, Sigmund Bauer, will take the passports from you. For God's sake, don't try some fancy scheme to rescue them. Leave it to Bauer and others, people who do a lot of this sort of thing.

Steve nodded. "I certainly don't think Eden should be mixed up in this."

"What? Gyp me out of the role of a lifetime?"

Leo smiled without mirth. "You are to do nothing. Lombard is to do only one thing, give the passports to Sigmund Bauer of the *Theatre an der Wien.* Unobtrusively—inside a music score or a book, that sort of thing."

"I'm not a complete fool," Steve assured him. "I'll be careful."

Leo sighed deeply. "You two make a good team," he said.

Steve held out his hand to her, and she took it. His smile meant so much that she hardly heard the words.

"We'll win through for Prysing, won't we, partner?"

"You bet." Then she thought of something. "I wouldn't trust Kurt Friedrich. Even if it's safe for Dr. Josef to leave, I don't think Kurt should know."

"Right you are, partner."

But Leo had less fear of the Austrian actor. "My father and his were very close . . . Though he *did* grow up with his mother, a Prussian junker's daughter. He may not remember anything about his early years . . . Yes. You are right. He could be crazy enough to betray us. Keep it from him."

Crazy? Eden wondered. Kurt Friedrich would never think it crazy to make trouble for a Jew. It would warm his Nazi heart . . . But apparently Leo Prysing had some hold over him, or thought he did.

# *Chapter Three*

BROOKE Friedrich arrived at the airport in a chauffeured limousine which she would tell him Kurt had provided as an honor to Steve. She would not be able to tell him the real reason . . . Kurt wanted his Nazi friend, the chauffeur, to listen to the conversation between Brooke and Steve, hoping to hear any political information Steve had.

As Steve and Eden were riding away from the busy airport, he remarked that everyone seemed anxious to get out of Austria. "The inbound plane was only half-full."

Brooke waved her hand in front of Steve, then leaned forward and tested the glass barrier that separated them from the driver. "Kurt was a darling to provide us with this lovely transportation. He wanted to meet you but he is so busy these days. Everything seems to be happening. The plebiscite Sunday, you know. Like our elections. Only this includes the issue of union with the Third Reich. A great day for Austria."

"Great for Hitler's gang, you mean. The way I hear it—"

Eden stepped on his foot. Steve caught himself, noting Brooke's eyes which were darting to the back of the chauffeur's head. He rubbed his hands briskly together. "Well, here we are in frigid Vienna. With all that sunlight out there, my bones are still cold. I'd know the feeling anywhere. How has the weather been?"

"Beautiful! Perfect! Really!" Brooke said this so quickly they both looked at her. "Cold but sunny. Great weather for the plebiscite, Kurt says."

"And your birthday is the day before this election business," Steve reminded her.

Eden, having been present at most of Brooke's recent birthdays, knew what a hullabaloo was always raised and what an assortment of expensive presents Brooke received; so it was with a good deal of surprise that she saw it had apparently slipped Brooke's mind.

Brooke agreed rather as an afterthought. "That too. Thirty-nine. How I've dreaded that mark!"

Eden had gone through this before and tried to signal Steve that there were certain "gentlemen's agreements" among women. "Thirty-nine?" Steve started to say, "You're only a year younger than—" He winced as Eden's toe came down hard again on his foot.

"Very true," he finished gamely. But he muttered to Eden, "When I leave here my feet will be killing me."

Eden grinned. Her stepmother had celebrated her thirty-ninth birthday six years ago. But Eden was wondering what had come over Brooke. She was extraordinarily nervous and almost seemed scared. Was it possible the political situation had finally reached her? It didn't seem likely—unless some danger touched her personally . . . Eden wished she could warn Steve who was likely to blurt out their plan concerning the Preysings.

"Do you know whether any operettas are on? I'd like to see one while I'm in town," he asked.

Brooke was vague. "Possibly the Kalman *Maritza* or the Strauss *Zigeuner-Baron.*" She added, "*Die Lustige Witwe* is nearly always on. In spite of the troubles."

"*Die Lustige—*" Steve began. "*The Lusty Widow?* Oh, *The Merry*—That's the one. My favorite."

"A taste you share with the führer," Brooke said lightly.

"Can we see *The Merry Widow?*" Eden asked.

"One of the violinists was arrested last night. They say he is a Communist. Or was he a Social Democrat? I forget."

Steve and Eden exchanged anxious glances.

"Man named Bauer?"

"I believe it was Sigmund Bauer. Well now, what do you want to do first?" Brooke seemed much too excited. "A trip through the Vienna Woods? Kurt and I bought a chalet on the edge of Baden only ten minutes from town. There's even a streetcar that runs to Vienna. You will love the place." She clapped her hands. "But you always adored sidewalk cafés, Steve. I know what will really make you happy. A stein of beer at the Café Mueller, and it's within walking distance of the hotel. Ernst, stop the car." She tapped on the glass partition.

To Eden's immense relief, Steve made no objection. The car rolled to a stop. Ernst, the thin-faced chauffeur, got out and opened the passenger door.

"You will not take long, please, Frau Friedrich? I will be blamed if I do not deliver you promptly to Herr Friedrich. He is always concerned when you are not at his side."

"Really, Ernst, my brother has dreamed of this café for years. Would you deprive him now? Run along. Tell Kurt we will be arriving in half an hour." The chauffeur had nothing to do but get back into the limousine and drive off through the empty square.

None of the café regulars were sitting out on the terrace with its four-foot geranium hedge separating it from the sidewalk, but Brooke marched to the outermost table.

"Ah!" she breathed the bright crisp air. "Isn't it what you wanted?"

Steve ignored her question. "What the hell is this all about? Why are you afraid of that chauffeur?"

"Stevie, keep quiet. Eden understands, don't you dear?"

"I think so. You're in trouble—political trouble. Aren't you?"

"Oh, God, am I! And not through any fault of my own, believe me. I'm no heroine. But I've been trapped into it, and if I'm not careful Kurt will suspect." Her frightened face quickly changed, and she was all sparkle. "*Guten tag,* Frieda. A beer for my brother and a new wine for my stepdaughter and myself. Of course, it won't be any of the really new wines yet, will it?"

As soon as the red-cheeked waitress had gone, Steve leaned over to Brooke. "Tell us," he whispered. "What have you done? What can we do?"

"Easy," Eden warned him, "this isn't Paris. Every passerby on this street may be interested in us, watching us."

Brooke's smile flickered. "Sarah Preysing called me yesterday. They had heard Josef was about to be arrested last night when Herr Bauer was taken. I said what could I do? I haven't any way of helping people like that. She would be taken too. A Jew, you know. But she was most insistent. His life, she said. His very life was in danger."

Eden and Steve both stiffened. "Where are they now?" Steve asked.

Brooke threw up her hands. "I had no say in the matter. Sarah knows all about the wine cellar of our chalet, so that's where they are, if you can imagine. Kurt would kill me if he knew." She added with a weak smile, "I'm only exaggerating a little. You see, if I were accused, they would come down on him too. Unless he informed on me."

"But the Nazis aren't here yet. I don't see how—"

"On the borders, Steve. Every border between Austria and the Reich. And in the south it's Mussolini's blackshirts. No help there. Steve, I've got to get out of here."

"Of course you're going to leave." Steve was furious that his sister was threatened with such danger—Brooke, the last person in the world to be mixed up in escape plots.

Eden tried to contain her fears and concentrate on the matter. "I don't suppose Czechoslovakia would be safe. They're surrounded by fascist states."

"They are next in line, Kurt says. Something about the Sudetenland belonging to the Reich."

Steve pounded the table. "Oh, great. And the West sits and lets it happen."

Eden chose not to remind Steve that he himself hadn't been too concerned until the danger struck his own family.

"I think we can get the Preysings out," he told Brooke. "Never mind how. Brooke, is your passport up to date?"

"I can leave any time. I used it at Christmas when Kurt and I visited Berlin. But the airports will be monitored."

"How about making reservations to fly out the night of the twelfth. Day after tomorrow. The Preysings will have tickets for the flight tomorrow night."

"But how . . . their passports—"

"Never mind. None of us will use the plane. But the reservations will be made anyway."

So the train tickets would be used instead, Eden thought as she recognized a sensation of fear, not excitement . . . This was no Hollywood scenario.

"Where is your birthday party to be held?" Steve asked.

"The chalet. The night before—tomorrow night—we are to have a family dinner at the chalet."

"Tomorrow night we leave. The eleventh. We'll shake Kurt somehow."

"But Brooke," Eden ventured, knowing the ties that held Brooke to her husband. "Can you leave Kurt like this? Sneak off?"

Brooke looked at her with all the confidence of the born beauty. "He will come after me to Paris, naturally. If he thinks I'm bluffing, I'll go on back to America. But I know Kurt. He needs me more than he needs his precious führer. And I certainly have had enough of this place."

Steve was deep in thought. "I've got to make a phone call when we get to the hotel. Business. I'll be calling André de Grasse. He'll understand what's needed."

"The operator may listen in," Brooke warned him. "They do that a lot lately."

"André will know that."

"Dear André," Brooke murmured, to Eden's annoyance. "I wish we were with him in Paris now."

"We soon will be. Don't worry."

Eden wished she shared Steve's confidence.

KURT FRIEDRICH had never behaved better. He outdid himself in fawning over Steve and, relieved that Eden was causing him no trouble, he was especially nice to her as well. She could almost feel his relief when he took her arm and insisted on escorting her to her hotel room down the hall, not far from the Friedrich suite.

"Really next door to my brother-in-law," he joked. Eden played this up, laughing.

"Thanks for thinking I need guys his age . . . you seem awfully chipper."

"But of course. I am a happy man." His very exuberance seemed to Eden to serve their purposes. He was much too interested in his own goings-on to suspect anything was wrong, least of all that his wife was about to leave him.

"Career going well? How I envy you, Kurt. Big movie deal coming up, I suppose."

"Yes," he said, his eyes sparkling. "We have great plans for combining Austrian and German talents in the cinema industry that will completely eclipse the old UFA films and outclass Hollywood in every way. Jews ran those outfits before. We will use only Aryan talent now. You have seen the work of Riefenstahl?" Eden had seen the German Olympics film and had been impressed by the woman's obvious genius. Kurt went on. "Who can say? If you play the cards right, my dear Eden, you may one day be a part of our work."

"Play my cards? That will do it?"

"That and my help." He sat down on the bed, and Eden willed herself not to shrink away. He took her hand and brought it to his lips.

Next he'll be clicking his heels, she thought . . .

"Eden, *Liebchen,* how often I have wished to make amends for that little misunderstanding so many years ago. How very foolish of me to have drunk too much that night. I might have shown you a time you would never forget."

"Oh, but you did. You certainly did. You were so naughty." My God! she thought . . . If Prysing could see me now I'll bet I'd be a star in no time.

But she didn't want to carry this charade too far. She turned quickly to look at the corridor door beyond the foyer, and as she had hoped, he looked too. He was nervous. Living as he did to a great extent on his wife's income, it wasn't surprising that he preferred to keep his talk of a rendezvous with Eden a secret from Brooke.

Eden realized that Brooke's attachment to her third husband could be hard to break; her track record with him far exceeded those with her first two husbands. Eden decided that she must warn Steve not to tell Brooke too much . . .

At the same time Eden also decided it would be helpful to their plans to find out how strong Kurt Friedrich's attachment to his wife was. She challenged him impudently. "You look scared. Don't tell me you're afraid of my little old stepmother."

His smile was forced, and he let her hand go. "No. I have a club meeting tomorrow night. I must attend. I will, of course, be present at dinner. But I do not want Brooke to be hurt. I wish it were not necessary to leave her the night before her birthday."

"How sweet of you to care, after all these years."

"We suit each other. You must understand that, my dear. One may find attraction elsewhere. But there is always the warm hearth—for me, at least. Do I make myself clear?"

"Like crystal. You don't care for any other woman. Just Brooke."

He had started for the door, but stopped now and gave her a long, penetrating look. "I do not say that. Not entirely. Perhaps, if I were not so busy at this time . . ." He saluted her. "Come to visit in six months. You will find all of us very different. And I, most of all."

She gave him her biggest smile. "Six months. I'll remember that." She still wasn't at all sure of his feelings about his wife, wasn't sure if there was some attachment to Brooke other than her money. She could be sure of only one thing . . . He was certainly counting on Sunday's election and the triumph of the Nazi party. She worried over what was planned for the following night . . . probably a celebration to gloat over the future.

That evening proved to be nerve-wracking for Eden and Steve, but even more so, apparently, for their host.

An excellent dinner of veal and ham, crêpes and champagne was served in the hotel's elegant dining room. But Kurt and the others were constantly interrupted by urgent telephone calls, and at one point, Kurt was summoned to the adjoining cocktail lounge where Steve caught a glimpse of two soldiers in heavy, belted black coats and shiny boots. He pointed them out to Eden.

"Not soldiers," she told him quietly. "Hitler's S.S. They're not too popular with the workers and the general public. They've got their nerve appearing now, bold as brass."

Brooke dabbed a napkin at her mouth. Her hands were trembling. "They aren't wearing swastika armbands. It's nothing official. Oh, my God, what will happen to me—to us? They mustn't find the—"

Steve cut her off. "Never mind. I want you both to listen. Things are going to pop suddenly tomorrow night, if André understands the call I made to him today. Brooke says Kurt has to be gone after dinner tomorrow night, to some political club. Nazi, no doubt."

Eden nodded. "I know. It seems as if they've got something planned for tomorrow night. A rally, or something bigger. I'd bet on it."

"Good. The more rallying the better. André is ordering tickets for me on the International Express leaving Vienna tomorrow night."

"Steve!" Brooke whispered hoarsely, "Not the Express through Munich. We'd be spending the whole night crossing Germany."

"No. To Zurich. We will take your two servants, Franz and Hilda Hofer, Swiss citizens." He saw the expression of doubt shared by Eden and Brooke, and went on confidently. "If you are recognized you will say you are on your way to Paris for spring clothes."

They were now on ground Brooke knew very well. "Summer clothes," she corrected him. "The couturiers are almost into their fall collections by now."

Eden thought it providential that Kurt would be out of the way tomorrow night, the evening of the eleventh, though she couldn't help feeling anxious about the political meeting.

Kurt returned to the table and proposed a champagne toast to "the future of the Austrian Reich." Steve and Eden raised their glasses to their lips, but only Brooke, laughing nervously, managed to swallow a mouthful . . .

The all-important call from André de Grasse in Paris didn't arrive until the next morning, as Brooke and Eden were about to be driven to the Friedrich chalet in the Vienna Woods. The call barely caught Steve as he was setting out at Kurt's insistence to see how "pro-German" Vienna had become . . .

"I must show you what may be accomplished, my good friend, by one leader, one people, one Reich. A peaceful Europe in which a German-speaking Reich will have its proper place. You will be impressed."

"There seems to be no doubt who will win the election—sorry, the plebiscite—on Sunday," Steve remarked.

"None whatsoever. Austria is tired of its position as a tiny buffer with no strength, no influence. But as part of the German-speaking Reich, with a dynamic and inspired leader . . . Need I say more?"

"No. You've convinced me." Steve felt certain that the sooner his little group got out, the better. As soon as he got back to the States, he would make these developments known. He was sure that all America needed—unlike Britain and France—was the truth and she would act to bring the Germans to their senses . . .

Steve heard the welcome voice of the chambermaid. "Herr Lombard! They demand you on the telephone. From Paris." Eden and Brooke glanced at each other briefly, afraid they would betray the anxiety in their eyes. Eden saw that Kurt Friedrich was not interested. He was still wrapped up in his own political plans for the day and evening, and went over to the big windows opening upon the square. The street below was littered with leaflets apparently dropped by planes, and Kurt studied the men and women, especially the children, picking up the leaflets. In a small notebook he jotted down notes.

Steve looked at Eden as he talked. By the changes in his expression from carelessness to boredom to disgust, Eden suspected that he hoped to fool his brother-in-law.

"Yes. Not settled? What do you mean, not settled? No, I can't make it tomorrow. You don't understand, Count. I don't care what your problems are. Who? I know. From Cologne. I don't care if he is a friend of Hitler's. It's my sister . . . I see, I see. But I can return immediately after the signing. Well, I suppose I can get away. As long as I'm guaranteed to get back. Things are happening here. Great stuff. My brother-in-law is taking me around today . . . All right. I'll pick them up, fly out and return the following night, the twelfth. Well, Count, let's hope we have a real three-way deal. France, Germany and the good old U.S. of A. I do understand. Every word of what? Clicking sound? I didn't hear it. Can't thank you enough. This may be the biggest deal of our lives. *Au revoir* to you, too."

It was obvious to Eden that both Steve and André knew the Austrian operator was listening in. Bless André, she thought. He just might save them all.

She had the two Swiss passports in her large handbag. Josef would have to shave his shaggy sideburns and trim his hair to match the severe photograph of his Swiss passport. Sarah's picture looked pretty much like herself. Her face was not well-known, and it was unlikely to be challenged.

But the possibility still existed: what if they were all caught smuggling out two "wanted criminals"?

*We could deny we knew they were wanted, act innocent,* Eden thought . . . The Preysings had been good to her ever since '29 when they had met her at the Westbahnhof after her awful train ride through Germany. She didn't know them well, and seldom saw them in the past few years. Eden tried to pin down the time the Preysings and the Friedrichs drifted apart, and all of a sudden realized the answer was simple. The split between Kurt and Dr. Josef, who had given him his start in light-opera, had come shortly after the Nuremberg Laws against the Jews were passed, not in Austria, but in Germany. Kurt must have had Nazi leanings that long ago . . .

That knowledge did not make it easier for Eden to smile into his smug face now. But she hadn't been born an actress for nothing, she told herself, and tried to forget her anxieties. Steve looked over at her, grinned and winked. He was so sure of himself.

*We are going to get out, all of us . . .*

Steve and Kurt Friedrich left at once. Kurt seemed enthusiastic over the idea of Steve's big wine deal . . . It had been a clever ploy by André de Grasse, Eden thought. He must have realized that Kurt might not wish to make difficulties with a powerful American who had involved Germany in his big-money deals.

Meanwhile, there was this day, March 11, to be gotten through. Brooke took Eden's arm as they strolled along the narrow lobby with its rich marble and gold baroque decor.

"We won't get a chance to talk in the car. Not really. Kurt trusts me, but I know that driver of his doesn't. I haven't had a chance to tell you, but my own car is parked in a garage at the edge of town. I told Kurt it had to be overhauled. It's ready to be picked up any time I want it—My God, Eden. That's tonight!" She clung to Eden's arm. "But Kurt will come to Paris after me. You wait and see. We've had too long a marriage for him to give me up over some stupid political party."

Eden was skeptical about Kurt. Although she knew that Kurt cared for his wife, perhaps even loved her, in a choice between his Nazi friends and his wife, Brooke would be the loser. Eden would have bet on that.

"What do we do about the Preysings? How can they avoid your servants?"

Brooke gave her a catlike smile. "Because Kurt told the Preysings, long ago, that he thinks the servants steal his liquor. And my dear, they certainly do! So he and I have the only cellar keys." Her bright look faded with the memory of their danger. "Sarah asked for my key to keep anyone out, and to be sure she and Josef get out if they have to . . . if for some reason she can't count on me."

Eden thought that since they didn't dare involve Kurt's chauffeur and limousine, it had been surprisingly clever of Brooke to arrange for her own car to be handy.

"I did that so I could sneak away on my own, if I wanted to keep Ernst from knowing where I go. There's the most heavenly sable coat at Kellermann's. I've been planning to get it and fib a bit to Kurt about the price. But of course, if Ernst took me there, he'd manage to find out the truth."

"Brooke, whatever your reasons, you are wonderful!"

They went out to the big car parked at the curb on the Kartnerstrasse. Here too the crowded street was paved with leaflets—reminders of the plebiscite coming Sunday.

Obviously, the government still believed Austria would be able to run her own election without the armies of the Third Reich poised on her borders . . .

"I can't get out of here quickly enough," Eden whispered.

Brooke was bolstering her own courage. "Honey, do you realize that by this time tomorrow we'll be safe in Switzerland?"

"Don't say it. I'm superstitious." She put on a big smile for the chauffeur but it had no effect. He stood impassively beside the open door, saluted Brooke and ushered the two women into the car.

The conversation between the women was sparse. Brooke pointed out the Schonnbrunn Palace, the lovely green countryside, the darker green of the woods that covered hill after rolling hill. Somewhere in one of the clearings was the little town with its neighboring country house where Kurt and Brooke lived. The women trod gingerly through the wet leaves that lined the path to the blue-painted front door of the house.

"I meant to have all this cleaned up," Brooke apologized. "Kurt will be cross. He thinks I'm not a very good housekeeper. But good heavens, Randi always handled that at home. And in the islands, it was Tamiko . . . Are they happy? Nigel and Tamiko?"

"Awfully. They should have married when Chiye and I were children." Eden caught herself. "Sorry. I know you made dad happy. It was just that he never seemed to be your type."

"He wasn't. But I'm fond of dear Nigel. And I really have nothing against Tamiko. An excellent creature, in her way."

Eden wondered if all this chitchat was deliberate. Ernst looked bored and after opening the door for them, went back to the limousine.

"Will he hang around?" Eden asked.

"No. He has to go to pick up Steve and Kurt."

There were other servants, however, to worry about—a cook, a maid and the old yardman, half-blind and slightly deaf. They tolerated him, Brooke said, "Because he was in Kurt's family. Loyal retainer. You know the type."

Eden was anxious to get to the Preysings, to fill them in on their plans for that night. Brooke managed to corral the servants in the huge, old-fashioned kitchen to discuss her birthday party the following night.

Eden found her way down two flights of creaking wooden stairs. She looked around, and saw in the darkness a deep hole where coal was piled. On her left were shelves, ceiling-high, crowded with canned vegetables and meats, paint, brushes, varnishes and a bicycle wheel. There had been a vague noise when she first walked into the cellar, like an intermittent hum, but it stopped abruptly.

Straight ahead was the locked reinforced door to the wine cellar. Eden looked around, made certain no one had broken away from Brooke's little group upstairs and then knocked on the heavy oak door. She was not heard by the two within and tried again, her mouth close to the lock of the door.

"Dr. Josef? It's Eden Ware. You are leaving tonight with us. Brooke has the servants cornered upstairs . . . Can you hear me?"

A key turned in the lock. The door opened a crack and she saw Sarah Preysing's violet blue eyes studying her. The heavy door opened, and she slipped in. Sarah closed the door, locked it again.

"You look just the same, Miss Ware. I remember you back in '29. You were just a child. Something had happened on the train. You were upset."

The parallel wine racks gave the place the feeling of a prison. Dr. Josef came out from behind one of the racks. He had changed shockingly since Eden's last meeting with him two years ago. His hands trembled and there was a twitch under his right eye.

"It's so unfair! So rotten and unfair!" Eden said as she shook his hand.

He smiled sadly. "Yes. One may say that."

"He should have gone," Sarah protested. "Long ago when Leo first wanted us to go in '33. I told him that a hundred times."

Dr. Josef reminded her with infinite patience, "Mama, you tell me all the right things. But my poor Austria needs me. Can I abandon her when she is beaten and bullied? The party will die without me. You know it. We all know. When I am gone the Social Democrats will be dead."

"It is conceit, my old man," she said tenderly, "to think only you can keep the party alive."

Eden motioned them to the far end of the room between two wine racks, where about an inch of candle burned in a saucer.

"We take the International Express tonight. We'll take Brooke's car. Kurt Friedrich will be at some kind of rally. Something is going on tonight. We don't know what. But at least he will be out of our sight. Your brother sent these for you. You are Swiss citizens, servants of Mrs. Friedrich."

"How like my brother," Dr. Josef murmured, amused as he looked over the passports. "He loves intrigue. I am to disguise myself?"

Eden opened her handbag again and gave Sarah Preysing a pair of scissors. "Make him look like this passport picture."

"Easy enough," Sarah agreed. "Hold still, old man. I don't want to take off your ears along with your hair." She got to work. "We used only one candle last night. But it became so depressing today that we used two at once. Brooke—Mrs. Friedrich—was very kind to let us stay here. She gave us blankets . . ."

"Food. Are you hungry?"

"Thank you. We have eaten. The blessing was the coffee the first night. It stayed warm. Now we are not hungry. Nerves, I think. I will eat like a heifer when we are across the border. And my old man—he too."

"I miss my reading," he admitted.

"Tried to read by candlelight a new text on the removal of stones of the bowel. That man!"

He shrugged. "That was a failure. But I wrote letters to my party. When we are in Switzerland, I will see if they can be printed. In German, of course. To be read by my brave friends who remain behind." He squeezed his wife's plump waist beneath the heavy wool coat she wore. "Thanks, mama. In so few hours we are safe. Warm food. Lights. A warm room. Books to read, and pen and paper to tell the world what we have seen. Only eight hours if the train leaves as planned. We can be patient eight hours. What can stop us now?"

# *Chapter Four*

LATE that afternoon Steve returned to the chalet with an irate Kurt Friedrich. Trying hard not to upset his host, Steve still found it hilarious that a parade of about fifty black-clad youths wearing swastika armbands had been met on the Kartnerstrasse by rotten eggs and ripe fruit.

"It was not meant to be so," Kurt kept saying. "The police, the army, they are on our side. The timing, I think. It was the wrong timing."

Steve's spirits were raised by what he had seen. Maybe somebody in Europe was finally standing up to Hitler, he thought with new hope.

In the several hours after their arrival at the chalet, Steve and the others in the conspiracy waited anxiously. Kurt's evening appointment was still on schedule.

By evening their nervousness began to grow. Kurt had not left yet and it was almost six o'clock. When the call came for him, everyone in the sitting room jumped, and Steve was relieved by Kurt's sudden enthusiasm, knowing that whatever the news, it would get him out of the house and back to Vienna.

Kurt said nothing to his guests beyond a quick excuse. "I am expected in town. Please, my apologies." But in the doorway he called to Steve. "It will be different this time. You will see. There must be celebrations. No plebiscite. No election. It is settled tonight. The führer has seen to that. When I return we will drink to one führer, one Reich, one people. In fact, I have collected some choice vintages for this very night. But I am afraid it will be very late. Near dawn."

Brooke wished him well, kissing him with more ardor than the situation seemed to warrant.

When they saw him drive off in the limousine, Steve asked Brooke to show them the garden, where the servants could not hear them.

"When he comes back he will go to the wine cellar. We've got to be away and over the border long before. We can gain time if he goes to the airport first to look for us."

"What in the world caused Kurt's excitement?" Brooke wanted to know.

"How bad is it?" Eden asked dryly.

Steve had heard very little on the radio except that there would be no election Sunday. Hitler had put on the pressure. Within hours the Austrian chancellor would announce the *Anschluss,* the union of Austria with the Third Reich.

"The German army seems to have succeeded where the Austrian Nazi party failed. Chancellor Schuschnigg will surrender the country tonight. Probably he is doing so at this minute."

Eden gasped. "But they will stop the planes. And the trains, too, until things settle down. They always do."

"I know. Eden, you keep monitoring the radio. Brooke, keep the servants occupied. I'm going to call the railway station."

The station proved to be chaotic. A female clerk answered his question with an abruptness that could not conceal her fear.

"The Express leaves inside the hour. You are here, you go. Your tickets are reserved. But we do not go on schedule. Any minute the word comes—no departures."

Steve hung up. It was barely dark outside but there wasn't a minute to lose. He signaled to Eden. She understood at once and passed close by him on her way to get the word to Brooke. "I can't go and get the car. It must be Brooke," he said.

She nodded. "I've got the keys. I'll borrow one of Brooke's coats and that black halo hat of hers. I've been thinking. There's a path into the woods behind the barns. I'll drive there. You get the Preysings and Brooke."

Another problem remained. "I don't know what we'll do about the servants," Steve frowned.

Eden winked. "Leave that to Brooke. Right now she's discussing whether all the bedclothes upstairs should be changed. Even the cook is going to be roped in."

Although Steve took a new pride in his sister, he was let down when, some twenty minutes later, he saw the suitcases she wanted to take on this escape attempt. He frightened Brooke into leaving all but one behind, and hurried her out to the car where Eden waited. It was now fully dark, and there were few lights around.

Steve escorted the Preysings out of the wine cellar without difficulty. There was no sign of the servants, although once, looking back, Steve caught sight of a shadow at the attic window. It was the old gardener . . .

"We must take the front seat, Herr Lombard," Dr. Preysing said. "It is the place of the servants."

"Too dangerous. Someone may recognize your profile when we cut across the city to the station. I've a feeling every Nazi in Austria will be out on the streets tonight."

There was no time for argument. Eden took the front seat beside Steve. They had previously discussed the danger points, and now all agreed that crossing the huge interior of the Bahnhof was the worst.

"Except that the place will be jammed. We won't stand out so much," Eden pointed out.

The city was a madhouse. Every sidewalk café was knee-deep in celebrants. All the civil authorities of Vienna had donned swastika armbands, and rowdy young Nazis in uniform paraded the streets of the Inner Ring singing beer-hall songs and stopping cars, forcing the occupants to shout their triumph.

"One führer! One Reich! One people!" came the chorus.

"Shout whatever they say, even with your rotten accent," Eden ordered Steve. "Don't give them trouble."

"I'm not a fool," he snapped. But when a young student in a black belted coat and a Nazi armband reached in and caught him by the collar, it took all Steve's will power not to shove a fist in his face. Eden grabbed Steve's arm just in time.

*"Heil Hitler! Ein Führer! Ein Reich! Ein Volk!"*

Steve managed to spit the words out, but the crowd roared at his accent. Eden did much better, with full voice, though Steve noticed that, while she spoke, she had her fingers crossed, like a child telling a lie. Echoes came obediently from the back seat.

The crowd in the street swarmed on to the next car, and Steve maneuvered the car around a platoon of marchers and turned off to a dark side street. The car lights picked up half a dozen young men and women running along the sidewalk. Their shouts were audible to everyone in the car.

*"Juden! Juden!"*

It was the Third Reich incarnate . . .

Steve felt Eden stiffen. "Don't look!" he commanded furiously. There was no sound from the back seat.

In a few hours' time carefree Vienna had become a Nazi satellite. The cancer had spread, and before morning every national barrier separating the Reich from Austria would be down . . . The German army was now in complete control . . .

The old baroque railway station loomed up before Steve expected it. Cars were parked in a melee everywhere, and Brooke's car would be only one among many. She insisted that when she telephoned Kurt from Zurich he would have it brought home to the garage. Steve wasn't at all sure her husband would even take a call from her, but he didn't want to discourage her at this point. Her belief in her own irresistible charm was still a strong one . . .

Steve hated to burden the frail Dr. Josef with their luggage but all the porters were busy and, as the doctor pointed out, he was supposed to be their servant. The more baggage he carried, the less he himself would be observed. His wide-brimmed Swiss hat shadowed his face, and he walked as stiffly as possible. It seemed unlikely that he would be recognized by anyone not on the lookout for him.

The high-roofed, echoing concourse was swarming with people trying to flee Vienna. Steve also saw the men in black uniforms with the now familiar armband of the Nazi party. He heard English spoken everywhere and decided that his group would be less conspicuous if they played up their American nationality.

He tried to make his way to the desk where people pushed, shoved and wept, trying to obtain tickets.

"Too late, please," the harassed young female behind the counter announced. "The Basle-Mulhouse-Paris express has departed." A cacophony of voices followed in every European language.

Steve reached over heads and tapped on the counter with a fifty schilling note. "Tickets paid and reserved for Stephen Lombard. The Zurich train." For a few seconds he was aware of his own heartbeat.

"Lombard . . . Lombard. I do not find—"

He felt a surge of anger. Could there have been a mix-up? Had someone else gotten the tickets that were arranged by André and his connections? He felt Brooke's trembling hand on his arm.

"Aren't they here?"

He felt helpless. The train might pull out at any minute. Suddenly, the clerk looked up from her file.

"Please, they were cross-filed. Herr von Secht of Köln ordered them. You are friends of Herr von Secht?"

"Business acquaintances. We are going into a partnership to sell wines in the United States."

"So. That is good, Herr Lombard. The führer will be pleased. Good trade relations." She slapped the tickets into his palm, and he left her the fifty schillings.

Rounding up his four charges, Steve rushed them past the desperate crowd who pleaded to get the attention of the few ticket sellers who had nothing to sell except space on trains traveling into the Reich.

"Poor devils!" Steve muttered to Eden. The enormity of the tragedy struck him when Dr. Josef, close beside him and carrying four overnight bags, explained in a low voice.

"Many of them are Jews. For them it is too late."

The long blue train stood waiting for them.

"I could kiss the dear thing," Eden cried as they all walked quickly through the chilly night air. The puffing train threatened to slip out from under the roof at any moment. Crowds on the platform clung to the extended hands of those lucky passengers in the train corridors. The noise of the steam, the engine and the human voices was deafening.

Without taking time to look for their own compartment, Steve pushed everyone up the steps of the first car they reached. Dr. Josef and Sarah went into the next car, a compartment for six which was already filled by a Frenchman, his wife and two well-behaved children.

Brooke and Eden shared one sleeping compartment whose upper and lower berths had already been made up. Steve was about to take the next sleeping compartment, which he would share with a slightly drunk Englishman, but Brooke insisted that she would not sleep and they must all sit up in the lower berth. She was still arguing when they felt the train give a jerk. The last International Express pulled quietly out of Vienna . . .

Steve pushed his way through the crowd at the corridor windows. Eden was behind him, and let out a heavy sigh.

"Poor old Austria. When do you suppose we'll ever see Vienna again?"

Others around them were still waving to the luckless ones left behind who were running alongside the moving train until they reached the end of the platform. Eden watched as the train moved on, and the faces melted into the cold, clear night.

The train porters began to check the tickets, and the crowd in the corridors returned to their respective compartments. Brooke had already stretched out in the lower berth, and Eden tried to comfort her.

"It's all okay now. Relax."

There were no further problems. Their tickets and passports went unchallenged, and Steve was relieved when the attendant, after examining their tickets, saluted, bowed to the ladies and congratulated Steve.

"The news has preceded you, Herr Lombard. A proposition involving three nations. Such a deal should bring peace to Europe. A good thing, such a deal."

News certainly traveled fast, Steve thought, even news of an imaginary deal. Trying to hide his nervousness, he strolled along the corridor to the next car. The Preysings seemed quietly secure. Dr. Josef played his servile role with dignity, but Sarah found it harder, and chattered with Steve in English.

"You must own a great deal of the United States, Mr. Lombard. How do you keep track of all your territory?"

He grinned. "It's not easy. Every day those little valley cities spread just a bit further. That's in Southern California. When I bought that acreage it was nothing but rabbit holes and Black Widow spiders. The ground still isn't worth much, but it will be. It's just a matter of time."

"We heard from Brooke that your losses in that dreadful earthquake were severe. The death of your father—"

"The Monte Carlo was a total loss. But though the courts were badly cracked around the foundations, they've been repaired and are perfectly safe now. Most of them are occupied. One of them belongs to your—"

He had almost blurted out Leo Prysing's name. They must be cautious until they were across the border, and there were still hours of suspense ahead . . .

But surely, he thought, the worst was over.

SOME TIME before midnight Steve fell asleep. His companion in the compartment had fallen asleep in the upper berth before they left the outskirts of Vienna. When Steve awoke with a start, fully dressed and instantly on the alert, his companion's head peered upside down at him from the upper berth.

"I say, old man! Easy does it. Never saw anyone wake up with such a jolt. But then, I've never slept with another man since my school days."

The fellow had a youthful face that annoyed Steve. "What the hell is going on? Where are we? Why are we stopped?"

"Border coming up. Thought you'd like to know. Just a friendly warning. My name is Weydon, by the by. Harry Weydon. *York Daily Herald.*"

Steve resented the tone of this easygoing Englishman, and so it took a minute for the warning to sink in. When it finally registered, he set his feet on the floor and reached over to raise the blind. He saw no city but only darkness, then a couple of blinding lights and men in uniform walking past his window. They appeared to be Austrian, but they wore the insidious armband.

Steve's heart sank. He knew that border guards often strolled the length of the train and, in normal circumstances, he would not have been worried. But he now was deeply concerned about the false passports.

The Englishman swung down beside him.

"Don't tell me you are smuggling something across. You don't look the type, if I may say so."

"Don't be ridiculous. But I have my sister and her stepdaughter and two servants in the next car. I don't want them to worry. Border inspection is always nerve-wracking."

"Quite so. Sorry." Harry Weydon shrugged, started to climb back up to his berth, but stopped halfway up the ladder when they heard the heavy pounding on the compartment door.

"They seem to mean it," the Englishman murmured. "It's always a bad sign when they use their palms instead of their knuckles."

Steve was in no mood for the man's humor. "Thanks. I've got my family to look out for, so let's not kid about it."

"Who's kidding? That your wife? The beauty next door?"

Steve assumed he was referring to Brooke. "No. My sister. And her stepdaughter."

"The younger girl looks familiar, somehow. Nervy, too. I'll bet these bullyboys won't scare *her.*"

Steve opened the door, and to his relief saw that the Austrian customs official wore no swastika. But the security man who popped out from behind him wore the armband. The two men saluted Steve. While he and Weydon produced their passports Steve could hear the next compartment door unlock. Eden stuck her head out. She too was fully dressed but her red hair looked wild and unruly.

"It's all right," Steve said calmly. "Tell Brooke it's only the border police."

From inside the compartment Brooke's voice quavered. "Police from which side? Are we over the border yet?"

Steve looked at Eden; they shared a common fear of Brooke's indiscreet tongue. Eden ducked her head back in an attempt to be reassuring.

"It's those nice Austrians, Brooke. Give me your passport."

The security official slapped the Englishman's passport back into his outstretched hand.

"You are a journalist, Herr Weydon?"

"That's what it says there. There may be some doubt among my readers."

"And what will you report of our great *Anschluss?*"

"Fantastic, I'd say."

"Excellent, Herr Weydon." Evidently, the official heard nothing but approval in Weydon's response. "And you are Herr Stefan Lombard." He studied Steve's face, then thumbed the passport's pages to the entry stamp. You found our country boring?"

"Far from it."

"Unpleasant? You were treated badly? Offended?"

"Not at all. Everyone was most pleasant." Steve could not tell what the guard was getting at.

"You arrive 10 March 1938."

Steve suddenly remembered another March 10 . . . the day he had lost both his father and Randi . . . Not a lucky date for him . . .

"Yes. I arrived March 10."

"And you depart 11 March."

It was awkward, to say the least, but Steve leaped to the subject that had served him so well. "Well now, it didn't take me long to find out that my new company, DeGrasse-von Secht-California Wines, had made a mistake."

Both the customs and the security man stiffened.

"So? You do not find the German wines worthy of your company?"

"Quite the contrary. We are going to have to add some of your Austrian wines. The ones you folks call new wines. Or May wine. Light on the tongue. They'll be real sellers. I'm on my way to Paris now to convince my partners that I was right. We've missed a great bet."

Smiles broke out as both officials thawed. When Steve got his suitcase up for the customs man to search, the official waved aside the formality. He barely glanced inside Weydon's valise before going on to Brooke, who had pushed Eden away and now stood there clasping her negligée loosely over her nightgown. Green satin had never been more successfully employed, Steve thought. Passing their two passports to the security man, she leaned over to Steve.

"You didn't tell me they would be so good-looking," she whispered loudly.

The customs official blushed and avoided her eyes. Eden passed their bags to him but he waved them aside and moved on.

Steve worried about the Preysings, but didn't want his concern to call unnecessary attention to them.

"You will find two of my household employees in the next car. Named Hofer."

"Austrians?" the security guard asked.

"Swiss."

Both officials nodded and went on to knock at the next compartment door. Steve did not dare to remain in the corridor, but he left the door ajar and sat down on the edge of the lower berth, waiting and listening.

"You know something, old boy?" Weydon remarked as he climbed back up to his berth. "You're a damned mysterious fellow."

Steve looked at him. The Englishman shrugged, freed one hand and held it out as if to ward him off.

"Don't tell me. I don't want to know. Not, at least, until we are safe in sober little Switzerland."

Steve heard a door slam at the end of the corridor and got up. He opened his own door only to find Eden standing there, still dressed. She looked scared.

"Is it all right?"

"Sure. Fine. You saw them."

"They're taking so much longer than usual. And this isn't the usual stop, either . . . Steve, come here."

He followed her to the long corridor window, sensing trouble. She motioned him close to the glass.

"Look back to the end of the train. As far as you can. What do you see?"

He squinted. "Some kind of railroad workers' shack. There's someone in front of it, in uniform." He glanced at her uneasily. "What's going on?"

"A minute ago they hustled five people into that shack. I think they're rounding up more as they move through the train."

"They're weeding out the ones without passports. Or those with false passports."

"Or Jews."

His fingers made marks on the window. "Not if they're Swiss."

She waited a moment too long before she agreed. "Of course not."

"I mean—how could they? These people may be citizens of other countries. How can they detain them?"

"Those people in that shack are probably Austrian citizens. Maybe you don't know how it's been done in Germany. Jews are not allowed to leave. They can't work or live like the rest of us. So what is happening to them? What will happen to those people they've just rounded up? That's what the world ought to ask. You could make them ask, Steve. You're rich and powerful and respected."

"Later," he dismissed her irritably. "Right now I'm interested in just two people. Two Swiss citizens." He started along the corridor, but she caught his hand.

"Be careful, Steve, for heaven's sake." He ignored her.

He had just reached the open steps at the end of the next car when he met the customs official starting down the steps. The man gave him a stern glance, then softened when he recognized Steve.

"It's you, Herr Lombard. You'll soon be on your way to sign that excellent contract."

"Thank you. All in order then?"

"All matters attended to. *Auf Wiedersehn,* Herr Lombard."

"Then I can see my valet now? He seems to have forgotten to pack my razor. I may have to borrow his."

"Ah. Often the trouble with servants. Good luck."

Steve considered his departure a good sign, and hoped that as soon as the security man left, the suspense would be over. He went on into the corridor. The compartment the Preysings shared with the French family was closed and the curtains pulled down. The French family was lined up along the corridor.

Steve hesitated, then spoke to them. "My employees are in there with the security police?"

The woman only shrugged, but her husband, who understood English, answered impatiently.

"Always, they take our time. Only a search of the suitcase of these Swiss. Our cases were searched. It is nothing. A formality. This *flic,* maybe he is Gestapo. But if there is nothing to find, maybe they leave soon."

Two security police in black with swastika armbands strutted through the corridor from the other direction.

"All is in order. The Express starts in five minutes. The corridors must be cleared when the border is crossed. The Swiss are very precise. They demand it." They motioned Steve back the way he had come.

"I've got to see my valet."

"Once you cross the border, all is in order, Herr Lombard."

By this time he wasn't too surprised that they knew him. "There is no problem about my Swiss valet? I can vouch for him."

"None whatsoever. But the corridors must be cleared. You may return in ten minutes."

Behind him he heard the compartment door open. The first security man began to raise the compartment curtains while he reassured the French family.

"Inspection is completed. You may return in a minute."

Steve could see Dr. Josef's profile, pale but composed. At least the Preysings were still in the compartment, he thought with relief. Then Steve was forced to move out of the car, and Eden and Brooke met him outside his own compartment.

"Is—is it okay? We were so scared. We th–thought they'd arrested you," Brooke stammered.

"Good Lord, no! They went through everyone's baggage, that's all. We'll be over the border in ten minutes. The officials told me so. In fact, I don't know what the delay is right now."

"What a relief!" Eden whispered.

Moments later, the train began to move, slowly, then faster, until it was speeding, the wild shriek of the train whistle trailing behind it. Steve pressed his nose against the window, and saw that the little railroad shack was now far behind them.

Steve could see no indication of a border ahead.

"Twelve minutes. I'm not going to wait any longer."

"Suppose we're still in Austria?"

"So what if we are? I just want to shake Preysing's hand. Kind of welcome him to Switzerland."

Amid bright searchlights near the track, the train suddenly pulled to a stop. Swiss officials came aboard. They looked frighteningly like the Austrians, but there was no denying the flag that drooped over the entrance to the small railroad station. Its white cross on a red background represented safety . . . They were in Switzerland.

Steve started to go to the next car, but was stopped by two businesslike Swiss officials who examined his passport, gave his suitcase a brief inspection, and went on to Eden and Brooke. Steve waited with the women, who were still shivering.

When the officials moved on, he went quickly to the next car. The curtains of several compartments were pulled down, the occupants trying to sleep sitting up. He knocked at the compartment the Preysings shared with the French family. The husband opened the door an inch.

"Go away. We are asleep."

"Excuse me. I want to speak to my friends."

"No friends here. Please to go."

"My valet, Franz Hofer, and his wife."

The Frenchwoman called something to her husband. The man

tried to close the door, but Steve got his hand in and forced it open. The compartment was dark. "Franz? Mrs. Hofer?"

Before he finished speaking he knew they were not there. Across the Preysings' seats the two children were stretched, sound asleep. The wife was huddled in her seat, her head propped against the window.

Steve snapped on the light. "Where are they?"

The train lurched forward. They were on their way again.

"They were taken off by the Austrian police just before the train left the border station," the Frenchman told him.

*I knew it all the time,* Steve told himself. *I let them do it. That's what the police were here for. The two bastards outside the compartment . . .*

"What did—" He cleared his throat. "Why?"

For the first time, the Frenchman showed signs of sympathy. "They searched his case very carefully. They perhaps knew him. Or guessed they would find something. One of them—I do not speak German well—but he said, 'This is the one. The actor's description suits. There will be evidence here. Always.' They tore off the top of his case. They found papers. Notes, I think."

The poor fool, Steve thought with a hopeless frustration welling up inside him. Hadn't Preysing known that if the officials were at all suspicious, they would pull apart the entire suitcase?

"What did they do with my friends?"

"We could not see. The train moved on."

Steve turned and left the compartment. He was looking for an emergency brake somewhere, and ran into Eden in the corridor. She was shaken.

"I heard. Steve, you can't do anything now on the border. It's closed. I know. It was that way with Germany years ago."

"I'm not going to stand for this. Not by a damned long shot!"

"They'll shoot you. They have their orders. That's all they know."

In his pain and anger, he almost despised her at that moment. "And I'm to just stand by and let them be imprisoned, maybe tortured? Maybe murdered? Thanks! You certainly know me well."

"Don't be so pigheaded! Didn't your beloved Randi ever tell you that? Now, listen. You've got to use your influence. *Buy* them from those bastards. They want to deal with you about the wine and all. If you wait until Zurich, you can get some big shots to help you. All you can do here is spin your wheels."

He shook off her hands and strode on. He found the porter making up a bed at the end of their car.

"I must leave the train. Will you have it stopped? It's an emergency."

"Impossible, Herr Lombard."

"Now, see here—"

The porter straightened. "It is necessary to proceed. We too are on emergency. It is possible the *Anschluss* of Austria and the German Reich will bring war. France and Britain will not stand by. For us, with so many refugees on this train, it is necessary to move away from the border as fast as we can."

# *Chapter Five*

STEVE had telephoned Leo Prysing's hotel in Zurich during one of their stops. He had rehearsed the briefest report possible so that the producer could instruct him.

"My name has some weight in the Reich and in Austria, thanks to a wine deal the Comte de Grasse set up. I could threaten to cancel the deal. Make a trade," Steve suggested.

Leo had received the news stoically. "Do nothing. Wait for me in Zurich. I'm flying to the border. I'll meet you later, I hope. We may need your name and your business connections before we are through."

When the train pulled into the Züricher Bahnhof that foggy morning, Leo Prysing's powerful figure was striding up and down the station platform.

"How ironic," Eden said. "He looks like a Nazi *Gauleiter* in that belted coat." But fearing for Dr. Josef and Sarah, she could only feel joy at the sight of Prysing.

He and Steve wasted no time in greetings or expressions of regret. "What can be done?" Steve asked at once.

Eden and Brooke followed the two men quickly through the noisy station, where the possibility of war was being discussed everywhere.

"The borders are impossible," Leo explained. "And they all know my face. There was some unpleasantness. None of the Austrian border guards will talk. One of the Swiss told me that my brother was separated from the others because of his record. His radical record, they called it." His voice seemed to lose some control. "And the false passports. Which means that I put them in this spot."

"No. Not you."

"Don't tell me you're responsible. I pressured you."

Steve glanced over his shoulder, and saw the women were hurrying along.

"I feel my responsibility, believe me. But neither of us betrayed them. I didn't tell the girls, but the French family heard a remark by one of the police searching your brother's suitcase. Something like 'the actor described him.' Kurt Friedrich betrayed your brother and Mrs. Preysing."

Leo hesitated for an instant. Then he caught himself and they went on to the taxis out on the Bahnhofplatz.

"How did he find out?"

Steve had had hours to think it out. "There was an old man, one of Friedrich's servants, who may have seen us from the attic window as we left. When my sister and Miss Ware didn't return after presumably seeing me off at the airport, he may have notified Friedrich."

"And the servant saw Josef and Sarah get in the car?"

"I didn't think so at the time. But it's the only possible explanation. If Friedrich thought his wife had betrayed him politically, I wouldn't put anything past him."

"Ah!" It was a curiously alarming sound, like a chuckle heard in a moment of grief.

"In dealing with these lice we must forget about getting even. At least, until we have the doctor and Mrs. Preysing safe," Steve reminded him.

"But you see, my dear fellow, I have a hold upon this Kurt Friedrich. I will let him know that I do not hesitate to use it. You have my word, he will be happy to help us."

Steve wasn't sure of anything. "You know best. But it's my belief that bribery is the best way. They really fawned over me about the wine deal."

The two women took the taxi up to a hillside hotel. Leo and Steve remained in the city to communicate with Vienna through the Austrian Consulate. The conquered city seemed to be a madhouse and telephone connections were constantly breaking down. There was also the problem of the press . . . Numerous reporters and correspondents for the powerful American and European radio networks besieged Steve the second he and Leo visited the consulate.

Steve's recent bedfellow, Harry Weydon, was among them. "I say, old boy, for old time's sake, could I get a medium-sized—all right. Make it a brief interview with you and the movie man? Rumor has it that you're heroes, trying to rescue your friends. I'm at the Hotel Ile du Lac."

"Beat it," Leo ordered him.

"Really, sir, you've no idea how large a readership we have. And radio. I'm representing the BBC and your own American CBS at the moment, until Murrow and the big boys get here."

Leo grabbed Harry Weydon's lapel. "Stick around today. We may need you. Later." He turned to Steve. "That will make a very pretty threat when I talk to Friedrich."

No official in Vienna would speak to them, nor could they reach Kurt Friedrich. The embassy and the consulates throughout Western Europe were in a state of confusion about the situation in Vienna. Even Berlin itself officially knew nothing.

For the moment, it seemed as if there would be no war. Great Britain was making noises of indignation and France insisted it could do nothing alone. Steve was convinced by noon that the war scare was over. The führer's gamble had paid off at the price of Austria's enslavement.

There was still another string to pull . . . Steve tried to reach André at his lodgings in the de Grasse village and left a message. Then he tried the Paris hotel where André occasionally stayed and was desperately trying to figure out where else he might leave a message when he gave his first report to Eden, also by phone.

"How is Brooke?"

"I got her to lie down a little while ago. Steve, I have a feeling. Brooke keeps saying she wants to call Kurt and reassure him. But I heard some of what the Frenchman told you. Is it true? Did Kurt betray the Preysings? How could he have known?"

"Guesswork. Something they left in the wine cellar. Some identification the old man in the attic made. Don't tell Brooke yet. She's liable to have hysterics. Christ! I just don't see how any human being could do a thing like that."

Eden spoke quietly. "It didn't happen overnight. It's been happening day after day, hour after hour, while the rest of the world was worrying about whether Mrs. Simpson would marry King Edward or not. André says it could have happened in France or anywhere else, given the same conditions."

He leaped onto that. "You know André well? Eden, I've got to reach him. He may be able to help us. Do you know any hotel or office, any girl friend where we could leave a message?"

Eden was silent for a moment. "Yes. There is one place, a small room. He stays there sometimes. He's probably there now. Anyway, leave the message with my concierge."

"Your—?" He didn't think he had understood her. Then he apologized. "Sorry. I didn't know you were so well acquainted. I mean, that might do it. I'll call your concierge. You'll never know how much you've helped Leo. And all of us."

Her voice was cold, and he realized it must have hurt her to tell him this.

"I'm glad it may help. Good luck."

Fifteen minutes later his call was cleared to Paris. André came hurrying down from the attic room, notified by Eden's grumbling concierge. Even after twenty years of friendship, he continued to surprise Steve. He needed only a few words in order to put it all together.

"You are right. We do have—*I* happen to have a contact or two in the higher echelons of the Nazi party. It was arranged long ago. Never mind how. My job, as you say, is to let them know you will make a trade. This German wine thing, and perhaps money. You and Prysing can pay?"

"If necessary. We've got to get Dr. Josef and his wife back before they are lost in some forgotten prison."

"Concentration camp," André corrected him. "They have them, you know, in the glorious Third Reich."

"Yes, yes. I'm not a complete innocent."

"Good. I will get started at once. I take it the von Secht name helped you. Is Eden safe?"

"Perfectly."

"And Brooke, of course. You say she has left Friedrich for good? Otherwise, it could be awkward."

Steve was about to hang up but caught André at the last second.

"One more thing. Leo Prysing threatens to blackmail Friedrich to get his help. I don't know the nature of the threat, but it's there."

*"Merci. À demain,* my friend."

Steve checked back with Eden late in the afternoon.

"Brooke has ben trying to get her husband. The servants say he won't take her call. She's pretty upset," she told him.

"I was afraid she would be. Hysterical? Crying a lot? What does she see in that son of a bitch?"

"Just the opposite, Steve. She's furious. Says she can't wait to get home."

"Home?"

"I think she means the islands. I certainly don't want her disturbing father and Tamiko, but I'll work something out. Don't worry. I've always been able to handle her."

Steve laughed. "Sounds like Brooke. Running to whoever might coddle her. I'm sorry you're saddled with her right now, but we think we are getting through. The vice-consul, I think, says they may hear from Dr. Seyss-Inquart himself."

"Oh, my God! That Nazi snake? He's Hitler's buddy."

"Please. You're speaking of a gentleman with whom we hope to do business."

"I suppose they've murdered Chancellor Schuschnigg."

"Not so far, but I wouldn't write any life insurance on him. By the way, the German army, in all its glory, is occupying Austria. To preserve order."

Leo Prysing signaled to him from doorway of the room in the hotel suite where they were trying to conduct negotiations. Two Austrian businessmen had been with Leo, and were now huddled around his phone. Neither man wore the Nazi armband, and they both looked anxious, knowing they would be replaced any minute . . .

Leo called to Steve. "They are willing to trade. In principle. For a fifty percent share in that wine corporation of yours."

"With or without von Secht?"

"Including the Cologne bunch. They say they're all one now. There will be financial payoffs, too. They want that first. But I'll handle that."

"Go to it, if Dr. Josef and his wife are safe. Can you find out where they're being held?"

Leo had relaxed. "Of all places, that fancy Emperor Hotel near the Kartnerstrasse, in the Inner Ring. Seyss-Inquart himself wanted to question Josef. Obviously to find where other Social Democrats are hiding out. They have them on the sixth floor. We've got to move fast, before Hitler arrives in Vienna. They wouldn't dare make a deal once he's around."

Though he didn't want to take anything away from Leo's evident relief, Steve knew they still risked much . . .

While Leo arranged for signatures on the contracts, and a meeting with Dr. Seyss-Inquart's agents on the border, where the money would be paid, Steve was called to the phone in the foyer. It was André.

"Bad news, Stephen."

"How bad?"

"The worst. They are dead."

"Dead? Both of them?" Steve's voice cracked in disbelief. These people had trusted him, he thought with pain. "Not Sarah, too! For Christ's sake, why?"

"My informant says Dr. Preysing was being questioned. They brought his wife in. He agreed to tell them what they wanted to know. They must have threatened her. He was expected to betray his friends. He began to talk. The Boches were offguard. Mrs. Preysing took his hand. It was a signal. They plunged out one of those long front windows of the Emperor Hotel. From the sixth floor."

"Suicide?"

"A suicide pact. They must have discussed it before. It was all very sudden. The lady was smiling. The Boches could not understand that. My informant says they were puzzled. They asked each other, 'Why did she smile when she was going to her death?' Incredible, these Boche minds. No understanding of the human heart."

Steve's voice was shaking. "I had better tell Leo. He's still making deals with that gang."

"Tell me what?" The anguished look in the producer's eyes told Steve that he understood. Steve handed over the receiver.

Prysing listened to André's voice, saying nothing. Finally he hung up, turned, called to the Austrians as if he had just completed filming a scene.

"Gentlemen, that will be all. I won't need you, after all. Thank you for your trouble." He turned to Steve. "How do I reach your newspaper friend? Is it true he represents the BBC and the CBS network?"

"He says so. I believe Edward Murrow is in Prague or Warsaw with CBS. The other important ones must be in Vienna and Berlin. Some American correspondents are in Geneva."

"Would a broadcast be picked up by the Austrian Broadcasting Company?"

If he had in mind a condemnation of the Nazis by European radio he would hardly get far, Steve thought. They would see that no one in the Reich heard him after his first words.

"Berlin will pick you up. Especially if you speak in German. But the minute you start attacking them, they'll jam the broadcast."

"Oh, no," Leo said with deadly conviction. "Those who count will hear every word. And they will ask for a transcription, so they can study it and not miss the salient points."

"I'll get Weydon for you. You will want to talk to the local radio people, I suppose."

"I don't trust them. They are too neutral. I need an anti-Nazi country. Outside Hitler's reach. If I have to, I'll use Geneva, but I prefer the BBC or an American network. Tell your friend this is to be an interview by someone describing courage and bravery in the recent takeover of Austria. A secret revealed. That sort of thing."

Whatever he had in mind, he seemed very sure of the results. Relieved to be doing something, even if the broadcast should be jammed, Steve went off to the Hotel Ile du Lac to give Harry Weydon a scoop he would never forget.

IN THE end, perhaps because of his desperation, Leo Prysing managed to persuade the Zurich radio facilities to give him a BBC pickup. Harry Weydon, delighted to get hold of what promised to be a sensational program, agreed to interview the famed producer.

Steve stood by, trying to guess what Prysing had in mind.

Looking around at the curious crowd, many of them newsmen from France, Great Britain and the American newspaper syndicates, Steve wondered what they expected the flamboyant movie producer to do and say. There were several German and Austrian newsmen present, and they had even more reason for interest. The knowledge of the Preysings' deaths had spread already, and already Berlin was broadcasting condemnations of the "criminals" . . .

"Pick up your cues from me," Leo Prysing told Harry Weydon.

"I say, you're not going to declare war between Britain and the Reich, I hope," Weydon said, only half-kidding.

"No. It will be a eulogy to a brave man."

"Fair enough." Weydon supposed, as did most of those listening in the crowded room, that Leo would give an emotional tribute to his valient brother, Dr. Josef Preysing, chairman of the Social Democrats, the only moderate force in Austria that had fought the Nazis to the last.

Only Steve wondered. He knew what Leo Prysing was capable of . . .

Two of the microphones had been set up, and Leo and Weydon were seated, each before a microphone . . . It reminded Steve of Alec Huntington's first tryouts back in the early days of radio. Alec should be here now. It would be something he would appreciate . . . Weydon jotted down a few questions while Leo was apparently committing to memory whatever he intended to say.

The Swiss in charge nodded to Weydon, whose hands were trembling enough to make his page of notes rattle. He glanced over at Steve and grinned weakly.

The formalities were covered, and after clearance from London, Weydon began. He introduced Leo Prysing as a man who had just lived a story of sheer horror far more dramatic than anything created for his two Oscar-winning films or his early German classics. Leo shifted impatiently in his chair.

"Excuse me, Mr. Weydon, but my purpose here is to recount the bravery, heroism and sheer dogged courage of a man who once appeared as leading man in my early films. I mean, of course, one of Austria's unsung, unsuspected anti-Nazi heroes, Kurt Friedrich."

The two German reporters looked up, startled. There was no reason for them to believe Leo, but in their suspicious minds, the first seed had been planted.

Leo's interruption made Weydon nervous. The newsman leaped to cite the brilliance of Dr. Josef Preysing, his importance as a leader of the last democratic party in Austria, and his failed escape attempt on the last Express from Vienna to the West.

"This brilliant man, the last hope of Austrian independence, was taken off the train and died today under the threat of torture. Mr. Prysing," he said, turning to Leo, "besides the actor you mention, did any member of the Schuschnigg government do anything to protect a man of your brother's stature?"

"Nothing. Though Kurt kept my brother and his wife safely hidden in his wine cellar, the government itself did nothing. Friedrich escaped last night by plane, I believe. That was the plan. He used a ticket in the name of our friend, Stephen Lombard, while his wife, Frau Friedrich, came by train at his instruction. I expect to meet my old friend in London, where I hope his status as a refugee will not be questioned."

Steve didn't see how Leo could pull this off. The Nazis would see through it at once as a lie to discredit their loyal party member. Still, the little drops of poison added up . . . the departure of Kurt's wife, the fact that the two fugitives had actually been hidden in Kurt's wine cellar . . .

Weydon read off the statement Leo had given him. "Sorry, but my broadcasting associates in Vienna list Kurt Friedrich as a well-known Nazi sympathizer. Some say he is—or was—a party member."

"Naturally," Leo agreed. "But that is over now. It was part of our strategy. International Jewry must do many things to survive. But if you are in London now, Kurt, old friend, I do not hold you responsible for Josef's death. It was enough that you did what you could in so many other ways for your people . . ."

"You can't mean that the actor Kurt Friedrich is not German," Weydon said incredulously.

"Perfectly true. His mother was Prussian. But, of course, Meyer Friedrich and my father, the Rabbi Jacob Preysing, grew up together. Somewhere at the synagogue in the Inner Ring is the record of Kurt's birth. Unfortunately, Meyer Friedrich died when little Kurt was barely a year old. But the records remain. Kurt, my brave anti-Nazi friend, is one of us . . . Welcome to freedom, Kurt, wherever you are at this moment. You must know I am thinking of you."

Steve watched three newsmen push their way out of the room. All of them represented the German or Austrian press.

Leo did not even raise his eyes. He touched the microphone in front of him with one finger. Weydon said something to him, but Steve did not think he heard. His vengeance was complete, and only the pain of loss remained.

# *Chapter Six*

TONY Lombard insisted that he accompany his mother to Hollywood to greet Leo Prysing. Leo had said that he was arriving with a new starlet, and Randi wondered if that was why Tony was interested in going.

Prysing was due to arrive by plane after a fast flight from New York with only two stops. Much was made in the press of his ambitious plans. The Hollywood trade papers hinted at daring productions. Tony read an article aloud while they waited for Leo's phone call in Randi's large apartment in the Villa Eugenie, a four-story stucco building on Franklin Avenue above Hollywood Boulevard. Randi spent nearly as much time here as she spent at home on Nob Hill, though there were nights when she felt that she had traded Steve's love for this cold independence. He had never made an effort to visit her here, and now threatened in his European letters to spend even more time traveling, carrying his political message of the necessity for preparedness. He hadn't returned from Europe yet, insisting he had to be briefed on the situation there. But he was obviously also waiting for Brooke Friedrich to pull herself together and leave Paris, where she still expected her vanished husband to contact her.

"What do you think, mom? Is Leo bringing back a wee dram of sex from that cloak-and-dagger business in Europe? What else does it mean, all this talk about his daring plans? I'll bet he intends to star his little starlet."

"Don't ask me. He always sticks me with his B-scripts."

Tony flicked the newspaper under her chin teasingly. "Why not use some of that sex appeal on him? I know he's got a yen for you."

"Don't be silly. You're not talking to Heather. You're talking to your mother. I'm certainly beyond using such wiles, even if I ever had them."

"Well, if we are talking about Heather—" He laughed and slapped the arm of her chair with the rolled-up paper. It made her jump and she started to say something but he cut her off by his next words. "I always told you our little Heather had big ideas. She's not sixteen yet, but she pictures me as the first Mr. Heather Burkett."

"Tony!" The idea had alarmed her from the beginning. Randi suspected it had always been Stella's dream to get complete control of the house on Nob Hill and the Lombard interests, but she did not trust Heather either. Since the earthquake, the girl had used her appalling experience to gain the attention and sympathy of any man she set eyes on. No one could resist her . . .

Tony waved away her fears. "Don't worry. I've got her where I want her. She's a cute kid, but she's never going to do to me what she's doing to Alec. She plays us off against each other. But he doesn't see it."

"Poor Alec."

Tony looked bored. "Well, he's got only himself to blame. Anybody with half an eye could see through her."

She studied him with some curiosity. "I hope you aren't interested in this starlet Leo is bringing back from Zurich."

"Why not?" Again that mischievous gleam. "You see, mom, I happen to know who the starlet is. She wrote to me and told me all about her triumph. It seems she did Prysing a great favor, and he promised to repay her. So he's doing it this way."

"She wrote to you? Why would she do that? A girl friend of Leo's?"

"Nope. She isn't, and I don't think she would be. Not the type. I happen to know her."

"You know a European starlet? You mean, you've seen her in the movies. Tony, I hope you aren't going to get involved with anyone like . . ."

In his lively eyes she read the old familiar truth. No girl had ever made a fool of him. She could only hope none ever would.

"Leave it to me. I've pursued this one before. Like they say, she's a foeman worthy of my steel."

When the phone rang she was greatly relieved to hear Leo Prysing's harsh voice.

"Made it. Had an unscheduled stop at Denver, but I'm here now. I'd like to talk to you. Shall we come to your apartment?" He went on in his imperious way. "Why don't you come across the street to the chateau? My place is a hell of a lot bigger than yours. And I'll have food sent over from Chasen's or Perino's."

Tony would insist on going with her, but at least he would be kept busy eating while Randi and Leo discussed whatever ideas he had in mind. She only hoped Leo's starlet had the good sense not to interfere with the conference and not to try her hand at Tony.

They crossed the busy avenue and entered the ten-story apartment hotel which, like the Villa Eugenie, had been built in the early twenties, but with towers, turrets and cornice to make the movie industry seem to be located in the Loire region of France. In the ornate lobby Randi saw two pretty blonde bit-players given Tony the eye. He responded with a crooked grin and the wiggle of four fingers.

In the elevator Randi shook her head at her flirtatious son. "You never miss a trick, do you?"

"Not if I can help it. Life is short, mother."

"You are impossible."

"So are you," he came back.

"Me! That's not very respectful of your aged parent."

"Teasing Leo about dad and holding dad against Leo. What do you call that?"

"Our floor," Randi snapped and hurried out of the elevator almost before the doors were fully opened. Tony leaped after her, trying to lock arms with her.

Leo came into the hall to meet them, and Tony was amused to see that the producer greeted Randi with a kiss on each cheek and a hug that lifted her off the floor.

"Lovelier every day, Mary-Randal. Are you sure you won't let me star you in some great epic?"

"I'll ignore that as ill-timed sarcasm. I'm afraid my son feels that life won't be worth living until he meets your pretty starlet."

Tony shook hands with Prysing.

"Nothing easier. Matter of fact, she's had a bit to say about you. Why are you called 'Mad Tony'?"

Randi laughed. "That was his great-grandfather. Tony may be many things but if he's crazy, he's crazy like a fox."

Tony pushed past them and into the producer's old-fashioned apartment. Eden Ware was standing in the middle of the living room.

Even Randi recognized a certain photogenic quality about her and noticed that in her odd way, she sparkled.

Leo presented her. "My starlet."

Randi laughed and returned Eden Ware's warm embrace.

It wasn't for several minutes until Randi could get a good look at Leo Prysing and Eden. They had changed, she thought, aged in some subtle way that had nothing to do with wrinkles. Eden was confident in a more sophisticated and subdued way. But Leo seemed damaged. His eyes were sunken, his manner and speech brittle, more harsh than ever. She knew then that the horrifying double suicide of his brother and sister-in-law had marked him forever.

Almost immediately, the food arrived. Tony and Eden waited on their elders while Leo, at Randi's prodding, laid out his plans for future films.

He surprised her with the remark, "Your husband is involved, by the way. I have plans to glorify him. Heroic endeavor. Stood up to the Nazi gangsters and all that."

Tony burst out. "Mom, it's the way dad tried to save Dr. Josef. You're going to film the train ride, sir?"

"Much more." Leo did not hesitate to speak of the tragedy. "We'll begin by interviewing your father on Fox Movietone News, and Paramount—"

"The Eyes and Ears of the World," Tony quoted.

"This isn't funny," Randi reminded him.

Leo waved away her objection. "I'm not sensitive. Lombard feels as strongly about this as I do. We have what is virtually a partnership. He invests, and we tell the world through several movies what is going on. Steve has been busy in Europe trying to whip up some preparedness in the Western countries. He says he's made a little dent in London, at least. And he visited Winston Churchill at his estate not long ago. Of course, Churchill has been preaching the danger of Hitler's ambitions for years. But Lombard says it gave him a good feeling to know someone agrees with the two of us. He couldn't get anywhere with the Chamberlain government, though."

"He wrote me some time ago. Said he'd had threats while he was in England. He was amused. Said he's stepping on someone's toes."

"Aristocrats," Leo murmured, "maybe I can use that. With Lombard returning next week."

"What!" She felt crushed by the knowledge that Steve had confided in Prysing before telling his own wife he was finally coming home.

"Didn't you know? Anyhow, he has persuaded his sister to come back to the States."

Eden froze. "Has she heard anything about Kurt?"

There was a moment of silence. "I still can't picture Kurt Friedrich being a hero. I mean, he seemed like such a heel-clicker to me," Tony said carelessly.

Randi agreed. "And to me. It did come as a surprise, your tribute to him on the radio. It was broadcast all over the country. And then, when he didn't show up in London after all, everyone understood how you must have felt. Not that anyone blamed you. It was just a tragic mistiming. I know you wanted to let the world hear how helpful he had been so he would be welcomed as a refugee."

Before she finished speaking she sensed an odd atmosphere in the room. She caught Tony studying Eden Ware with a puzzled expression, and became aware herself of an understanding of some kind that existed between Eden and Leo Prysing . . .

Tony voiced his mother's suspicion. "Looking back on that broadcast of yours, Mr. Prysing, it doesn't seem too smart. Not like you at all. I mean, suppose Kurt hadn't gotten out of Austria in time. The Nazis must have heard your broadcast. Imagine what they'd have done if they'd caught him."

"Yes," Leo admitted. "I should never have mentioned poor Kurt's father. As a Jew, Kurt would have no more chance than Josef had."

Randi eyed him suspiciously. "And where is Kurt now? Why hasn't he at least called Brooke? You'd think he would want a divorce, if nothing else, given the way she left him so abruptly."

"You would think so, wouldn't you?" Eden's tone was unusually arch.

"I keep getting the notion that everyone is in on something except me," Randi said, her eyes fixed on Leo.

He was immovable. "It will all be in the movie. Shall we eat?"

Randi refused to be diverted. She let him fill her plate and her wine glass, but she never took her eyes off him.

"All this isn't telling me what I came over to find out. Everyone is talking about your daring new movie plans. Since these are obviously A-movies, how do they affect me?"

"Because, my angel, they are to be the biggest in my career and you are to write them. The first, at any rate. The rest will depend upon how well you do on the first."

"You give me one chance and then back to the busy B's? Thanks." Her sarcasm was real; she would not let herself get her hopes up.

"That's right. You're going to do a film about your husband's attempt to rescue Josef and Sarah. Part of it told through Lombard's eyes, some through Mrs. Friedrich's eyes, and a third perspective—Sarah's."

"But you can't do it. They won't accept it." She was shaken by the sheer daring of it. No studio in Hollywood had ever released a purely anti-Nazi film, fearing that an insult to the Third Reich would cut off an enormous slice of their business. Only Warner Brothers dared to make a film now and then that demonstrated some villainy by Nazis, usually in America.

Leo Prysing waved away her objections. "But if we succeed! If we make our films so romantic, so intimate, so full of box office stars they can't fail."

She wanted to applaud. If he was right, what things they might do to bring the truth before the public! But Randi wondered how Steve really felt, how Leo had ever persuaded him to take part in this movie propaganda.

Leo seemed to guess her doubts. "The Nazi bullyboys attacked your husband personally when they murdered my family. Your husband's grudge is personal. Do you understand?"

"I suppose so." She changed the subject, asking Leo about the first script. It would have to be extraordinary, she thought, with a fabulous cast to overcome the powerful isolationist sentiment of the American people.

The intricate dealings of studio heads were never better demonstrated than in Leo's discussion of available stars. This was important because as scriptwriter, Randi had to tailor her characters to fit the big-name stars he would sign.

"Goldwyn owes me one for my Huston deal several years ago. He has an option on Stanwyck. I'll take her. Zanuck won't lend out Tyrone Power unless I can get him an equivalent. I can get Taylor for Fox and borrow Power. The Nazis I can get from Korda in London. I'd like Conrad Veidt and Anton Walbrook. Both have Jewish backgrounds and both fled the Nazis. I'll want Wyler to direct."

"You'll never get him from Goldwyn."

"We'll see. Maybe LeRoy from Metro. Mayer owes me a favor or two. And I'd like young de Havilland from Warners in Mrs. Friedrich's part. Beautiful but vulnerable. And either Herbert Marshall or Franchot Tone. Or maybe George Brent to play my part."

She managed to get through the staggering miscasting without a smile. It was incomprehensible that he could talk so calmly about casting his family tragedy, but she wrote everything down. Meanwhile Tony asked Eden where she was going to be living in Hollywood.

She gave him an ironic look that he took for amusement. "If you mean, am I sleeping with my boss, the answer is no. Not my type. He did get me an apartment in your mother's building, the Villa Eugenie across the street. By the way, I have a genuine part in this film of Prysing's."

"Really? Stand-in for Stanwyck?"

"I'm playing myself in the plot. Eden Ware playing Eden Ware. Some names will be changed, but not mine."

"I'll walk you home. You'll need your beauty sleep."

"Thanks loads."

"Then I'll return for mother. I'd just as soon not leave him alone with her."

Tony carried Eden's two suitcases across the street, puzzled by the disparity between them. One was a shabby overnight bag with faded labels plastered all over it, while the other was elegant black leather with brass locks and her initials. She explained that the ancient one had been all she could take out of Vienna. The other was a present from her new boss.

"Aha!"

"Nothing of the sort. He's never even kissed me. I think he's got a secret love."

"Never mind that," he frowned, and dropped the matter.

Her apartment was on the first floor. Tony noticed that the long windows with dramatic crimson velveteen drapes looked out on a stone wall six feet high, but Eden didn't care.

"You should have seen my attic in Paris."

"I wish I had." He set her bags down and took her hand. "Shall we try everything out once, just to see if it works? The kitchen stove, the drapes, the pulldown bed?"

"The dressing room. The bathroom. The shower."

Despite the humor, there was excitement between them. They both felt it, a physical tension they wanted to prolong . . . Eden had always been a challenge to Tony. There was a free-spirited quality about her that made her sophistication magnetic. Now that she was a true heroine, her allure seemed irresistible . . .

He insisted on putting her empty suitcases away on the high shelf of the closet behind the bed, which required opening the door with the bed clamped to it. He tested the bed, pulling it out and sitting down.

"You really like these awful one-room holes, don't you?"

Eden knew exactly what he was leading up to. "How many Eden Wares do you see?"

"One is enough for me." He reached for her, but she slapped his hands away.

"Then why do I need more than one room?"

He laughed. "You don't mean that. Now me, I want as many rooms as I can get."

As she stretched to reach the high shelf, he pulled her backward down on the bed. She struggled, hit him in the stomach with her elbow and then rolled over on top of him.

"You want me, okay. But when you play rough you're not in my league. I've played with some tough hombres. Now, what's it to be?"

He welcomed her into his arms. Once more she had surprised and tantalized him.

"Look what you're doing to me, you beautiful thing!"

She looked. He was young and virile. Her pulse quickened . . . She had a sudden vision of Steve Lombard here before her, a young man. Tony's age. And belonging to her . . .

She knew he was not used to women who took the initiative in sex, but he responded rapidly, inspired by the excitement they shared. Before she quite knew what was happening he was inside her, moving with her, clinging to her as they both tried to prolong their ecstasy . . . For Eden, it was the first, the only time she had experienced such a deep fulfillment of desire.

He lay with his lips close to her throat and it was with enormous effort that she managed to end the precious contact.

"Didn't you say you were going to walk your mother back over here to the villa?"

"My God!" He swung off the bed, buttoning up his slacks. "That Hollywood big shot has been after her for years. Mother doesn't know these guys and their angles."

She sighed and rolled over on her side, and he bent over to kiss her bare shoulder. She murmured dreamily, "Steve . . ." Then her eyes fluttered open.

He was very close to her face, his own eyes blazing. "Not Steve. Tony is the name."

She instantly regretted the stupid mistake . . . What Eden did not know that night was how stubbornly the tradition of jealousy remained in the Lombard family, how every son seemed bound by the deadly determination to conquer his father.

But Eden could tell by the look in his eyes that Tony had finally grown up . . . He was determined to have her in such a way that she could never again utter his father's name after he had made love to her.

FROM THE notes Randi had taken and her own incomplete knowledge of what had happened on the train ride and the aftermath in Switzerland, Randi felt that a popular thriller could be made. But she had one serious objection.

"You'll pardon my pointing out, Leo, that your American hero has a wife somewhere; what do we do with her?"

"Let's not clutter up the scene with nonessentials. We've got two married couples. We'll have our hero single. Then there's our heavy. He's very much married. And our Austrian heroes—their marriage will be the tragedy-romance."

"But who is your heavy? Your villain."

He stared at her. "Well, that bastard Friedrich, of course."

She sat up straight, evidently shocked at the revelation.

"It was Kurt who betrayed them? I thought it was the servant. But your praise of Kurt, the way you spoke about him on the radio . . . Oh, my God. It was deliberate on your part. You wanted the Nazis to destroy him."

"I thought Steve would have told you. I discovered only tonight that he hadn't."

"He told me nothing." She realized that she hardly knew Steve any more, and for the second time that night she was aware of the chasm between them that had become deeper with the years.

Leo was watching her intently, and she couldn't help but show her jealousy.

"I suppose he has some girl friend. That's why he spends so much time away from home. Does he have a mistress? You met him in Paris, didn't you?"

Leo paused. "Why should he come home?" he said finally. "You're never there."

"But you ought to know. I have my work. Besides, the house isn't big enough for both Stella and me."

"Then get rid of her."

"My dear Leo, she owns one-third of the house and she loves the feeling. I understand it—I was the same way once."

She was aware of his presence over her shoulder.

"Is it still Lombard? That schoolgirl crush you dramatized into the romance of a lifetime?"

His mouth was disturbingly close. She raised her head and her lips touched his. Leo's embrace was powerful, almost angry, and she responded with a passion of which she was immediately ashamed.

"I am a Victorian. I was born before the turn of the century. I wouldn't satisfy you unless I felt absolutely free of Steve. And I don't yet."

To her surprise he moved away from her, saying calmly, "I am more Victorian than you. Or let's say I am a product of Franz Josef's day. So I have no such complex . . . Back again, I see, Tony."

Randi turned and saw her son in the doorway. He was smiling but in her embarrassment she knew he didn't like what he had seen.

Undisturbed, Leo welcomed him. "Come in. You are just in time. I was about to propose to your mother—" He paused deliberately, "—that Prysing Films hire you during your summer vacation. Give you a start in the business."

It was such an obvious bribe that Randi wasn't surprised when her son refused. But he was forced to reconsider.

"Your father made it a conditional provision. He thought you might like it. Nothing much at the start, but an assistant director's title would certainly help you with the girls."

"Well, sir . . ." Tony was having a change of heart. "There are advantages, as you put it. I could see more of Eden. And it wouldn't hurt to earn a little money. And of course, I'd like to please dad." He laughed over his first reaction, playing it lightly. "Who knows? I might make good. I doubt if dad figured that. Or a few other things." Randi was still seated, and her son reached over her head to shake hands with Leo Prysing.

"It's a deal," the producer agreed.

Randi stared at Tony. "Aren't you forgetting that you live in Northern California? And then, there's Heather."

"Oh, Heather. Why shouldn't I be a decent guy for once? She's Alec's whole life. Leave her to Alec. I only hope he knows what he's getting into."

# *Chapter Seven*

ALEC Huntington had no need for such cautiousness as Tony advised . . . He could hardly believe his own luck . . .

Alec knew that Heather's determination to marry him had something to do with Tony's new job with Prysing Films. Heather, wanting desperately to visit the movie studio, had been refused, and Alec understood her disappointment.

He had recently suffered a setback himself when his hopes of representing his radio network at the Munich talks fell through. Britain, France, the Third Reich and Italy had decided peace was possible as long as Hitler was permitted to keep Austria, the Saar, the Rhine border and a large chunk of Czechoslovakia. So Alec tried to get assigned to cover the Pacific, but here too, men with seniority over Alec or better name recognition were preferred.

Heather had never been more charming than when she cuddled up next to Alec on the wicker couch in the sunroom of the Nob Hill house and they listened together to the Hollywood radio broadcast of Prysing's film *Journey.* There had been predictions that its daring attack on the Nazis would be disastrous at the box office. But the world had just heard that twenty-five thousand Jews had disappeared within one week into "camps" of which little was known outside the Reich. With such knowledge it was difficult to fault Prysing Films for painting a brutally critical picture of the Third Reich . . .

A few days before the premiere, when Randi told her about Kurt Friedrich's depiction in the movie script, Brooke Friedrich took to her bed in the Nob Hill house. The script destroyed her steadily growing, romantic memories of her husband, and she blamed Randi for blackening Kurt's reputation. There was still no word from Kurt himself, no correspondence, and during the year they were separated, Brooke had convinced herself that he was merely hurt by her desertion. None of her letters had been returned; so, she reasoned, unless the government was holding them for some reason, he must want to keep them . . .

When the movie was released, though, and the truth about her husband made known, there was a painful break in Brooke's relations with Randi and Eden. Stella Burkett Lombard set about filling the void, pampering Brooke and in general making herself indispensable. Alec wondered if she hoped this would encourage the relationship between their two children, which was fine with Alec. Only Heather's age kept him from proposing to her now. He was not blind to the nature of her attraction for him, though . . . she was so like his own mother, a helpless beauty incapable of living life alone.

The film *Journey* premiered in the summer of 1939. The cheers that went up on the radio when Randi and Steve arrived with the producer were chiefly for Steve, whom Leo presented as the real-life hero of the film.

"He's so handsome. I can just see him now when I hear his voice," Heather murmured, snuggling up close to Alec. "But actually, you're handsomer than him or that dumb Tony."

"I wouldn't go that far. Uncle Steve has more class. But the kid's not bad-looking either. I wonder if there's anything between him and . . ." He remembered whom he was talking to. "Probably not."

"Eden Ware." So Heather knew what he was hinting at. "How did she ever get in the movies? She's nothing to look at, and yet she's already in another movie, they say. I wish I could see what she's wearing. They ought to describe their clothes. They usually do."

Stella came in to listen to the Lombard triumph. Through the years the one-time Lombard parlormaid had developed into a woman who was no longer shapely but impressive, almost handsome—and more bossy than ever.

The telephone rang and Stella jumped up to answer it.

"It's for you, Alec. Calling from New York. Some fellow says he's back from London."

Alec picked up the phone but knew at once that his mother had taken up the extension in her bedroom. "I'll take it, mother," he said. But her voice was more uneven than usual.

"No. I want to hear. It's about Kurt."

The voice of Chuck Simon, NBC's London man, came on. "Sorry, Alec. I thought I'd tell you the bad news first. I didn't mean to break it like this."

"It's about my husband," Brooke cut in shrilly. "He's dead. They killed him."

It always pained Alec when he heard that desperate tone in his mother's voice, or Heather's when she found herself alone in a room with the door closed . . .

"Mother, don't." He signaled to Stella. "Get her off the phone."

Stella left the room. "It's something bad," Heather whispered.

"Depends on your viewpoint." He then spoke into the phone. "Chuck, is this about my stepfather, Kurt Friedrich?"

"He's dead, boy. Happened months ago, but I heard it from Shirer the night before I left London. They say the war's coming any day. If the *Wehrmacht* crosses the Polish border, it's war."

Alec heard a click and knew Stella had hung up Brooke's phone. "No Munich this time?" Alec asked.

"Not a chance. If only they could convince the führer that Britain and France mean business at last."

Alec's mind raced . . . *If the war comes, and I'm not there to report it* . . . He said, "How come you're back home?"

"They're sending the big guns in. I was never more than a little popgun, you know."

"Tell me about Friedrich."

Chuck Simon cleared his throat. "Lousy business. The rumors were all over London that Friedrich wasn't exactly the hero Prysing's radio message painted. Even so . . . Anyway, he died on what's being called *Kristallnacht.* It was last November when Berlin went nuts on a regular orgy of breakage and killing."

"I know. It was triggered by the assassination of a Nazi in Paris. Had Friedrich been in prison?"

"No. That's the weird part. There was a lot of suspicion against him but Goebbels and his gang insisted that the story he was a Jew was a lie. And then, one night a gang of S.S. beat him to death. They called it a tragic mistake; they killed the wrong guy. I quote."

Hearing no sound from Alec, Chuck Simon ended lamely. "Just thought you'd like to know. Well, fella, if Mr. Hitler gets his war I hope you get that London assignment you wanted so badly."

"Thanks. You never know. And thanks for the news. It's bad, but almost anything is better than not knowing."

When he hung up he went in to see his mother. Stella bustled around, removing Brooke's dinner tray. Brooke lay with her head buried among the satin-cased pillows, tears streaming down her face.

"It's all my fault. I shouldn't have left him. He would have stayed in Vienna. Why did I let Steve talk me into deserting him? Why?"

Alec took her delicate hand and leaned over to kiss her cheek. "It wasn't your fault, mother. You mustn't think that."

She obviously wanted to be convinced.

"I had to leave, you know. I was terrified of those Nazi friends he had. You do see that, don't you?"

"I certainly do. Would you like a toddy or something to help you sleep?"

"No, dear," she sniffed. "You've always been a good son. Never gave me a minute's worry." Brooke gazed from him to Stella. "Dear boy, after all that's happened, that horrid movie and all, I think Heather deserves better than Randi's son. She is a sweet child and deserves my good boy."

Stella smiled grimly, and Alec could read her thoughts . . . It had been a long, hard struggle to get her illegitimate daughter set up among the Lombards as their equal. She had almost made it . . .

"How right you are, mother. You were never more right." Alec sensed Stella's body relax beside him. Heather came up behind him, put her arms around his middle and tucked her cheek against his shoulders.

"Sweet, sweet Alec," she whispered.

The two mothers basked in the sight.

STEVE LOMBARD had flown home to San Francisco to new fame. He had pictured a reunion with Randi that would cancel out all past problems, but Randi wasn't home. She was over four hundred miles away with Leo Prysing. Even Tony was gone, though Steve could hardly blame Leo for hiring the boy. It had seemed a good idea to Steve when he first broached the subject, thinking it would keep Tony busy during that summer. Steve could not have guessed that Tony would quit college in order to pursue a career in the movies, behind the camera . . .

A year later, Steve's situation was much the same. His properties had skyrocketed and the films he invested in were money-makers. But his real ambition, rousing America to an awareness of the Nazi menace, had not changed from where it had been when he returned home in late spring of 1938. The calm, decisive voice of air hero Charles Lindbergh, backed by respected isolationists, senators, writers, men and women of many fields, had organized powerful public meetings, and had managed to counteract Steve's every warning . . .

Steve considered it a good sign when Randi promised to be present for his talk before a large audience in a big valley town south of Oakland. Scenes from *Journey* would be shown, along with newsreel shots of a recent Nuremberg rally. Alec Huntington was going to cover the affair for the network and Leo Prysing had made a deal to cover it for Fox Movietone News. Bridget Gallegher, Steve's mother-in-law and his staunchest supporter, would be there in spite of a flareup of liver trouble brought on, she said, by her doctor's insistence that she lay off the liquor and stick to water.

"That water'll kill you every time," she insisted, "but no doctor's keeping me from my son-in-law's speechifying."

Alma Gault Ottinger and her oilman husband were in the opposite camp and the Hearst papers reported that J. Henry Ottinger regularly contributed to the isolation groups and to the campaigns of the senator from Montana who spearheaded the drive to keep America out of any European entanglements.

Randi flew up to Fresno from Hollywood with a reluctant Tony, who complained that by leaving now he was giving Eden Ware time to find somebody else.

"And she will, too. You simply can't pin her down."

"Eden doesn't strike me as promiscuous, but of course, she is popular. I wouldn't be surprised if she became another Hepburn before she was through."

"Small comfort. While I remain a flunky for Prysing Films."

Randi smiled. "You really are smitten, aren't you?"

"Smitten! Now there's a bright new 1939 expression." Tony turned to study her. "You're looking mighty happy. Seeing dad certainly brings out the sparkle in your eyes. These last few years it seemed like you were on the outs more than usual."

"He needs all of us now."

Tony was fed up with his father's politics. "Family solidarity is all that's getting me to this damned rally. I'm all for keeping our noses out of Europe. No war for me." He shrugged. "And unfortunately for dad, practically all my friends feel the same way."

She didn't argue with him. "Fasten your seat belt. We're coming into Fresno. To show you what a sport I am, you can drive me the rest of the way."

"Thanks. I can't stand women drivers. Eden scares the hell out of me the way she zooms right along, never paying any attention to anything on the road. Is Alec driving down? I wonder if he'll bring Heather. It's about time he was making an honest woman of that girl."

"Do you want to see her?"

Tony considered. "Not really. She's trouble. And I don't want any stories to get back to Eden."

Nor to Alec, Randi hoped.

THE SCOTTISH Rite Auditorium, a barnlike hall with excellent acoustics, was one of the largest gathering places in San Joaquin County, and on that summer night in 1939 it was packed. Several army officers from San Francisco's Presidio base were prominently displayed in the front rows but to Randi, the audience looked like common-sense, middle class citizens, far too staid to fall for the blandishments of a handsome man who wanted to pull them into a war. The movie scenes could help, though, as well as the spectacular shots of the last Nuremberg rally.

Proudly escorted by Bridget and Tony, Randi went backstage where she found Steve surrounded by local and Hollywood reporters, and radio people, including Alec who seemed very much in his element. Steve welcomed Randi enthusiastically, and as they embraced she thought of how close she had come to letting Leo make love to her. As long as Steve was honest with her he would move and excite her as only he could do.

He insisted she sit on the stage with her family and those who introduced him. She felt shy there, but if it would help him, she was willing. Bridget sat next to her.

"Good crowd. Ought to be a nice take. Plenty of moolah." Randi hoped no one else heard her mother's remark.

Alec Huntington and a man representing another network from Hollywood shared the bare stage along with an army general and several distinguished refugees. There was great applause when Steve was introduced by the general. But then, to Randi's horror, a few "boos" could be heard. She felt Tony, on one side of her, raise his head angrily. Randi remembered the tradition: whatever their political differences, a Lombard always defended another Lombard when the chips were down.

Steve ignored it all. He told the now familiar story of a young actor who married into his family and gradually turned into a Nazi and a betrayer. His message was that it could happen anywhere.

There were yells from the floor. "Not here! Not here!"

"Not if we keep ourselves and Western Europe strong. Not if Congress votes to increase Lend-Lease to Great Britain."

Bridget whispered to Randi, "I'm not so keen on that. I never was one for the givin' of guns to England."

"Ships, mama. Old ones we don't need."

"Still and all, England?" Her Irish blood still ran strong, but Bridget perked up to cheer when Steve continued.

"We can't allow ourselves to remain blind to the danger these fascist governments present. Spain has discovered that, and Austria now knows the heel of the jackboot. And Czechoslovakia. Poland is next in line. And after Poland? France? Britain?"

"No war. No war," came the chant from the floor.

"I agree. So why not give Britain some of our support in their effort to strengthen themselves. Let's prevent the war from starting. Strength is the only deterrent the führer understands."

Thunderous applause, led by the military, greeted this. But suddenly, amid the applause, an overripe tomato flew through the air from somewhere in the auditorium. It struck Steve on his right sleeve and shoulder. He flinched, and Randi and Tony were on their feet instantly. Tony rushed in front of his father to deflect any further attacks, but Steve calmly moved him aside.

The audience was in an uproar. Uniformed men swung around in their seats to find the culprit.

"Wait!" Steve's voice rang out. He picked up the remnants of the tomato and held it up.

"In the concentration camps of the Third Reich this is more wholesome food than they get in a month. Don't waste it." He flipped it over his shoulder to the floor.

His contempt cut to the bone, and the applause that followed was deafening. Steve chose this moment to give the brief buildup for the movie reels being shown. When the screen descended and those onstage moved to the wings to discuss the event, Steve was overwhelmed by hugs and kisses from his family and the admiration of the media and his supporters. He looked at his son with special pride, but Tony was staring at something backstage.

"I got it all, it's great," Alec boasted. "You're a real hero tonight, Uncle Steve, for the way you turned it all around."

As Steve held her and Bridget close, Randi uneasily discovered Leo Prysing and Eden Ware backstage waiting to congratulate Steve. Tony had seen them too, and was frowning.

Eden shook Steve's hand. "You were splendid. We were so proud of you, Steve. We got here late, but you really made the night."

Leo added his congratulations, but Steve had other things to think about. "Excuse us. Randi and I thought we'd take this opportunity to have a second honeymoon. How about one night, sweetheart?"

Though she could feel Leo Prysing's penetrating eyes on her, she agreed happily.

"Hardly the place I'd have chosen, but who knows? Our first honeymoon hotel was the . . . what on earth was it, darling?"

Steve grinned. "The Cedar Hotel, Strand's finest."

Leo shook hands with Steve. "Anyway, it was a great job. By the way, Prysing Films will pay for a new jacket. That stain looks permanent."

"I'll hold you to it. Alec, are you still taking Bridget back to San Francisco?"

"I'm sleeping in the car on the way," Bridget explained. "Got a heavy date tomorrow with Doc Hernsdon."

Everyone began to ask anxious questions but she waved them away impatiently. "Checkup is all. Now go along."

Randi and Steve kissed her, then hurried away. Randi felt guilty about leaving her, but she knew her mother wanted her to be with Steve.

They reached the dark street and saw the old building with its faded sign: MARTITA PALACE HOTEL. It was a four-story frame building with a wooden porch and a rocking chair.

"The Cedar Hotel, Strand's finest!" Steve and Randi shouted together.

Laughing at the memory of their honeymoon hotel, they ran along the sidewalk and rushed into the lobby, waking up the sleeping desk clerk.

"Martita Tourist Court's down the street," he said.

"We want a room," Steve insisted.

"Here?"

"Yep."

The young man sighed, reached for a key on the board behind him and gave it to Steve. They hurried up the wooden stairs.

"The Cedar to a *T*," Randi joked.

They finally found the awful front room with its creaking brass bed, aged lace curtains, green window shade and camphor-smelling closet. But it didn't matter . . . They were newlyweds again.

Steve undressed Randi and lay her on the bed. Her skin was cool to his touch, even on this hot August night, and the sight of her still-youthful body stirred him.

"I never loved anyone but you. Never. I swear it."

"Long ago maybe you might have . . . There was Alma What's-her-name."

"I've forgotten. But that certainly wasn't love."

"You must have had women in Europe." She pretended to be

casual, but longed to be reassured. "I could understand. Just as long as you didn't lie to me."

"Not a one. I thought about you constantly."

Randi reveled in his words. She knew that the affair with Alma was many years old, buried now, and that Steve knew she would forgive anything but a lie . . . They made love tenderly, as if it were the first time, and soon fell asleep in each other's arms . . .

By the time Randi woke up, Steve was gone. He had left a note near her pillow.

"Sweetheart, I'm out buying a razor. Unless you prefer bearded lovers."

She looked out the window at the busy street below, and to her surprise, saw Eden and Tony. They were standing in front of the hotel entrance, in the middle of an arm-waving argument. They disappeared into the hotel lobby.

Randi finished dressing and went down to meet them, wondering what the problem was, hoping to play peacemaker.

Their voices carried halfway up the staircase.

"I'm sick of it," Eden said. "I live my own life. If I want to sleep with a dozen men in Paris—or in Hollywood—I'll do it. Anyway, your imagination is one for the books."

Randi figured that Eden was probably exaggerating her exploits to impress Tony. She rattled the bannister to warn them that they were being overheard, but they didn't hear her . . .

"It wasn't my imagination that you let my father lay you," Tony snapped.

Randi froze.

"You're out of your mind," Eden yelled. "Where'd you get that crazy story?"

"From you, that's where! You sleeping with me and forgetting who I was, thinking I was Steve. That's what you said. And you're forgetting you told me about the night Leo found you together, loving it up. The night he got you two lovebirds to rescue his family. Well, don't count on me being as forgiving as my mother. I'm not that cold-blooded."

Randi retreated quietly up the stairs. In a daze she returned to the room, felt around the foot of the bed for her handbag. She wondered if she had brought enough money to pay for a plane to Oakland, and then for the harrowing business that lay ahead in San Francisco.

She had to clear out the part of her life encompassed by the house on Nob Hill.

# *Chapter Eight*

ONE week later, on a sultry September day, Hitler marched into Poland. Britain and France immediately declared war on the Third Reich, but the isolationist feeling only increased in the United States.

Steve Lombard had never known such bitter frustration as now. Randi had walked out on him, announcing politely that she wanted a legal separation.

Tony had been easier to reason with than Randi. He almost believed Steve's explanation of his relations with Eden, and if he didn't believe it completely, still he accepted it.

Randi left the Nob Hill house shortly before Christmas. Steve had business at the Fairmont Hotel that day which kept him across the street from the Lombard house for most of the morning. He stood outside the hotel for hours, waiting for her to come out. Late in the afternoon he finally caught sight of Randi walking to a waiting taxi. She was accompanied by Stella, and carried a battered old valise.

A carpetbag . . . She had brought that carpetbag to the house twenty-one years ago, the day before her wedding . . .

She stopped outside the wrought iron gate and looked back. So she did share his memories, Steve thought, and was relieved. He stepped into the street to go to her, but the clanging bell of a cable car made him jump back. By the time the car rattled on down the California Street hill, Randi's cab had roared away down Taylor Street.

Nothing went right these days, he thought miserably.

Stella Burkett called to him, and there was no way to avoid her.

"Come in, Steve. Have a drink. Your boy is here making eyes at Heather. He wouldn't dare if your sister was here, but Brooke's gone off to have lunch with that Baccagalupi man from Alec's radio station. Now, I wonder why." Steve thought her coyness ridiculous, but he played along.

"Well, why?"

She took his arm and ushered him into the house—*his* house. "Lord, I wouldn't know. Not exactly, anyway. Come in and see Tony. He's been picking up a few things his mother left and he's going to ship them later. But you know that minx Heather. She's got him spinning already. He's no match for my girl."

While Stella fussed around the living room getting Steve a drink, he went upstairs to see what was going on between Tony and Heather. Steve knew that Tony could have only one reason for playing around with the girl, and that was out of jealous spite against Eden. Tony had probably not even given a thought to Alec's feelings . . .

Walking into Randi's room, Steve saw his son and Heather.

"Cleaning up? Be careful you don't throw away any of Randi's treasures. When she comes back, she's going to want to know where every hairpin is."

Tony had been staring vaguely out the window, and turned now to look at his father.

"According to mom, she isn't coming back."

Steve ignored the cruelty of his son's words, and turned to leave. But Heather fluttered over to him.

"Oh, do stay, Uncle Steve. You're never here any more. We love having you."

Tony looked at Steve and rolled his eyes. "She acts like the place is hers already." Heather glanced up quickly. "You've still got a little way to go, honeybun. Don't overdo it. Dad, do you need company?"

"Certainly not. Do I look like I do?"

Steve knew that his son must care for someone, but despite her beauty, it wasn't Heather Burkett. Yet when Steve reached the stair landing, he heard Heather give a squeal of pleasure. Steve stopped, glanced over his shoulder, and saw at the top of the stairs the two in an embrace. He went on down the stairs, but Tony broke away and called after him.

"Where to, dad?"

"The station. The manager is sending someone to New York. It's the first step in the London assignment. I want to ask him about the power of these isolation rallies while he's at it."

"Let me go with you. I'd like to talk to Baccagalupi. I can show him that with my Prysing connections I'm a perfect choice for the London assignment after New York. I can work with the radio network and film the news for Prysing on the spot."

He was already halfway down the stairs. They both heard Heather as she ran down to join them.

"Let me go too. Oh, Tony! I'd rather go to New York than anything in the world."

Steve didn't want her along. Neither did his son. But they had no choice . . .

As they drove down to the radio station just off Market Street, Steve wondered what strings Tony would pull to get his favor from Baccagalupi. They found Alec going over the notes of an interview he had conducted with the famed American hero, Colonel Charles A. Lindbergh. Alec stood up and kissed Heather, who smiled shyly over his shoulder at Tony. Tony wandered off, but Steve was curious about the interview.

"Uncle Steve, you're in trouble," Alec warned him. "The Lone Eagle is no fool. He was right about German preparedness, wasn't he? Long ago, he warned us the Allies weren't able to match them."

Steve groaned. "And I'm no match for him. I'll admit that. Did he say anything new?"

"The usual. No foreign entanglements. No involvements, et cetera. In a lot of ways I'd rather believe him than you."

"So would I. Is Baccagalupi still at lunch with your mother?"

Alec knew nothing about it. "What the devil—they're an odd couple."

"Maybe it's a romance," Heather interrupted.

"He's no Don Juan," Steve explained. "And his five kids might object. Not to mention Sylvia, his wife." They all laughed.

Brooke and the station manager arrived soon afterwards. She was looking especially beautiful in a green crêpe outfit under a sable coat, and greeted Steve and Tony with reserve.

Tony approached Baccagalupi anxiously and Steve suddenly had a paternal desire for his son to win whatever he wanted.

"I'd like to have a word with you, sir. In private, if I could."

"Sure, boy. But later. I've got an announcement to make. Hey, everybody. Get in on this." Brooke smiled mischievously.

"I guess you all know the network's taking in one of our San Francisco boys. With London in the offing."

Alec had stopped rustling his pages. He stood frozen, staring across the room at Tony.

"A great break," Steve agreed.

"Well, we had the choice in mind earlier, but I wanted to enjoy my lunch date beforehand. Now, I think I'll be the first to give you a wedding present, Miss Burkett."

Heather gasped, and her blue eyes were enormous. "*Who*—I mean, please don't make us wait."

"Not a minute more. You're it, Alec. And we're mighty proud of you. Hell, all San Francisco is proud of you."

Steve tried not to look at his son. He was happy for Alec, and kept thinking how pleased Randi would be when she heard the news.

Heather remained still for a couple of seconds, then turned to Alec and kissed him softly. "Dearest Alec! How wonderful for us. Let's get married in New York. It would be so glamorous. Can we go soon?"

Alec looked stunned. Tony thrust out his hand. "Great work, Alec. They couldn't have made a better choice. I was going to suggest you myself."

As he moved back to make room for Alec's eager coworkers eager to add their congratulations, Tony stepped on Steve's foot.

"Sorry to be so clumsy," he grinned. "Must have been thinking of something else."

DURING THE eight months between the declaration of war in September of 1939 and the bombing of open cities in May of 1940, Hollywood found itself far more consumed in the Academy Awards than the stalemate then being called the Phony War in Europe.

*Journey* was one of the nominees for best picture of the year, and until the end of the year Leo Prysing felt that his film, its stars and urgent message had as much of a chance as *Ninotchka, Wuthering Heights, Goodbye, Mr. Chips* and the others. But in December *Gone With the Wind* opened. Prysing quickly saw the writing on the wall.

Randi fully expected to attend the awards ceremony with Leo Prysing at the end of February. He had entries nominated in seven categories, though, unfortunately, none of the nominations included her screenplay. She, too, recognized that their film was hardly a rival to *Gone With the Wind* . . .

Randi spent that Christmas Eve with Prysing. She had tried not to let him guess that she was desperately lonely for her family. Tony had gone off to Tijuana with a studio crowd, and Steve was in New York working on a big Madison Square Garden rally to aid Bundles for Britain. He called her only minutes before Leo arrived, and was very friendly, repeatedly letting her know he was having a great time. Randi could hear in the background the sounds of a party.

She put the phone down and looked around the room, ready to burst into tears.

Just then Leo Prysing arrived. He met her at the door with the snow-white beard and red stocking cap of Santa Claus. She laughed, but her nerves were still strung tight. He set down on the table a little Christmas tree loaded with ornaments. She was touched—painfully so—by his gesture. He slapped her hands away.

"Not yet. There must be lights." He pulled a string of tiny lights out of his overcoat pocket. "Used to be switchboard lights. I had them made specially in the prop department. String them around. I leave that to you."

"Oh, thank you. What a darling you are!" She hugged him until he pretended to groan.

"Don't thank me. The studio created it. Just remember me next Hanukkah. You're elected to light the candles."

"It's a promise."

Randi marveled at her friend's generosity in everything large and small. At one moment he could be Santa Claus and the next be responsible for bringing dozens of refugees out of Europe, mainly through the judicious payment of "ransoms" to influential Nazis . . .

As Randi strung the ornaments, they discussed their upcoming films. Leo told her that he would be renewing Eden Ware's contract, and Randi's stubborn resentment of the girl reared up.

"What do you think people see in Eden Ware? She isn't pretty or glamorous. She isn't the greatest actress in the world. Do you think she will last?"

Leo was amused. "My sweet, she and the camera were made for each other. Within a year or so she will be bringing in audiences to see her alone. That's star power." He slapped her hand gently. "But you aren't interested in her star power. You are still thinking of her as your husband's mistress—isn't that true?"

"I have no interest whatsoever in Steve's girl friends."

"Then, for God's sake, don't knock her until after the awards. She's my ace in the hole. I'm hoping that if Hattie McDaniel and de Havilland are nominated for *Gone With the Wind,* which is likely, they'll cancel each other out and Eden will chalk up a win in the Prysing column."

"You're as bad as Steve. Everything leads back to your work."

He was wrong about the awards. Hattie McDaniel canceled out everyone in her category and won. Prysing Films brought home the Oscar for two less publicized categories . . .

Shortly afterward, with the bombing of undefended Rotterdam in a country still at peace with Germany, the war took on the bloody aspects Leo had foreseen. He took a crew to London for a first-hand documentary of what was coming.

Nevertheless, it was not the world-famous film producer but the almost unknown San Franciscan, Alec Huntington, who was talked about on the Pacific Coast and throughout America during the Dunkirk retreat.

Tony Lombard told Eden about his cousin's first network broadcast to America.

"How about listening to my cousin Alec's broadcast tonight, darlin'? At mom's apartment."

Eden had put him off the last two times he cornered her on the set, but she very much wanted to patch things up with Randi Lombard, so she jumped at the offer.

Eden thought less often these days about that evening in Paris with Steve Lombard, though she still wondered what would have happened if Leo Prysing hadn't been there . . . It didn't really matter anymore—not since she had fallen for Stephen Lombard's son. But Tony's self-centeredness still made it easy for Eden to detach herself whenever she thought she was getting too fond of him . . .

Randi greeted them coolly.

"Sit down. Alec is coming on. It's been terrible. The surrender of the Belgians took place so quickly the French and British armies had no time to retreat and regroup. They're stranded at the Channel between the German lines and the sea."

Tony waved away explanations. He had plotted out the positions of the armies during the last desperate May days and went to the kitchen now to get drinks while Eden and Randi settled around the radio, listening to the announcer.

"Alec Huntington was there. He found himself a part of the miracle. And a miracle it is. Plans had been implemented for sixty thousand troops to be drawn off the beaches between Niewport in Belgium and Dunkirk in France. But three days ago almost one hundred twenty-five thousand reached the coast, thirsty and half-starved, plus the wounded. Nor did this include the remnants of the French army, the French Third Corps, and the two French regiments which hold the perimeter along the canals.

"Among other brave men arriving in London hourly throughout

this fog-shrouded day and night, by train, ambulance and lorry . . . Here is Alec Huntington."

Alec's voice seemed curiously flat after the buildup.

"I hitched a ride on one of His Majesty's destroyers the night before—" His voice faltered as he pulled his thoughts together. "Yes. Night before last, it was. We found five thousand men in one line, waiting to be taken aboard our ship alone. A few hundred made it. They say there were still over eighteen thousand waiting in that hour. And nothing. No way to take them off on our single ship. By dawn my ship had sailed with a full load. I wandered along the beach to the hospital set up near La Panne in Belgium. We got quite a few wounded out. Some brawny Scots tore off a door from the latrine and used that when the hospital wing blew up. The Jerry guns were on target . . . .

"Anyway, we carried two fellows on that door. We finally got it to a dingy. About a dozen men were lying in the dingy like logwood. Some of them were layered crisscross over the others. The dingy took off. We kept making the trip until we couldn't see where we were going. The hospital got a direct hit. Those patients that could walk, walked . . . They were strafed when daylight came and the *Luftwaffe* had a great target.

"The clouds parted. The fog lifted. The Jerries could see the whole bloody mess. But they missed too. Boats, ships, everything that would float was pulling off into the Channel loaded to the gunnels.

"After the hospital blew up I found a bike. I made it to some one-horse village outside Dunkirk. I'd made it across the French border and didn't even know it. They had set up tents for the wounded and the fellows in shock. You see, there were no orders to save the French. Only the British. And a certain French officer was there, a nobleman I have known since I was a child. He'd been a flyer in the Great War. But he was overage now, serving in the ground forces. He was pleading with a Royal Navy officer to save some of his men."

Alec stopped. Eden leaned forward. But she didn't notice Randi's gasp. Randi too had guessed.

Memories flamed in Eden's mind. She whispered, "Dear God! It's André."

Alec resumed. "The navy boys wanted to help my French friend but they had no orders. We all made a big commotion. They got on the phone. They got the new PM himself. Mr. Churchill said 'Save 'em.' So we started loading on Frenchmen too, naked and dirty like our British boys, all piled in wherever you could stick them. Two of our boats got strafed. But the other Frenchmen began to sing. Very low. Pretty soon the others took it up. Even to us it was stirring. The 'Marseillaise.' Some of us went back for another load. My friend, the French count, waved to me from the beach. Raised four fingers. That meant he had four more wounded for that load.

"The big guns behind the canal—they found their target. Next minute the beach was all white and blinding ahead of us. We were deafened by the concussion. By the time we got on our feet, there was nothing left where my friend, the count, had been. Just a crater in the sand. But we had gotten a lot of his men out.

"So we pushed off . . . That's about it. This is Alec Huntington, for UBC."

The UBC's now-familiar voice from London thanked Alec and signed off by telling the listening audience that Mr. Huntington would be hurrying off to his bride at their residence outside of London.

Tony came out of the kitchen to hear only the concluding remarks. "That's our Heather. I knew he wouldn't get her to stick it out in all that danger. Depend on it, she's found a safe haven."

"Yes. It does sound like her," Randi quietly agreed. "I think your father's friend, André de Grasse, was the French officer Alec mentioned."

Eden was chilled . . . Memories of the day she and André first made love in the ruins of the de Grasse chateau assailed her. She saw him then and years earlier, handsome, kind to a gawky twelve-year-old girl alone in Paris for the first time . . . Now André was dead. Her beloved Paris would go next. Her grief was too deep for tears. . . .

Eden responded to Tony with deep tenderness that night when he took her down to her apartment. Their lovemaking was as it had always been, as perfect and as fulfilling as she could wish. Tony had become a part of her, inseparable from everything she did and all that happened.

So despite all her resolutions and ambitions, Eden found that with the fall of France and the voting in of draft registration, she could not bear to see him leave her.

Marriage seemed the only solution . . .

Two weeks later, Eden and Tony drove to the small desert town of Las Vegas and were married.

Randi was not surprised. She had known it was inevitable. But she did ask about Steve's reactions, and when Tony told her about the thousand-dollar check he had sent from Washington, D.C., along with the deed to a small but profitable new motor court on the Long Beach Highway, she seemed relieved.

That night, though, as they celebrated together in Los Angeles, they turned on the radio and heard Walter Winchell's radio bulletin.

"Good evening, Mr. and Mrs. America and all the ships at

sea . . . Flash! Looks like wedding bells are in the offing for Meribel Connaught and Pacific Coast wheeler-dealer, Stephen Lombard as soon as the prospective groom untangles his marital affairs. The beauteous Meribel is the widow of the late Senator Connaught and an outspoken supporter of Bundles for Britain."

Tony and Eden looked over to Randi, but her face was buried in her hands.

# *Chapter Nine*

RANDI listened to Winchell's broadcasts every week with a tension even greater than she felt during the daily news bulletins of the war. The German invasion of Russia had shaken the world, but Randi remembered that the news came the very day Winchell mentioned "the beauteous Meribel" again in connection with the pressure from pro-British sympathizers.

Randi knew from the photos she had seen in *Harper's Bazaar* and *Vogue* that Steve was a vital part of the pro-British lobby. Steve continued to write to Randi, mostly about his work. He was working closely with Alec, who was now second man in the London office of his network. In one of her letters, Randi asked Steve about Alec and Heather.

His reply was amused and tolerant.

> *Frankly, Alec seems prepared to deal with her. She leans on him for everything. He makes all her decisions—anything goes, so long as she is kept happy. She wants more than he can afford, and I know he is dipping into his other income. I've tried to do a little maneuvering, but he is sharp and won't take anything he calls charity.*
>
> *Remember the awful mess about mother's money that he paid to Stella? I always wished I'd never mentioned it to him.*

*Anyway, Heather costs him but she seems to be making him happy. And he certainly needs something to take his mind off his job.*

*It's brutal over there these days.*

*I saw your latest film and I liked it. How is Leo?*

*Tony and I keep in touch. I guess you know that. And Bridget and I have long talks by phone every once in a while. You know Bridget—lively as ever. I'm glad Thorgy is back looking after her. Bridget says Stella was nice about letting her go. Surprising how well Stella and Brooke get along. Maybe because the Nob Hill house is so big.*

*Has Tony told you he sees himself as a father? He seems to think that is one way to hold Eden. She was upset when she wasn't nominated this year. Her fourth film. Ambitious girl.*

*Love always,*
*STEVE*

He hadn't once mentioned divorce—or Mrs. Connaught. But the gossip continued . . .

Late in June Tony rushed to Randi with the news that Eden was pregnant.

"I never objected to babies. Only husbands," Eden reminded both Randi and Tony. She reached for Tony's hand. "He's going to be just like his father. I don't suppose you'd approve of our christening him Tony Junior."

Tony kissed Eden and held her close. Though it warmed Randi to see them as they teased and loved each other, it also made her a little sad, bringing back as it did so many memories of her happy times with Steve.

"She's going to be a girl," Tony said. "Seems to me the daughter of Eden ought to be called Eve."

Eden wrinkled her nose at the idea. "A boy!"

"Girl!"

"Either way," Randi interrupted them, "the question is—when?"

"Late November, probably."

"She—I mean *he* is going to be born in the islands," Eden announced. "Father and Tamiko insist. I called them an hour ago. And Chiye promises to stop all her peacemongering long enough to play godmother. You must come over for the christening, Randi. It will be a vacation for you, if nothing else. Bring Leo. He'll probably do a whole movie about the big event."

"Isn't she a doll?" Tony asked. "She's taken a leave of absence for six months. Won't take another role until February. We'll have to find a nice apartment, maybe out near Westwood. I forgot to tell you, I'm cramming all the courses I can get. I've got my credits from Cal. I'll finish at UCLA if I can before I'm—God forbid—drafted."

The next important matter was to tell Bridget she was going to be a great-grandmother. Leo Prysing offered to fly up to San Francisco with Randi, but much as she enjoyed his company, she refused him. Bridget had taken a dislike to him and since she was still having liver trouble, Randi was anxious not to upset her.

"And what'll be the meaning of this, I'd like to know," Bridget asked when Randi came to the rooming house.

"Mama, get back to your bed, and stop running around in your stocking feet. I thought Miss Thorgerson was taking care of you."

"Thorgy's all right. She's up at your old house on Nob Hill again. Stella sent for her."

Randi didn't hear the rest. She hugged her suddenly fragile mother, and they walked into Bridget's parlor arm in arm.

"I'm sitting up, so I am," Bridget said. "No bed for yours truly. Take your coat off and tell me if this is true."

Randi glanced at the magazine Bridget held. There was a photograph of Steve with Mrs. Connaught.

"There. Who'll that be? I'd like to know."

"She is a senator's widow. She has been working with Steve to help Britain. You do want to help Britain, don't you?"

"The hell with Britain. So she's got her hooks in Steve. I never thought he'd do this to me."

"To you!"

"Well," Bridget reminded her, "you made the choice to leave him. I didn't. He's still my boy, but not if he takes up with this dame."

Randi threw the magazine onto Bridget's old-fashioned round table, and Bridget watched her, smiling grimly.

"Still care?"

"I just don't want him to make a fool of himself. Oh, ma, I can't keep the news any longer. Guess what? You're going to be a great-grandmother."

"I already got the news from himself," Bridget admitted.

"What? Tony agreed to let me tell you."

"Himself, my girl, will always be Steve. He just called me. I was that happy I forgot to ask him about this dame of his."

Randi walked into the kitchen and poured them both mugs of coffee. When she returned, Bridget had brightened.

"You'll never guess, my girl. Old Stella Burkett wants me to move in with her. That's what Thorgy is doing today. After Stella's kid got married she got real lonesome, what with Brooke out every night. Anyway, Thorgy came back to live here, and now old Stell and Brooke need company, they're saying. Picture me living in that fancy Lombard house."

"You could have lived there with Steve and me," Randi reminded her.

"Don't be silly. I couldn't have paid you. I pay old Stell. Would you believe it, now? She needs that money for when she goes to England. Brooke says she's going to be lonesome."

"Stella is actually going to England?"

"Oh, that's another story. Stell wants to go to see her girl. She thinks maybe I've got pull with Steve. He might get her across to London. He told *me* he'd try."

Randi remained in San Francisco long enough to settle Bridget in the Nob Hill house. She saw for herself that Stella was relieved to have Bridget within the big, lonely mansion.

"We'll look out for her, Randi. Lord knows, we've got enough people we're paying around here. And when Steve arranges for me to go off to England, well, there's Thorgerson and the servants to take care of her, and Brooke will keep her company."

"I wish I could get ma to Hollywood."

Bridget walked into the room with Brooke.

"I wouldn't be caught dead in L.A.," Bridget insisted. "Somebody might see me. I'd be shamed for life."

They all laughed. Brooke hugged Randi, who was relieved to see that her sister-in-law had finally thawed toward her.

"Bridget says you're going to Hawaii for the baby's birth," Brooke said.

"At least for the christening. I take it she is having an army of godparents."

"I've decided to sail with you. I need a change of scenery. And I did love the islands when I was married to Nigel. What a nice man he was!"

Brooke received a special invitation from Eden and was ready with bag and baggage that late November day in 1941 when the *Lorelei* sailed from San Francisco . . .

Eden and Tony's first daughter had been born a week earlier and would be christened Eve Andrea Lombard . . .

It was only Brooke who wondered if Andrea was named for the special man in Eden's early Paris years.

STEVE LOMBARD reached Honolulu on December 4, the day before the christening. For weeks he had prepared himself to handle the meeting with Randi. He had made up his mind that things would go well. The affair with Meribel Connaught meant little to him compared to this.

Randi looked drained when she greeted him along with the others on Dr. Ware's long lanai. He went to her immediately. She brushed his cheek with her lips, and then joined Tony and the women as they whisked Steve off to see the new baby. But Steve's eyes were on Randi alone.

There was a large, informal dinner, with everyone full of pride and laughter for the newest member of the family. Chiye left early with Jim Nagumo, who was driving her to her class. Eden heard them arguing as they left, and laughed.

"Some day when they're old and gray, they'll probably get married like Tony and me. All that arguing is a very good sign."

"Chiye's ideas have a lot of good in them," Dr. Ware explained seriously. "God knows what will happen when the war comes, but you can count on the loyalty of our Nisei population. I'll agree with Chiye on that."

"Do you think it will come?" Steve asked.

"No question. Our own people are loyal. But out here in the Pacific we've got an enemy as ruthless as the Nazis. I'm talking about the war party in Japan. Steve, you can do us a big favor here if you will talk to some groups about your European experiences. Have you been in London since the Blitz?"

Randi turned her head. Even in her silence Steve was aware that none of his moves, nothing he said, escaped her. He loosened his collar, suddenly warm.

"About British war relief, Brooke's son is the real hero of the family."

Brooke jumped in to add tales of her son's broadcasting heroism and Steve glanced over at Randi. Her mind seemed elsewhere, he noted, and her eyes were fixed on Tony.

"I'm 1-A, in spite of my two beauties. Father, do you suppose I'll wind up a hero like Cousin Alec?" Tony asked.

"I sincerely hope not," Randi said in an even voice which disguised her anxiety to everyone but Steve, who recognized the tone in her voice.

Eden was more hopeful. "He's going to be reclassified. I'll bet on it. I don't want him loose in one of those boot camps where any female can get hold of him."

Tony grinned and, leaning over, he kissed his wife. Everyone beamed. Randi turned to Steve for help exactly as she might have during their good years.

"Do you think so? You have influence in Washington. Could you have them reclassify him?"

He wanted to say yes, but he knew she was too smart for that. He got out of it the best way he could. "Don't worry about Tony. He'll land on his feet."

Tony looked around and saluted him. "Amen to that. Still, I don't want old Alec getting all the glory. So don't do me any favors."

After dinner, the family went down to the water to watch the tide roll in. Steve watched the dark waters and remembered that it was here, long ago, that Irita Vallman Prysing had been fatally injured . . .

"I wonder why Leo Prysing didn't come with Randi. Aren't they pretty close?" Steve asked Eden as they sat off to the side of the group.

Eden watched Randi carefully. "I wrote to Leo. I told him you would be here. I said it was a surprise reunion and I guess he understood. He figured you were entitled to your time with her."

"Thanks. Not that it's done a hell of a lot of good. I thought she would stay at least until the next sailing."

"She's worried about her mother."

Steve was worried, too. It seemed to him that the best part of his life had included Bridget Gallegher . . .

On the christening day, Friday, December 5, the house was crowded with people. The Wares seemed to know everyone on Oahu and they all showed up at the ancient and royal Kawaiahao Church.

Steve watched the ceremony as it was given in both Hawaiian and English, standing beside his sister and Tamiko Ware, while Randi stood on the other side of the font with Dr. Ware. The parents and Chiye Akina, as first godmother, surrounded the baby.

It came as a shock to Steve when he learned that Randi and Brooke were going directly from the church to the ship. They were due to set sail at 4:00 P.M., in the tradition of the Honolulu-San Francisco passenger liners.

Holding Eve Andrea between them, Tamiko and Eden said goodbye to Randi and Brooke at the church before driving back to the Ware house. Randi was in tears, and Tamiko was moved as they embraced each other.

Randi and Brooke were loaded down with leis when they started up the gangplank to the sleek white ship. Steve remembered Randi's passion for gardenias and had presented her with a lei of the blossoms.

Randi was moved, and when he kissed her, she made no objection, though her mouth trembled.

Steve took her face in his hands and looked at her for a long moment.

"I wish you could stay and return by Clipper with me next week. I promised Ware to give some talks and to counteract all the propaganda going around. We want to alert everyone to the real danger in the Pacific."

"If I could stay—But I can't leave ma too long. Not now." At least she didn't refuse flat out, he thought with some encouragement.

"I'll be sure and see her when the clipper gets in. Are you and Leo . . . Do you have any plans?"

"He is my boss." She searched his face for something, and started to speak, but the "All ashore" blasted their eardrums. "You'd better go," she said, "or you'll never make those speeches."

The horn kept on blasting.

"Can't hear yourself think. All right. I'm off. Have a good sailing."

"Have a good flight. Give my love to baby Eve, won't you?"

"Give mine to Bridget. Tell her I'll be seeing her in a week."

Randi smiled and blew kisses to him and to the family below on the dock. Brooke was already standing close to the handsome purser, weaving her not inconsiderable spell.

Steve saw Randi glance up at the clock in the Aloha Tower as the last gangplank was being pulled down. The Royal Hawaiian Orchestra had begun playing the traditional song of parting, "Aloha."

The clock tower read 4:00 P.M. The December 5, 1941 sailing had begun.

# *Chapter Ten*

RANDI'S first night at sea was a little unsettling. She no longer got seasick, as she had long ago on her first sailing with Steve. But on the night of December 5, her sleep was often broken by the ship's movement, the slap of winter seas against the hull, and the hum of the *Lorelei's* powerful engines. As she dozed fitfully, she kept remembering the words of the ship's officers: *We are one of the twelve monsters . . . The Japanese have the* Lorelei *on their list . . .*

Her old fears remained to haunt her. She had not forgotten the year when Steve Lombard was overseas and every day she feared he might be killed and never know she loved him . . . A war now might take both Steve and Tony.

Please God, she prayed, not another war in my time . . .

By morning, her fears had receded with the night, and the voyage became a pleasurable escape from her problems.

The next evening, after a convivial dinner with Randi and Brooke, the assistant purser promised Randi he would show her a passing ship if she would take a stroll along the deck with him. Reckless and swayed by the wines at dinner, she agreed. When they reached the deck, Randi was surprised to find a ship this far out, the only lights on the vast Pacific horizon.

"A Japanese freighter. The *Asama Maru,* probably headed for the islands. Or maybe she will bypass Honolulu and sail direct for Yokahama."

"It seems a long way off."

"She isn't. About ten miles."

"Do you think there really will be a war?"

"No question. Just a matter of time. Wait 'til that peace mission leaves Washington after Kurusu and Nomura report to Tokyo. By Christmas, say, we'll be in it up to our necks."

"Sorry. Let's talk about something else." She could concentrate on nothing but the blackness of the waters beyond the ship's wake. "It looks deep."

He laughed. "Tomorrow we will be further from land than at any other spot in the world. Except straight down, of course. Why don't we have a nightcap and I'll see you to your cabin."

She glanced at him.

"Your cabin door. How's that?"

"Thank you. I'd like that."

Brooke got back to their stateroom late, still dancing. Randi laughed and went back to sleep, making a mental note that she must send a cablegram to Leo . . .

Sunday morning, the halfway mark of the voyage, was a blue-sky, blue-water day. As Randi walked the length of the deck on her way to the services conducted by the chief pursuer, Clyde Hatch, she suddenly saw the assistant purser pass her at a fast clip, cutting between Randi and two women, and heading for the radio room.

By the time she reached the lounge doors, Randi began to sense that something was wrong. Of the ship's company, always seated in the three front rows, several stewards had their heads together.

Almost all the Sunday worshipers had gathered and were seated before the chief officers appeared. Like many of those present, Randi guessed suddenly what had happened . . . The captain had been wearing a white tropical uniform, but now he appeared in his blues. It may have been the traditional change at the halfway point, but it was the first confirmation of their growing fears. The long, elegant room was completely silent when the last officer joined the lineup behind the makeshift altar.

Chief Purser Hatch, who was to have conducted the service, stood behind the altar with the captain on his right. His usually urbane voice was somber.

"Ladies and gentlemen, before our service begins, the captain of the *Lorelei* has an announcement to make. Captain Creasey, United States Naval Reserve."

Captain Creasey took the nervous purser's place.

"Ladies and gentlemen, we have just received a radio communication from Honolulu. At approximately 7:50 this morning, Honolulu time, our installations at Hickam, Wheeler, Schofield, Kaneohe and the Pacific Fleet stationed at Ford Island, Pearl, were attacked by Nakajimas and Aichi bombers, and by Zero fighters of the empire of Japan, flying at low altitude and inflicting some casualties. Oahu is still under attack as of our latest report."

Somewhere in the room a woman gave out a small scream, quickly silenced. The others only sat there, like Randi, stiff with dread.

"Sir," one of the stewards asked, "the damage. Was the city hit? Waikiki? The Halekulani? I mean—"

"No further information has come through," the captain replied to them all. "Bulletins will be relayed through the public rooms as they are received."

"Are we at war?" a young stewardess asked.

The captain waved away this question but the officers in the line behind the altar were looking at him expectantly.

"No information received on that point. Information will be posted as received."

He gestured to Chief Purser Hatch and stepped back, passing behind the officers and out through the door at the back of the bandstand. Clyde Hatch read from a note pad in his hand.

"The ship will operate under war conditions. All outboard lights forbidden. No smoking on any outside deck. All portholes remain closed. These will be covered and remain inoperable. Lifejackets will be worn at all times—"

A murmur arose from the audience.

"At all times. Including children. All children will be kept under watch, within sight."

There was another groan. He ignored it and went on.

"The hospital facilities will remain ready at all times. Every physician and nurse aboard will give his or her name and cabin number to the ship's physician. Meals will be served promptly. Please be on time." He hesitated, staring at his note pad. "Also, all passengers are requested to keep their clothing on when they retire. No nightgowns or other night garments to be worn."

Everyone laughed. It was amusing to watch Clyde Hatch struggle with this particular instruction, but they all knew it made sense. Everyone aboard knew that the Germans had sunk the *Athenia* and other passenger ships in mid-Atlantic, and the implications for the *Lorelei* were clear. At this moment she was the number-one civilian target of Japan's navy.

"All instructions will be posted in the public rooms," the purser concluded rapidly.

A woman's voice called out from the audience. "Can't we be told? We all have our men at Hickam and Pearl."

"And Schofield," another voice called.

"And Honolulu."

Soon there would be panic, and the chief engineer spoke up. His easy manner calmed them. "Every scrap of real news will be posted. There may well have been a token raid. A flyover and some scattered shooting. They wouldn't dare attack Pearl. They'd have the entire Pacific Fleet to contend with."

No one reminded him that the fleet itself had been attacked. They settled down, and the purser took over again.

"We came here for Sunday service. We will begin with hymn number 56."

While she sang with the others, Randi knew that she shared their haunting fears . . . *How much damage was done? The casualties. Where? Were my loved ones among them? Steve. Tony. The Ware family . . .*

Half an hour later, when she returned to the cabin suite to tell Brooke the news, she found a young sailor unlocking their door. He explained with brisk authority.

"Got to black out the windows, ma'am."

"Is it that bad?" Randi asked.

"There's reports we're being stalked by a sub, ma'am."

"Then for heaven's sake, go ahead."

He painted the windows while Brooke sat up in bed and grumbled in protest.

Randi silenced her. "Never mind, Brooke. We're at war."

ON OAHU, Saturday had been a lovely day, hazy and warm as September. Eden and Tony walked the long shoreline that evening, arguing about the future.

Tony had his plans all laid out. "If they skip over me and I'm not drafted, I'm sure to land a better job. If not at Paramount, then I've been sounding out Leo Prysing."

She pulled away. "You know why Leo offers you these breaks. Because of your mother."

"Well, old girl, mother loves him. The least he can do is pay her back by giving her son a break. Look, it isn't as if I wasn't good at my job."

Eden walked to the water's edge and let the tide wash over her feet.

"You don't seem to be aware of it but Randi doesn't love Leo. She loves your father."

"Does that bother you?" he shot out suddenly.

She smiled. "Don't be silly." Eden knew Tony very well and wanted to keep him on his toes. As long as he was never sure of her, she thought, he would never look elsewhere . . . She surprised him by kissing him on the ear. "Let's go back and see the baby."

Arm in arm, they retraced their footsteps in the wet sand. "It's been a beautiful evening," she said, hugging him.

They stood over Eve Andrea's small white crib that had been in the Ware family since the arrival of the first Ware missionaries back in the 1830s. Jim and Chiye came home and stopped to visit the baby, explaining why Dr. Ware and Tamiko were late.

"It's my landlady," Jim explained. "Doc Ware says it's going to be rough—a breech birth."

Eden thought her pretty stepsister looked more tired than usual. "Are you worried about Jim's landlady?"

Chiye made a quick gesture, brushing aside her own disquiet. "I'm in a foul mood. My car is in the shop again. And then, Jim kidded me all the way home. He says the Japanese have been burning papers all day at the consulate. However . . ." Chiye broke off thoughtfully.

Tony and Eden excused themselves and went up to bed.

Only Steve had business in town early that Sunday morning. Eden got up to feed Eve Andrea, and Tamiko had been up since dawn preparing the big family breakfast before the two maids arrived. She was the first to answer the phone when it rang at 6:15. Jim Nagumo was on the line, and Tamiko started to call Chiye.

"No, Mrs. Ware! You and the doctor. Mrs. Hanama was taken bad. Labor pains, they say, but it's too early. Henry Hanama and I got her to the little Ilii Plantation Hospital. Tell doctor to make it fast. And please come, too. She keeps asking for you."

Tamiko dropped everything and hurried to rouse Dr. Ware. She passed Chiye.

"Mrs. Hanama. Very bad, Jim says."

"I'll talk to him."

He had already hung up. Eden, coming in to heat Eve Andrea's bottle, could see how disappointed she was.

"Don't worry. Don't you have a date with Jim Monday night?"

"Who cares?" Chiye split the papayas and set them on glass plates with lemon wedges.

Meanwhile, Eden heard her father discussing the transportation problem with Steve. Tony put the baby into Eden's arms and volunteered to help.

"Why don't I drop you off at Ilii and drive Steve on through town to Waikiki. Then I can pick you up again at Ilii."

Ten minutes later they drove away, Tony and Steve in the front seat of Dr. Ware's green Chevrolet, with Nigel and Tamiko in the back.

Chiye grumbled. "Well, our nice Sunday breakfast is shot to hell." She scraped the uneaten food into the sink and sat down at the kitchen table opposite Eden and the baby's crib.

Shortly after eight, Tamiko's two Filipino maids arrived out of breath, running up the beach steps onto the lanai. "Big fire, Mrs. Ware. Down Kaneohe Bay. Come see."

Eden got up, then stopped. A sound like thunder shook the air. She went to the door.

"Sorry, Mrs. Ware isn't here now. Come in. Have some breakfast, girls."

Eden looked toward Kaneohe Bay in the south and she was shocked at the huge plumes of smoke pouring up from the grounds of the Kaneohe naval air station. The planes, which must have cleared the fire, were circling the station. One of them took off northward toward the Ware property. Eden opened the screen door.

"Chiye, the fire! It's enormous. Thank heaven the planes got off— Here they come."

Both women saw the planes approaching. Eden moved down the steps to the sand, shielding her eyes against the morning sun. She was trying to identify the make of the first plane.

"Is it a bomber or a fighter?"

An instant later Chiye screamed. As the plane roared overhead, Eden caught sight of the red circle on the wing and fuselage.

# *Chapter Eleven*

STEVE had never seen any hospital quite like the long, low one-story wooden building with screens and jalousies for walls, all surrounded by pineapple fields. Tony came out and down the wooden steps after checking Mrs. Hanama's condition with Jim and Tamiko.

"All set, dad? Here we go. Off to shake up the good admiral. When Steve gets through with all his propaganda, Dr. Ware, we'll have the admiral shaking in his boots."

"We?" Steve asked as Tony drove off in the doctor's car with Steve beside him.

"Sure. You two are going to need a little levity. It sounds like a heavy breakfast to me, in every way."

Headed toward Honolulu and Waikiki beyond, they passed Wheeler Field. The usual early morning activity had begun. A farm truck pulled into the base and onto the field where the fighter planes were neatly lined up.

"Sleepy Sunday for everybody but doctors and speechmakers with an ax to grind," Steve remarked.

"And their chauffeurs."

"That was your choice, boy."

"You sound just like Grandpa Red," Tony told him and looked through his rearview mirror. "Not all of the island is asleep. About a dozen planes just cut through Kolekole Pass. Headed this way. No.

Looks like they're going to buzz Battleship Row. You won't have to worry about your admiral making it on time. They'll wake him up. Been a lot of complaints about it lately . . . You're not listening to me."

With his head back Steve had closed his eyes. "Sorry. I was just wondering what your mother is doing along about now. Probably going down to breakfast. I can see her this minute. I wonder if she's wearing that blue slacks outfit I liked last Thursday."

"I wonder what Aunt Brooke is doing. I can see her, peacefully slumbering with her curly henna head buried in pillows. She's a great old girl."

How she would hate to hear that dubious praise, Steve thought with some amusement, quickly returning to the subject that interested him most. Would Randi go back to Prysing? Steve and Prysing hadn't met since Steve used a little arm twisting at Immigration to get two Jewish professors into the country. It was hard for Steve to explain the ties that bound him and the producer together. They certainly didn't like each other. Jealousy was always in the background. But they had done some worthwhile things during their informal partnership . . .

A thunderclap jarred the car. Tony looked out. "What the hell! The sky is clear, except over Ewa way. That's the big sugar plantation. They've got a marine base there."

"Is it on fire? Look at all that smoke."

"They usually burn the cane off earlier. Not this late in the season." Tony sat up. "That's not Ewa. That's Pearl!"

The car shot forward.

Suddenly the car swung over a ridge and they caught a full view of the Honolulu harbor, including the installations beyond Pearl City. Everything was shrouded in black smoke.

Tony pulled the car to a halt inches from the turn in the highway.

"My God! Is it real?"

"Maybe it's some gigantic accident. An explosion could have set it off." Steve's words were hopeful, but in his heart he knew none of them were true. The thunder, the massive destruction over enormous areas . . . He hadn't really believed it would happen—not this way on a quiet Sunday, far from Randi.

The scene before them, the distant sea a deep blue-green with lacy foam, had become a smoke-screened background for the valley below. Pearl Harbor had vanished in the smoke while dive bombers and fighters circled overhead.

They studied the Nakajima bombers still hovering over the area, the protective Zeros buzzing above, now banking, leveling off to retrace their deadly paths.

Again the sound of thunder shook the car. Steve put one hand out, not quite touching the wheel. "Let's get back to your wife and the baby."

Tony turned around and shot back along the road over which they had traveled in safety only minutes before. They could see funnels of smoke ahead at Wheeler Field where its near row of fighter planes must have been easy targets for the enemy.

"You don't think they hit the girls? And the baby?" Tony asked suddenly, his voice rising as the ground shook and the car jolted to the right.

The air ahead over Wheeler Field was alive with planes and flying debris. The earth rumbled under explosions. Steve could make out the red circles on the planes now . . . There was no longer any shred of doubt. It was war.

"The girls should be safe. There are no installations on that side of the island. Are there?"

"Only Kaneohe. God, you don't think they'd get the flak from Kaneohe!"

"We'll soon know. Keep an eye on the road. Looks like several Zeros coming down from Wheeler."

The fighter planes zoomed out of the inferno of the air field and headed for Pearl Harbor, coming in low over the highway. Around the harbor area the sun was blotted out by billowing black smoke and debris. Tony forgot the massive holocaust behind them, his attention concentrated on one concern: his own wife and daughter . . .

An army truck racing toward them blew up on the road. Wreckage rained through the air. Overhead the planes flew on.

Steve ducked his head. "They're strafing. Pull over."

Tony swung over again, skirting the blasted hole where the truck's fuel tank had been hit. He headed for the roadside, among wild ferns bordering a small, flooded taro patch. Overhead, the planes buzzed onward. The bombers ignored the battered, debris-covered road, and the strafing began from the second wave of Zeros.

Glass burst and spattered the length of the car from the windshield to the taillights on the driver's side. Tony yelled and flung one hand up to his neck and cheek as blood spurted across the dashboard. Steve grabbed Tony with one arm, bracing him, and with his other hand guided the steering wheel. They ran into a ditch and remained there with the engine idling.

"I'm all right," Tony insisted, fighting off his father's arm. "Scratched by the window glass."

Steve squinted up at the smoke-filled sky. The wave of planes had passed over. He got out of the car, went around to the driver's side, examined the damage. Both windows on that side and the corner of the windshield were shattered. Blood ran between Tony's fingers, and Steve knew it was more than a scratch. He stuck his handkerchief between Tony's fingers.

"Hold it. Press tightly and slide over."

Tony obeyed, his fingers trembling. "Must be an artery. Doesn't hurt much."

"Don't talk. Where is the closest hospital?"

"Ilii. Nigel's there waiting for me to pick him up."

Steve got behind the wheel, but the car had lodged deep in the mud. Swearing, he got out of the car, broke off dry twigs and stuck them behind the rear wheels. The car pulled out. Half a dozen times on the road, men in ditched vehicles, some carrying wounded, waved to him for help, but there was no time. The handkerchief in Tony's fingers was saturated. He closed his eyes, and his lips moved as he tried to make himself understood.

"Soon, boy, soon," Steve said without looking away from the road.

Ahead was another bomb crater. He swerved around it, gave what remained of Wheeler Field a quick look. The hangars had been torn and ripped wide open, and everywhere the fires still burned. Piles of twisted metal junk loomed up in crazy, abstract designs. But the place was alive with running men dragging axes, broken hoses, machine guns.

Steve searched for the pineapple field in which the little wooden hospital was located. He started to peer ahead through the cracked windshield, trying to make out what lay ahead beyond the pall of smoke.

When he saw the extent of the fires and the damage blazing along the road he thought he must have overshot the hospital. He slowed and looked out.

"Don't stop, for God's sake," Tony pleaded hoarsely.

A Zero had been shot down over the pineapple field. Spiraling to earth it had set fire to the entire field. Within the perimeter of the fires, Steve saw the hospital at last.

"Hold on!" Steve threw the car door open and raced across the road between smouldering rows of dead vegetation. But the hospital was devastated. Men in army uniform were working with a doctor in a stained white apron who directed the soldiers and several women trying to bring out the dead. Steve called to the doctor.

"I have an injured boy—my son. He is bleeding badly. Please help me."

"Nothing here," the doctor said harshly. "Take him on toward Wahiawa. They've set up something beyond Schofield."

Steve caught him by the elbow. "I can't. He may bleed to death. Where is Dr. Ware?"

The doctor shrugged off his frantic grasp. "Dr. Ware has been removed with the other victims. They are in that truck on the other side of the building. Take your boy somewhere else."

Steve shifted. Gritty sounds underfoot made him flinch. The calamity had finally begun to hit him.

"How many died here?"

"All but one. A Nisei named Hanama."

*"All?"*

"The damned place was nothing but tissue paper. Took three direct hits. Dr. Ware and three Nisei, a pregnant woman, an older woman and a young fellow named Nagumo. You're in the way, mister. Either help us or get out."

All of them gone . . . Nigel Ware, Tamiko. Jim Nagumo. He couldn't believe it . . .

Steve pushed aside the young worker in overalls who was climbing out of the back of the truck. Inside, the bodies lay like cordwood. He covered the bodies as he found them.

Going back to the car with a handkerchief he borrowed on the way from a Nisei soldier, he found that Tony was now somnolent. Steve tried to shake the boy, then saw that his shirt and rib cage had been slashed by shards of glass. He got in and put his free arm around Tony, holding him carefully upright, and took off at a tearing speed.

He reached the small mid-island plantation town of Wahiawa only minutes later. He was directed by an impassive MP to the makeshift hospital outside town. Again, an ancient plantation owner's house had been converted into a hospital. The building swarmed with patients, and more were pouring in.

Steve lifted Tony out and carried him across the grass, up the steps and into the low tropical house.

Two women waved him to a long plinth, then pushed him away.

"Out! Out!" one of the women said. "You go. Help those men with stretchers."

He would go, but first there were two phone calls he had to make.

CHIYE WAS standing by the phone. She had been standing there with folded arms since the radio's first announcement. Eden knelt on the floor by the radio, playing absently with the baby's tiny fingers while the radio voices repeated the story of the attack for the hundredth time, ending the same way every time.

"This is no drill. This is no maneuver. Repeat. This is no drill."

Chiye said nothing. Eden got up and put the baby in her crib. Chiye turned her head.

"Is it my fault?" Her dark eyes burned.

Eden was indignant. "Your fault because you wanted peace? Because you wanted *haoles* to understand Japanese culture and vice versa?"

"It *is* my fault. I should have known. Jim will have something on me now. He teased me about the consultate burning things . . . Were they papers? Did they know this was coming? Eden, embassies and consulates always do that just before they go to war. I should have known."

"What could you do? You told all of us. Jim is always teasing you about something. He likes it. It's a form of lovemaking with him."

Chiye's face softened. "Yes."

"He loves you. You'd better grab him this time."

Chiye shrugged. "I would. But now, with the war breaking over our heads—"

Eden turned away, paced up and down. "Where *are* they? Daddy should be fairly safe, but Tony and Steve could have been passing Pearl Harbor about the time they first attacked. Why don't we hear?"

Minutes later, the phone began to ring. Chiye grabbed it.

"This is Steve Lombard. It's bad, Chiye."

"How bad? Who?"

Eden ran into Dr. Ware's bedroom and heard the three names: her father, Tamiko and Jim Nagumo. She heard Chiye's voice with hardly a change in its flat, unemotional tones that acknowledged the wiping out of all those she loved.

"Where are they?" Chiye asked.

"Don't come. There may be another attack. Stay where you are until we learn more."

"Where are they?"

"Near Wahiawa, I think they call it. Let me talk to Eden."

"I'm on. Steve, where is Tony? Why didn't he call?"

"He's here. He got cut. They strafed some of the cars."

"Alive?"

"Yes, thank God! But he's lost a lot of blood. They're still working. Have to remove bits of glass. He got a blast of it. Don't come here. They're going to get him to the hospital as soon as he can be moved.

Do me a big favor, Eden. I've got to know about Randi. I know the *Lorelei* will be in trouble. Can you find out if she's safe? I've been trying to get the steamship company, but they seem to be tied up. Lines busy."

Eden cut him off impatiently. Her father was gone and she had to get to Tony. Steve was taking up precious time.

"Yes. Yes. All right." She hung up.

Chiye set the phone back slowly. She looked up when Eden came in. Her smile shattered Eden.

"Don't!" She tried to take Chiye in her arms but Chiye backed away, warding her off.

"I was so sure of Jim—"

"Chiye, don't! I can't bear to think about what we've lost. Not now. I'm going to borrow the Kinaus' truck and find them. Find Tony. Are you coming?" She must get to Tony.

She made a token call to the steamship company, got a busy signal and after giving instructions to the nursemaid, hurried out along the sand to the Kinau beach house. She drove the open vegetable truck past the Ware house, and Chiye climbed up beside her.

They were cut off the main highways and had to reach the mid-island town by an old plantation road. They found Steve employed as stretcher-bearer. He finished his task of removing a young Hawaiian woman from the temporary hospital to an ambulance and went in with Eden.

"Was it really daddy?" she asked. "Couldn't there be a mistake?"

He had his arm around her. "I saw him. I'll take you there when we know Tony is coming around."

She could hardly see through her tears when Steve brought her to Tony's army cot. His smooth features were now haggard and stitches marred the left side of his face from his cheek downward. But when he opened his eyes he gave her a lopsided smile.

With his first relief since the enemy attacks began, Steve left them together and went out to help Chiye. She was still trying to start the truck. He got in beside her.

"Honey, I told you and Eden not to come. You're in no condition to drive."

She was silent. They had already pulled out of the lot and were maneuvering around an ambulance when Chiye spoke.

"At first, I wanted to die. But when I look around here, I see that a lot has to be done."

"I know."

"Have you heard about your wife and your sister?"

"Not yet. But they'll be all right. They've got to. They are my life."

# *Chapter Twelve*

"YOU'VE played the hero, dad. I'll be all right now. But for God's sake, see if you can head off mom in San Francisco before Prysing gets her back to L.A.," Tony told Steve from his hospital bed.

After three days of trying Steve had still been unable to contact Randi and Brooke. The *Lorelei's* radio was reserved for official matters; so he cabled Randi about Tony's recovery and the personal tragedies in the Ware family. He received no reply.

Having managed to persuade the right parties that he would be more useful to the war effort on the mainland, he hitched a ride on a coast-bound B-29 and arrived in Oakland in the midst of a blackout, three days before the long delayed arrival of the *Lorelei.*

Steve had concentrated during those three days on some special present for Randi, something that would touch her and make her realize what they still meant to each other. The first evening that he spent with Bridget Gallegher he knew what that present must be. Looking yellow and piqued but still herself in spirits, Bridget chattered away, making him feel as he had twenty-three years ago, when he wanted to give Randi the world. Bridget always had that effect upon him . . .

That morning, while he waited on the dockside when the large white ship, camouflaged with ghastly gray slabs of paint, sailed into San Francisco harbor, he was ready. Steve had not felt so hopeful in years as he did this December morning.

Then he looked down the dock and saw Leo Prysing . . .

Randi and Brooke were among the first to crowd the promenade deck as the ship eased into its berth alongside the pier.

"You got a cable this morning. Was it from Steve?"

Randi smiled, showed her the folded paper. "From Leo. He says he's been frantic. He says he will be here to welcome us."

Brooke sighed. "I must say, it's been quite a voyage. Ten days when it should have been four and a half. And talk about speeding cars! Twenty-four knots when they usually cruise along at a nice, romantic eighteen."

"A lot you cared. You and the purser."

Brooke shrugged. "Once I get ashore, poor old Clyde won't look quite so irresistible, I'm afraid. Still, he came in handy."

He and the entire crew had been more than handy . . . Randi remembered all too clearly the fifth night out when they were called by an alert at 3:30 in the morning and the entire ship's company showed up on deck faster than at any drill in the ship's history. Fully dressed and with lifejackets correctly tied, they had stayed there, cold with fear and the unexpected slap of the icy North Pacific, until they were dismissed some twenty minutes later. They would never know whether a submarine had had them under surveillance. They had been moving with such unexpected speed, and in waters never sailed by the *Lorelei,* that it was possible the enemy never did discover their whereabouts . . .

Brooke peered over at the dock below to the great throng gathered there.

"I see your boy friend showed up. There he is. Looks tough; doesn't he?" Brooke did not like what she saw.

Randi saw Leo Prysing waving to her as he elbowed his way toward the gangplank. She waved and smiled. The lines were thrown out and tied, the ship made fast to the pier after nearly ten days of terror in unknown waters.

Hurrying down to the disembarkation deck, Brooke managed to get into the line and make room for Randi. Leo rushed up, and Randi held out both hands to him.

"Leo! We're back and we're safe," she called. Almost before their fingers touched, she added, "Have you heard anything about Pearl Harbor?"

Steve and Tony were never out of her mind, and Leo knew it. He was about to pull her into his arms but she rattled on.

"Tony was hurt, you know. And so many of our friends and relatives lost. You knew Dr. Ware. And his wife. But I can only be grateful Tony and Steve came through."

He got in a few words for himself. "You know how I felt, Randi? All that talk about you sinking and being tracked by subs? But think of the script we can make out of it."

He must have felt the sudden tension in her body, and was about to make a joke when he saw her staring over his shoulder. Her face was alight with a joy he had never seen before. Leo swung around, and knew then that he had lost . . .

Steve Lombard stood at the foot of the gangplank. Leo dropped his arms and watched Randi run the last few feet into Steve's arms. He saw tears in Steve's eyes . . . Maybe he loved her after all, Leo thought as he squeezed past them.

"I'm glad I didn't know you would be here. I'd have died of happiness," Randi murmured.

"Sweetheart . . . Oh, sweetheart . . ."

Leo strode beyond their hearing and evaporated into the crowd on the street.

"Is Tony really all right? Really?" Randi asked.

"Still has to have the stitches removed, but he'll be up and around soon. Poor Chiye lost both her mother and Jim. And Eden lost her father, that great old Nigel Ware."

Brooke was quiet. Her memory of Nigel Ware would always be associated with the warm, dreamy Hawaiian years she had traded so easily for her European travels . . .

Having hugged and kissed Brooke, Steve crossed the pier shed with his sister on one arm, his wife on the other.

"Now for your surprise, sweetheart. Maybe yours too, sis."

The women didn't need to be told what the surprise was when they reached the big limousine parked on the Embarcadero. Bridget Gallegher, swathed in a full-length mink coat, waved to them from the back seat. Her feet were wrapped in a baby blanket and the car door was held open by a uniformed chauffeur.

Randi and Brooke went into the arms she held open for them both.

"Get me! Old Bridget Gallegher ridin' high, wide an' handsome in a limousine with a chauffeur."

"Where to, sir?" the chauffeur asked, not cracking a smile.

"Let's go home," Brooke said, her brightness returning.

Steve glanced at Randi. "Stella is gone, you know. I put her on the plane yesterday. She should be in New York today and London probably tomorrow night."

They all waited, holding their breath, watching her. Randi took her husband's hand and smiled.

"Well, darling," she said finally. "Twenty-three years ago, we all started out at Nob Hill together. Let's go home and start again."